PRAISE FOR *THE STORY SPINNER*

'Barbara Erskine is one of my favourite writers. *The Story Spinner* is another delicious feast of love, drama, suspense, mystery, history and a ghostly magic that is Barbara's alone. She's simply unputdownable! I think this book is very special'
Santa Montefiore

'I enjoyed *The Story Spinner* hugely. Intriguing, dramatic, beautifully researched, with characters that bring past and present alive, it shows Barbara Erskine on excellent form'
Rachel Hore

'Barbara Erskine is the Grand Dame of the time-slip novel and this is her best yet. Gripping, constantly intriguing and brilliantly satisfying'
Peter James

'There is romance, mystery, history, long-buried feuds and secrets all wrapped up in Barbara's marvellously evocative descriptions. For lovers of top-quality historical and time-slip fiction, I highly recommend *The Story Spinner'*
Carol Drinkwater

'A thoroughly enjoyable novel – Barbara Erskine at her best. I looked forward every day to my reading time knowing this was waiting for me – what a treat! Definitely going on my best books of the year list'
Elizabeth Chadwick

'Barbara Erskine is a divine storyteller, a clever spider who spins a golden web around her readers. This is a glorious dual-narrative tale, full of wonderful characters, atmosphere and magnificently researched history. I absolutely loved *The Story Spinner*: one of her very best books'
Jane Johnson

'What a wonderful book! Unputdownable. It has all the ingredients Barbara Erskine's fans would expect; real history, myth and mysticism all sewn together into a gripping plot. Cadi and Elen are fantastic characters, each distinct and belonging to their respective periods, and I was particularly fond of Uncle Meryn!'
Deborah Swift

The Story Spinner

Barbara Erskine is the *Sunday Times* bestselling author of seventeen novels and three volumes of short stories. Her first book, *Lady of Hay*, has sold more than three million copies worldwide and has never been out of print since it was first published nearly forty years ago. Her books have been translated into over twenty-five languages and are international bestsellers. Barbara lives near Hay-on-Wye in the Welsh borders.

To find out more about Barbara and her books visit her website, find her on Facebook or follow her on X.

www.barbara-erskine.co.uk
 /barbaraerskineofficial
 @Barbaraerskine

Also by Barbara Erskine

LADY OF HAY

KINGDOM OF SHADOWS

ENCOUNTERS (SHORT STORIES)

CHILD OF THE PHOENIX

MIDNIGHT IS A LONELY PLACE

HOUSE OF ECHOES

DISTANT VOICES (SHORT STORIES)

ON THE EDGE OF DARKNESS

WHISPERS IN THE SAND

HIDING FROM THE LIGHT

SANDS OF TIME (SHORT STORIES)

DAUGHTERS OF FIRE

THE WARRIOR'S PRINCESS

TIME'S LEGACY

RIVER OF DESTINY

THE DARKEST HOUR

SLEEPER'S CASTLE

THE GHOST TREE

THE DREAM WEAVERS

BARBARA ERSKINE

The Story Spinner

HarperCollins*Publishers*

HarperCollins*Publishers* Ltd
1 London Bridge Street
London SE1 9GF

www.harpercollins.co.uk

HarperCollins*Publishers*
Macken House
39/40 Mayor Street Upper
Dublin 1
D01 C9W8
Ireland

First published by HarperCollins*Publishers* Ltd 2024

2

A catalogue record for this book
is available from the British Library

ISBN: 978-0-00-856090-4 (HB)
ISBN: 978-0-00-856091-1 (TPB)

Typeset in Meridien by HarperCollins*Publishers* India

Printed and bound in the UK using 100%
Renewable Electricity at CPI Group (UK) Ltd

For Fergus

The
ROMAN EMPIRE
Late 4th Century

N

ALLEMANI

PONTUS
EUXINUS

Constantinopolis

ERNUM

AEGYPTUS

BRITANNIA
Late 4th Century

OCEANUS
GERMANICUS

OCEANUS
HIBERNICUS

HADRIAN'S WALL

Eburacum

Deva

Dinas Dinlle
Segontium
Castell-Dinas Emrys

ORDOVICES

Ynys Enlli

Virconium

DEMETAE
SILURES
Venta Silurum
Isca
Cardiff

Camulodunum

Verulamium

Londinium

Rutupiae

OCEANUS BRITANNICUS

N

Roman Place Names

Armorica	Brittany
Augusta Treverorum	Trier
Caesarodunum	Tours
Camelodunum	Colchester
Deva	Chester
Dubris	Dover
Eboracum	York
Isca Silurum	Caerleon
Lugdunensis	Northern Gaul
Lugdunum	Lyon
Lutetia	Paris
Mediolanum	Milan (there were several places called Mediolanum including one in England)
Poetovio	Ptuj in Slovenia
Rutupiae	Richborough
Sabrina Flumen	The River Severn
Segontium	Caernarfon
Urbs Aeterna/Roma	The Eternal City – Rome
Venta Silurum	Caerwent
Viriconium	Wroxeter

It all started with a story.
The dream of a handsome man
The emperor of Rome, no less.
His name was Macsen
And he came to Wales to find a wife.
Or that is what they say . . .

Cadi Jones

Wormhole: *physics* A tunnel in the geometry of space-time postulated to connect different parts of the universe

Collins English Dictionary

Prologue

She had begged to learn how to see the future. It was the hardest of lessons and yet it seemed to come naturally as she held the clear glass bowl on her lap and watched the water swirl and settle in the flickering lamplight. For a while nothing happened, then she realised slowly that she was no longer in her bedchamber in the palace; she could feel the sun on her back and hear the gentle breeze rustling in the trees and she could see in the water the reflection of clouds, white and gentle, soft as swansdown. Nervously she cradled the bowl between her palms as she had been shown. For what seemed an age she could see nothing but the clouds but then, between one heartbeat and the next, she saw a sword. She caught her breath. It hung, suspended in the water, glowing in the darkness of a cave. The hilt was studded with gems, the blade shone like silver. Staring at it unblinking, she felt for one precious moment its inestimable power, its timeless magic. But almost as soon as she had seen it, it was gone, snatched away to some other time and some other place. The water rippled and cleared and now she could see instead a woman, writing. She was sitting on the grass in a peaceful meadow and she looked up and smiled. Her eyes met Elen's for a brief second and then she too was gone, fading into the mist. 'Where are you? Come back!' Had Elen called out loud? She didn't know, but for that brief instant she had felt a link with this unknown figure that was almost visceral.

The water in the bowl grew slowly murky. Now, Elen heard the tramp of armies in step, the rhythmic crunch of hobnails on the road and she smelled smoke. She gasped, stifled, sick with sudden fear. The cohorts were coming, but they were too late; somehow she knew they always would be too late. Too late to the fire. Too late to the battlefield.

As she watched she felt her hands shaking and her whole body started to tremble. She could see faces now, shouting, screaming with fear, as the water swirled, thick and scarlet with blood, and she felt herself overwhelmed with a sense of utter, irredeemable loss.

Clutching the bowl, she heard herself gasp. She scrambled to her feet. If this was the future she did not want to see it. She looked desperately for the woman sitting quietly on the grass, writing. She had been at peace. She was not afraid. But there was no sign of her. She had no part in this. She had gone. The water held nothing but anguish and horror.

Raising the bowl above her head, Elen smashed it down onto the mosaic stones of the floor at her feet in a shower of splintered shards. By the time her teacher reached her and put her arms around Elen's shoulders, comforting and reassuring, all memory of what she had seen was gone, fading and drifting from her consciousness like a bad dream.

Sitting on the grass in the summer meadow the woman sighed and looked down at her notebook. Her pencil had fallen from her fingers as she dozed, without a word being written. It was strange. She had a distinct memory of scribbling something down, but it must have been a part of a dream.

Climbing to her feet she turned towards the gate and, conscious of a dark cloud drifting across the sun, she felt an apprehensive shiver. It was time to go home.

1

It all started with a knock on the door.

Cadi Jones threw down her pen with an exclamation of annoyance and, pushing back her chair, she stood up. Her next-door neighbour Sally Price was standing on the doorstep clutching a handful of letters. She held them out. 'I'm just coming back from work and I met Gethin at the gate. He's later than ever today.' Gethin was their postman.

'Someone's off sick, so he's covering two rounds.' Cadi was already turning away.

'Sarnelen Cottage.' Sally read the address off the top envelope out loud.

'Yes. That's my address. You know it is.' Cadi stepped back, wanting to close the door, wanting to go back to her desk but acknowledging reluctantly that it wasn't going to happen. Not yet. Sally was already in the room.

'Do you have the deeds, Cadi?'

'The deeds?'

'The Land Registry deeds of your house. Sorry, it just occurred to me.' Belatedly Sally took stock of the untidy room, the scattered papers on the table, the piles of books on the old bureau, more books and files on the floor. The desk lamp was on. 'I'm sorry, were you in full flow?'

Of course she was. 'What on earth do you want to know about my deeds for?' Bewildered, Cadi walked over to the round table that stood in the centre of the room and pulled out a chair for her visitor, then sat down opposite her. It was too late to go on working now anyway. Her thought process had been interrupted, the fluent flow of words dammed.

The two women were complete contrasts in every way. Cadi was tall with wild, prematurely grey hair and vivid green eyes. Stunningly beautiful eyes, her ex-husband David always said, but the woman who went with them was far too complicated, too much of a dreamer, for him to handle. Sally on the other hand was short, whip thin, with dark straight hair, neatly bobbed, and steady brown eyes, and sensible with it. She fixed Cadi with what Cadi always thought of as her headmistress look. One glance from her at the children in her primary school probably ensured instant silence. Cadi was silent now as Sally went on, 'It's this house. It might be our only hope. David did give you the deeds?'

Her divorce, ten years before, had proceeded inevitably and completely amicably, with David keeping their London flat and Cadi, the cottage. The flat was worth probably twenty times as much as the cottage, so he had thrown in a lump sum as well 'to balance things out a bit and tide you over'. She had been living off the lump sum ever since and she hated London anyway: win-win. They were still close friends.

'To be honest, I have no idea about the deeds.' Cadi stood up restlessly. 'I expect the solicitor has them. Why on earth do you want to know?'

'I was wondering if by some wonderful chance you owned Camp Meadow.'

There was a long pause. Camp Meadow lay beyond their small terrace of houses at the end of the village, ten acres or so of flower-studded grass, bordered by a line of ancient willows and beyond them a rocky brook. It ran along the far side of the meadow and down the shallow hillside, following a tributary that bisected the village near the church, driving the ancient mill wheel from which the village took its name, Cwmfelin, before turning sharply south-west and winding for miles towards the distant Severn Estuary. Beyond the meadow rose a steep over-grown hillside, topped by an Iron Age hill fort. 'I'm pretty sure I would know if I did. Why?'

'Because someone has applied for planning permission to build an estate of new houses on it.'

There was a shocked silence as Cadi registered what she had said.

'They can't!' Her anguished cry, when it came, was heartfelt. Too shocked to move, Cadi stood immobile staring down at her friend.

'So you didn't know. Thank God! Everyone in the village thinks it's you.'

'Of course it isn't me. How could anyone believe that for a single second.' Cadi threw herself back into her chair. 'I always thought it belonged to Dai Prosser,' she said at last. 'It must be his, surely.' Dai was the local farmer.

Sally shook her head. 'Someone has asked him. He knew nothing about it either. The whole village is stunned. He says he's got grazing rights; the sheep are his, but he's admitted he has never paid any rent. He assumed it belonged to the Caradoc family. He says his father and his grandfather have always had the use of it and he had sort of assumed that, after your divorce from David Caradoc, it belonged to you and you were happy with the arrangement. Knowing Dai, I don't suppose he tried too hard to find out. He wouldn't want to pay rent if he didn't have to, would he.'

Cadi sat still, her mind a blank. When at last she looked up, she shook her head slowly. 'Why don't I know about any of this, Sal?'

'Because your head is always in the clouds.' Sally gave her an affectionate smile. 'And someone had to drag you down to earth to make sure it wasn't you who sold it to the developers.'

Stone-built, with low ceilings and small windows, the end-of-terrace cottage had a single open-plan room downstairs, a kitchen one end, with a pantry and back door leading out into a passageway with a gate into the garden. The other half of the downstairs space formed a living room-cum-study, with French doors onto a pretty terrace with beyond it a long thin strip of garden, while upstairs there were two bedrooms plus a box-room. Sarnelen had originally been a labourer's cottage on the Caradocs' vast estates until, as more and more of the land was sold off and farm after farm disappeared, at last only the one cottage remained. It finally became Cadi's husband's family holiday retreat, their only foothold left in Wales, but even so no one had seemed to miss it when he gave it to her as part of the divorce settlement. No one else was interested in it anymore. She loved it. It was home.

She rang David that evening.

'Dear God, it never occurred to me to even wonder about the meadow.' He sounded as shocked as she was. 'I don't think we owned it. Leave it with me. I'll find out what's going on.'

He rang her back two hours later.

'Bad news, I'm afraid. Once upon a time the family owned practically the whole valley, as you know, but the last bit, the home farm, was sold off after the war. I'm afraid Camp Meadow was part of that deal. The only thing my grandfather kept for old time's sake was Sarnelen Cottage. I gather the whole estate was split up after it was sold and that included the other cottages in your terrace. The largest slice of land, which included Camp Meadow, last changed hands four years ago. It was sold to someone or something called Meadow Holdings. Apparently they applied for planning permission for this development a few weeks ago.'

'But Camp Meadow isn't development land!' Cadi's cry was desolate.

He sighed. 'I think you'll find it is. I've looked it up online and they've submitted outline plans for forty-eight houses. You can put in an objection, Cadi. The whole village can, but in the present climate I'm afraid it's unlikely the developer will be turned down. I'll forward you the links so you can do it asap. I'm so sorry, darling.'

He still called her darling even though they had been apart for ten years, more than five times as long as they had been married.

With a sigh she switched off the phone and walked out into the garden. The summer night was very still. Beyond the hedge the meadow stretched out in the twilight towards the trees that lined the brook. From somewhere in the distance she heard the hoot of an owl and seconds later she saw the bird float silently across the grass.

Across the houses.

She could visualise them clearly in her mind's eye, neat rows, there in the shadows, identical roofs tiled with identical slates, a straight road leading north where the footpath ran towards the ford. It couldn't be allowed to happen. It just couldn't. There was someone standing in the field, she realised, the figure with its back towards her, staring as she was towards the distant hills. The sun had set, the red glow of its parting turned to cold clear palest pink and then to yellow. The evening star hung bright and low in the north-west and in minutes would follow the sun down behind the black line of the hills. There was a flash of green light across the horizon and the colour had gone, leaving only the memory of silhouetted trees on the hillside where two thousand years ago an Iron Age tribe had built their township. A horizontal band of cloud appeared black against the sky and then everything faded into obscurity. She smiled ruefully, turning her attention back to the figure in the field. It was Sally walking her dog.

Cadi woke to the sound of rain pattering on the roof of the porch below her bedroom window. She had worked late, hunched over her desk in the pool of lamplight, aware of the silence of the village around her. Sally always went to bed early; the other two cottages in the terrace were second homes now, too small for a family these days but resolutely refused planning permission for extensions by the same authority which was presumably happy to grant it for the development of an ancient meadow.

She was almost asleep again when she heard the distant marching feet. She froze, her heart thudding with fear, then she sat up, straining her ears. She had heard it before, this strangely sinister sound and always she had thought it part of a nightmare.

Marching. Marching. Soldiers marching.

She was fully awake now and the sound of marching was in her ears, not in her dreams. Men in hobnailed boots. In step. In the street outside. Throwing back her covers she slid out of bed and, tiptoeing over to the window, drew back the curtain, staring out into the night. The road was deserted. Slowly her pulse rate steadied, her terror subsided. A shadow moved on the tarmac in the moonlight and disappeared. It was a cat. There was nothing else out there. After a moment's hesitation, quietly, she pushed the window open. She could hear it again now, further away, the sound of marching growing eerily fainter. It was still raining. The air smelled of damp earth, wet grass. There were no street lamps, but there was enough filtered light in the street outside to see that there was no one there. The sound came from the rain, the empty echoes, the very silence of the night itself. She shivered. It was so real, so immediate it had confused her brain. Or her ears. She pulled back into the room and shut the window with a bang. Outside, the sounds stopped immediately.

2

David rang again next morning. 'I don't know if this will help but I mentioned the development of the meadow to Donald.' He paused for dramatic effect. Donald was David's cousin, the family's self-appointed archivist. 'I remembered he was furious when he realised the family estate, as he called the farm, had been split up before we were born. I think he had illusions about us buying it back one day. I seemed to remember he had once told me there was something special about that field. Apparently, it's got archaeology, Cadi. There was a family tradition that it was the site of a Roman villa. And he thinks there was an earlier Roman marching camp there as well. And he thinks if it was proved, that might stop them building on it. At the very least they would have to do an exploratory excavation.'

Marching.

Soldiers.

'Cadi? Are you there? Did you hear what I said?'

'Yes. Sorry.' She sat down abruptly. 'I was thinking about something—'

She heard him chuckle. 'Keep your feet on the ground, girl. Anyway, listen. Donald reminded me. There's a guy in the village – Arwel Davies. Something of an amateur historian.

I couldn't stand the chap. He was an arrogant shit, if I remember, but if he's still around he might know something about it.
He used to claim he knew everything there was to know about
the village. If there is something there like a fort or a villa, it
might stop any development in its tracks. You never know. It's
worth a try.'

Arwel. She put down the phone. Oh yes, she knew Arwel.
Arwel, with whose son she'd had an intense and ultimately
horrifically unhappy affair after the break-up of her marriage.
Arwel, who mocked her at every opportunity for her 'little
books', pointedly scorning people who 'thought they were
Welsh just because they had married a Welshman and read a bit
of the Mabinogion'. People who claimed to be poets as though
it were a real job. Poets like her.

As it happened, she was Welsh, born and bred, but of course
in one thing he was right. For most people, poetry wasn't a real
job; as it wasn't for her. She couldn't have lived off her earnings.
Were it not for David's input after their divorce and the somewhat sporadic payments for her journalistic efforts, she would
have needed a real job. Real job. That phrase made her toes curl.
Being a poet was a real job, especially in Wales where the bards
of old had been honoured and presumably richly rewarded in
kind. The fact that she had won prizes for her work and was
acclaimed in certain circles led to a few of her neighbours looking at her romantically starry-eyed, but that was it. More often
than not people glanced at her askance, like Arwel. Except for
Sally. Sally understood. And it wasn't only Sally who had been
enthusiastic about her latest enterprise. The reviewers too had
been enchanted.

She was working with her cousin Rachel on a new poetic
translation of the stories from the Mabinogion, hence Arwel's
unpleasant dig. She was rewriting the text in simple verse, and
Rachel, a talented artist, was providing the illustrations. One
book per ancient story. The 'little books' Arwel had mocked so
scornfully.

Rachel Pritchard was a painter and illustrator by trade and in
her lowest, most self-deprecating moments Cadi sometimes suspected it was the wonderful, magical illustrations rather than

her own words that made their books so popular. Rachel also lived alone in an old cottage. Hers was on the west coast and from it she ran a thriving business selling her sketches and cards online and in local art galleries who were happy to display her larger works.

The Mabinogion was a collection of ancient stories and legends, medieval, but much older in origin, first written down in Middle Welsh and now translated in many versions. Cadi's poems were a unique take on the stories, intuitive and full of charm. The first four titles had sold surprisingly well; stories of Celtic gods and goddesses, of love and war, of fairies and magic, the strange, complex stories of ancient Wales that Cadi loved so passionately. And now she and Rachel were about to embark on the fifth.

She sat down at her desk and looked at the books lying open before her. Three different versions. One in Welsh, the other two, translations into English. She idly turned the pages. The difference between fairy stories and legends was that fairy stories were made up; legends were, however loosely, based on history, or so she had been told – by someone, she thought with a chuckle – who obviously didn't believe in fairies.

The first four stories she and Rachel had published had been mythical and magical, the next in the most usual sequence was based, if only loosely, on history, and at least two, if not more of the characters were based in fact. The story was called 'The Dream of Macsen Wledig'. Macsen, meaning Magnus or Great, Wledig being the title of a ruler or perhaps even a prince.

The real-life hero of the story wasn't Welsh, he was an officer in the legions, called Flavius Magnus Maximus, who became Roman emperor of the West, a man who had genuinely lived for at least a time in Wales towards the end of the fourth century AD and who, according to the story in the Mabinogion, had fallen in love with the Welsh princess he had seen in a dream and had come all the way from Rome to woo her.

When she and Rachel had first discussed their project, Cadi had been doubtful about including this story in the series at all. Perhaps because it contained so much real history, it lacked the magic of some of the others, lacked the profusion of shape-shifting animals and birds that Rachel was so good at depicting, and also because it was very short, perhaps too short for a whole book. But then she had turned back to it. After the dream described in the original, Macsen was so enchanted by the lady and so convinced she was real that he sent messengers from Rome to the four corners of the world to find her. Cadi reached for her notebook. She had been intrigued enough by the story to look it up and make notes about him.

In reality Macsen had never actually been to Rome; he was a soldier and his family probably came from Spain. He was a senior officer of the Roman legions who had fought in North Africa, among other places, and latterly he was stationed in Northern Britain to fight the Caledonian tribes. Only then did history and legend begin to overlap. At some point in his tour of duty in Britannia, he did come to Wales, and there he had found his princess. Her name was Helen or Elen.

Cadi looked up. Elen. The name resonated at the back of her mind. But then of course it was part of the name of her street, of her house. She frowned thoughtfully. It was more than that though. Something important she ought to remember. No, it had gone. If it was that important it would come to her.

She turned back to her notebook. Elen was probably the daughter of a tribal leader or king, known by the Romans as Octavius. In the language of his native country, he was Eudaf, king of the Silures, the tribe who inhabited the south-eastern corner of an area of Britain that would one day be called Wales, the local tribe who had had one of their main townships here, in a hill fort called Bryndinas, outside her windows, on the far side of Camp Meadow.

Romans. A Roman marching camp. Marching. Soldiers. She shivered. Had her new interest in the soldiers of Rome conjured the sounds she had heard in the night? And if so, why? Where were they going?

It was early evening when she reached for her phone. 'Sal. Are you busy? Can you come over? I want to discuss something with you.'

* * *

'Well, we knew it was called Camp Meadow because there was a Roman military camp here.' Sally sat forward on the edge of the chair, rolling the glass of wine between her palms. They were sitting outside in the garden. 'I would have thought the county archaeologists would have known that as well.'

'Perhaps they do. For all we know it's not important enough for it to stop a rich developer. If it's even true.' Cadi hesitated. 'Do you believe in ghosts, Sal?'

Sally raised an eyebrow. 'Interesting question.'

'And the answer?'

'I've never seen one. Have you?'

Cadi shook her head. 'Not as far as I know. It's just' – she took a thoughtful sip from her own glass – 'I've been hearing things. Don't laugh.'

'I wasn't going to.'

'At night. The sound of soldiers marching down the street outside. I've heard it several times. I thought it might be rain on the roof at first, or a dream, but—' She stopped uncomfortably. 'I wondered if you'd heard it too?'

'No, not a thing.' Sally grinned. 'But you know me. I'm so shattered by bedtime I would sleep through an earthquake. Gemma would have barked, though, if she'd heard anything.' Gemma was Sally's dog.

'Do you think? But what if all the extra interest in the meadow has stirred something up?'

'You haven't actually seen anything?'

'No.'

'When you say soldiers marching, how do you know they're soldiers if you haven't seen anything?'

'They march in step. Hobnailed boots. On stone.'

'No shouted commands? In Latin?'

Cadi smiled. 'No, no shouted commands.'

Sally sighed. 'I honestly don't know what to say, but I do think we should follow up the proper history, if there is any.' She hesitated. 'I wouldn't say anything to anyone else about ghostly noises. It might muddy the water.'

'Emphasise the dottiness of the poet next door, you mean.' Cadi smiled ruefully.

13

'Not dotty. Wonderfully otherworldly. I certainly wouldn't mention it to Arwel. You will go and see him, I presume?' Sally's response was robust.

'Unless you would like to do it?' Cadi said hopefully. 'No. I'm not that much of a coward. I'll do it. Tomorrow.' She reached for the wine bottle and topped up both their glasses.

'He's jealous of the fact you're a successful author,' Sally went on. 'So, ignore his sniping. I love your books and I can't wait for the next one. Have you decided which tale it's going to be?'

'"The Dream of Macsen Wledig".'

'Aha. A chunk of Romano-Welsh history. That will be good for the box office. I shall look forward to reading it.'

So, Sally had heard of Macsen. But Sally was well read. Her primary school pupils might not be into medieval literature, but she most definitely was.

Macsen.

The name hung in the air, seeming to reverberate around the room.

'What's wrong? You look as though you've swallowed a wasp.' Sally was still smiling.

Cadi put down her glass and rubbed her face with the flat of her hands. 'Sorry. It's the heat.'

The June day had been building up towards a thunderstorm and, right on cue, as she spoke they heard low rumbling in the distance.

Sally drank the last of her wine and stood up abruptly. 'I'd better get home. I've got some marking to do and you know how Gemma hates thunder.' The little dog would already be cowering behind the sofa.

When Sally had gone Cadi sat down again.

'Macsen,' she whispered.

It was raining again, slow heavy drops, falling on the narrow flowerbed at the front of the house under her open kitchen window. The scent was magical – petrichor – that was what it was called, a word she treasured. The smell of wet rock and earth, the smell of the liquid that flows through the veins of the gods. A word to go in a poem one day.

But until that day came, there was Macsen.

She looked round uncomfortably. The word drummed with the rhythm of the rain.

Of the marching feet.

'No!' She pushed back her chair and ran to the front door, pulling it open. Beyond the gate the road was empty. She flinched as lightning zigzagged across the sky in the distance.

She could still hear them marching. Marching. A troop of men, carefully in step. Left right. Left right. In the distance. Menacing. Inexorable.

There was another flash on the horizon and the sound stopped. Silence except for the rain drumming on the ground.

She slammed the door and stood with her back against it, listening. There was nothing to be afraid of. It was her imagination playing with the sound of the rain. She could hear a car now, its tyres swishing on the wet road. It approached, passed the house and the sound faded into the distance.

Cadi went over to her desk and stood looking down at her notebook. Macsen. Marching feet. Roman soldiers. She shivered.

3

'What can I do for you?' Arwel's expression when he opened his door and saw who was on his doorstep was not encouraging, but after a moment's hesitation he stood back to let Cadi in.

His house was several doors up from the terrace where Cadi lived, in lonely splendour on the opposite side of the road, small and determinedly detached behind a wild hedge of untrimmed hawthorn. Behind it a narrow lane led up to the village's ancient church.

The room into which he led her was full of books. It smelled stale and the window, she noticed, was firmly shut in spite of the building heat of the morning. A huge partners' desk took up most of the floor space, apart from two deep armchairs placed on either side of the fireplace. She walked past him and perched uncomfortably on the arm of the chair furthest from the door where Arwel remained, standing in silence, his arms folded. A wiry man with thick pepper-and-salt hair, short in stature with sharp, very dark eyes and a prominent, slightly hooked nose, he reminded her of a bird of prey about to pounce. There was no reason for either of them to mention his son, Ifan. She hadn't been in the house since she and Ifan had finally split up. This room at least hadn't changed.

'I wanted to ask you about the history of the village.' She forced herself to relax. 'Specifically, I wondered if you knew anything about there being a Roman villa in the area. In Camp Meadow.'

'Ah.' He walked over and seated himself on the corner of his desk. 'So, you do know about the planning dispute.'

'I didn't realise until recently that there was a planning dispute. I had no idea building permission had been applied for. I think it's terrible.'

'Is it?' He glared at her.

'Well, isn't it?' She took a deep breath. 'So, was there a villa there? Surely if there is archaeological evidence for something like that they won't be able to develop the land at least until they've done a proper survey.'

'There was no villa.' He gave an exaggerated sigh. 'Why do you think it's called Camp Meadow?'

'I gather there was a military camp there as well. To be honest, I hadn't really thought about it before.'

'No, of course you hadn't.'

She forced herself to stay calm. She could feel the heat rising in her face. 'So if there was a camp, would that be enough to qualify for some kind of rescue dig?'

'There was a Roman camp, yes. There was a trial ditch dug before the last war. But if they did find anything it had presumably left little or no trace because they filled in the ditch. No doubt the planning people will check before they give permission for any development. I believe they do ground radar tests of some sort. But even if they deem a rescue dig worthwhile, they would in the end cover it up and go ahead with the building. Don't worry. If you have a financial interest, you'll still get your money.'

'I don't own it, Arwel,' she replied as calmly as she could. If he thought that, it would be yet another reason for his hostility. 'Neither does my ex-husband's family. I gather the farm was sold soon after the war. David checked yesterday. Then apparently it changed hands again about four years ago and is now owned by a development company. I had so hoped it was the site of somewhere important.'

'If it was the site of somewhere important we would all know about it, wouldn't we.' He stood up and walked towards the door. It was clearly a signal that she should leave.

'It's no good. He wasn't interested.' Cadi went straight over to Sally's. Her neighbour had just returned from a walk with Gemma. It was Saturday so there was no school.

'Well, everyone else is interested even if he isn't.' Sally led the way into her living room. 'Dai Prosser is getting up a petition and Christopher and Mel at the mill have already lodged a formal objection.'

'Good.' Cadi hesitated. 'They don't all think I owned the field, do they? Arwel did.'

Sally shook her head. 'Don't worry. I've put them right on that one. Couldn't Arwel think of anything we could do?'

'He says there was a marching camp there but it wasn't worth excavating.'

Sally thought for a few seconds. 'It sounds as though he was in curmudgeon mode.' Sitting down she patted her knee and her little dog jumped onto her lap. A cross between a West Highland terrier and an unknown suitor, Gemma, white, fluffy and, according to her mistress, with the super-intelligence of a Nobel prizewinner, appeared to be listening intently to the conversation.

Cadi laughed. 'Isn't he always? Wretched man.'

'Never mind.' Sally was philosophical. 'There must be other experts about. Maybe we could find something ourselves. Do you know anyone with a metal detector?'

'As I expect you know, a marching camp was a temporary military camp they set up when the legions were on their way somewhere. Probably early on, before they had built any proper fortresses or towns to suppress the wild Welsh.' Chris Chatto had obviously been doing his homework. He was finishing tidying up the mill kitchen, his face red from the baking ovens. He set the timer and led the way out onto the narrow terrace that bordered the millstream. Behind them the great mill wheel was stationary. It obviously wasn't a day for grinding flour.

He sat down on one of the wrought-iron chairs and stuck his legs out in front of him with a satisfied sigh. 'That's the last batch. Mel did most of the baking first thing.' Chris and his wife Melissa ran a popular little café, shop and bakery as part of the working watermill that ground local flour several times a week. He pushed a tall glass of fruit cordial across the table towards Cadi. 'I've become an expert on the Roman invasion of Britain in the last few days. God bless the internet! Arwel's right. There probably isn't anything left in the field but the name.' He paused. 'I've checked the planning application. It implies there has been a preliminary survey of the site and that it showed nothing of interest. They claim there is no need for further investigation. Oh, Cadi.' He sighed. 'I don't know about you – and after all, you live next door to the place – but as far as I can gather no one around here, no one at all, has seen or heard anything that might amount to a survey going on. But then of course it might have consisted of nothing more than a quick walk through the field. Call me cynical, but I can't help wondering if it ever happened at all. One hears about schemes being waved through all the time.'

'Oh Chris, if you're implying what I think you're implying, that's awful. But I certainly never saw anything that made me suspect the field was being surveyed,' Cadi shook her head, 'but then, I'm not watching it every second of the day. Far from it. Although, shouldn't there be yellow planning application notices stuck on the gate or in the hedge somewhere?' She thought for a moment. 'So, why would the Romans have had a temporary camp here when there were places like Caerleon with all its wonderful Roman remains a few miles up the road?'

'Either this was here first, or they were on the way somewhere else. There's a Roman road running straight through the village – you of all people should know that, living in Sarnelen Cottage.'

Cadi nodded. Sarn Helen or Sarn Elen was not only the name of her road, it was the name of several roads in Wales, Roman roads, one in particular, from the south coast to the north, built, so legend had it, by Macsen's wife, the Welsh princess of the Mabinogion, the princess about whom she was about to write.

Chris glanced at his watch. 'You know how stories get around. Memories of a camp with a few wooden buildings might have escalated into a villa over the centuries. Far more glamorous. That's how legends develop.' He sighed. 'Four more minutes and I'll have to go back to the kitchen. The girls will be in to prep for lunch soon.' He drained his glass and stood up. 'By the way, you might hear the wheel in action later this afternoon. There's a party of kids coming to see it. A birthday treat for one of them. This mill has Roman foundations, did you know? I think there are a lot of places round here like us. Just think, the noise of that wheel turning the millstones won't have changed much in two thousand years. Whatever Arwel says, we may not have had a villa, but there was certainly some kind of settlement here. And I mean to find it.'

Cadi stood in the middle of the meadow staring down at the ground as if it could show her the outline of whatever building had stood there so long ago. The grass was long, lush, full of wildflowers. Presumably Dai would come in soon to mow it for hay. Normally, once the bales had gone he would bring in his sheep to graze for a few weeks, growing fat on what was left. But who knew what would happen this year? She loved this space next to her house. It was somewhere she could come to be alone, to think, to compose her poetry, to absorb the glorious peace as she sat on the grass or wandered around, following the faint tracks left by the rabbits. They had to save it, they just had to. Not just because she loved it so much, but because everyone in the village felt the same. Turning onto the narrow public footpath that threaded its way through the grasses across the centre of the meadow she made her way down towards the brook and the diverted leat that served the mill.

There the midday sun glinted in the water as it rippled across the rocks to fall into a deep pool in the shade of the alders and willows. The footpath led on towards some stepping stones across the brook and from there climbed through the scrub towards the steeper hillside. There was nothing to be seen of the remains of the hill fort from here, but up there, on the flattened summit, hundreds of feet above the spot where she was standing, there was a stunning view for miles across the countryside, north towards the mountains and hills of the Bannau Brycheiniog and south towards the distant Severn estuary and the Bristol Channel, and there one could still see amongst the heather and gorse the concentric deep ditches and an outline of the ramparts that had sheltered an entire community. Who did the hill belong to, she wondered. Was that too in danger? Surely it was an ancient monument of some kind. She would need to check the notice at the foot of the path from the lane. She left the footpath and pushed on down through the long grass and nettles towards the shingle beach where Dai's sheep always congregated to drink.

The sound of hoofbeats seemed to come out of nowhere. One minute she was listening to the quiet splashing of the water and the repetitive echoing call of a song thrush high in one of the trees, then the ground was shaking with the drumming of hooves and she heard the angry scream of a frightened horse. Spinning round with a cry of alarm, she automatically leapt out of the way, but there was nothing there. It had gone. Silence settled around her again, broken only by the gentle gurgle of the water. The thrush had flown away.

Retracing her steps, her heart thudding with fright, she stared round but the meadow was empty.

'I don't know where it went. It must have jumped the stream.' Still trembling with shock, she called Dai Prosser on her mobile. From the frantic baaing noises in the background she could tell he was with his sheep. 'I'm so sorry, I must have scared it. But to be fair it scared me. I didn't realise there was a horse in the field. Will it be safe up there in the woods?'

'There isn't a horse in the field—' Dai cut off in mid sentence and she heard another man's voice in the background.

'Sorry. Are you busy?'

Dai laughed. 'I'm always busy. Right now I'm shearing sheep, my lovely. Look, I don't know anything about a horse. It shouldn't be there. It hasn't thrown its rider somewhere, has it? Was it tacked up? Best you have a quick look round. Sorry, I've got to go.' She heard the sound of electric shears in the background and then the phone went dead.

She gazed round helplessly. There was no sign of anyone or anything in the gently swaying long grasses. All she could hear was the hum of bees.

Cadi told Sally what had happened that evening as they strolled together up the lane with Gemma.

'I rang Dai in case he had let someone graze a horse in here. He said not. He wasn't much interested, to be fair.'

'He's shearing.' Sally opened the gate and they walked back into the meadow. She bent to let the little dog off the lead. 'Do you want to walk down to the stream to make sure there's no one wandering around concussed?'

Cadi laughed. 'I suppose it would put my mind at rest. And if there was someone lying unconscious in the grass somewhere, wouldn't Gemma find them?'

'Some hope. Tracker dog she isn't, although, she might be up for it if they were eating biscuits.'

The two women followed the path across the meadow, with Gemma in front of them, nose to the ground, indeed giving the impression of a dog on the trail of something interesting. The something turned out to be a rabbit. Sally called her back, laughing. 'I doubt a rabbit could snort and thump and shake the ground enough to sound like a horse's hooves, and if there was a human round here the creature would have fled long since.'

'Rabbits do thump with their back legs,' Cadi put in. She stopped. 'What's the matter with Gemma?' The dog had frozen in her tracks, crouching low to the ground, staring ahead. They could both see the hackles bristling on the back of her neck.

'Come on,' Sally whispered. 'We'd better go and see.'

They tiptoed down the path. 'I can't see anyone.'

'I can hear the horse,' Cadi murmured. 'Listen.'

Sally shook her head. 'There's nothing here.' She turned round slowly. At her feet Gemma was panting, eyes wide, ears flat against her head.

'Let's go back.' Cadi could feel her skin beginning to prickle. 'There's something here; something weird, and Gemma can sense it.' She didn't wait for Sally, who paused to glance once more over her shoulder around the empty meadow before following Cadi back towards the lane, Gemma close at her heels.

'Do you think there's a big cat out here somewhere?' Sally said as she unlatched the gate. 'You hear about them from time to time.'

Cadi shook her head. 'It's a horse,' she insisted. 'I heard the wretched thing.'

'A disappearing horse? A magic horse? Ceffyl Dŵr – a water horse? A beast of ill omen.' Sally loved the Welsh legends. She gave an involuntary shudder.

'No. A real horse, heavy enough to make the ground shake as it galloped.'

'But invisible.'

Cadi shook her head in mock despair. 'If you say so. More likely I suspect it's in a field across the brook somewhere or perhaps even further away than that and there are some kind of strange acoustics at work. Vibrations in the earth. Or—'

'Or you imagined it.' Sally laughed. 'A ghost horse. Think of that.' She glanced over her shoulder. 'Where's Gemma?' She gave a whistle. 'Where's she gone? Whatever it was, let's hope it drives the developers away. Gemma!' she called again. 'Come on. Time to go home.'

The meadow behind them was deserted. There was no answering rustle in the grass, no sharp bark in response.

'Where is she?' Sally was growing anxious. 'Gemma! Come on, Gem! She was here a minute ago.' With a quick glance at Cadi she turned back along the footpath, whistling as she went.

Twenty minutes later, after splitting up and searching the path all the way across the meadow, along the brook and up the lower slopes of the wood, they met up in the centre of the meadow again, still scanning the grass. 'She could be anywhere. Supposing she's gone down a rabbit hole and got stuck.'

'We'd hear her barking, surely,' Cadi said. 'I don't understand it. She followed us to the gate. She did, didn't she? There's no one else around. No other dogs. Do you think she's gone all the way up to the fort?'

'I suppose she might if she was chasing something.' Sally was distraught.

They turned and made their way back to the shingle beach on the edge of the brook, jumped from stone to stone to the other side and began to walk up the path through the trees. After ten minutes Sally stopped. 'It's no good. She wouldn't have come this far. She never goes this far away from me.' There were tears in her eyes.

'Look, Sal. Think about it. She's a clever little dog. She knows where she lives. If she's lost, she'll find her way home. Something frightened her out there—' Cadi stopped and swallowed. 'If she was scared, she would run home, wouldn't she? Perhaps she lost her bearings momentarily.'

'But she would come to me. She would want me to pick her up and comfort her.' The tears were falling now.

'If she's not at home we can ask around the village. Everyone knows her. Lots of other people walk their dogs here. If she's trapped somewhere, one of them will find her.'

'Do you think someone could have stolen her? She's such a beautiful little dog.' Sally had found a tissue and was mopping frantically at her eyes.

Cadi shook her head slowly. 'We'd have seen if there were strangers around. Or anyone else at all.' She knew as well as Sally the news was always full of stories about stolen dogs. Best not even think about it. 'I'm sure she'll come home by herself. She might already be there waiting for you.'

* * *

She heard the marching feet again that night. There was no rain this time. She was woken by the moon shining through the crack in the curtains. She listened as the sounds drew closer. They were louder this time, somehow more sinister. A large group of men, in step, heading towards Camp Meadow. She lay rigid, not daring to move. They were right outside now. She clenched her fists, terrified they might come to a halt outside her cottage, the crunch of boots inexorable, threatening. Closing her eyes, she held her breath but they marched on up the road. Only when the sounds had died away completely did she slide out of bed and tiptoe to the window. The road was empty.

As she looked out a light came on at the far end of the street. Arwel was awake too.

4

'Well, I think it would be lovely. Lots of young new faces in the village school. That's what this place needs.'

The views on the housing development were polarising in the post office on Monday morning.

'Don't be daft, woman. They would be bought by people from off as Airbnbs.'

Cadi took her place in the queue with some trepidation, wishing she hadn't come in. But it was already too late to retreat. 'I thought that field belonged to your ex.' Maggie Powell turned to face her. The old woman's round cheeks were pink with indignation. 'It must have gone for millions.'

Cadi forced herself to smile. 'The family sold the farm decades ago, Mrs Powell. Whoever put it on the market, it wasn't us. We didn't know anything about it.' She changed the subject quickly. 'Did you know Sally's little dog Gemma is missing? Please can everyone keep their eyes open. We went for a walk in the meadow on Saturday to see what was happening. Something frightened Gemma and she ran off. She just disappeared. We spent all yesterday looking. There was a horse in the field too but that has disappeared as well, Dai said it was nothing to do with him.'

'There have never been horses in that meadow,' Bet Evans joined in. 'There is something in there that scares the daylights out of them. Remember?' She turned to Maggie Powell. 'When we rode our ponies as kids, we were always told to keep out of there. Horses know, you know.'

'Know?' Cadi was nearing the front of the queue. She reached for her purse.

'People were killed there, in the old days.' Maggie nodded. 'They found bones.'

'Bones?' Cadi's mouth went dry.

'Don't listen to her.' Bet gave her friend a punch on the shoulder. 'Hundreds of years old, they were.'

'But horses know.' Maggie wasn't to be deflected. 'They can sense death. Maybe that little dog felt it too and ran away.'

'They did some excavating.' Bet turned back to Cadi. 'Before the war, I think it was. It wasn't just one grave, was it? There was lots of old bones.' She glanced around the post office. The queue had fallen silent, transfixed. 'And wasn't there some kind of fancy floor they found too? Then the war came along and they covered everything up. I don't think anyone ever came back to go on with the digging . . .'

Her voice trailed off. Everyone in the post office was thinking the same thing. 'I'll speak to Chris at the mill,' she said at last. 'Maybe he ought to tell the police or someone, if it's bones. And you can tell them about the little dog as well.'

Cadi sat in the garden that night watching the moon rise behind the hills. The village was silent. The lights in Sally's cottage had gone off an hour ago. The silence had been awful since Gemma had disappeared. She hadn't been a noisy little dog – quite the reverse – but the occasional sharp bark of excitement or Sally's voice as she called her was part of the soundscape of Cadi's life.

There was a line of pale light in the northern sky. With a sigh she watched it fade. If a body had been found before the war, the chances were that was when the meadow had still belonged to David's family. Surely his cousin must know something about it. She glanced at her watch. It was too late to ring him tonight. She would call him in the morning, and in the meantime she would start thinking about the story of Elen, the daughter of Eudaf, king of the Silures, and if she was going to write a poem telling Elen's story from her point of view rather than that of the macho Roman emperor, it was time to start making some notes about the possible real-life backstory of her heroine. Wandering inside, she sat down at her desk and picked up her pen.

Elen, princess of the Silures, had waited until it was quiet that evening before slipping into her riding trousers and sturdy boots and creeping outside, her pouch stuffed with treats. Her father and her brother were preoccupied with the forthcoming visit of the commander of the troops stationed down at Isca and paid no attention as she slipped from her couch, leaving them to talk over the final course of their meal. Only her groom, Rhys, knew how often she went to visit the young horse and how much training they had done together as they practised the moves again and again in ever more complicated manoeuvres, the girl riding bareback, pivoting the animal on his haunches with just the touch of her toes, no whip, no spurs, no raised voice. Only a whisper. And only Rhys knew that, though the girl had set her heart on this horse for her very own, the horse she called Emrys, it had been promised to her brother.

'No!' Her response to his gentle warning had been so angry the colt had thrown up its head, eyes rolling. 'Never! That is not going to happen.'

He sighed. It was not his place to come between the children of the high king. When she went out alone into the dusk he pretended not to see.

The colt was waiting for her on the far side of the meadow, by the stream. She lured him to her with a crust of bread and talked to him gently as he snuffled up the reward before allowing her to scramble onto his back and, her hands wound firmly into his mane, kick him into a canter, riding circles on the grass, left, right, neatly drawn figures, round and round.

She never saw the strange reflection of bright lights across the field in front of the colt, never heard the cacophony of voices, the roar of the engine as the animal reared up with a scream of fright and she flew off to land with a thud almost under the animal's hooves.

'Are you all right?'

Elen was aware of the ring of faces looking down at her as she lay on the ground. A file of legionaries had marched up the lane from the road. They had come to an abrupt halt at the sight of her lying on the ground and three of the cavalry officers, riding at the head of the troop, had turned into the field, followed by two or three of the men, while the rest halted some distance away.

She scrambled to her feet. 'You scared him!' She rounded on them furiously. 'With your noises and your lights! Don't you know better than to terrify a horse like that? He's only young.' The colt had galloped off to the far corner of the meadow and had come to a halt staring at the group of men surrounding his rider. His rein was trailing and his coat was streaked with sweat.

The senior officer dismounted. 'You ride well for a peasant chit. And for the record, it wasn't us that spooked him. We were riding up the lane to the king's palace. There was some kind of bright light in the field. A reflection off a polished surface.'

She felt his gaze run up and down her body, taking in her hair that had come loose from its tight plait, and her furious, mud-stained face. She grew hot with shame, self-consciously aware for the first time that she was wearing a short sturdy overtunic and loose checked trousers of the kind worn by her father's poorer tribesmen, and instead of sandals her feet were clad in sturdy boots.

'Don't let anyone else see you riding that horse,' the officer went on sternly. 'My guess is that animal was sired by one of the legion's Arabs. It will be worth something if you haven't maimed it.'

'He belongs to my father,' she retorted. 'I have every right to ride him.'

'A likely story! Shall I catch it, sir?' One of the officer's men stood forward.

'No, leave it. It will be safe enough.' He turned back to Elen. 'Hop it, you! Back to the village with you.' He nodded towards

29

the hill beyond the brook. On top, the thatched roofs of the tribal settlement were just visible behind the stone and brush-wood ramparts. 'And be glad I won't report you to your king's household.'

Elen felt another surge of incredulous fury sweep over her. How dare he talk to her like that? Her anger was swiftly replaced by relief. He thought she was a villager – and what else would he think with her roughly spun trousers, her coating of dust and her tangled hair? 'Thank you, lord,' she said meekly, and she hid her smile behind a downcast gaze.

He grinned. He wasn't fooled. The girl had as much spirit as the horse. He watched as she turned and walked away. She was limping, too proud to admit how much the fall had shaken her. As she moved away towards the gate, the yearling raised its head and whickered at her. It trotted towards her and nuzzled her shoulder. With its silky black coat and the give-away dished face of a legionary Arab stallion that had been allowed to run in the hills with the sturdy native ponies, it did indeed have the makings of a fine horse. He grinned to himself again. The wild Silurian girl too had a touch of the exotic about her with her tangled curls and flashing eyes.

Octavius, high king of Britain and lord of the Silures, studied his visitor with care. The two men were alone. The commander of the Roman armies in the province of Britannia was a seasoned soldier, victorious after defeating the Pictish inroads into North Britain and before that, campaigns in North Africa and Germania and Gaul. Rumour had it he was the son of the Hispanic pro-consul, a close relative of the Emperor Theodosius himself. Though he was head of the legions of Britannia, it was no secret that he wanted more.

Flavius Magnus gave his host a frank look. 'I want to be honest with you. The connection would suit us both. Britannia is threatened from all sides and my expected support from the emperor is so far less than helpful. I have defeated the Picts and Caledonians in the North. I expect more raids from Hibernia and we are endlessly threatened by the Saxons. If your son, heir to you as high king, with royal blood in his veins, were my son too and brought the support of the tribes of the west with him—'

Octavius scratched his chin. 'And my guess is, it is the king of Cornwall who put this idea in your head,' he commented thoughtfully.

'We discussed it, certainly.' Flavius Magnus did not miss a beat. 'You are the most powerful of the kings in Britain and as such you were elected high king as a client of Rome. It would make sense for both of us. My fortress at Isca is in your territory—'

'Your fortress.' The thoughtful repetition of the pronoun came with only the slightest emphasis on the first word. 'So, tell me about your daughter.'

'She is my only girl. Flavia Maxima is beautiful. Biddable.'

'And her mother?'

'Her mother is dead. Of a fever. Sadly,' he added almost as an afterthought. 'And I have two sons by her. Victor and Constantine.'

Octavius raised an eyebrow. 'So, my son has little to gain from such a marriage, though you yourself gain immeasurably from being son-in-law to the high king.'

His visitor stiffened. 'I am a relative of the Emperor Theodosius.'

Octavius was not impressed. 'I will consider your offer and consult with my kinsmen and advisors. And my son. It may be that he has other ideas.'

Magnus allowed himself a smile. 'I am sure your son will do as he is told.'

'My son is a grown man, sir. And he is already promised to another. I somehow doubt he would favour your offer, however great the compliment.'

Octavius rose to his feet. After a brief hesitation the general did likewise. He saluted with a click of the heels. 'I thank you for your hospitality.' There had been none to speak of, he had noticed. No more than an offer of a chair and the acknowledgement for the need for privacy during their exchange. 'I have to return to my duties at Isca.'

Octavius waited until the door had closed behind his visitor before calling for refreshments. His preferred beverage was metheglin. With a glass in his hand, he walked out into the atrium and stood staring at the fountain. The water was beginning to stutter and fail. Unless they had rain soon the channels bringing the water to the palace down from the springs on the steep hillside would cease to flow and the basin would run dry. He sighed. He had much to think about. But first he had to talk to Conan.

Flavius Magnus mounted his horse and gestured to his men to follow as he rode away from the high king's palace. He snorted. Palace indeed! It was no more than a villa, smaller than many private residences in Gaul or in his native Hispania, or Roma itself for that matter, not that he had ever been there. The king's other residence, a town house in Venta Silurum was even less impressive, a grace and favour building to appease a native ruler once Rome had acknowledged it would be wise to keep these men and their wild tribes on side. After all, this man's ancestors had lived in a round house on top of a hill. He glanced up at the fort. It still overhung the valley, an impressive and dominant position in the landscape, and he could see the conical roofs of the houses showing above the palisade, houses only there by permission of the Roman rulers of the province once the native tribe had finally and with difficulty been subdued. He took a deep breath to calm himself. He could not allow his daughter to be disparaged by some petty jumped-up Brituncullus who thought himself too good for the most senior officer of this part of the Western Empire.

His brother, Marcellinus, acting as his second in command, had ridden up alongside him. He was pointing towards the neatly fenced paddocks, paddocks that, like the entire villa complex had been part of a marching camp, donated to the Silures two hundred years or so before. 'The horse we saw earlier, sir. Is it worth suggesting it might be an acceptable gift from the king?'

Had anyone overheard their conversation? Apparently not. Marcellinus did not realise that Octavius had not thought his brother worthy of a glass of wine, never mind a valuable horse.

'Is the girl still there?' Magnus reined in his own mount, a fine chestnut stallion every bit as good as the yearling that had stopped grazing and was watching them, ears pricked.

'No sign of her, sir.'

Magnus smiled. He doubted she was supposed to be anywhere near that horse, but she must have been brought up with them. Probably a by-blow of one of the grooms or even of a British charioteer. The Brits were good with horses, there was no denying that, and formidable in battle, which is why it was so important to keep as many of these tribes pacified as possible. Octavius's tribe, the Silures, has taken long enough to subdue. Octavius. For all his ostentatiously Roman name the man was still at heart Eudaf, king of the Silures and of the neighbouring district of Ewyas. He sighed. He must not antagonise Octavius, especially if the intelligence that had brought him down to the fortress town of Isca with a full legion of men was correct and the Déisi from Hibernia were planning yet more raids up the River Sabrina. This was something that had to be dealt with once and for all. He had been a senior officer in the army that had pacified the northern border beyond Hadrian's Wall, an area that was once more seething with unrest, and now he needed to sort out this threat to the western shores of Britannia, the furthest outpost of the Roman Empire. His kinsman, Theodosius, was emperor of the eastern half of the empire, but he was not the man Magnus had to deal with. In the year 330 the Emperor Constantine had decided that the empire was too large and unwieldy to be ruled by one man alone and had divided it into two. The emperor of the West, based in Rome, was Gratian, from whom Magnus had again and again demanded more men and money to help keep his troublesome province on the edge of the world under control. So far none was forthcoming. Gratian had enough to distract him with the increasingly hostile tribal incursions into northern Gaul. For now Magnus had to rely on his own army and his own usually very efficient skills in diplomacy.

He was still absent-mindedly watching the black colt. It had moved off, heading towards the stream. He saw it striding purposefully across the meadow, its gait elegant and confident.

It stopped abruptly, staring ahead. He could see its eyes rolling and then it was away, frightened by something he couldn't see. He grinned to himself as the young horse galloped across the grass, bucking. Whatever had spooked it was on the same spot where it had thrown its girl rider. He wondered briefly what it was. Some animal? Dead or alive? Horses didn't like the smell of death. Or perhaps it was some old piece of metal glinting in the sunlight. A bronze shield, maybe, dented and discarded, from the days of the marching camp. He considered whether he should send a couple of men in to search the meadow. On the whole, he thought not. He turned his own horse's head away and raised his arm to signal the men behind him as he set off along the long straight road towards the fortress town of Isca Silurum.

5

Cadi awoke with her brain obsessively whirring. She had lain awake for hours and eventually she had given up trying to sleep and gone back downstairs, switched on her desk lamp and picked up her pen again. She must have come back to bed in the end because she lay now, staring up at the ceiling, wondering what time it was. Outside it was dark, but dawn was near; she could hear the tentative calls of a bird. She had spent most of the night writing, wild, half-literate scrawls, her hand barely able to keep up with the story unfolding on the page.

She had become fascinated with the original story behind the dream of Macsen in the Mabinogion – fair enough, but this was ridiculous. She had been thinking about how the story might have started and somehow her musings had become entangled with her worries about the meadow and the development and finding a way of stopping the builders in their tracks. She sighed. She was a poet, with a book of poetry to write, but what she had been writing last night had not been poetry. It was barely prose. It was a combination of notes from the history books and internet references, as far as they went, combined with strange compulsive nonsense as though the story was unfurling unstoppably inside her head, the kind of story she used to write as a child, undisciplined excited adventure stories, hidden in exercise books under her pillow, in this case, the story of the meadow. The horse had been in the meadow; their meadow, but it had been smaller then, a paddock; the characters had mentioned the marching camp and there had been a villa there, in her story, a large beautiful villa with gardens, lying at the eastern half of the present meadow. She heard Arwel's scornful reference to a palace again in her head. She had seen soldiers, Roman soldiers, foot soldiers, like the men she had heard marching in some ghostly column down her street, but now led by mounted officers. And the man who led them – had that been Macsen? She needed to discuss the new book with Rachel as soon as possible, tell her how the poem would pan out, and that because the original story was so short she was going to incorporate some extra detail the original bards had left out, details they would undoubtedly have included had they thought of it, details like a feisty black horse and a handsome stranger.

It was still barely light. The meadow was lying silent under a blanket of mist. Cadi opened the field gate as quietly as she could and let herself in, latching the metal bolt carefully behind her. She waited for several minutes looking round, listening, still half hoping she would hear a joyful bark, see Sally's dog bounding towards her, but there was nothing there, just the sound of the dawn chorus drifting in waves from the woods on the hillside on the far side of the brook. The path was wet with dew, soaking through her sandals in seconds, and she swore quietly, wishing she had thought to wear something more sensible. Her feet were freezing as she walked through the long grass towards the alder brake where the mist was even thicker, muffling the sound of the water.

Every so often she stopped and looked round. Even if Gemma was not there, there was still the chance she might see the elusive horse grazing in the distance, the horse that in her own mind had taken the form of a wild black colt, but the meadow was empty. There was no sign either that a cohort of marching soldiers had passed this way. As the sun slowly rose and broke through, the mist began to thin and dissipate and it became clear there was nothing there. Even down near the water it was easy to see now. The mud at its edge, the pebbles, the long grasses were all untouched. No footprints, no paw-prints, no hoof marks, and even as she stood there looking down at the water she saw the little dumpy brown-and-white form of a dipper standing on a rock. It did not appear to have seen her. It was concentrating on the still pool of water at its feet. As she watched, it jumped off the rock to swim underwater in strong unbirdlike strokes after some prey she couldn't see. It was near here she had heard the horse, felt the ground shake under its hooves. There was nothing here now. No sign. No trace, no breath of wind, only the birds.

It was a magical place, inspirational. And safe, even when Ifan had tried to spoil it for her. Their relationship had begun so well. He had been there for her when the reality of splitting from David had begun to sink in. She had been lonely and the occasional drink and meal with Arwel's son had been a comfort, enjoyable, a distraction. And the inevitable sex had been incredible. Passionate. Wild. She stood staring down into the water, lost in a flood of unwelcome memories. It had been her own fault; the relationship had intensified without her quite realising what was happening. The occasional overnight stops had become more frequent, until he suggested he move in full-time. She had tried to backtrack – she valued her space – but he insisted. For the first year it seemed to work, but after a while he began to change. He grew more and more controlling. He started following her out here to the meadow. He accused her of meeting other men. She had tried to end it; asked him to leave. He refused. He shouted; he lost his temper, and she realised she was becoming afraid of him.

Then his strategy had changed. He told her he was planning a great future for them both, a future which did not include living in some poxy village in Wales. They were going to move to London. He had ambitions. He hated the cottage, the countryside, her writing, his father. She shivered at the flood of memories.

In the end, somehow she had found the courage to stand up to him. No one in the village knew what was happening.

She was too proud and he was too clever. Although Rachel knew, of course. They had been working closely together on the first story from the Mabinogion – excited, full of plans. Twice Cadi had gone to stay with her cousin for a few days. The first time to talk about the potential series of books and the fact that they had found a publisher. They were happy and optimistic about the future. Ifan was furious. She wasn't sure if he was jealous, or if it was because she had gone away without him, or if it was because her poems were beginning to receive proper recognition. The second time she went to see Rachel it was to get away for a few days' peace by the sea. He rang Rachel afterwards and threatened that if she had anything to do with Cadi again he would rip up her paintings and burn her cottage to the ground.

Sally guessed what was happening, and so probably did Arwel. The day Ifan hit her was the final straw. She threatened to go to the police. It appeared he had more to lose than she did. He left the next day. Their affair had lasted barely more than three years.

That had not been the end, though. There had been months of phone calls. Letters. Online threats. In all that time if he visited his father she never knew about it. His name had not been mentioned again and in the end slowly the threats had stopped. It was Chris Chatto in the village who, not knowing of Cadi's history with him, had mentioned casually in passing that Arwel's son had married a rich heiress. It appeared he was now the successful businessman he had told her he would be. Cadi had sighed with relief. She had tried to forget she had ever known him.

The threat to the meadow had presumably released this unexpected and unwelcome flood of memories and she shook her head unhappily, trying to rid herself of them. It was as she retraced her steps slowly towards the footpath that she saw a stranger walking across the grass in her direction and for one terrible moment, still distracted by her thoughts, she wondered with a shock of fear if it was Ifan. But of course it wasn't. Almost at once she realised the man was nothing like him. This man was tall, broad shouldered, with a weathered complexion and sturdy outdoor gear, something Ifan would never have contemplated wearing. He greeted her cheerfully as soon as he was close enough. 'You're not the owner of the field, by any chance?'

She shook her head. 'No. Are you looking for the dog?'

'Dog?' he seemed perplexed. 'What dog?'

'My neighbour has lost hers, here in this field. We're desperately worried.'

He frowned. 'I haven't seen any dogs, I'm afraid, but I'll keep my eyes open, I promise.' He had a kind face; friendly eyes.

'And while you're at it,' she added, 'there was a horse reported in here. You weren't looking for that, I suppose?'

He smiled. 'No, I'm not looking for a horse either.' As he glanced away as if searching for the missing animals, she examined him. She did not recognise him so he was almost certainly not local. Late forties, early fifties, perhaps, with grey hair and a neatly trimmed beard. Nice enough looking. She was suddenly suspicious. Was this someone from the developers, or perhaps the planning office? On the other hand, he might be nothing more sinister than a harmless walker. And yes, he had the obligatory backpack slung over one shoulder. He turned back to her. 'You're right, I was looking for something. To tell you the truth I was going to do a bit of dowsing. Do you think anyone would mind?'

'Dowsing?' She had not expected that.

'A bit like metal detecting, but without the mechanics,' he added.

'Oh, I know what dowsing is,' she said. 'Are you looking for the camp?'

'A villa, or so I was told.' He lifted the pack off his shoulder and pulled out the forked stick that had been poking out of the top. He held it out towards her. 'Hazel. People usually dowse for ley lines, earth energy, that kind of thing, and of course lots of water companies use it to find burst pipes, but it can be used for almost anything. In my case I look for lost buildings.'

She smiled. 'My uncle was a dowser.'

'Was he any good at it?'

She didn't answer at once, thinking about her father's

brother for the first time in ages. 'He was very good. He probably still is.' She shifted her attention back to the stranger. 'Are you?'

He nodded with a shy smile. 'Not bad.'

'Well, in that case you might be able to help us. This field is threatened with development.'

'I heard.'

'There was a marching camp here apparently, hence the name, Camp Meadow, and my husband's family, who lived hereabouts for centuries, had a tradition of there being a villa here, but our local historian says not.'

No villa. But there was a palace. In her strange stream of consciousness dream or vision, there was a palace. The word came back to her with a jolt.

'So, is it all right with you, if I wander round for a bit?' The stranger looked anxious.

'Well, this is a public footpath and, as I said, it's not my field, but as far as I'm concerned, you're welcome. If you found something it would be a godsend. It would perhaps help with our appeal against the development.'

He gave a smile by way of acknowledgement and shifted the hazel twig into position, the arms of the fork braced against his thumbs. Almost at once the main shaft of the twig moved sharply downwards and twisted out of his hands.

'There's something there!' Cadi exclaimed.

He shook his head dismissively. 'Too soon to tell. I need to get myself tuned in.'

With a faint flicker of excitement she watched him as he wandered off. If he had heard about the villa, maybe it was true. She wondered belatedly where he had heard the story and where he came from, but it was too late to ask now. He was striding purposefully away from her and it was time for her to go home.

'Don't tell me the virgin poetess has fallen for someone at last!' Cadi had met Sally at her gate. 'I've taken the day off. Paper-work. And to be honest, I needed a bit of downtime to get my head straight.' Sally gave a guilty little shrug.

Shocked at her friend's miserable face, Cadi insisted she come in for a coffee. After listening to Cadi's description of her encounter with the dowser Sally had laughed.

Cadi felt a leap of pleasure. Sally had not laughed since little Gemma had disappeared. But then she shook her head. 'Hang on a minute,' she said. 'What do you mean?'

'You have described him in minute detail – eye colour, hair colour, speech patterns, historical nous, even clothes, for goodness' sake, all without a hint of criticism.'

'I meant, what do you mean by the virgin poetess?'

'Didn't you know? That's what they call you down the pub!'

'No!'

'Oh, it's kindly meant, fondly even. Only because you steadfastly ignore all attempts to chat you up. Oh, Cadi, don't be cross. They are proud of you in the village. You're famous. You're our local celebrity.' Sally shook her head in mock despair.

'They can't think I'm a virgin!' Cadi responded with a laugh. 'If nothing else, they must know that I've been married.' She paused. And then there had been Ifan. But nothing since. She had never even looked at anyone since. She doubted if she ever would again. Ifan had made sure of that. Sally was right. She was unapproachable.

'So, who's tried to chat me up?'

'You really don't know? Well, if you haven't noticed, I'm not telling you, girl. We don't want to embarrass anyone, do we. So, what's his name, your mystery man?'

'I don't know. I never asked.'

'Oh, Cadi.'

'I told him to tell Chris at the mill if he found anything.'

'Ah. Playing hard to get.' Sally tapped the side of her nose.

'No!' Cadi jumped to her feet. 'That's it! On your way. I have work to do.'

Sally's laughter rang across the road as she let herself out of the gate and turned towards the post office. Automatically she looked round for Gemma. Her laughter died and her shoulders slumped as she remembered the little dog wasn't there. She had rung the police, the vet, the nearest dog sanctuary, posted on the missing-dog sites and the local community noticeboard.

She had put up a sign on the meadow gate and another in the post office. There was nothing else to be done.

It was a couple of hours later that the nameless dowser appeared at Cadi's door. 'I'm sorry to call like this but Christopher Chatto at the mill thought it would be all right.' The man's jaunty confidence had disappeared. 'After you'd gone, something weird happened in the field. Christopher thought I should tell you about it.'

After a moment's hesitation she asked him in. Halfway across the room he held out his hand. 'I'm Charles, by the way. Charles Ford.'

'Cadi.' She smiled. 'Cadi Jones. So, what happened?' She waved him towards the sofa by the French doors that overlooked her garden.

'You told me you saw a horse in there and Christopher said people were asking about it in the village.'

'Yes,' Cadi sat down opposite him, studying his face. 'That is, no,' she contradicted herself. 'I didn't actually see one. I heard it.' She could see the faint tic of a muscle under his eye. He was actually quite handsome. And he was tall. She had noticed how he had had to fold up his legs as he lowered himself onto her sofa. 'What happened?' she repeated.

He swallowed hard. 'I had been walking up and down for a while, and I was heading steadily towards the far hedge, following the twig.' He gave an embarrassed half smile. 'I was distracted when a bird flew up at my feet and I lost concentration and the twig flew out of my hands. At that moment I saw something . . .' He paused, seemingly lost in thought.

'A horse?' Cadi prompted.

'No. It was more a trick of the light. A shimmer on the grass, then it was as if I was looking at – I don't know, a puddle, a reflection, some kind of mirror. And yes, there were horses there. Men and horses. Real horses, saddled and bridled. I could hear people talking. Not loud enough to make out what they were saying. Just a murmur and the jingle of harnesses. Just for a split second. Then . . . then, it was as if someone had flicked a switch The sounds had gone. The whole scene disappeared.

I was standing there up to my knees in waving grass and there was total silence. Absolute total silence, and then a skylark started to sing way up high.' He was staring down at his hands.

'And you told Chris this?'

'No.' He smiled as he looked up. 'No, of course I didn't. I said I heard the sounds coming from beyond the hedge. He knew there was a lost horse around here and he thought you should know about it; that I should drop in and tell you. But, I sensed . . .' he hesitated, looking straight at her now, 'that I could tell you the truth.' He gave a shudder. 'Please tell me I'm not going mad.' He rubbed his hands up and down his face. She heard the rasp of his beard against his palms.

'You look as if you could do with a drink,' she said, taking pity on him. 'Whisky?'

There was a bottle in the cupboard beside the kitchen window. Finding a glass, she brought it over, aware as she handed it to him that his hands were shaking.

'Thank you, that's kind of you.' He had an attractive smile.

She waited until he had taken a sip, then asked, 'So, tell me, again. Slowly. What did you actually see?'

'Nothing.'

'But you mentioned horses.'

'It was only a second. A trick of the light. Some kind of reflection. A mirage. It was like a mirage.'

'In a puddle, you said.'

'I suppose so. I couldn't find the spot again and then I was suddenly very cold and frightened. It made me feel like a child.' He sounded angry. 'Caught doing something it shouldn't.' He tipped the glass and drained it.

Cadi stood up and went to fetch the bottle. 'I heard some old ladies in the post office saying there was always something odd about that field, that when they were young their ponies wouldn't go near it,' she said cautiously. 'And apparently, none of the local children would play in there in the old days – still don't, now I come to think about it. At least, not on their own.'

'So, I suppose the locals think it's haunted.'

'I'm beginning to think it might be.' She laughed. 'Sadly,

I don't suppose that will put off the builders. A ghost horse is, if anything, rather romantic.'

'It's a very beautiful site. I walked up the hill first thing, before I met you, and one can see the sea far away in the distance.'

Cadi nodded. 'The estuary,' she corrected gently.

'It would be a shame to build there,' he said almost absent-mindedly. He stood up and put his glass down on the windowsill. 'Thank you for that. Much appreciated. I must go. I'm sorry to have burst in on you like this. I was completely rattled. Your neighbour at the mill was too busy to listen, but he could tell I needed someone to talk to.'

'I'm sorry I couldn't help.'

'You did. That's good whisky.'

'And strong. If you're driving, can I suggest you go back to the mill and get yourself something to eat. Chris serves good food. Grounding.' My goodness, she was sounding like a schoolmistress, she thought, hearing herself. It was the sort of thing Sally would say.

He didn't seem to be offended. 'Point taken.'

Cadi followed him to the door. 'Will you go back to the meadow?'

'Maybe. Another time.'

She wondered if he was going to suggest she joined him down at the mill, but he was already outside. 'Thank you again.'

She watched as he headed up the road and out of sight before closing the door and slowly making her way back to her desk. Within a few minutes she had forgotten him. She thought better with her pen in her hand and the story was lying in wait.

6

It was all arranged, apparently. Elen was to have no say in the matter. The Roman general had returned to the palace some eighteen months after his first visit with a full detachment of cavalry and this time he had made an offer her father would not hesitate to accept. The general wanted the suggestion of an alliance with Octavius's son forgotten. It was the high king's daughter he wanted and not as wife to one of his children. He wanted her for himself. The alliance would benefit them all. The foreign general from a distant land who had won his rank and position by power of arms and popularity with the vast armies he led in Britannia needed to form an alliance by marriage to the daughter of ancient kings, descendant of the gods themselves.

Elen and Magnus had never been introduced.

'No!'

Her father had at least had the courtesy to tell her at last the night before her future husband arrived for the ceremony.

Octavius's eyes hardened. 'It is my decision.'

'Conan?' Elen appealed to her brother, seated next to her father near one of the braziers. They were at the far end of the reception hall. Groups of people, talking quietly in the body of the room fell silent at the sound of raised voices, glancing at the royal family then, anxious not to be caught watching, returning to their own conversations. Until Octavius's decision that it might be prudent to warn his daughter what was to happen the next day he and Conan had been playing gwyddbwyll, a board game they both enjoyed. 'You turned the offer of the general's daughter down,' she cried indignantly. 'You didn't like him. You said no!'

Conan was by blood the son of the high king's sister, adopted by Octavius as his heir when it became clear he would have no sons of his own. The young man shook his head slowly. 'She did not suit me. And I was not sure he was right for you, Sister. I argued against the marriage when our father first told me of the offer, but don't forget I have met the man, and now I have had the chance to think about it, I agree with him that maybe he would be a good match for you.' He gave a somewhat cryptic smile.

'Meaning?'

'Meaning,' their father interrupted sharply, 'the decision is made.'

'But he is—'

He cut her off mid-sentence. 'He is a soldier, Elen. You knew you would one day marry a soldier.'

'But he is not one of us.' She finished the sentence under her breath.

It appeared that her father had been doing his research. 'He is head of the legions in Britannia. His mother was sister to the father of the emperor of the East and he is representative of the emperor of the West in Britannia. He is a great man. And the marriage will take place tomorrow.' Drawing his mantle around his shoulders, Octavius rose to his feet and, pushing the gaming board aside with such force that the table overturned, scattering the carved pieces on the floor, he stalked out of the hall, leaving brother and sister alone.

Someone was waiting for him in the atrium. At the sight of the woman, swathed from head to foot in black, the king's attendants drew back and one by one melted into the shadows.

'You must not proceed with this alliance.' Her voice was

husky. 'It bodes no good for your kingdom, or for greater Albion. Your foreign general bears the mark of the doomed on his forehead.'

Octavius shuddered. His wife had brought Branwen into his household when Elen was a small child as her nurse, her attendant and her teacher. When Aurelia had died, Branwen effortlessly filled the gap in the child's life. Daughter and grand-daughter of wise men of the Silures – and, he strongly suspected, a follower of the long-forbidden native Druid traditions of the country – Branwen had remained at Elen's side ever since, and all his efforts to dislodge her had failed. In only one thing had he managed to override the woman's malign influence. He had seen to it that his daughter and his adopted son had been brought up in the Christian faith, of which his wife had been a staunch follower.

He took a deep breath. 'You speak rubbish, woman. The arrangements are made; they cannot be changed.'

'And does Elen know what kind of man you propose to give her to? You cannot, you must not marry her to him.' Branwen stepped up to him, her eyes blazing. 'Don't you understand what you are doing?'

'I understand perfectly well.' The king pushed her away with a shudder. 'He is a great man. He may one day be even greater. He may be emperor himself.'

She gave a disparaging hiss. 'No. Elen deserves better.'

'There is no better,' he snapped. 'I acknowledge that it is largely due to you that he would consider her as his wife, inex-perienced and young as she is,' he added in a conciliatory tone. 'Thanks to you, my daughter can read and write, she is an educated young woman, probably a lot better educated than he is, truth be told, but it is not up to her now.' He paused, thoughtful. 'You can go with her as her attendant. There, does that reassure you?'

She shook her head. 'No. I will never serve Rome. She must go without me.'

'Then what will you do?' It didn't occur to him to insist. If he was honest, he never quite dared insist anything with this woman.

She gave a grim smile. 'Don't worry, my lord king.' Her voice held a note of mockery. 'I won't stay here. I will return to my own people up at the oppidum. From there, I plan to retire into seclusion in the forest where I can serve my own gods.'

He opened his mouth to protest but already she had walked back into the pillared shadows of the walled garden.

The oppidum. The ironic Latin term the local people used for their ancient towns on the hilltops, fortified, safe from attack, sanctuaries for people and stock, and only defeated finally by the massed Roman armies. It had been a long time before the Romans had conceded that the local tribespeople could once again use the ruins of their base as a town, but slowly they had returned and slowly they had rebuilt their houses and turned it into a thriving centre, far more their own than the Roman concessionary market town of Venta would ever be.

In the king's reception hall Elen was staring pleadingly at her brother. 'I can't marry him,' she whispered, watching a slave pick up the pieces from the abandoned game, very conscious of people still glancing anxiously towards the brother and sister after the high king had stormed out of the chamber. 'I know nothing about him. I've never seen him. He will take me away from everything I have ever known. If Mama was here, she would speak for me. She would understand.' Elen's mother had died five years before when Elen was twelve.

Conan moved across to his father's chair, indicating that Elen take his own before leaning across and putting his hands over hers. 'I can tell you a little, but as I said, I met him only briefly all those months ago when he came to ask father for my hand for his daughter Flavia.'

She stared at him, wide-eyed. 'So, go on, tell me about him.'

Conan sighed. 'Well, I know he virtually rules the country, Elen. He is a legate, general, Comes Britanniarum, head of the field armies of the entire province. He was Dux Britanniarum in the north.' He paused, aware of his sister's gaze fixed on his face. 'He has been married before, obviously. His wife died. He has two grown sons and a daughter who is probably about the same age as you. I fear he is much older than you.' He did a quick calculation in his head and scowled. 'Probably more than twice as old. But he is popular with his men, which is a good sign.'

'What does he look like?' It was a whisper.

Conan laughed. 'I think you'll find him handsome. I'm no judge of a woman's view, but from a man's I see him as tall, taller than you.' He cocked a glance at his sister, huddled as she was in her chair. She was tall for a woman, slim and athletic with dark blond wavy hair, restrained now by several carved bone pins. With hazel eyes and a clear pale complexion, he had to acknowledge, if she hadn't been his sister, he would have found her almost beautiful. As it was, they had scrapped too often in the nursery for him to be impressed by her fiery temper and her passionate outbursts. He felt an unexpected wave of compassion. In her shoes he would probably be scared. 'He has regular features, a man of presence. Strong. A man to respect.'

Elen was silent. 'Is he a Christian?' she asked at last.

'I've no idea,' he admitted. 'Does it matter?'

'I don't suppose so,' she conceded.

It was dark when Elen slipped out to the stables. The colt was there, brought in from the paddock, his coat glossy, a soft leather head collar over his ears. He was fully grown now and trained to bit and saddle. He nuzzled at her, searching the folds of her shawl for the titbit he knew would be hidden there.

'I hear you are to leave us.' The voice from the shadows made her jump. Rhys was there, sucking on a wisp of hay as he leaned against the doorpost. 'I shall miss this chap.'

'Why? Where is he going?' Elen tried to keep her voice steady.

'With you. He is your wedding gift from your father. Did he not tell you? You may think you've hidden it from him and your brother, but they know how much you love that animal and how much time you have spent schooling him.' He moved over to scratch the horse's neck. The girl's misery was coming off her in waves. 'I doubt you'll be able to ride him much,' he went on firmly. Better she come to terms with it at once. 'He will be, to all intents and purposes, your husband's horse.

You will have to behave like a princess all the time in your new life.' He hid a smile. Someone had to tell her, and he doubted anyone else would dare. 'To show the Roman general how lucky he is to have a royal bride.'

She scowled, burying her face in the horse's mane. 'Will I have to go to live at Isca?'

He chewed his lip. This was way beyond the limits of his experience. 'I suppose you will follow him like any officer's wife but with more dinner parties. Are you taking your own servants and slaves?'

She hadn't even thought of that. She hadn't had time to think of anything except running to the stables for comfort from her beloved horse. 'Will I go tomorrow, straight after we are married?'

'I am only your father's horse master, Princess,' he said softly. 'I know nothing of how these things are managed. Is there no one else you can ask?'

It turned out the servants and slaves knew far more than she did, which was not unusual. The palace was a hotbed of gossip at the best of times, but news of the wedding, unexpected and exciting as it was, had travelled the corridors and courtyards with the speed of light. When she returned to it, Elen found her bedchamber was warm. The hypocaust had been fired up and already a trunk was lying open on the floor, half full of tunics and mantles and shawls.

'There you are at last!' Delyth, Elen's senior attendant, her confidante and friend, hurried towards her with an audible sigh of relief. 'There is so much to do.'

Elen sat down on the end of the bed and kicked off her sandals. Her silk tunic and her smartest mantle were already hanging up ready for the next day's ceremony. The gold embroidered girdle that had been her mother's was lying on a side table. Delyth followed her gaze. 'I thought you would like to wear that,' she said gently. 'But if you would prefer something else?'

Elen shook her head, trying not to cry. Delyth took in the situation at a glance and, turning towards the room, clapped her hands together loudly. 'Leave us, please. Nia, Sian, go to the kitchen and bring something for our princess to eat. The rest of you may go. The last items can go into the travelling chests tomorrow.'

She waited for the women to leave the room then she came and sat down next to Elen. 'I am to come with you, if you wish it. The general has ordered that you can bring your own household. Servants, slaves. Me,' she added. 'He seems kind.' She glanced across at Elen.

'Where will we go?' Elen swallowed hard.

'We follow the army now. But at first we will be at his headquarters at Isca. He has requisitioned the commander's house there. Not so far away,' she added.

'It seems far away to me.' Elen reached out her hand and clasped the other woman's fingers. 'I'm glad you're coming.'

'Don't fret. I'll be there as long as you need me.'

The older woman and the girl looked at each other for several long seconds. Both knew their future was in the hands of a stranger.

'And Branwen. She can come too?' Elen whispered at last.

There was a long pause. Delyth bit her lip. 'Branwen has gone,' she said after what seemed an eternity. 'I'm sorry. I don't know what happened, but it appears that the king your father has sent her away.'

'Why?' The word came out as a cry of pain.

Delyth shook her head. 'I didn't see her. All I know is that the servants watched her pack her bundle and leave the palace.'

'She can't have gone. She wouldn't go without saying goodbye.'

'She was escorted off the premises, Elen. Sent on her way down the road.'

'So she will have gone up the hill, to the oppidum, to find her family.'

'I don't know if she has any family, sweetheart. We, you, were her family.' Delyth sighed. 'I believe . . . that is, someone overheard her with your father. They were quarrelling. No one quarrels with the high king.'

* * *

It was much later and the lamps had almost burned down. Elen lay tossing in her bed, wishing now that she had asked for one of the girls to come and sing to her as she tried to sleep, when the door opened again and someone slipped into the room. She sat up. 'Who's that?'

'It is me, child.' Branwen, wrapped in her black mantle, tip-toed across the room. 'I couldn't go without seeing you.'

Elen slipped out of bed and ran across the room, the mosaic floor warm beneath her bare feet. She threw herself into Branwen's arms. 'You have to come with me. I can't go without you.'

Branwen held her close, then gently she pushed her away. 'No, Elen. This is goodbye. Your father has spoken and you must obey him. I have done all I can for you and he has thanked me. He has told the man who will be your husband that you are an educated young woman with a mind of her own.' Branwen smiled. 'You will bring authenticity to his position as a leader in Britannia. Your blood is royal, your children will be kings.'

Elen stared at her. 'You can see the future?'

'Sometimes.'

'But you didn't see that I was going to be married tomorrow!' Elen knew she sounded petulant, but she couldn't help herself.

She swung round as the door opened. A slave girl came in carrying a tray. On it were two flagons, one of warm wine and one of water, and a flask of oil with which to replenish the lamps. The two women fell silent until she left the room. Branwen smiled. 'I came in through the kitchens. I asked Stella to bring the wine. My friends there will make sure we are not disturbed.'

'Please come with me.' Elen leaned forward and caught Branwen's hands in her own.

The woman shook her head. 'My home is with my people, Elen. I have taught you all you need to know. You have to be strong now. You don't need me anymore. You are ready.'

'Ready?'

'Ready, child.'

'But I can't read the future like you. I can't see what is to happen.'

'That is a power you can well do without, Elen. You are too young—'

'No!' Elen stamped her foot. 'If you won't come with me, then you must teach me the art of scrying, so I know what to expect, just as you do.'

'No, child!'

'Stop calling me child. I need to know. Here.' Elen ran to the side table and grabbed a glass bowl full of fruit; tipping the contents onto the floor, she reached for the goblet of water, pouring it into the bowl. 'So, show me what to do.'

Branwen sighed. 'It is simple. Sit down and hold the bowl, so. Then make yourself quiet. Look into the water and allow the pictures to come.'

'It can't be that easy.'

'It is easy if you still your thoughts and wait.' Branwen walked over to a stool by the door and sat down, folding her arms.

Elen glanced at her, then down at the bowl of water.

How it slipped from her hands she didn't know. One moment she was sitting quietly waiting for the revelations to appear and the next Branwen had her arm around her shoulders and with tears pouring down her face Elen was staring at the broken glass at her feet. One of the maids came running. A brush and pan was brought, the glass swept up and a beaker of warm wine was pressed into her hands.

Branwen shook her head. 'It was obviously not to be,' she murmured. 'Leave it now.' She would never tell Elen that she had slipped easily into the waking dream and that whatever it was that she had seen had terrified her. 'Whatever the goddess has decided,' she whispered, 'she will not be deflected.' She stepped back and stared down at the floor where the head of the goddess stared serenely up at them from the mosaic. 'Whatever happens, she will be with you, child. Yours is a sacred and a special bloodline. My gods and yours will protect you, I promise you that, and if ever you do need me, really need me, I will come to find you.'

* * *

Was that how it had happened? The scene seemed somehow familiar. As though she had seen it before. Cadi stared down at the pages in front of her. So many scribbled notes. The crude sketch of a rearing horse – she was no Rachel – and the birth of a story. She gave a grim smile. That was how it had been when she was a child. Stories. She was always writing stories, illustrating them herself, her tongue clamped between her teeth as she concentrated hard on the page, reaching for her coloured chalks, then abandoning the pictures in frustration for the greater flexibility and complexity and sheer accuracy of the written word, the stories which never seemed to stop, the stories that became ever more exciting as she covered page after page in her exercise books with the weird and wonderful tales that endlessly and effortlessly emerged from her imagination.

With a sigh she tore the pages from her notepad and screwed them up, hurling them towards the wastepaper basket. She hadn't done this for years – writing almost unconsciously, carried away by the power of some half-remembered story when she should be concentrating on the spare, pure verses that were her trademark style as a poet.

And now it had happened twice.

She sat for several minutes staring into space, then she bent and retrieved the pages. Slowly she flattened them out on her desk, and after a moment slipped them into the back of one of her folders. It might be interesting, one day, to read through what she had written. And in the meantime she had thought of someone she could talk to about all this. Maybe.

7

'How are you, Dad?'

Cadi was standing in her back garden. The meadow, now mown and the hay baled, was populated with fifty or so sheep. No one had told Dai Prosser not to put them there. There had been no sign of strangers eyeing up the land. Charles Ford had not, as far as she knew, returned.

'I'm good.' Her father had picked up the call almost at once this time after she had spent several days trying in vain to leave him a message. He obviously didn't believe in switching on any answering gizmos on his phone. 'When are you coming to see me?'

'Maybe in the autumn, Dad. That would be nice.' Her father, long widowed, had decamped to France several years before. The slight note of reproach in his voice cut no ice with Cadi. She knew he was having the time of his life out there in his Provençal cottage.

After all the preliminary chat and questions as to his welfare, which as expected he answered with practised vagueness, she got to the point of her call. 'Dad, do you happen to know where Uncle Meryn is?'

'Why?'

The coldness in his tone was clear even in that one word.

'I wanted to ask him something.'

The two Jones brothers had never got along, but even so, they kept in touch. 'At a safe distance', as her father, Owen, described it. They came, as Owen constantly reminded his daughter, from different planets. How could they be friends?

'Don't tell me you want to talk gobbledegook!' Owen grumbled.

Cadi laughed. 'Yup. Exactly that. I know he's in America. I wondered if you had an email address or something for him.'

'Last time I heard, he was back at his cottage in Wales.' The reply was grudging. 'I suppose I can find his phone number if you really want it.'

'Oh come on, Dad, what's he done now?'

'Nothing.'

She sighed. The brothers barely spoke. Never would, but she realised as she glanced down at the number she had scribbled in her notebook, her father hadn't had to look it up. He had known it off the top of his head. A mobile too. Who would have thought her dotty uncle Meryn would own such a thing. Dotty as in psychic. Dotty as in expert on the weird and wonderful and, wonderfully, back in Wales after his long sojourn in the United States.

'Hello, Cadi. How are you?' Meryn was obviously outside somewhere. She could hear the wind echoing in the phone.

'I was wondering if you could give me some advice.'

'About?'

'I'm not sure.'

'Right.'

The reception on the phone improved as she heard a door bang. He had obviously gone indoors.

'I keep hearing things,' she said cautiously.

'And since you've called me and not your doctor, I take it it's not tinnitus?'

'It's marching feet. And a galloping horse.'

'Interesting.'

'Actually, it's a bit scary. You couldn't come over, could you?'

'I'm busy, Cadi.'

'I know. It's just – it's urgent. They're threatening to build houses on the meadow next to my cottage and the noise of soldiers marching is getting closer each time I hear it. Closer and more urgent. I think they're Roman soldiers.'

'Coming to the rescue of the meadow?'

'No. Yes. Perhaps. I don't know. But there's something weird going on. I need, we need, to prove there was a Roman villa here.'

'And you want me to stand the middle of the meadow wearing my cloak and pointy hat and tell them the field is haunted so they can't build there? You know what, Cadi, they would be ecstatic. They would charge double for houses in a haunted field.'

She scowled. 'I wasn't suggesting you do that. As if I would! You are a proper professor, aren't you? You could prepare a real scientific professory sort of report. You don't have to be specific.'

'Cadi – "a real, scientific professory sort of report"! What on earth do you think it is I do?'

She grinned to herself. 'Not sure. Dad thinks you're a ghost hunter. I know you have super powers. Please, Uncle Meryn.' She was doing a mock wheedle. 'You could just demand another, more thorough survey. A proper one. What is it they do on the TV? Geophys or something?'

'I think you'll find it's called ground-penetrating radar. And they haven't done that?'

'Not as far as I know. Chris, one of my neighbours, has been in touch with the planning office and demanded to see the survey, and I gather they came up with all sorts of stuff about it being unavailable. He doesn't believe there is one. Not a proper one. Either that or there is something there they don't want us to see. You'll be my secret weapon. I won't tell anyone how we know we're right, we'll just insist they come and do the investigation again with us there to watch.'

'And so far your only reason for thinking they're lying and there was a villa there, is that you have heard a ghostly army marching to the rescue?'

'And there is a long tradition in the village of something there, and in David's family too. We know there was definitely something called a marching camp, which might explain the marching footsteps, but I gather that isn't important enough alone to stop the development.'

'Who owns the field?'

'The developer.'

'Oh dear. And what does the council say?'

'The community council is one hundred per cent with us. The county council seem to think there's no good reason to say no to the application. Chris thinks that in itself is suspicious. He thinks maybe someone has slipped someone a backhander.' There was a hopeful silence. 'Please.'

'I suppose I could come and take a look.' He sighed.

'That's brilliant. I thought you were still in the States. I thought you would have to write to them. But if you can come, that is perfect. I won't tell a soul, obviously. We could just go for a walk. At the moment there's a footpath across the field and there are sheep in there. It all seems quite normal. Oh, Uncle Meryn, it will be so good to see you again. When can you come?'

'I'll drive over tomorrow.' She could hear the laughter in his voice. 'And, Cadi, for the record: I am an emeritus professor and I hold two doctorates. That professory enough for you?'

8

Elen recognised him as soon as he walked into the room at the head of the procession. She remembered clearly the amused face of the helmeted commander who had bent over her as she lay in the field covered in mud and extended his hand to pull her to her feet in front of all his men. At first he saw only the beautiful composed young woman who rose to greet him and it was a moment before he identified her as the wild young woman who had so spectacularly flown off the spirited black colt to land at his feet in the mud. This was the girl who had dressed in tribesmen's trousers, her hair tangled, her eyes at first furious at the fall, then perhaps a little embarrassed, then indignant as she had pulled her hand away from his. But never afraid. At no time had she been the slightest bit afraid of him.

Neither betrayed any sign of ever having met before. He was in the uniform of a general now, the crested helmet under his arm being passed to his attendant, a scarlet cloak draped over his shoulder; she was wearing a long white tunic belted with an elaborate silk girdle and a matching mantle bordered with silver thread. Her hair, neatly coiled round her head, was covered with a veil. He noted the heavy carved gold necklace and earrings.

She was not required to be present at the protracted final-isation of the wedding contract between her future husband and her father, swathed as he was in the full formal toga, but then came the blessing in the chapel with its mosaics and fres-coed pictures of ancient weddings. The bishop had come in the general's party from Venta to intone the prayers, place the floral wreaths – hers redolent with wild mint and roses – upon the heads of bride and groom, and to supervise the exchange of rings before at last the groom was permitted to lift her veil. As he looked down into her face for the first time that day, he winked.

The feasting would go on for several days but at last Flavius Magnus and his wife withdrew to the wing of guest rooms which had been put at their disposal for their wedding night. Even as they reached the door it appeared they were not yet to be alone. With a bow in her direction he allowed himself to be led away towards the palace bathhouse while she entered the bedroom to be prepared for her husband. Her wedding garments were removed, her skin anointed with scented olive oil and a shift of softest silk slipped over her head. Her own attendants, slaves and freedwomen brushed out her hair and at last left her alone. She stood looking around. The bedchamber was lit by a single lamp. Someone had arranged vases of flowers in the alcoves and there were refreshments on the table, a jug of wine with two golden goblets and a plate of almond cakes. She looked around uncertainly. She hadn't expected to be alone. She could hear the faint sounds of the party going on in the distance and the splatter of water from the fountain in the courtyard. The scent of roses drifted through the half-open doors.

She could feel her wedding ring, strangely tight on the fourth finger of her left hand. Her women had removed the rest of her jewellery with her clothes and the wreath of flowers on her hair. She twisted the ring uncomfortably and shivered as a gentle breeze blew in from the peristyle. She reached over to the couch by the wall to retrieve the embroidered stole Nia had left there, perhaps suspecting she might feel cold. Wrapping it around her shoulders, she stood in the doorway looking out. The whole area was deserted, lit only by two cressets placed discreetly on the columns, amongst the pots of honey-suckle and bay. The shadows danced. No one came. She assumed the guests had been steered away from these rooms to give the newly-weds some privacy, but the privacy was becoming frightening. Where was her husband? He had barely spoken to her. She had felt his fingers, strong and somehow reassuring, grip hers as her father put her hand in his, and she had met his gaze as he lifted her veil to kiss her forehead, but that was all. They had not exchanged as much as a word in private. Her thoughts flew back to that other meeting in the field when she had been lying at his feet and she felt a moment of total panic.

Behind her the door from the corridor opened and he was there at last; not the eager bridegroom she had been half expecting, half dreading, but a fully armed soldier. Only his helm was missing as he strode towards her and caught her hands.

'The gods are against us, sweetheart, but only for a while. I have just received intelligence that pirates from Hibernia have landed an invasion force in the land of the Demetae on the south-west coast. I have spoken to your father and he agrees it is safest that you stay here with him. I will return as soon as I have sent the invaders packing.' He leaned forward and kissed her forehead for the second time. 'Did you ever succeed in training that colt?' His eyes danced as he looked down at her. 'This will give you more time.'

And with a swirl of his cloak and a brief waft of the cedar oil with which his skin had been massaged in the bathhouse, he was gone. She heard him shouting to her servants to attend her, and the tramp of his heavy sandals receding down the passage, then the room fell silent. She had not uttered a word.

As Delyth appeared in the doorway the silence was broken by the distant sound of barked commands, of troops falling in and then marching in step down the stone driveway towards the road. The general and his attendant cohort was gone. His bride was left alone slowly twisting the ring on her finger.

It was Rhys who found the little dog. It was wet and cold, cowering under some bushes in a corner of the paddock. He had heard it whimpering as he turned the colt out to graze.

Picking the little thing up, he carried it back to the stables. The animal was wearing a collar, otherwise he would probably have knocked it on the head as a stray from the hill fort, but the collar intrigued him. It was made of soft leather and was the colour of the palest wild rose. Attached to a metal ring near the buckle was a medal, engraved with strange symbols. The little creature seemed friendly and lonely and very hungry, and an idea dawned on him. He took it, bathed, brushed and fed with scraps from his own plate, to find Nia. 'For the princess. To cheer her up in the absence of her husband.' And, he thought quietly to himself, to help if she had to part from the colt. He knew how men worked. If the general fancied the horse for himself as he had warned her, it would remain hers in name only and even that for no time at all.

Elen was enchanted. The little dog and she took to one another at once. 'Gemma.' The name carved on the medal was easily read, but the other symbols defeated her. It didn't matter. If they were there to bring luck to the little jewel of a dog they had certainly done so. She now belonged to the greatest lady in the land.

Elen's husband returned to the palace a month to the day after he had left for the west. The bulk of the legion marched on to Isca while he turned north with a hand-picked troop of men as escort, to collect his bride.

He had brought her a gift. Alone together at last in the court-yard garden after he had given his formal greetings to her father, he produced the package with a cautious smile. 'Our marriage has had an inauspicious start. I'm sorry. I'm afraid the life of a soldier is never predictable. I hope this will convey my respect with a promise to try and do better.'

She was astonished at the flood of anger that swept through her. 'I hope you will do more than try! Presumably you have officers below you in your command who could have led a sortie against the pirates – who fled, I hear, without so much as a blow struck. Some invasion!'

He recoiled slightly. If he had expected a submissive bride ready to welcome him into her arms, she soon clarified the situation. 'I have waited for a message; a sign from you that you had survived some fearsome massacre and instead my father told me – from a message he received, not me – that your hasty departure had not been necessary. You humiliated me, a princess of the royal blood of Britannia! And you think to make good with a paltry present!' She stormed away from him and stood staring down into the alabaster bowl of the fountain, her fists clenched.

His amazement was genuine. For a moment he was speechless. She heard the creak of the leather base of his breastplate as he moved towards her. 'Forgive me.' Luckily she did not see his smile. By the time he was standing beside her he had managed a note of contrition. 'My behaviour was ungracious and unforgivable. Your father has so often emphasised how young you are. I was trying to spare you. I had understood I was marrying someone not long out childhood.'

'Childhood!' She spun round.

'No.' He took a step back. This young woman was far from childish. Even in the short month he had been away she had filled out a little and he could see the womanly curves beneath her tunic. 'I can see you are no child. I have married a great lady. A royal lady. And I have come to fetch you back to my headquarters. I hope one good thing has come from our extended nuptials – my men have had time to supervise the last stages of building a palace fit for a queen.'

'At Isca?' She was dismissive.

'At Segontium.'

She was taken aback. 'And where is that?'

'Beyond the mountains to the north. No more than three or four days' march from here,' he added hastily. 'Perhaps five or six.'

'But why there? Why not here?' She managed to stop herself from stamping her foot. That would indeed be childish.

'Because I need somewhere to keep you safe. If nothing else, my sortie to the land of the Demetae has shown how vulnerable the coast down there is to attack. I have requested again and again for the emperor to send extra field army units, but so far I have had no response. The empire is threatened on every

63

side. Here in Britannia alone we have to contend with Saxon raiding parties in the east, Picts and Caledonians to the north, tribes from Hibernia who may come in force next time. In Gaul they face even greater threats and the emperor seems unable or unwilling to face up to them. At Segontium you will be safe. We'll travel the land together, you and I, north south, east and west, but I need to have somewhere secure as a base for my family.' He smiled down at her. 'Your father would find me remiss if I let anything happen to my royal princess.'

Her snort of derision was anything but royal. Again he managed to hide a smile. 'Will you not open my gift?'

'If I must.' She turned to face him and he was surprised to see the amount of hostility held in that slim body. Grudgingly she stretched out her hand and he placed the package in it. It was heavy and awkward in shape, wrapped in rough flax-blue linen. She tore off the silk ribbon, dropping it at her feet and unfolded the cloth. Inside was a miniature statuette of a prancing horse. It was made of solid gold. She stared at it for several seconds. 'It's very beautiful,' she said at last. She glanced up at him. 'Did you have it made specially?'

He nodded. 'Your horse is the colour of ebony, but I felt gold was more suitable. It was made by a craftsman in the hills where the gold is mined.'

'My people are clever craftsmen.'

He noted the possessive pronoun.

'Indeed they are.'

'Is he a slave?' Her tone sharpened.

'A freeman and so a citizen of the Roman Empire. As you are.'

She raised an eyebrow. 'Then I thank you for the gift. It is beautiful.'

'And it will be one of many.' He stooped and picked up the dog that had crept up to sit near her feet. It wore a pink collar, and his fingers rattled the medals that hung from it. One carried the symbol of luck and blessing, the other, the dog's name, Gemma, engraved in careful script. On the reverse was a sequence of other symbols. He stared at them. 'How strange. Your dog carries a message similar to those I saw used in Arabia to represent numbers. She must be a well-travelled little creature.' He bent and set the dog down on the floor. Then he reached out for Elen's hand. 'Can we start again? Our relationship needs to be built on rock. May I call you Elen?'

'That is my name. I am Elen ferch Eudaf, my father's daughter. And I shall call you Macsen, that is Magnus in our language. Macsen meaning greatest.' She raised an eyebrow.

He smiled. 'So what does Elen mean?'

'A ray of sunlight.'

'Perfect. Together we will rule the world.'

They looked at one another in all seriousness for a second, then both burst out laughing. 'Come,' he said, 'your father has ordered a second wedding feast to celebrate our union. Let us go in together, then together we will set off on our new life tomorrow at dawn.'

But after the feast and before dawn would come their wedding night. And that, he thought with a tingle of anticipation, was going to prove interesting.

9

The sheep had gone and the gate into the meadow was padlocked. But next to it the stile was still accessible and the footpath fingerpost remained in place. Cadi climbed over and stood just inside the hedge, half expecting to hear a shout of objection, but the field was empty. She began to walk across it, listening to the birds, as always keeping a hopeful eye open for Gemma. The brook was running deep after all the rain, the water gurgling greedily over the stones. The sun was only just up, rising out of a bank of mist, promising heat later in the day. She followed the footpath over the brook and began to climb through the wood on the far side. Towards the top the trees began to thin out and the hill flattened. This was the site of the ancient pre-Roman fort and presumably of Branwen's oppidum. An atmosphere of mystery still clung to the overgrown banks and ditches that circled the summit. She was panting as she reached the top and paused as she always did to admire the view. To the north and west there were banks of distant mountains, the Bannau Brycheiniog, to the south a stunning glimpse of the Severn Estuary, a strip of silver, bronzed by the early sunlight. She glanced up as a buzzard drifted overhead, letting out a lonely yelping cry, then she turned and looked back the way she had come, down towards Camp Meadow and she tensed. There were horses in the field. Several of them, clustered together. She could just glimpse someone holding the reins as though they were waiting for their riders. A cloud covered the sun and a dark shadow ran over the grass. When it passed the horses had gone.

Cadi's Uncle Meryn arrived later that morning. Leaving his car in the village, he called at the mill bakery to buy pastries before strolling down the road towards Sarnelen Cottage. He hesitated for several seconds outside the gate before reaching over to unlatch it and walking up the short path to the front door.

He was an elderly man, slim and wiry, with white hair, his face tanned from the Californian sun. For the last two years he had been a visiting professor at UCLA but now, as he told Cadi while they waited for the kettle to boil, he was planning to settle down for a peaceful retirement.

'Retirement?' Cadi repeated incredulously as she reached for plates and mugs. 'You?'

He was, she knew, quite a bit older than her father, but had always looked ten years younger.

He laughed. He had pulled a chair out to sit down at the kitchen table. 'Point taken. I'm writing a book. But no more lecturing. I need to recharge my batteries and take my garden in hand. I've been away too long.'

He lived in a remote cottage in the Black Mountains, high on the hillside above Hay-on-Wye with a view over four counties.

He emptied the paper bag onto the plates and edged the pastries into position, wadding the bag into a ball and hurling it unerringly towards her recycling bin. 'Right. The story. From the beginning please.'

She told him everything that had happened, including the disappearance of Gemma, then, almost as an afterthought, described her walk that morning and the fleeting glimpse of the horses in the distance in the meadow below. As she retraced her steps earlier, she had searched the place for hoofmarks or horse dung, signs of trampled turf, but all she could find was clear evidence of the sheep that had presumably been taken elsewhere the night before. There was absolutely no sign that any horse had ever set foot in the meadow.

Sipping his coffee, Meryn pulled off a piece of pastry and stuffed it into his mouth, chewing thoughtfully as she finished her story. 'And nothing else significant has happened? You are sure?'

She shook her head. 'Mrs Powell in the village said she thought an excavation was carried out somewhere round here just before the war, then filled in. She thought they found bones and maybe a mosaic floor, but there seems to be no record anywhere. I checked with David and he asked his cousin Donald, the family historian, but neither had ever heard anything about it. Donald said there was no official record of any excavations.'

Meryn nodded thoughtfully. 'The war got in the way of so much. I expect it was completely forgotten and they weren't great on keeping archaeological records in those days anyway.' He thought for a minute. 'So, what are you working on?' He nodded towards the piles of books on her desk.

'I've been writing stories.' She hesitated, then ploughed on. 'Strange, almost stream-of-consciousness stories about the history, as if I'm watching it happen. It's weird. Compulsive. And I'm writing some poetry based around the stories in the Mabinogion.'

'Ah yes, I heard about that.'

'Who from? Not Pa?' She was astonished.

He shook his head. 'A colleague in LA. Something of a poetry buff with a passion for Celtic legend.'

Cadi digested that information for a second then went on, 'I thought I might—' She broke off. 'That is, one of the stories, "The Dream of Macsen Wledig", seems to fit the Roman vibe. I wasn't even going to use the story originally. I love the tales of Celtic gods and goddesses, and Macsen and Roman history didn't seem to work for what Rachel and I are doing, but now . . .' she paused, groping for the right words. 'The story I'm writing, it's as though it wants to write itself. I can't seem to stop. It's compulsive, fascinating.' She took a deep breath. 'It's not frightening, although in a way it should be. Elen is not dictating the story to me. It's as if I'm ducking in and out of her life. I'm not her, but I feel as though I know her. It's as though I met her once . . . It must have been in a dream, I suppose. Her dream or my dream.' She shook her head. 'I can't quite remember. For some weird reason I associate the memory with the sound of breaking glass. I don't know why. I'm not anyone in the story, but I'm seeing what's happening in real time. I'm seeing a parallel universe. Except that I know what's going to happen because in my world hers is in the past and it's already happened.'

'Macsen is the link,' he interrupted.

She smiled. 'Is he? That's your department. I'm not sure. Maybe it's just that I've heard soldiers. And this house is called Sarnelen Cottage. The woman in the story, the princess who became his wife, Elen, is the heroine of the story, the heroine of Macsen's Dream and so of course the heroine of my poem as well.' She stopped, thinking over what she had just said. 'But that's all too much of a coincidence, isn't it.'

'Why? What coincidence?' He returned her smile, his eyes twinkling. 'No such thing as a coincidence. The link was there, ready for someone to see it. All it needed was something to set the telegraph wires trembling.'

She felt his gaze on her face and glanced up, anxious now. 'Is that how it works? It's as easy as that?' That was what he did. Psychic stuff. Ghosts and energies. Magic and paranormal activity. And of course the technical stuff, the quantum physics behind it all that he taught at university.

He nodded slowly as he leaned back in his chair and folded his arms. He thought for a moment then reached for his mug. 'But, as you guessed, there had to be something there to forge the connection in the first place and that could well be the new threat to the status quo. Let me finish this, then I think you had better show me this famous meadow.'

Every time she went to the meadow now Cadi felt more and more desperate. Everyone was doing their best to find a way of saving it, but that did not stop her feeling tearful on each occasion she came and saw afresh just how much they were in danger of losing. 'That was where Charles Ford was dowsing.'

She glanced back at Meryn. They were standing just inside the gate. The padlock was still in place and they had had to climb over the stile. 'He saw something that shook him so much he needed a stiff drink to get over the shock.' She watched her uncle as he strode ahead of her a few paces and stopped. He had his hands in his pockets. In his well-worn serviceable Barbour jacket he looked anything but a wizard. It was beginning to rain, a soft mist across the grass.

'What sort of something?' he asked at last as he stopped and looked back.

'He didn't seem very sure. He talked about reflections in a puddle.'

Meryn nodded. 'And you mentioned flashing lights and horses. Wait here. I'm going to walk across the field.'

She stood where she was and watched as he moved slowly and steadily along the footpath towards the stream. Every now and then he stopped and looked around him. The path was barely visible now the grass had been mown, but enough people had walked it in the past, she supposed, for it to remain as a clear track. She sighed. She was missing the cheerful bouncing little dog with her flying ears and wondered, as she always did when she came out here, what had become of her. Sally was inconsolable. There had been no more unscheduled days off as far as she knew, but her friend was obviously burying herself in her work as the summer term wore on; they walked together far less often these days, perhaps unable to bear being reminded of the terrible gap in their lives.

Meryn had almost reached the brook and was standing, gazing around. After what must have been several seconds, he set off back towards her, walking only a few metres before he stopped and moved sharply off the track. He had taken his hands out of his pockets and she saw him stretch them out in front of him as if he were patting the air. She felt a sharp tingle of excitement, tempted to move towards him. Somehow she made herself stand still. It was several long minutes before he returned to the path and headed back to where she waited for him near the gate.

'Well?' she breathed.

He turned back to face the field, leaning with his elbow on the top bar. 'Interesting.'

'Do you think there is a villa here?'

He gave a slow smile. 'I've no idea. I'm not an archaeologist.'

'But—'

'But,' he repeated the word quietly, 'there are thin places in this field. Places where time is, shall we say, inconsistent.'

'I don't understand.'

'Of course you do. You are my niece. You must have inherited some of our ancestors' gifts and talents even if your father blatantly hasn't. Think of how you feel when you go into an ancient church. There is no one else there; you can smell dust but you sense the generations who have worshipped there. Their prayers. Their hopes and fears are all anchored in the stone. When that happens in an outdoor environment, the stones, the buildings have gone; perhaps they were never there, but the link remains, and that is largely because, in the old days, places of worship, sacred places, were always positioned at special sites. Thin sites. Not now, of course. Most people have lost the art of the sacred. Planning committees are renowned for their lack of acuity. Even if someone raises an objection, their opinion will not be counted, probably not even noted. The intangible doesn't exist in our current cartesian culture.' He grinned.

She came to lean against the gate beside him. 'So, what does a thin place look like?'

'You tell me. You've seen it.'

'A shimmer. A trick of the light. A reflection in a puddle?'

'Exactly that.'

'And always in the same place?'

'Usually. More or less.'

'Like in *Doctor Who*?'

He smiled at the thought. 'I think it's fair to say CGI sometimes lacks subtlety, but yes, in a way, fantasy and sci-fi can often get it fairly right.'

'It's a gate into the past. Somewhere ghosts hang around?'

'Yes, to the first. Not necessarily, to the second. Ghosts have many different forms, origins, explanations, definitions.'

'I saw horses. Down here. From the hilltop. And I've heard

horses, in the meadow. Here. Felt the ground shake beneath their hooves. Surely, they're not ghosts?'

'Why not?'

She gave him a sideways glance. 'You're being serious?'

'Isn't that why you asked me to come over? You didn't want a rational explanation?'

Their eyes met and they both smiled.

'None of this helps, Cadi, for your hopes of an archaeological breakthrough. Sadly, the mention of my name would not aid your cause and I doubt whether even the intervention of a battery of TV cameras would delay builders for more than a few weeks or perhaps at most months once they have planning permission.'

Cadi bit her lip. 'No, you're right. But can you try again? See if you can tell what it is you're sensing.'

Pushing himself away from the gate, he nodded. 'Follow me.'

It was exactly the same place where he had hesitated before. He held out his hands. 'You try. Do this: imagine you're feeling for the heat from a stove. Gently, cautiously, put your whole attention into the palms of your hands. Don't try to prejudge the situation; empty your mind of thoughts and let the energy of the grasses brush your skin without going near enough for it to touch you.'

'Oh!' Cadi jumped backwards. 'Oh my God! I felt something!'

'Well done. Now try again. Don't be afraid. Calm acceptance is what we're looking for.'

She gave it a try but almost immediately dropped her hands and shook her head. 'No. I'm scared.'

'Scared?' He sounded appalled.

'I'm sorry. I'm obviously not a chip off the old block after all.'

He smiled. 'Oh, I think you are. Try again.'

But it was no good. She couldn't feel it. They spent twenty minutes slowly circling the spot but, whatever it was, to her secret relief, it had gone.

Walking up the lane later to have lunch at the mill, Meryn shrugged his shoulders. 'Don't worry about it. You've done it once, it won't be so hard next time. Sometimes we want these things so much our own heads act as a barrier to our sensitivity. And besides, I could no longer feel it either. It may be that the energies of the earth or the universe had moved on for the time being. These things can depend on so many parameters. Maybe we're just hungry!'

As they sat waiting for their food, sipping elderflower pressé, Chris stopped by their table. 'Did you find anything?' he asked with a grin.

Cadi put down her glass. 'Find anything?'

'You were spotted. Dowsing, was it? Any luck?'

''Fraid not.' She glanced at Meryn.

'You were in here this morning, buying pastries,' Chris went on. 'Cadi's famous uncle, right?'

Meryn remained impassive as Cadi reached for her glass again. 'Who told you that?'

'Arwel was in earlier. He said he'd seen you.'

'Do I know Arwel?' Meryn put in at last. He leaned back in his chair. 'Why do I sense he is not a fan.'

Chris laughed. 'You could be right.'

'What did he say?' Cadi interrupted.

'He was his usual snide self, but I thought I'd warn you, not everyone is against this development and for some reason he seems to be one of its backers. He told me he can prove there's nothing of interest in the meadow.'

'How? No one seems to have seen the results of the archaeological survey.'

'I doubt if there was one.' Chris pulled out a spare chair, spun it round and, sitting astride it, leaned forward, his elbows on the hooped back. He lowered his voice. 'I got a mate at the council to have a glance at the planning application. It's been marked for fast-track approval. And they've applied to have the footpath rerouted round the outside of the meadow. As soon as that's done, the "no trespassing" signs will go up, mark my words.'

Cadi's heart sank. 'The sheep were gone and the gate is already padlocked,' she put in. 'Can they really do that?'

'I dunno.' Chris stood up and pushed his chair back into

place. 'Don't let it spoil your lunch, but just be aware that there are eyes everywhere in this village.'

He grinned as his wife Mel appeared with two plates of food. '*Mwynha dy fwyd,* or as we also say in Wales, bon appétit, my friends,' she said with a smile.

'So, there are lines being drawn in the sand,' Meryn commented as Mel followed her husband back through the swing doors into the kitchen.

Cadi sighed. 'I'm not sure why. The only people to benefit, surely, are the developers.'

'New lifeblood in the village; much-needed housing; more children in the school; nimby versus all kinds of progress, however spurious some of it is. Will there be affordable housing?'

Cadi gave a bitter smile. 'I doubt it. I've heard so many stories in other places of fulsome promises made, only to be forgotten later.'

'I think you will find the council will insist,' he said reproachfully. 'And to make themselves look good the developers will pop in a few less well designed and more tightly grouped houses and, lo and behold, the planning will be confirmed.' He tore a corner off his bread roll. 'The trouble is, this really is your backyard. You will be affected more than anyone else.' He chewed for a moment. 'This food is excellent. We'll go back after lunch and walk the meadow again. Our host may well be right: if the footpath is diverted, we won't be able to work there so easily.'

'So easily?'

'Not in daylight, anyway.' He gave her a boyish grin. 'I'm not against development on principle. On the contrary. But I am against it being imposed on places which are special, and this meadow of yours is special. So let's go and find out exactly why.'

When they returned an hour later they found the gate wide open and a group of people standing in the centre of the meadow.

Cadi stopped abruptly, her hand on the gatepost. 'I don't recognise them.'

'The enemy reconnoitring, you reckon?'

She nodded ruefully. 'One of them has a clipboard.'

'Let's go and see. Find out what we're dealing with. This is still a public footpath, presumably. Until it says otherwise.'

There were four men and a woman, talking earnestly together. As Cadi and Meryn approached they fell silent and looked round. 'Can we help you?' The youngest of the men was wearing a suit. It seemed to show a measure of authority within the group. His gaze shifted from Meryn's face to Cadi and back to Meryn.

'We're looking for a lost dog,' Cadi announced firmly.

'We'll keep our eyes open.' Was it her imagination or did the man look relieved at the banality of her reply to his question. His attention on her at last, he gave her what he probably assumed was a reassuring smile.

'Thank you.' She forced herself to smile back. 'Are you the new owner of the meadow?'

'In a manner of speaking.'

'And what exactly does that mean?' Cadi found herself clenching her fists in her pockets.

'It means we are doing a site inspection for the owners.' The woman stepped forward. Wearing green wellies and a fleece despite the heat of the day, she looked every bit as much in uniform as the man in the suit. She was workmanlike and calmly in control of the situation. 'We'll look out for your dog. Please excuse us, we're busy people.'

'And that's us dismissed,' said Cadi under her breath as the group moved purposefully off to the far side of the field.

'And we'll go quietly,' Meryn put in gently. 'We don't want to draw any undue attention to ourselves. Let's follow the path on down to the stream. Presumably they can't buy the woods and the fort. We'll have to check, but they will almost certainly belong to Cadw.' Cadw was the Welsh government's organisation for the protection of the historic environment. He led the way into the shadow of the woods without stopping to look back.

'We are busy people!' Cadi mimicked the woman's voice as she followed him. 'Who the hell does she think she is!'

'A busy person, obviously.' Meryn stopped and turned to put

his arm around her shoulders. 'Take a deep breath. Don't waste any energy on them. There will be a lot of surveyors and people walking around here over the next few weeks and months. You'll have to get used to it. Their people and council people and archaeologists and objectors and sightseers. And ghosts.'

'Ghosts?'

'Of course. I told you. This is a thin place. A place where time zones collide.' He gave a happy chuckle. 'Wonderful.'

They walked slowly on up the track to the far edge of the woodland, then paused to look down at the meadow. The five figures in the distance were walking towards the gate and out into the lane. From up here they could see the large four-by-four parked in the lay-by further up the narrow road. They watched as the group climbed in.

'Right.' Meryn turned back down the path. 'Let's take the chance while the field is empty. My guess is they will have left some uneasy echoes behind them, but you never know, they could be totally benign beings who have left nothing but peace and goodwill.'

'Here!' Meryn stopped abruptly. 'Can you feel it?'

The meadow was very still, a shimmering heat haze lying over the grass. The intense silence was emphasised by the shrill sound of grasshoppers and crickets, and somewhere high in the glare a skylark had begun to sing.

Cadi held out her hands, palm down. 'What am I feeling for?' she whispered.

'Empty your mind. Have no expectations. Feel the quality of the air against your skin but don't prejudge it. Be passive and at the same time receptive.' He watched her for a few moments, nodded, then turned away and walked on. 'This path has been here for many centuries. Can you sense it?'

She shook her head. 'I can't feel anything.'

'You will. You already have. Relax. It's not important.' He glanced up at the sky and then looked at his watch. 'I'm sorry, Cadi, but I can't stay much longer. There is somewhere I have to be this evening, but don't worry' – he added, observing her look of disappointment – 'I'll come again. And I want you to keep me posted. This place intrigues me beyond measure and I intend to continue to work on this from home.' With a grin he tapped the side of his nose. 'If there is a villa here, we are going to find it. There is a leaky space-time continuum in this meadow, and it will lead us to the right place.'

It was as he climbed back into his car half an hour later that he looked up at her again. 'From what you've told me, your poem is already telling the story. And your story is dictating the poem. You and your Elen have some kind of a link. Follow the flow of your pen, Cadi. Trust the inspiration. The channel is open and you are the conduit. All you have to do is listen. I caught the echo of a quarrel in that meadow. It's part of the story. Or maybe it's where the story starts. All you have to do is read your own narrative.'

10

Had she meant to put Gemma into the story? Cadi read through her notes with a smile of recognition. She didn't think so, but after all, the meadow was the last place the little dog had been seen, and it was comforting to imagine that she might have somehow traversed one of the thin places in the meadow to which Meryn had alluded and turned up in the palace of the high king. She sat back in her chair staring out of the window into the garden where a brisk breeze, coming seemingly out of nowhere, was shaking the hedges, scattering a white confetti of petals from the seringa bushes across the lawn. A palace. Not a villa, but the state residence of a king. And yet in her imagination the building looked like a Roman villa, with a classical pediment, statues and fountains, an atrium, mosaics on the floor. The native tribespeople were living up on the hill in the fort, firmly dated in her own mind and in the description of the place inscribed on the sign at the bottom of one of the footpaths up the hill, as Iron Age, but obviously still surviving into the late fourth century AD.

She reached for her research notebook, the place she had begun to write down anything she thought relevant to her story as she read up on the actual history behind the legend of Macsen Wledig and his Welsh princess. As far as she could see he had entered the historical record in the late 360s early 370s as a senior officer under the Count Theodosius, father of the man who would later be emperor of the East. About Macsen's wife there was very little information. His second wife, and the mother of most of his children, was only 'probably' called Elen . . . or maybe Helen . . . and was often confused with another Helen of an earlier generation, Helena the mother of Emperor Constantine I. Cadi sighed. So little certainty about this woman who had been, surely, one of the most important in the early history of this island.

She flipped through her pages of notes. The Iron Age, she had noted, came after the Bronze Age and before the Romans. The Romans had arrived with Julius Caesar in 54 BC and left Britain in the early 400s AD. Magnus, she had written, had become emperor in AD 383. Or not emperor. Or sort of emperor, elected by his own men to be emperor in Britain, then emperor of the West. Her notes were wildly conflicted. He was popular, elected by general acclaim. He was not popular. His name was on the list of proper emperors; his name was not on that list, and he had never been recognised by historians as anything more than a usurper. She shook her head. Too much. Too much history. Too much history that contradicted itself. The original story was a Romance. In the original sense of the word. She was not writing an academic treatise. She was a poet, like the original bard who had first recited the tale, probably centuries before it had ever been written down in the Red Book of Hergest which dated from about 1375. Perhaps the story had been doing the rounds within living memory of the protagonists. In which case, it was the poet's story that held the truth, and she by her very calling was entitled to expand on it or to redact bits as she saw fit. Facts as they related to her meadow. And they did relate to her meadow, she felt it deep inside herself, just as she felt that once in a dream she had seen Elen out there face to face.

Surely it was possible to find out whether in reality a villa – a villa large enough and beautiful enough to be a palace – had ever stood there?

* * *

There were bats flitting across the grass in the dusk. She had a torch in her pocket but she didn't need it. The luminous dusk was light enough to show her the outline of the meadow and the trees along the brook. She could hear the faint burble of the water in the silence. The wind had dropped as darkness approached and she could see the diamond-bright glitter of the evening star above the distant mountain peaks. Soon it would have dipped out of sight. Somewhere nearby an owl hooted and she shivered. She wished she had asked Sally to come with her. The night was very lonely and she was feeling nervous. She stopped, listening hard. Supposing she heard, or felt, the drum-beat of the horse's hooves? Was someone out there watching her? She felt very exposed. There was nowhere to hide and presumably, if she could see the trees from here, anyone lurking at the field margins could see her. Her mouth was dry as she slowly turned full circle, straining her eyes against the encroaching darkness.

And then she saw it. The horse was grazing only twenty metres away, its head lowered to the grass; she could hear the crunch of its teeth as it pulled up mouthfuls of lush meadow grass. She froze as it took a few steps forward and raised its head, ears forward. It wasn't looking at her. She followed its gaze and saw a man standing on the far side of the meadow. He was opening the gate. He stepped into the field and called softly. The horse whickered in reply and trotted towards him. She saw the man hand it a titbit as he reached out with a halter, pulling it over the animal's ears. For a moment it seemed to resist, then it gave in gracefully and turned to follow him as he led it out through the gate and up a broad track. She could see it all clearly, the man and the horse, the distant huddle of buildings, a barn, and the great house itself, the villa, two storeys high, with a lofty roof, the pointed architraves, the flaring torches that lit the driveway and flickered shadows onto the red tiles and the grey slates of the rooftops, a line of stone statues . . . And was that a little dog, trotting out of the shadows? With a visceral shock of recognition, Cadi took a step forward. 'Gemma?' she called.

The night shivered and froze, and the scene was gone, but not before she recognised the man who turned towards her, desperately trying to pacify the frightened, rearing horse, his face rigid with fear. It was Rhys.

'Sally!'

Cadi rang the bell again, then thumped on the door with her fist. A light came on inside the house and after a few moments the door opened. Sally, her hair rumpled, wearing cotton pyjamas, had obviously been asleep. 'What is it? What's wrong?'

'I saw her, Sal. I saw Gemma!'

She saw the incredulous blank of shock on Sally's face too late, and then the leap of joy. 'Oh my God! Where is she?'

Cadi shook her head. 'No. No, I'm sorry. She's not here. She's . . . she's out there in the meadow. I saw her with the horse Emrys, with Rhys.'

Sally studied her face and Cadi saw the hope fading in her eyes. 'Who is Rhys?' she asked at last. She turned away from the door and Cadi followed her inside. Sally turned on the kitchen lights and automatically reached for the kettle. 'Go on,' she said with a sigh. 'Tell me.' She hitched herself up onto a stool at the worktop.

'I couldn't sleep and I thought I'd go for a stroll in the meadow. They're going to close it off any day now.' Cadi stopped, aware that she hadn't spoken to Sally for several days, and why. Her friend was avoiding the painful reminders of walks in the fields around their houses. 'I assumed there wouldn't be anyone there so late and I wanted to clear my head.' There was a long pause. 'Have I ever told you about my eccentric uncle Meryn?' she ploughed on. Another moment's silence. Sally didn't react. 'No, perhaps not, but I asked him to come over a couple of days ago. I wanted to ask him to do some dowsing. He's an expert on the subject. I told him about Charles Ford, my mystery man dowser, and his experience in the field.' She hoped to see a smile on Sally's face at the reminder of her crack about the virgin poetess, but there was no response. 'He thinks it's the type of place one might see ghosts, and that a villa might have left traces. He could feel strange energies out there, memories perhaps from the past.' It was no use. Sally didn't believe in this stuff. How could she explain the leap of joy she had experienced when she saw Gemma running towards her, heard the little dog's yelp of recognition before her own shout had brought the moment crashing out of time. 'Sorry. It was stupid of me to come rushing round like this. I shouldn't have got your hopes up.'

Sally shook her head. She slid off the stool as the kettle boiled and reached for a couple of cups. 'No. I'm glad you came. I've missed our walks and our chats. It's been busy at school and I suppose I've been burying myself in work to distract me.' She gave another deep sigh. 'It's just the house is so empty.'

Cadi leaned forward and put her hand over Sally's for a second. 'I know.'

'Thank you for looking for her.'

'I will always look for her, Sal. You know I will.'

They sat together in silence, sipping tea. 'So,' Sally said at last. 'Do you really believe in these memories from the past? How do you know it wasn't a dream?'

'I know it's not logical, but I think I do believe it, yes.' Cadi caught a glimpse of the scepticism in Sally's eyes and looked away. 'Besides I was outside in the meadow, so I can't have been dreaming. I can't explain it, and perhaps that is part of it. I love the thought of the unexplained being all around us. My uncle has studied the subject all his life. He practises what he preaches. He does dowsing and deals with intrusive ghosts and things, and studies all the supernatural stuff which is so mocked today. My dad thinks he's completely dotty, but his brother is a proper professor.' She smiled. 'They haven't talked for a long time. Which is sad as I love them both.'

'I thought your father lived in France.'

'He does. And Uncle Meryn lives over near Hay. So they can co-exist in the stratosphere quite happily.'

'Wow. What an interesting family.' Sally didn't sound particularly sincere.

'It does it for me.' Cadi surveyed her friend's face. 'I know it wasn't a dream. I was outside in the meadow and my feet were wet with dew and freezing.' She was making things worse with every word, she realised. 'I'd better go, Sal. It's late and I woke you up.'

'She's dead, isn't she. If she's a ghost?'

Cadi didn't have to ask who Sally meant. 'I suppose she might be. I'm so sorry.'

'Did she look happy?'

'She did, yes. And she recognised me. Stupidly I called out to her and the whole . . .' she hesitated, searching for the right word, 'the whole dream or vision, whatever it was, just disappeared. If any of it is true, be comforted that it looked as though someone was looking after her.'

She stood in the street outside for several minutes before walking the few steps next door to her own gate. The night was very still. There was a faint streak of pale light on the far horizon but otherwise the village lay in total darkness.

Cadi couldn't sleep. She lay for a long time staring up at the ceiling, her thoughts whirring back and forth from the meadow with its dark sweet scent of mown hay to the appearance of the horse, so real, so wild, so – smelling of horse – the glimpse of Rhys the groom, and of Gemma, her joyous bark of recognition and then of the total blankness of the scene as she found herself once more alone in the empty field. She rolled over and picked up her phone. It was 3.20 a.m. With a groan she sat up and dragged herself out of bed.

It was strange how different the living room looked at night, the darkness, the emptiness, the silence holding no echoes of the previous day. She made her way over to her desk and turned on the lamp, leaving the rest of the room in shadow. She was half afraid of hearing the soldiers marching in the night, but there was no sound outside. Or inside either. She recalled the grandfather clock in her father's old house, always ticking, that slow monotonous steady sound counting away the hours and days, chiming every quarter, revving up to chime extra loudly on every hour. She'd hated it as a child. It was somehow too inevitable, too full of doom. She wondered briefly what had happened to it. Had her father taken it with him to France to continue to count down his days for the rest of his life? Maybe it had been company in its own way. Here, there was nothing but silence. Clocks didn't tick anymore.

If she couldn't sleep, perhaps she could write. She reached for her notebook. 'So, Elen, princess of Britain and soon to be empress, what happened next?' she whispered. 'Presumably you left our beautiful meadow with its sprawling villa that was more like a palace, with its mosaic floors and its fountains, and you headed off for a new life with your soldier husband.'

Could she even follow Elen once she had left this, the land of her birth?

11

When her phone rang Cadi was so sure it was Meryn, picking up on her doubts, she almost greeted him by name, only at the last moment noting the caller's name on the screen. 'Hi, Rachel.'

'You sound tired.' Her cousin's voice was as usual almost drowned out by the sound of the sea. She was obviously standing in her favourite place on the veranda in front of her cottage, overlooking the wild beauty of Cardigan Bay. 'Can I come over so we can talk?'

When Rachel arrived the following day she gave Cadi a resigned smile. 'So, let me get this straight. You originally thought we should leave out "The Dream of Macsen", as it had too much history and not enough magic and, if I remember right, you said it was too short to make a book of it. Then you rang and told me you wanted to do it but with infills of real history to make it long enough for a book? And now you've started work on it, whether I agree or not.'

Cadi nodded guiltily. She should have discussed this more thoroughly with Rachel weeks ago. 'That's about it. I've become interested in local Roman history and Macsen's Dream seems to fit with what's happening round here. As with the others, we can say "loosely based on the story".' She glanced hopefully at Rachel, who was staring down at the pile of notes Cadi had pushed towards her. 'You can make it magical with your illustrations. What I want to do with this one is improvise, expand it a little. I've researched what happened in real life. More or less. And it makes a fantastic story.'

'Really?' Rachel looked her in the eye.

Cadi held her gaze. 'The first four books we've done are called the four branches of the Mabinogion. Now we have come to the histories. I've been looking it all up. We have "The Dream of Macscn Wledig" there in the original, which stops when his dream is realised and it has a happy ending, but what I want to do is carry on to the end of the story. Where Macsen's dream turns into a nightmare.'

'OK.' Rachel was still sounding cautious. 'So, we need to discuss this a bit more. I read the original story again yesterday; that's why I called you. And I agree, as it's only about five pages it's too short for a book. It's extremely sketchy. "And on the way he conquered France" – that's a bit minimalist, to put it mildly.'

'That's my point. Let me show you the rest of my notes so far.' Cadi walked over to her desk.

'So, assuming we go with your new idea, have you thought about the background?' Rachel was immediately practical. 'For instance, if it was written in medieval times, would you want the settings, the costumes, to be medieval or Roman? The poem talks about castles. The Romans didn't have fairy-tale castles with pointy turrets, like our other stories, did they? Tricky if we're turning it from myth to real history.' She sat down with the pile of Cadi's notes and began to leaf through them.

The silence was broken ten minutes later when Cadi's phone rang. She picked it up, glancing at the screen. 'Sally?'

'Come outside. Now. They're in the field. I think they're doing X-rays.'

* * *

There were three cars parked in the lane, their nearside wheels up on the bank below the hedge and a little further up there was a four-wheel drive towing a low loader. Its ramp was down. The gate was wide open.

'Oh hell! It's really going to happen. I thought we'd have longer.' Sally glanced at Cadi. Introductions had been made and Rachel was standing a little way behind them. As they walked towards the gate she had fished in her backpack for a camera and it was now slung prominently around her neck. 'I may as well look professional,' she had said with a grin as Sally raised an eyebrow. 'I am an illustrator, after all. Although I don't officially approve of photos I quite often use them for reference and from what Cadi has told me about all this, that might be useful.'

Cadi was staring at the group of people ahead of them. Two were gesticulating wildly. 'It looks as though some of them are as unhappy as we are,' she murmured. The strangers were standing in front of another man who was holding a square frame on a low, four-wheeled trolley.

'I hope you're not going to get involved as well.' Arwel had walked up the lane behind them without them noticing. He came to a halt in the gateway and stood, arms folded, his eyes narrowed against the sun.

'I don't think a few people shouting are going to stop them now,' Cadi said sadly. 'But at least they seem to be taking X-rays of the ground.'

'Ground-penetrating radar!' Arwel muttered. 'Pointless. I've told them there was nothing there.'

'You told them?' Sally glanced at him. 'I thought the developers said they had done a survey.'

'It appears the village doesn't believe it.' Arwel couldn't hide his scorn. 'Chris at the mill has taken it upon himself to say there was no survey, though how he knows I can't imagine. Presumably he's brought this lot in. Well good luck to him. There's nothing here.' He turned towards Cadi. 'If your wizarding uncle has an ounce of honesty, he would have to back me on that one. What did he think? Or did he pretend he had seen something? If so, I presume he put a curse on the meadow to keep the nasty outsiders away?' The sneer was loud in his voice.

'He was very interested.' Cadi refused to be goaded.

'Well, tell him to keep out of my way,' Arwel snarled. 'Everyone knows the man's a New Age charlatan. He writes woo-woo. His books are total rubbish.'

Cadi opened her mouth to retort but Sally jumped in ahead of her. 'Whatever you think of Professor Jones, there is no call to be rude,' she said firmly. 'Ignore him, Cadi.'

Cadi took a deep breath. 'I am.' She managed a smile.

Behind them a shout echoed across the field and they saw the group in the distance gathering around the machine.

'They've found something.' Rachel had been quietly snapping the scene. Arwel was already hurrying towards the group and she quickly took a picture of his retreating figure and winked at Cadi before setting off in pursuit. There were quite a few people in the field now, they realised. As word had gone round the village, more and more figures had appeared in the lane.

'I think it's the line of a wall, and I've already seen signs of post holes.' The man with the machine was responding to questions from some of the onlookers clustered around him.

'I forbid you to go on with this.' One of the men who had been waving his arms about stepped forward and put his hand on the frame. 'This is private property. You have no permission to be here.'

Arwel pushed the man aside. 'Let me see that tracing.' He leaned over towards the screen. 'Who are you, anyway?'

'I'm from the county archaeology department.' The man in charge of the machine let go of the handles and wiped his forehead with his sleeve.

'And we represent the owners of the field.' The gesticulator stepped closer, followed by his companion. His face was florid but whether from heat or fury it was difficult to tell. He was wearing an open-necked shirt and carried a plastic portfolio under his arm. 'I must ask you all to leave. Now. This public footpath is subject to a temporary closure order. The field is private. No permission has been given to dig here.'

He threw a malevolent glance towards the man with the machine.

'I think you're wrong there, my friend,' the archaeologist said firmly. 'Your owners applied to the council for planning permission to build on this field and nothing can proceed without an official survey. That's me.'

'Yes!' The single triumphant word from someone in the crowd seemed to echo in the silence that followed.

Both men looked up. 'I suggest you contact your owners.' The archaeologist's weary tone gave the impression he had been in this situation before. 'Tell them I'm carrying out the survey on their behalf as requested by the council. I gather mention of a previous survey had been made but nothing had been produced, so my department felt I should do a preliminary scan of the area. Just to be sure.' He glanced at the man with the portfolio. 'When I've finished I'll submit my findings to the planning office and they will take it from there.' He paused. 'It often takes quite a while for the department to process this type of request. There's a colossal backlog.' Was that a note of suppressed amusement as he turned back to his machine? 'Now, if you will excuse me, sir . . .' Arwel had once more been bending over the display.

'There seems to be a lot showing up.' Arwel stepped back, obviously puzzled.

'There is indeed. Very interesting site, this one.' But the archaeologist would say no more.

One by one the crowd dispersed. The owners' agents walked off across the field, one of them with a phone clamped to his ear.

Sally, Rachel and Cadi drifted away with the last few onlookers.

'She's the one you said had lost her little dog?' Rachel asked as they parted in the lane and Sally went on towards her gate.

Cadi nodded. This was not the moment to mention her sighting of Gemma in the field.

* * *

'So.' They were sitting in the garden, aware of the archaeologist in the meadow on the far side of the hedge still plodding up and down with his machine. 'From your notes, which I have to say are pretty random, I gather you're having some problems actually getting a sequence on this story?' Rachel reached for the coffee Cadi had produced. They had looked at her photos of the field and the group of people around the surveyor. Cadi had hoped she might see a little dog amongst the legs of the onlookers, but there was nothing there. Rachel had retrieved a folder of sketches from her car. She laid it on the table. 'Take a look. See if anything here helps with your decisions on how to move forward.'

Cadi spread them carefully out in front of her and smiled. 'These are so good.'

'But are they right?'

Cadi didn't immediately respond. Then at last, she slid one from the pile. 'This one. This is Macsen.'

Rachel considered it. 'He's not in the uniform of a Roman legionary, of course.' It showed a tall, grizzled man, his head bare, his black hair dishevelled, wearing a loose primitive shirt, open almost to the waist, his only identifying feature his raised right hand, clutching a broadsword. On his forefinger was a heavy ruby ring.

'I like him.' Cadi smiled. 'And so would Elen.'

Rachel raised an eyebrow. 'Good. OK. We'll use him. Now, Elen?'

Cadi shuffled through some more sketches. 'We need to keep her clothes ambiguous too. Informal. Nothing too medieval. No headdress. She's a princess but she's a Celt through and through.'

'But no red hair?' Rachel pushed forward a sketch of a robust young woman with tumbling wild auburn locks.

Cadi shook her head. 'No. No. She's darker haired. Not black like him. He's swarthy. Spanish. She's dark blond, I suppose you would call it.'

'In other words, mousey?' Rachel grinned.

'Far from it. She was quite a character. I think she should be tall, elegant if anything. Hazel eyes. Straight nose. Not someone to mess with. She has to be able to stand up to him. He respects her. I wonder if he's a little afraid of her. She is regal. She carries the royal blood he so craves.'

'Quite like you, in fact!'

Cadi let out a snort. 'Apart from the fact that my hair is grey, and I'm far from regal without a drop of royal blood, yes, I suppose so!'

Rachel laughed. 'And she's about seventeen, right?'

'At the start of their marriage, I think so yes.'

'So, very young. And the actual story we're working from only covers the start of their marriage.'

Cadi pushed back her chair and stood up. She wandered away across the lawn and stood staring up into an apple tree that stood in the hedge between her garden and the meadow.

'Cadi?' Rachel had followed her.

'You're right. The poem only really covers their meeting and the wedding.' She gave a rueful smile. 'But it does mention more history. Briefly. A few paragraphs. And those are wrong. It talks about him besieging Rome with her brothers. I don't think that happened. Although he wanted to. Time passes. She has children. We need to include that, surely. Wait. I'll fetch my notebook. You can see how the poem is progressing.'

She made them some lunch while Rachel sat outside with a glass of wine and worked her way through more of the pages of notes. The meadow was silent now. The archaeologist had finally packed up and left. When Cadi carried the tray out into the garden she found her cousin sitting in front of the folder, sipping thoughtfully from her glass.

'Weird, isn't it.'

Rachel nodded. 'You've been in touch with Uncle Meryn.'

'Yes.'

Rachel's mother was sister to Meryn and to Cadi's father.

'He's been over to see the field. Not that it's going to feature in our story. Once Elen is married she moves away to Caernarfon, which is where the legend is centred. The trouble is that my story actually seems to start here. It's only after they're married they go up to North Wales.'

'And even then, it's not Caernarfon as we know it.'

'No, and it's not North Wales either – Wales as such didn't exist. But one intriguing thing I've read somewhere is that the English king, Edward I, had heard the legend back then when he lived, in the thirteenth century, and he built the castle to fit his vision of the story, which is why it's sad that we can't use it, unless . . .' she paused, 'in a reference to the dream – which is after all what the poem is. You could then paint it as Macsen dreams it, with all its turrets and towers. Up to you!'

'And how does Meryn see it?'

'He doesn't. At least, we were concerned with the palace here. I haven't asked him about Caernarfon.'

'Your neighbour Arwel doesn't rate him, does he.' Rachel reached for the bottle and topped up their glasses.

'No. He obviously hates him. I think there must be some kind of personal thing going on there. Perhaps it's no more than jealousy – the fact that I gather Meryn's last book sold rather well.'

'It did. The one he wrote before that was slated by the serious history critics and I expect Arwel thinks of himself as a serious historian. People who talk about ghosts and energies and all that stuff are expected to keep their noses out of real history. Meryn's readers loved it. His last book was a magical herbal, lavishly illustrated with watercolour sketches by someone called Miranda Dysart, whose work I really admire and the next, due to be published next winter, will be a treatise on Welsh myth and legend. I checked on Amazon. Serious history or not, he writes bestsellers.' Rachel grinned. 'Arwel didn't sound as though he was your greatest admirer either.' She glanced across at her.

Cadi smiled. 'No. I'm afraid poets are almost as dodgy as mystics.'

'Especially bestselling poets? Do I assume Arwel is a writer too?'

'Not as far as I know. Just the local self-styled expert who needs to have his expertise validated by the facts. No one has ever called his views into question before. He wrote a guide to the village. They sell it in the post office. It doesn't mention the villa. I checked. Just the church and the mill. And some of the farms.'

'And now circumstances are putting him on the spot.'

Cadi sat down. 'I want to follow this story, Rach. See where it leads. It's hard to explain, even to myself, but there is a lot going on round here which seems to have linked me viscerally into the poem. And besides . . . I know it sounds silly, but sometimes I feel Elen knows I'm there. I feel as though we've met, somewhere out there in the past. I feel it's as if she talks to me and it's as if she knows I'm listening.'

Once she had started telling Rachel what had happened she couldn't seem to stop. Rachel listened intently, her eyes fixed on Cadi's face. She pulled a single sheet from the file. 'I especially like this one:

> 'The dog sat on Elen's knee
> Shivering with fear.
> But the reassuring hug
> And the ribbon on her collar
> Told her she was safe.
> She did not recognise the house.
> But the field was hers.
> The grass smelt the same,
> The cry of the circling birds
> Was steady and unchanged.'

There was a moment of silence.

'So,' Rachel said at last. 'What kind of dog was Gemma?'

'A bit of this and a bit of that. Small, white, quite fluffy but feisty. Energetic. And very loyal.'

'Ears pointy or floppy?'

Cadi grinned. Rachel was hooked. She had always loved painting the animals in the stories. 'Floppy, but pointy as well. I can show you photos.'

'So, we have the basis of several illustrations already. I can visualise them from your notes. You've put in a lot of detail. I will admit, the real history is fascinating.'

'I want to go on researching it. I want to write more.'

To her relief, Rachel nodded. 'I can see why. Can't you do both? The body of your poem is almost there. I can work with that. It's much as we imagined in our first talk about this tale. And we're working for a series, don't forget. We're producing the stories from the Mabinogion. It's part of a set and it's a successful brand, but that doesn't mean you have to restrict yourself to it. Go for it. Write the poem, of course write the poem in extended form to cover the way it pans out. In your head. Then you could write the rest of her story as a different, much more detailed project. A historical novel, perhaps. Or a poetic study. Or an academic enquiry into who Elen really was. You have to follow your interest in this, Cadi. That's obvious. All I ask is that you finish the poem, our poem, first.' She leaned back in her chair and closed her eyes. 'But then again, I have several commissions in the pipeline, so we don't have to hurry too much. As long as the publisher knows it's coming.' She waved a wasp away from the tray of food. 'And that gives us a template for the illustrations. They would be in the same style roughly as the first four stories. Hints of a medieval dream, in this case a Roman story. More legend than fairy tale, but set in a real place. Perhaps the castle can be there,' she glanced at the pile of notes, 'but as no more than a shadow on the horizon. So, I can go away and paint mountains and cloudscapes and dreamy ladies and handsome heroes?'

'You certainly can.'

'Excellent. And you go on with your research.' Rachel took a sip from her glass. 'How was Uncle Meryn, by the way?'

'Same as always. Ageless. Mysterious. But down to earth as well. I gather he's had enough of California and academia. I think he's dying to get back to some hands-on hocus pocus.'

'Great. I'll tell Mum he's back in Wales. She misses him when he goes away.'

'Unlike my dad.' Cadi gave a grimace.

Rachel nodded. 'Uncle Owen was always the odd one out of the three. How is France?'

'He's still enjoying it.'

'Good. So, I'll go home and wait for you to email me some

more of your early draft.' She glanced towards the hedge as she stood up. 'That sounds to me like a tractor.'

Cadi nodded. 'Dai had a few more hay bales to collect before he's kicked off the field forever.'

The house was very silent after Rachel left. Restlessly Cadi wandered round, then, almost without realising it, she sat down at her desk and reached for her notebook. *Follow the flow of your pen. The channel is open.* She thought back to Meryn's parting words, words she couldn't get out of her head.

'So, Elen,' she whispered. 'Talk to me. I'm listening.'

12

Their first argument occurred outside the entrance to the villa.

'I am not travelling in a litter!'

'The wives of officers always travel in a litter.'

'Not this one.' She said it very quietly. 'This one is a royal princess.' Turning away from the offending litter she scanned the line of horsemen behind them. 'Where is my horse?'

'Here, Princess.' Rhys appeared at once, almost as if he had been waiting for the summons, leading the black colt. The king had, it appeared, commanded that his head groom accompany the horse as part of his daughter's household. Emrys was regally apparelled with a scarlet bridle and saddle cloth. Without waiting for any further discussion, Elen walked over to him, took the reins and bent her knee for Rhys to throw her up onto the saddle. It was immediately apparent to those close enough to see that the elegantly embroidered tunic beneath her mantle was divided to allow for comfort in riding astride. Below the fine linen drapery she was wearing trousers.

Hearing the snigger that ran through the front line of his troops Magnus swung round. Immediate silence. Elen sat straight-backed, her face set. It was clear to everyone that all was not well between the newly-weds. The atmosphere between them was sharp with anger.

'Shall I ride at your side?' she demanded. Her voice was clear and proud and rang around the gravelled area with its lines of carefully positioned urns and clipped trees. The men of the legion stood as still as the stone statues in the entrance portico. 'Or would you rather I followed behind with my attendants?'

His fury evaporated as quickly as it had surged through his system and he found himself stifling a smile. 'A royal lady should ride at my side, no less,' he said, keeping his voice curt. 'You are right. Your groom may walk at the horse's head, and your dog' – he had noticed the small animal trotting nervously behind her, now abandoned on the ground as she sat on the horse – 'can ride in the litter with your ladies and your boxes.' Her father had impressed on him the fact that his daughter was a scholar and he had seen the trunk full of scrolls being hefted into one of the baggage carts. Something else about her he hadn't known. He pretended not to notice the gleam in her eye as she sweetly bent her head in acknowledgement.

Their first encounter the night before as husband and wife had left him with no illusions. His young inexperienced virgin bride was no shrinking violet. She was fully prepared to follow him wherever he led, throwing herself into the moment with an unexpected enthusiasm that had swiftly followed her initial hesitation. He had been gentle with her at first, testing and teasing. It had been her response to his quiet enquiry as to whether he pleased her that had, after a shocked pause, led them both to another of those sudden paroxysms of mirth. 'I know what to do. I have watched the horses often enough.'

'And you compare me to a stallion?' he spluttered.

'Oh yes, husband,' she had replied coyly. 'And I see you know your duty well.'

He found himself wondering now, briefly, as he watched her settle herself in the saddle, if the act of bestriding the horse gave her any pleasure. Sternly he turned his thoughts elsewhere. He had an army to lead. Raising his fist he gestured to his officers to take their places at the head of the procession and rode out of the palace gates as the men of the legionary escort fell in, two by two, behind him, managing to keep their faces solemn as they trotted after their commander and his new wife.

Behind the men of the legion came the royal escort, provided by the king from his cohort of tribal warriors, together with the personal household of the princess of Britain, something she hadn't even realised she possessed until the previous day, and securely in the litter with Delyth and Nia, her two senior ladies, was one small dog, her collar decorated with the silk ribbons that had wrapped the golden gift of a husband determined to make things better. At the front of the procession Macsen once again reminded himself that he had bought the allegiance of an entire province for Rome with this marriage.

Her father's parting words echoed in Elen's head as she rode north and west beside her husband towards her new life.

'Be proud. Be strong. You are royal, never forget it. Your blood is sacred and you hold the treasures of Britain in your hands. Before she left, that witch Branwen spoke to me in the words of a soothsayer. Macsen will one day be the ruler of all Britain and it is your power, as his wife, that he will use to go forth to rule the known world as emperor of Rome.'

Was that all Branwen had said? A prickle of suspicion had run down her spine at her father's words as his gaze had moved away from her face. Had he, as she suspected, sold his daughter for the sake of her bloodline, her descent from the gods? She would never know now. She was in all respects alone with her royal blood and her burden of responsibility for a nation that was not yet a nation, an empire that owed its epicentre to a distant world and her children as yet unborn who would inherit the symbols of sovereignty she didn't herself understand.

They headed east first, stopping briefly overnight at the fortress at Isca with its huge amphitheatre, the scene of so much blood-soaked entertainment for the legions over the long centuries of Roman rule, scarcely pausing to do more than eat and sleep, the army accustomed to overnight stops on long marches. They set off again at first light, heading north again, almost at once forging deep into mountainous countryside completely unknown to Elen, who had never before ventured so far from home.

The road wound ever northward, day after day of steady riding, with the tramp of marching men and the slow creak of the wagons behind them, following broad winding rivers through wild and lonely hills, traversing deep valleys and gorges, forests and mountain ranges, fording rushing, rocky streams, a route serviced at increasingly irregular intervals by staging posts and outlying forts until they reached the highest mountain range of all, with the summit of Yr Wyddfa, the burial place of ancient gods, towering over the steep narrow pass. In the daytime on the seemingly endless, exhausting route she rode defiantly and stubbornly at her husband's side. There was no sign of him at night and she found herself sleeping with her senior ladies in attendance, cuddling the dog instead of her husband.

The fort of Segontium was built a short distance from a north-facing shore; behind it lay the great mountain range of Eryri, Yr Wyddfa at its centre. Beyond the narrow Strait lay the sacred Isle of Môn. The fort had been built, so Macsen told her as they rode in through one of the arched entrances, some three hundred years before on a site especially chosen to overlook the Druid isle to the north and the main seashore fortress of the Ordovician rebels to the west; it had been constructed by the famous general Agricola to house a thousand men.

A guard of honour had been drawn up to greet them and lined the road across the parade ground which led towards the refurbished and extended commander's house with its stone walls and its newly planted garden courtyard.

'Welcome.' Macsen leapt from his saddle and came to stand at her horse's head. The long column of men had peeled off towards the legionary barracks while the baggage train and servants and slaves headed round to the back of the house.

This was a large fort, almost as large as Isca, and this house, the praetorium – extended and refurbished especially for the commander's new wife – though by no means a royal palace, was bigger and grander by far than the southern commander's house at Isca. Outside the walls of the fort sprawled the vicus, the township occupied by the families of the men of the fort, the workshops, the storehouses, the baths, bakehouses and smithies. Inside the walls, in contrast, the streets were regularly laid out, ordered and clean.

Macsen smiled. He took her hand and brushed it with his lips. 'You go and rest and settle in. I will see you later. No doubt a feast has been prepared for us.' Instead of accompanying her inside, he released her hand and turned away. She watched the swirl of his red cloak as he strode towards his men. There was nothing for it, disappointed and exhausted though she was, but to square her shoulders and walk alone into the shadows of her new home.

Cadi phoned Meryn that evening. 'The story has moved on. She's reached Caernarfon.'

'So, you were afraid it might stop when she left your meadow.'

'It hasn't stopped. She rode the whole way up to the north coast. To Segontium.'

'Excellent. I shall look forward to the next instalment.'

'Uncle Meryn . . .' She went on to tell him about Rachel's visit and the arguments in the meadow. 'Was it you who contacted the council about our field?'

'No.' He was outside again. She could hear the lone trilling song of a skylark in the distance as she explained what had happened. 'Interesting,' he went on. 'Did you see the outline of the villa on his screen?'

'Not really. It was hard to make out in the sunshine, and he didn't really want us to look. The developer's agent was there, trying to order us all off.'

'OK.' Meryn paused thoughtfully. 'I'm going to email you something. I did some dowsing for you over an Ordnance Survey map. See what you make of it.'

Five minutes later she found herself staring at her laptop screen in amazement. Superimposed on the much-enlarged OS map of the area to the north of Cadi's cottage was the neatly inked outline of a large building. It had two west-facing wings, a further two extensions to the east and various outbuildings around it. The building extended past the far hedge into the neighbouring countryside and part of it stretched across Cadi's border and under her lawn, almost as far as her cottage.

She stared at it in silence, trying to take in what she was seeing.

Her phone rang again. 'Important. I think we can all agree?'

'It's huge.' Cadi sat motionless, her eyes glued to the screen. 'What is it?'

It's a palace, Cadi. The seat of the king of the Silures, the high king of Britannia.'

'Eudaf,' she whispered.

'Indeed. I believe the Romans called him Octavius. At a guess, this was his country pad. I expect he had a townhouse somewhere. In Caerleon, or more likely Caerwent, and probably others further afield if he was high king. He must have had other places more central to the whole province. I've been studying the map and I think when they excavate the meadow they will find more than one mosaic floor. This is a quality building; it's sad you can't tell anyone.'

'But, Meryn—'

'Especially not your friend Arwel.'

She hadn't mentioned her neighbour's petty outburst and she gave a rueful smile. 'This is real though, isn't it. Dowsing is a thing.'

'Of course it's a thing! It's just not real unless you can find someone prepared to act on it in an orthodox way.'

'The archaeologist?'

'I suppose you might be able to link my ground plan to his own radar signals. But be careful, Cadi, my love. You don't want to make yourself a laughing stock.'

'So you're not confident yourself.' She knew she sounded crestfallen.

'I'm confident it was there once. But I recognise the fact that we're talking nearly two thousand years ago, give or take. It isn't there anymore. There might be no trace left. The field could have been deep ploughed long since. Ancient meadows were not always protected. During the last war many of them were intensively farmed.' His voice receded suddenly and she heard him talking to someone in the background. 'I'll leave this with you, Cadi, for now.' He was back. 'Take care, my love.'

'You will come again and see what's happening?'

He laughed quietly. 'Try and keep me away.'

She printed up the plan and stared at it for a long time. He was right. She couldn't go to anyone with what amounted to an imaginary sketch. But on the other hand, what was there to lose?

Chris came over as soon as the mill was closed. He had heard about the altercation between the new landowners and the county archaeologist and confessed he might have been responsible for the hunt for what looked as though it was a non-existent early survey.

They sat in the garden as the shadows lengthened over the grass, two glasses of wine between them on the garden table.

'Please, please, please, promise you won't mention this to Arwel.' She laid the plan on the table in front of him. 'Uncle Meryn dowsed the field yesterday.' She didn't tell him how Meryn had done it from home over a map. That would be pushing even his credulity too far.

There was a long silence as Chris pored over the map, carefully orienting it, looking up at her garden hedges, turning it some more. At last he pushed it away and sat back staring into space.

'If this is accurate, it would be something of world importance,' he said at last.

She nodded. 'Some of it seems to be under my cottage.' She leaned towards him. 'Don't say anything to anyone, Chris. We must keep this under our hats for now. Apart from anything else, people might arrive with metal detectors.'

'Which might not be a bad idea.' He leaned back in his chair and sighed. 'What a can of worms, Cadi.'

'When will we discover what the archaeologist has spotted with his machine?'

He shook his head sadly. 'I gather the report will go to the planning office and then the landowners – and their reaction to this doesn't convince me it will all go through smoothly.

102

But I wouldn't have thought they can override the council. If the planning department say there's got to be a rescue dig, or something of the sort, at least we'll know there is something there. All we would need to start with would be a couple of trenches. If it reflects your uncle's plan, we wouldn't even have to try to point them in the right direction.' He glanced back down at Meryn's map. 'This. This would be mind-blowing.'

He drained his glass and climbed to his feet. 'So, we have a secret, Cadi, agreed?'

She nodded. 'Agreed.'

It was only after he had gone that she noticed the tiny circle in the corner of Meryn's map, indicating a spot about fifty metres inside the meadow's gate. It looked like a well. He had marked the stream and sketched in the slopes of the hill fort beyond it, but the circle had a faintly scribbled note beside it, unreadable in the fading light. She carried the plan indoors and, switching on her desk lamp, held it close to the bulb. The area in question was marked 'paddock/perhaps Roman garden area'. The inscription beside the circle did not say 'well'.

It said 'wormhole'.

Meryn laughed when she rang him back. 'Sorry. I took it for granted you would know what I meant. It is a much-derided term meaning a thin place, a place where a hole or tunnel can open in the time-space continuum, both being favoured terms in science fiction. I'm afraid SF has a lot to answer for in that it detracts from the science part of the subject in favour of the fiction. Lovely to write about and tremendous fun to read, with the option of being hugely scary as a concept, but nonetheless, real.' He paused. 'There are lots of thin places which are not wormholes, and most wormholes are too small for large things, or people or animals, like a horse to travel through. In sci-fi they are usually depicted as a way of travelling forward in time, but they're far more often a way into the past. Don't go near it, Cadi, please. Seriously. It may be dangerous.'

She had no intention of going near it. She sat very still for a while, thinking. Was it possible Elen had been standing near the wormhole when they had met in her dream? If they met in her dream. If indeed it had been a dream. And was it really possible that was how Gemma had vanished? Had the little dog galloped, carefree, down an open time tunnel into the past? She shook her head. That was a flight into fantasy she had no intention of following up, at least for the time being. She was going to leave that part of the story to Meryn.

Sitting at her desk, her eyes had returned to her pages of rough scribbles. She had last seen Elen standing on the threshold of her new home in Segontium. Her married life was about to start. That was a part of the story she intended to follow.

Her women had been waiting for her; the hypocaust had already been fired up and the floors were warm; she was greeted with friendly faces, spiced wine and sweetmeats, and there was the little dog, Gemma, cautiously wagging her tail in this strange new place.

Throwing herself down in a chair, she patted her knee and Gemma jumped into her lap as Delyth stepped forward. Somehow she already seemed at home. 'The general's new house has been remodelled to give you your own suite of rooms here. It's lovely, Princess. It's small compared to your father's palace, but I think we'll be comfortable here. As soon as you've rested I'll show you round your new home.'

There were two reception rooms, just for her, one larger and more formal than the other that looked out onto a private garden with a fountain at its centre, carved from shiny black stone and with a powerful water jet. On the second storey were two bedchambers. 'I gather the general has his offices and the public reception rooms across the road,' Delyth explained. 'So you won't be bothered with army procedures and all his business affairs. I've been told he has asked two of the senior ladies of the garrison to wait on you and help introduce you to the way of life here. I believe they're the wives of high-ranking officers,' she added as they returned down the staircase and walked out into the courtyard. They stood looking at the fountain. 'I understand they are called Valeria Valentina and Julia Cassia.' She kept her eyes carefully fixed on the water jet.

Elen glanced at her. 'But they're not here to greet me?'

'I expect they will want to allow you to settle in first. Perhaps they'll be at the feast tonight.' Behind them a succession of servants and slaves were carrying boxes unloaded from the long line of wagons and pack animals drawn up outside the fortress walls, stowing them away in the apartments and storerooms and scurrying away for more.

'And these two ladies are going to show me how to behave as the wife of a high-ranking officer?' Elen said quietly.

Delyth glanced at her briefly and hastily refocused on the fountain. 'I believe the general wanted them to be your friends, Princess. He didn't want you to be lonely here, so far from your family. He wants you to feel at home.'

'Does he indeed.' Elen shrugged her mantle more closely around her shoulders as a gust of wind off the distant Strait penetrated the high walls of the little garden and whisked through the leaves of the carefully placed potted shrubs before vanishing as swiftly as it had come.

'It's cold out here,' Delyth said gently. 'Shall we go indoors?'

For a moment Elen didn't move, then she gave a brisk nod.

The feast turned out to be a small affair in one of the reception rooms in the principia, the administrative block of offices next to their house. Three of the general's senior officers and their wives were there, including the two ladies who had agreed to attend Elen. They had not, it was immediately apparent, been told that she was a royal princess. On the contrary, they intended to act as equals, perhaps even condescending equals in the company of a young, inexperienced woman who, although the wife of the commander of the fort and general in command of the entire armies of Britannia, was in their eyes little more than a child.

'You'll soon get used to life up here, my dear,' Julia Cassia, the wife of the senior officer of the resident garrison, Titus Octavius, said kindly as they took their places on the dining couches round the table. 'We're not formal very often. When the menfolk are away, us girls stick together.' She simpered across the table at Valeria Valentina, who greeted the remark with a stony smile. Her husband had been introduced as 'Claudius Valentius, tribune and third in rank'. 'One thing I must say to start with: we have you to thank for the updating of the bathhouse,' Julia went on. 'The dear general was not so worried about the temperature of the water before you arrived, even though we complained often enough that it felt as though it had come straight off Snow Mountain.' She gave a theatrical shrug and pulled her mantle more closely around her shoulders.

The general ignored her comment. He was too busy talking to the tall younger man next to him, who had been introduced as his brother Marcellinus, someone who until that moment Elen hadn't known existed. Marcellinus broke off the conversation and gave her a conspiratorial grin. 'We are all pleased about that. I'm sorry, this must feel very strange. You will grow used to us all, I promise, and if my big brother there is too busy to entertain you, just come to me and make a formal complaint.'

Elen grinned back. She liked him instantly and realised quickly that his intervention had at last attracted Macsen's attention. She managed a gracious smile. Feasts in her father's palace with their tasty food, vast quantities of alcohol and music, always music, from bards and harpists, and their own resident master of the crwth, one of her favourite instruments, and from local choirs and balladeers were much more fun than this stilted affair. But the food here was good and the wine of excellent quality; it was the atmosphere that was a disappointment and it wasn't all that long before Macsen rose to his feet. He reached for his glass and proposed a toast to his bride. It became obvious at once it was her duty to rise and lead the ladies from the chamber. She wasn't sure where she was supposed to go and it irritated her that Julia took the lead, guiding her out of the building and back next door to her new abode and on through to the smaller of her own reception rooms where a metal basket of scented woods and pine cones had been lit in the hearth in spite of the underfloor heating. It was Julia who demanded drinks from one of Elen's waiting servants.

Delyth carried in the tray. After handing round the steaming goblets she bowed before Elen. 'Will there be anything else, Princess?' The other women who had been giggling together over some private joke fell silent and Elen saw the astonishment on their faces. Did her husband think so little of her that he had told no one she was the high king's daughter?

'That will do for now, Delyth.' She managed to put some authority into her voice. 'I'm tired after the long journey. My guests will not be staying long. Please tell my maids to attend me in the bedchamber.'

To her relief they took the hint. Was there more respect in their voices as they took their leave? She wasn't sure. Julia seemed friendly but Valeria's tone was definitely frosty. *Like the water from the slopes of Snow Mountain*, she thought to herself with a shiver of apprehension.

Too exhausted to go on writing, Cadi dropped her pen. She stood up, massaging her cramped fingers. Her hand might be tired, but her mind was still racing, still fired up with the story she was following. Unable to contemplate going to bed even though it was so late, she rummaged in a drawer to find her torch, let herself out of the front door and turned up the silent road towards the field gate. It had been padlocked. The stile was wound round with barbed wire and a notice had been nailed over the fingerpost: *Footpath Diversion*. An arrow pointed up the lane. She frowned. What about the archaeologist? Had he finished his survey after they left or was he planning to return, in which case he would have to find his way into the meadow through a barrier of wire. She walked on up the lane through the dark of the summer night and found a new sign to the hill fort, pointing directly into the wood.

In the distance she could hear the trickle of water as the brook flowed around its tumbled rocks and lapped at the shingle beach. Otherwise the whole area seemed to be holding its breath. She walked on, following the track in the torchlight as it turned down towards the spot where the old footpath had forded the stream. Someone had nailed wire across there as well. She frowned, shining the torch upstream. The whole area was blocked now. It was going to be impossible to go back into the paddock.

She directed the beam of her torch out across the grass but it wasn't strong enough to pick out the area she wanted to see,

Meryn's wormhole. She didn't plan to go near it, she just wanted to know if it was visible. Was it obvious, like a whirlwind, or vortex, or did it just look like any other part of the field? Presumably it did, or they would all have seen it earlier. Perhaps it came and went like a change in the weather, or a mirage in the sunlight. She shivered. She had seen it, of course, from the top of the hill; she had seen the fluctuations of the light, the hazy vision of horses, horses from long ago. And Charles Ford had seen it too.

She glanced back into the undergrowth. It was hard to follow the track in the dark and suddenly she didn't want to. The silence was intense; no breeze to rustle the leaves, no gentle calling of sheep to their lambs, no owls hooting across the deserted wooded hillside high on the ancient fort. She would come back in daylight. Pushing her way back through the bushes she retraced her steps to the lane and only then did she hear a single sharp bark from a fox in the distance. It was as though a spell had been broken.

13

'You do realise the general was married before ?'

Julia had taken it upon herself to call on Elen most mornings. They were sitting in the courtyard garden sipping mint tea. Gemma was asleep, curled on a cushion at Elen's feet. On this occasion Valeria Valentina had joined them as well.

Elen gave Valeria a startled glance. There had been a tinge of malice in her tone. 'Of course; his wife died.' She held her breath, almost afraid that the woman would shake her head and deny it, but her guest nodded.

'Ceindrech. She too was of noble British blood.' She gave Elen a quizzical look. 'He himself is related to Theodosius, the emperor of the Eastern Empire – you know that, of course – and that should be enough for him, but he told my husband that for some weird reason he wanted to ally himself to the land where he's been posted, to feel he belongs here. Once, not so long ago, it was illegal for officers in the Roman army to marry local girls, but he has turned that ruling on its head.' The infinitesimal pause made it clear the words *local girl* were intended as a veiled insult, and Elen found herself wondering from where Valeria herself originated. 'Have you met his children yet?' the woman went on.

Elen ignored the dig at her origins. She was a princess and that trumped any supposed superiority Valeria might feel. She sat up straight. The absence of his children had been worrying her. She saw so little of her husband that when he did come to her bed it had seemed inappropriate to ask him about her predecessor. She had been too busy enjoying the feel of his body against hers, his strength as he took her, his practised mastery leading to her final helpless surrender, his kisses, at first fierce and demanding growing more tender as they fell apart in mutual exhaustion. She replayed Valeria's words in her head. *He likes to ally himself to the land,* and she felt a chill run down her spine. All she knew was that he had offered his daughter to her brother, an offer that had been rejected. His marriage to her had been the second-best option.

'Where are his children?'

'His sons are both in the army. I don't know where they're stationed. I believe his daughter, Flavia, has been married to a local war lord. They must be your age, if not older.' Valeria gave Elen a sideways glance.

Elen clenched her fists in the folds of her stole and took a deep breath. 'What happened to my husband's first wife?'

'She became ill,' Julia put in sharply. 'It was very sad. The best army doctors couldn't save her. She died when they were up north when he was in charge of the frontier forces on the great wall built by the Emperor Hadrian.'

'So, she went with him on manoeuvres?'

Valeria narrowed her eyes. 'Officers' wives usually do. Unless they're expecting a child. Then sometimes they remain with relatives if they're near their time.' She reached for her tisane and took a sip.

Elen saw the speculative look the woman had given in the direction of her slim figure and she laughed, unaccountably embarrassed at the implied criticism. 'We have been married only a few short weeks—'

A few short weeks and yet during that time he had visited her bed relatively seldom, pleading official duties and local manoeuvres training his men, promising when he did come that, as soon as the weather changed and training became more difficult, he would return home to spend more time with her.

Julia smiled. 'It won't be long, I'm sure, until you find yourself expecting another son for the general.' Another implied criticism. More time. Elen hoped she hadn't blushed. He might not have time to visit her bed often, but when he did it was easy to forgive and forget the long lonely nights. Even the thought of his eyes, intent on hers, signalling as the nights grew dark, that it was time to go to bed, whispering their private joke about Roman stallions and Silurian mares, laughing together as he kissed her breasts and teased her for her riding style, made her feel warm and desirable. But, when he was running his hand over her belly, was he too wondering, as probably half the fort was, why she had not conceived? She stood up abruptly. 'The sun is out. Why don't we walk in the herb gardens around the cook house while we have the chance. I would like to see the new planting and my little dog would much prefer to go for a run.'

Elen was only too pleased when Valeria, obviously bored by Julia's enthralled love of domestic trivialities, changed the subject as they stood in front of one of the new herb beds. She reverted to her favourite topic, which was talking about her travels with her own husband to the distant corners of the empire, even to the courts of the emperors. To Elen's shame, she had not realised there were two. Macsen had found time to explain that much to her. The ruler of the Western Empire, Gratian, had, it appeared, continued the tradition of appointing a co-ruler to manage the sprawling extremities of the vast empire and he had chosen his brother-in-law, Theodosius, to be the emperor of the East. And Theodosius was Macsen's cousin.

'The general has ambitions, you know,' Valeria murmured as she and Elen walked slowly down the newly laid gravel path between the beds, watching Gemma scamper ahead of them. 'He will not be satisfied with this posting in Britannia for long.'

Elen watched her thoughtfully. 'Is that what your husband says?'

Valeria was silent for a few moments. 'Flavius Magnus is the most senior officer in Britannia, but word is he could do even better elsewhere in the empire,' she replied cautiously. 'Would that please you? To go abroad?'

'This is my country,' Elen retorted. 'Flavius Magnus . . .' She paused at the unaccustomed use of his proper name, 'Flavius married me for my status as daughter and heir of the high king. I bring the loyalty of the British tribes to his standard.'

Valeria nodded. 'He is well aware of that. And values you for it. After all, that was the only reason he married you.' The remark had a cutting edge. 'So, perhaps he would not expect you to travel with him,' she went on swiftly. 'If he did go abroad, you could remain here, holding this province safe for him.' Realising Elen was scrutinising her face, she gave a tight smile. 'My husband is Flavius Magnus's most loyal supporter, you know that, don't you.'

Elen gave a small nod.

'I love it in the great centres of the empire. Augusta Treverorum, or Mediolanum or Urbs Aeterna, the centre of the empire itself.' Valeria's eyes sparkled. 'But for you I suspect it would be unpleasant to go so far from home. You have always lived in Britannia, so maybe it would be better for you to remain here.' Would the woman never stop putting her down? 'Let him know you would support him, but that you realise that if you did not accompany him but stayed here, your royal status would be undiminished and his would be increased tenfold, just by your presence at home.'

'Travel does sound exciting.' In spite of herself, Elen could not quite disguise the wistful note in her reply. She had listened transfixed on several occasions now to Valeria's accounts of life in an urban metropolis, where men of learning gathered and politicians argued in the forum.

'But you would do better to stay here,' Valeria repeated firmly. 'Especially if you were with child. That is why he's built this house for you in the centre of the most secure fort in the province. He wants to keep you safe.'

But I am not with child.

The words seemed to hover on Elen's lips and Julia, as if sensing her discomfort, adroitly sought to change the subject with a disapproving glance at her companion. 'As regards his children, tell him if you want to meet them. It is understandable that you should. If you don't, he has enough tact to understand that you might find it difficult. Either way, you must speak to him about it. And as for babies, ignore Valeria. There is time enough for that.' Impulsively she tucked her arm through Elen's. 'I'm sure you know how gossip flies around a fort. You're a new face. You're famous and exciting as the wife of our commander and a princess. Ignore them all.' She glared at Valeria, who sniffed loudly and tossed her head.

In the event the need to talk to Macsen about his children did not arise. Only a few days later a troop of soldiers marched into the fort. At their head was a young officer. With black hair, an aquiline nose and dark eyes, he was the image of his father. Vaulting from his horse he walked into the general's house alone and without ceremony, finding Elen in her favourite retreat in the courtyard by the fountain. 'So, this is my stepmama. Greetings.' He seized her hand and kissed it. 'I am Constantine, come all the way from Verulamium to meet you.' He stood back and gave her a formal salute. 'Forgive me for not being here to greet you when you arrived. We were out chasing a party of insurgents when I heard the news of father's marriage, and the roads are dreadful right across the province. Where is my pater? I assumed he would be at the side of his beautiful bride. Surely he's not gone back to work already?'

Standing up, Elen was pleased to realise she was as tall as he was. 'Greetings, stepson.' She smiled at last. 'Forgive me, I was somewhat surprised by your impetuous arrival. Are your brother and sister with you?'

He shook his head. 'My brother Flavius Victor is stationed at Eboracum and my sister Flavia is with her husband in the south where I have, it seems, a new nephew, another member of the family.'

Elen was taken aback. So these stepchildren of whom she had heard so little and of whom she had become increasingly nervous were indeed established young adults, and at least one of them was as curious about her as she was about them. She relaxed slightly beneath his charm. 'Then you must represent

them all. I am so pleased finally to meet my husband's family.'
She turned to the slaves who had been hovering in the background. 'Will one of you send a message to the general that
his son is here and then see we are brought refreshments.' She
had managed to collect herself. 'Sit down, Constantine. Tell me
about yourself. You are based in Verulamium, you said?'

'Only temporarily while the legion is posted there. When
my father was made Comes Britanniarum he thought it best
I broadened my experience of active service before coming to
work for him.' He smiled. He had his father's charm and probably his ambition. He had stooped to pick up Gemma, and was
tickling her under the chin.

'And are you married like your sister?'

He shook his head. 'It's too soon to settle down.' There was
a wicked gleam in his eye. 'My sister was ready for marriage.
My brother and I want to travel.' He put the dog down gently.
'My father has been to all the corners of the empire. I expect
he's told you. He used to tell us stories of his time in Africa and
in Gaul and Germania. Even his time fighting the tribes beyond
Hadrian's Wall sounds exciting.'

Where your mother died. Elen did not say it. She didn't want
to see the spark fade in the young man's eyes. Nor did she
want to admit that Macsen had told her nothing of his travels,
or of his ambitions. But that would change. She felt a wave of
indignation sweep through her. In every way but in bed, her
husband had been treating her like a child. Now he needed to
treat her wholly and completely as his wife.

'He's a restless spirit,' Macsen said later, a fond grin betraying
his affection for his younger son. The young man had chosen to
be billeted in the barracks with his men rather than join them in
the house, leaving his father and his stepmother to talk over the
remains of the wine as they sat out in the courtyard.

'I'm glad he came.' Elen realised this was almost the first
time her husband had sat down with her alone to relax. He
rested his arm along the back of the stone bench with a sigh,
beckoning a slave forward to refill his goblet. 'Will you let him
travel? It's obviously something he wants to do.'

He nodded. 'I've great plans for him.'

'He told me something about your career,' she said thoughtfully. 'That you've been all over the empire.'

He nodded again.

'And yet you're content to settle here in its furthest corner.'

'For now.' He gave her a mischievous grin, the mirror image of his son's. 'How about you? Do you like the idea of travelling, Elen? Would you like to see the world?'

She nodded. She was beginning to suspect she would like to go anywhere as long as it was at his side.

Cadi dropped her pen and massaged her hands together slowly. *Would you like to see the world?* Those were the last words she had written. Europe. North Africa. Egypt. The Middle East. Greece. Maybe even the Far East. The Silk Road. And how would Elen have reacted to that suggestion? Cadi was sitting up in bed, the writing pad on her knees. She glanced at the open copy of the Mabinogion lying face down on the bed beside her, and the *Oxford History of Roman Britain* beyond it, weighing down the bedclothes. She knew the answer of course. It was Rachel who had stated the obvious. Write the poem, her version of the mystical, poetic original, chosen by the bards of old to tell a story that was three quarters legend and perhaps one quarter fact, if that; the poem she was contracted to write, the poem which relied on Rachel's interpretation as much as her own. Then as a separate project, look up the known history – which was mainly about Macsen, of course, being a man and a soldier and an emperor. And then look up the many different theories about Helen/Elen, queen, empress, palaeolithic goddess crowned with antlers – difficult to visualise that version – and Christian saint, but only look them up out of interest to see what other people thought. Then close the books, pick up her pen and write the story as it flowed from Elen herself, the story of a dream. But not Macsen's dream; this would primarily be Elen's dream, the dream she, Cadi, alone, shared with a woman dead for probably some sixteen hundred years. She lay back on the pillows and smiled. She had finally made up her mind. The horrible sense of conflict was resolved. If her story was magically sourced through a wormhole in the middle of a Welsh field, so much the better. That was her secret. How did writers source their novels anyway? Where did their stories come from? Surely this was as likely an inspiration as sitting in a coffee shop with the literary pages in front of her, moulding each sentence into a work of art. She smiled. That last thought was aimed at Arwel, though he would never hear it.

14

'You did know Macsen was a follower of Mithras.'

Elen stared at Julia in horror. 'I had no idea.'

A year had passed since she arrived at Segontium. Today was Midsummer's Day. The Feast of St John.

The fort had two main shrines that she knew of: one dedicated to the goddess Minerva and one to Mars, the god of war; either or both could have been reconsecrated to the Christian faith after the decree of the Emperor Constantine that the whole empire become Christian, but it had obviously not happened in this faraway fort at the corner of the world. Macsen agreed instead that a room could be set aside for his wife's Christian worship, a house church, but nothing had happened and now she knew why.

'Where is it? The temple?' Her mouth had gone dry.

Julia shook her head. 'It's in the marshes down there, somewhere below the walls of the fort; a sacred place. We can't go there. No woman can. I shouldn't have mentioned it. I'm so sorry.' She noted Elen's confusion. 'Mithras is the soldiers' god. Most of the officers here are initiates.'

'Including your husband?'

Julia nodded.

'And yet you are a follower of Christ?'

Julia nodded again. 'Christ is a woman's god; at least, that is what the soldiers think.'

Elen stood up wearily. She was heavy with child, conceived at last in the previous winter after Macsen had finally returned to her bed. His attention had been determined and exhausting, and she had enjoyed it, the feelings she had experienced in their first months together re-awakening as her body responded to his, touch for touch and thrust for thrust, melting at his kisses and exchanging bite for bite. It was the moments of tenderness she treasured most, but also the new feeling of confidence and a profound belief in her own strength as a woman. She no longer felt inferior to the other wives, she was beautiful and strong, and above all she was fertile. But now the summer heat was draining her. Her instinct was to go and drag her husband away from his pagan god with its bloody rituals, but she knew that would never be possible. There was nothing she could do even if she had the energy. He would come to see her again in his own time. Which was less and less often now as the days passed. 'You need women around you, Nel,' he said kindly when she remonstrated at his neglect. 'When our son is born, then I shall return.'

Their son.

Delyth was sure it would be a girl. As was the midwife who had been in residence for a week now, sent from Deva, where the Celtic woman was widely regarded as the best birth attendant in the province.

'See how the child lies in your belly,' she said. 'And see how she kicks. She will be a horse rider like her mother.'

Elen's rides around the farms and woods, exploring the shore of the Strait, the meanders of the River Seiont and beyond into the wild mountainous countryside, often on the black colt, but lately on a more docile mare, had made her notorious amongst the men of the fort. Macsen did not try to dissuade her. He was proud of his beautiful princess. Her unconventional ways were explained by her royal blood.

She gave a wince of pain and put her hand to her back. There had been no riding for a few weeks now and she missed it, cooped up in the fort with its high stone walls trapping the heat. They had been built originally to intimidate the local British tribes, but of late, with the local tribes friendly trading partners, they formed instead a much-needed protection against hostile pirate attacks from the sea, from Hibernia in the west and from the far north, and they were a base for her husband's increasing ambition. He was frustrated by the continued failure of support of men or money from the mainland empire. As far as the Emperor Gratian was concerned, Britannia was a distant province, useful for its mineral riches and its taxes, but now too far away to be any kind of priority.

'Shall I call someone to massage your back?'

Elen became aware of Julia leaning towards her, her face full of concern, and she realised that she had groaned out loud. She managed a smile. 'That would be nice. I'm sorry. I'm not good company at the moment. Perhaps you could suggest to the others that I need a rest?' The chatter of the women, well-meant though it was, was exhausting. Only Valeria seemed to have got the message and stayed away.

Julia stood up. 'Of course. Anything you need, let me know.'

Mithras.

As Elen lay back on her bed, soothed by the gentle hand movements of the masseuse as she rubbed in the warm olive oil infused with lavender and by the quiet harp music played by the girl sitting in the corner of the bedchamber, her mind kept repeating the single word. The soldiers' god. Temples drenched in the blood of the slaughtered white bull. No wonder her mentions of Christ had left her husband unresponsive. Christianity had been a religion within the Roman Empire for seventy years now, permitted by the tolerant Roman occupiers as one of many. Only one religion was banned: that of the Druids, who had been too clever, too political, too fearsome for their Roman oppressors. They were educated, organised and inimical to the ambitions of their enemies. The most sacred place for the Druids had been the Island of Môn, over there on the far side of the Strait, within sight of the fort which was now her home, a fort built specifically to suppress them. They had had to go, massacred and officially wiped off the face of the map by

Agricola some three hundred years before. They still existed, of course. Everyone knew that. But now they were cautious. Their scholars even frequented the court of the emperor, but as philosophers and poets; only underground did they still present as a powerful force. Branwen was a Druid. And so, perhaps, was Elen's own father at heart, for all his lip service to Christianity. But now it was the Christian faith that was spreading. Christianity with its gentle god who no longer appeared to be a threat to anyone had been enthusiastically adopted throughout the empire, but mainly amongst women. Not all women. Elen had seen small altars dotted around the fort with their offerings of flowers and food and effigies of Minerva. Her own shrine to Christ and his mother was in the corner of the garden. She still had no chapel. But there was a little monastery along the coast. She had visited the monks there when out riding. And there was a holy man, a hermit, only half a day's ride away in the foothills of Eryri.

Macsen ignored the local Christians. Patrolling the mountain routes and the shoreline with his troops, his attention was directed towards signs of pirates, attacks from the aggressive tribes from Caledonia and from Hibernia, but his full concentration was fixed on distant ambitions. So did he pray to Mithras and the Unconquered Sun for success in his endeavours? She jumped as the baby kicked under her ribs and the masseuse laughed. 'Not long now, Princess. Your child is eager for the world.'

Elen's daughter, Maxima, was born on the Ides of July, a bouncing baby with a head of dark curls and a pair of lungs to outyell the shouts of the troops who had drawn up outside the house to drink the health of their general's child. Macsen hid his disappointment at not having a son well, giving her his name and his blessing. A message was sent south to tell Elen's father of the safe delivery of his first grandchild and on the eighth day, as was customary in Julia's household, and according to her throughout the Roman world, the birth of a girl baby was celebrated with special rites of purification that Julia as her patroness oversaw. Elen took part in the feasting and giving of gifts, but deep in her heart she wanted more for her daughter.

Those rites were pagan. The thanks were directed at the goddess Juno, and to the local goddess, Ffraid. She wanted Maxima to have a Christian baptism.

Only two days after the purification, when his daughter was ten days old, Macsen, with his son Constantine at his side, led the larger part of the garrison out of the fort. He had called for a meeting of field commanders and regional leaders in Eboracum. He left Elen and the baby behind, guarded by the remainder of the garrison under the command of Titus Octavius, Julia's husband. Valeria's husband, Claudius Valentius, and Macsen's ADC, his brother Marcellinus, rode at his shoulder at the head of the cohorts, together with the young prince Vortigern who had joined him from one of the local tribes.

Julia was full of importance. 'It's a fantastic promotion for Titus. Your safety, all of our safety is in his hands.'

Elen waved away the nursemaid in charge of the baby. As soon as the girl was sitting in the shade on the far side of the courtyard, rocking the cradle and well out of earshot, she leaned forward. 'But there is no danger, surely? My husband would not have gone if there was any intelligence of marauding pirates nearby.'

Julia looked offended. 'There is always the risk of danger. That is why he left his best officer in charge.'

'Of course. I didn't mean to imply otherwise.' Elen was only slowly learning to guard her tongue but sometimes she spoke without thinking and Julia was easily offended. 'I feel completely safe here.'

So safe in fact that with Delyth's help she had arranged a secret outing. It was a small group consisting of Rhys and two sturdy British grooms, Delyth, the wet nurse, and Nia and Sian, Elen's closest attendants. With them were four British slaves, armed with staves, all part of Elen's household, and one of the horse boys, a young man who had special care of Emrys and who, Elen knew, had been selected for training by Rhys with a view to one day being put in sole charge of this most special horse. Elen had already vowed to give the slaves their freedom as a reward for their part in today's ceremony. All of them had come with her from the south. All of them were Christians.

Gemma was left behind in the care of one of the younger house slaves. Their destination was the hermitage tucked up a narrow valley in the foothills, the site of a spring that had already been sacred for a thousand years.

The servants left behind were instructed to inform Julia and anyone else who called at the commander's house that the princess was feeling tired and had decided to spend the day in bed. Valeria Valentina had, it appeared, accompanied her husband to the meeting at Eboracum. Julia had conveyed the news with a quick glance at Elen, which was nothing if not embarrassed when she told her. Perhaps she suspected that Titus was after all not the most senior officer on the base. That accolade had left with Claudius Valentius, who had taken his wife and his own household with him.

The duty guard at the gatehouse had been sworn to secrecy, with suitable threats that if anyone betrayed news of the outing of the general's wife and her party they would be instantly demoted if not dismissed from the service, but the parade ground was deserted as they left, the guardsmen keeping their eyes carefully averted. Of Julia there was no sign.

The day was already hot and humid as the party set off just after dawn, following the road south through farmland and woods and then turning at last up the steep narrow track which led eventually between rocky outcrops and towering cliffs towards the hermit's cave. Little Maxima slept soundly, tightly bound in her swaddling shawl against her nurse's breast, lulled by the steady gait of the sturdy mountain pony. The party were all mounted, Elen on Emrys, happy to be back in the saddle at last, Rhys and the horse boy riding beside her, the others all following closely behind as the track climbed more and more steeply into the wild foothills.

The half-hidden cave opened onto a narrow rock platform beside a gushing spring. Offerings of coins and jewellery lay in the shallow basin below the jet of water and flower petals floated in the whirlpool before the stream ran over the edge of the rock and plunged down towards the narrow cwm below. There they halted and dismounted. The four slaves and the boy were detailed to remain with the horses, and the rest of the party climbed the long flight of rough-hewn steps towards the cave. The hermit greeted them with a blessing. He was an elderly man with a white beard and soft grey eyes. He stepped forward to take the baby from her nurse with a gentle smile.

Elen had chosen her baptismal name with care. Mair, for the mother of Christ. She knew the little girl would never go by that name – to her father she was already Maxima, but after her baptism the child was doubly blessed and safe, protected by her secret name and by the tiny gold cross which had been tucked beneath her swaddling bands when she was re-dressed, a squalling red-faced bundle who had not enjoyed her part of the ceremony one bit. Her sponsors were Delyth and Rhys, if not of royal blood, nevertheless her brother and sister in Christ, and as such, both kissed the little girl on the forehead.

The ceremony over, the party returned down the steep steps to the narrow strip of meadow at the valley's bottom where one of the slaves had been laying out a picnic on rugs on the edge of the stream while the boy took the horses, two by two, further down to a shallow pool where they could drink.

When the attack came it was sudden and vicious. More than two dozen heavily armed men with shouts and screams of defiance, most brandishing swords and daggers, some armed with quarterstaffs, surged onto the grass and before anyone knew what was happening the boy with the horses by the stream lay dead on the ground. Everyone froze. There was no escape, no chance for even one of their men to reach for a weapon. No one spoke. Their attackers fell silent as their leader, a man with wild red hair and beard and piercing green eyes, singled Elen out at one glance. Her mantle, her jewellery, her hair, marked her out as a rich woman. He approached with a ferocious fixed smile on his face. 'There is no need for anyone else to die. Tell your followers to put their weapons and jewels on the ground for my men to collect.' He spoke with a thick lilting accent.

Elen collected herself with difficulty, conscious of his knuckles tightening over the hilt of the dagger in his hand. Taking a deep breath, she straightened her shoulders and stepped towards him. 'Do you know who I am?' Her voice rang out clearly across the grass. She saw his eyebrows shoot up. He had not been expecting defiance.

'No, I don't know who you are, and I'm sure I don't care!'

'Well, perhaps you should.' She was aware of the total silence around them. Everyone was holding their breath. 'I am the daughter of the high king.' Her voice rang out over the gentle gurgle of water in the stream.

It was a gamble. She suspected he was a pirate from Hibernia or perhaps a Pict from Caledonia. Either way he would owe no allegiance to any king on the island of Britannia but Mammon. But another voice had lifted after hers.

'And I, my friends, am your father in Christ.' No one had been watching the hermit, standing above them on his rocky dais, his staff in his hand. He had declined the invitation to join in their picnic, retiring into his cave to pray, but now he emerged to stand above them in the full light of the sun. 'I command you to put up your weapons. There is no gold here. Even our king's daughter has little. I am sure she will throw you her woman's bangles if they mean so much to you. We came here to worship Christ, not to display our wealth. And what riches did that poor boy there have that he deserved to be slain?' He pointed at the young man lying in a pool of blood by the stream, the severed leading rein of one of the horses trailing from his hand. The horses themselves had fled into a rocky defile below the meadow.

There was an uncomfortable silence but the man's expression did not change. Elen stepped forward and pulled the bangles off her wrist. They were chased gold, a present from her father on her marriage, but she threw them down on the ground at the man's feet. 'Do you want my wedding ring as well?' she asked, her voice heavy with disdain. 'I advise against it as my husband is the leader of all the armies of Rome on this island and you have already done enough to incur his fury.'

This time the leader of the ruffians did react. Was it possible he hadn't known who she was? But of course she wasn't guarded by a troop of soldiers. Her small bodyguard of men did not wear any insignia. She saw the man's gaze shift slightly. One or two of his followers had grown restless and she wondered if they were readying themselves to commit murder or to flee.

Above their heads the hermit took a step forward. He raised his right hand and slowly and deliberately made the sign of the cross. 'Go in peace,' he cried, his voice echoing off the rocks behind him.

None of them had noticed Elen's colt walking steadily out of the rocky shadows towards his mistress. At the sound of the echoing shout from the man of God, so loud in the silence around them, the horse reared up, letting out a shrill whinny of rage. Instantly the attackers broke rank and fled. One of them turned back and with a challenging glance at Elen scooped her bracelets out of the grass, then he too disappeared after the others, lost from sight almost at once on the rocky mountainside.

15

Chris the miller arrived with a bag of croissants, still warm from the ovens, and they seated themselves in the garden with a large pot of coffee. He had left Mel in charge at the mill while he came over for what he described as a quick council of war.

'You see they've blocked off the field?' he said, plastering butter onto the flaking pastry in his hand.

Cadi nodded. 'The diversion leads up through the woods and joins the footpath up to the fort.'

'You've already been up there?'

She nodded.

'We've got to get our hands on the new survey.' Chris shook his head. 'I'll have another word with my mate at the council offices.'

'That might be difficult for him, Chris. He would be risking his job, surely.' She licked her fingers and reached for her coffee mug.

Chris gave a rueful smile. 'He knows the risk, but he's fully prepared to have a go. He thinks the cause is good. But in the meantime, has your uncle got any ideas?' He glanced at her. 'Arwel is expecting him to stand in the meadow, his raised staff in his hand, and pretend to curse the site.'

'Pretend.' She repeated the word thoughtfully.

Chris nodded. 'But he could do the real thing, yes?'

'I think that would go against the warlock's code.' She put her mug down. 'You do know he's a real professor, a proper serious author of books on some very esoteric science?'

'No, I didn't know that. I've been got at by Arwel. Sorry.'

'Then I suggest you look Meryn up online.' She relented. 'I know his is a bit of a specialist field, but I gather science is catching up fast. Quantum physics, the God particle, dark matter, the Hadron Collider, all that stuff. My cousin says he is much respected. And until we can lay our hands on that field survey, he is probably the best we can do – and that is a pretty good best.'

'Point taken.' It was Chris's turn to lick the butter off his fingers. 'One piece of news which may or may not be good: they agreed that Dai Prosser could top the grass at least once more. He contacted the land agent and told him he had a long-standing agreement with the previous owner. The agent seemed a very accommodating type of bloke, apparently. He agreed the current owner probably doesn't know one end of a blade of grass from another, but cutting it again would make it easier for everyone to find out what, if anything, is there.'

'Perhaps he'll find poor little Gemma. I've dreaded discovering her remains on one of our walks.'

Chris grimaced. 'I'm so sorry for Sally. Term ends soon. She'll miss her even more, being at home on her own.'

It was after Chris had gone that Cadi reached for her file of notes once more. She pulled out the scribbled poem about Gemma that at the time she hadn't even realised she was writing and ran a gentle finger over the words on the page as if she could comfort the little dog through the magic of her touch. She gave a rueful smile. That was something Meryn would understand. And Rachel. Spreading out the notes and looking at her file, stuffed with references and information about the historical Macsen and his rather too anonymous wife, she felt a shot of adrenaline. This was her story now. She was free to pursue it, beyond the limits of the poetic form and it could go anywhere she liked. She could dig deep into historical research and at the same time she could follow her own intuition. Follow her pen. Follow the ghostly story that was revealing itself in the meadow and in the misty mountains of a historical landscape almost two thousand years old.

Brennius, king of the Ordovices, came to see Elen the next day, attended by an escort of local tribesmen from their base in the great fortress of Dinas Dinlle, some four miles away, perched on its cliff above the Hibernian Ocean. Titus Octavius was called by the duty watch as the dozen or so fully armed men were halted at the gateway. Titus hesitated when the man demanded entry. He had heard about the attack by the pirates and was furious that Elen had gone out with so little protection, but she had been very clear that it was her decision and he was not to blame. She was also clear that whatever her husband had told Titus to the contrary, she, the daughter of the high king, was in charge at Segontium.

She received the king and his followers in the antechamber of the principia where Macsen held his meetings. The old man bowed. 'I have come to offer you the loyalty and protection of my people. This fort is not able to withstand an attack until the legion's return. With our presence known, you will be safe.' He glanced at Titus and his officers who had formed up behind Elen. 'I would ask you to dismiss your guard, if that is what they are.' He couldn't keep the scorn out of his voice. 'I have a gift for you, a gift from the gods, and this is for you alone. No one's eyes should fall on it but yours until due time. My men too will leave us.'

Elen sensed Titus tensing behind her. He had no intention of leaving her alone, but already the king's escort had fallen into some kind of order and were marching towards the door.

'Leave us!' Elen commanded as she turned to Titus. 'I am perfectly safe. The king is a man of honour and is due every respect.'

Titus hesitated then drew himself up and raised his right arm in salute. He nodded to his men and they filed out after him.

The old man gave a grim smile. 'I am glad he obeys you. He has an important task, to guard the wife of the general.'

She nodded. 'He is torn between his duty to my husband, and his recognition of my royal status. He will be outside within call.'

'And there will be no need to call. What I have brought you is a sacred relic. It has been in my care for many years, and in my father's and his father's before that. As the daughter of the high king and descendant of the bloodline of the gods, you should be its keeper now, and your children after you, until such time as it is needed to save the holy isle of Albion. This is a treasure beyond price.'

He was wearing a chequered woollen cloak fastened with a heavy circular topaz pin, as was customary for the senior men of the tribes; her father had one like it. He reached into the folds of the cloak and brought out an obviously heavy long package. To her astonishment he knelt before her and laid it on the ground, then he began carefully to unwrap it.

Almost at once she saw it was a sword. A very beautiful sword different in shape from its Roman counterpart, with a delicately carved hilt, set with crudely cut amethysts and garnets and clear sparkling quartz crystals. The blade, decorated with strange otherworldly swirls, had been polished to a dull grey sheen. She stared at it, stunned. Surely she had seen this sword before. She groped in her memory. How could she have forgotten something as beautiful, as powerful as this? But the memory had gone. King Brennius carefully picked it up and laid it across his palms before presenting it to her. She reached forward and took hold of the hilt. It was very cold. 'I am honoured,' she whispered.

'Its name is Caledfwlch. I don't know how old it is, but it was held sacred by the men of the oaks on the Isle of Môn. I heard it was forged by the gods themselves. When the Druids were attacked and slaughtered by the Roman armies three hundred years ago, this treasure was already hidden and survivors of the slaughter gave it to my ancestor and his descendants to keep until the time came for it to be passed on.' He gave her a gentle smile. 'To you. I sense the time is coming soon when it will be needed. The attacks such as we had yesterday are happening more and more frequently, but the auguries warn the worst will come from the eastern shores, and they will threaten the whole island of Albion. Not in our time, perhaps, but soon.'

She was staring down at the blade. The flame of the oil lamp on a stand behind her was reflecting in its polished surface. She could feel the sacredness of it. She could see the shapes of men and horses, she could hear the shouts and screams of dying soldiers and she could see, faintly but clearly, a young man, the sword in his hand, a coronet on his head. She looked up at the old man kneeling before her and he nodded slowly. 'You too see its future.'

She bit her lip. 'We have to keep it safe.' She held it up to the flickering light, feeling its weight. 'What is it made of?'

'I believe the metal fell from the stars, and the gems in the hilt came from the womb of Mother Earth, found somewhere long ago in this the land of eagles.' He frowned. 'This precious thing is not for your husband the general, lady. However high he rises as lord of this isle, this is not for him. He was not born of this holy earth and he will not die here.'

Deep in her heart she had already guessed as much. She lowered her voice: 'There is nowhere in the fort it would be safe.'

He nodded, acknowledging the truth of this.

She had already made the decision. 'I want you to take it and hide it again. You have kept it safe for so long, it's right you remain its keeper until the time comes for one of my children to take over the sacred trust.' She held out the sword and he rose to his feet, accepting it with a bow.

'I will return it to its resting place on Ynys Enlli, the sacred isle, where it can lie in peace,' he said gravely.

'I can feel its power,' she said almost regretfully as he rewrapped it and secreted it once more beneath his cloak. 'But its time hasn't yet come. For now we will let it sleep in the dark.'

Macsen returned four weeks after the raid on the hermit's shrine to find his wife in charge of the fort. The parade ground was neatly raked, the garrison immaculately turned out, but more to the point, some two hundred British tribesmen were drawn up outside the gateway in ragged ranks, and more within the outer ramparts, ranged in a tight squadron under the leadership of someone who was obviously the headman of the tribe.

'Word went out to raise the host.' Elen greeted him formally in front of the men. Macsen's troops had drawn up outside the walls. 'The Hibernian raiders were captured. They await your judgement.' She lowered her eyes demurely. 'I have ordered that they all be chained.'

Macsen studied the assembled troops. The brigade he had left behind reinforced now by the British host – men drawn presumably from the ring of great hill forts, nominally subservient to the empire, but he realised almost instantly, loyal to the woman who stood so poised at his side in front of them. The bedraggled prisoners were huddled together on their knees.

'Did they threaten my daughter?'

'No. Only her mother.' Elen gritted her teeth, waiting for a rebuke for leaving the fortress without a suitable escort. It didn't come and she glanced up at his face, which was, as always, inscrutable.

'Where is Titus Octavius?' Macsen's keen eye had noticed at once there was no sign of his commanding officer.

'He is in the hospital block with a high fever.' Elen refused to meet his eye.

Macsen looked around once more. The remaining officers in charge of the garrison were, he thought, looking sheepish. As his eye ran over them he could see them all visibly straightening their shoulders.

His wife's ragtag army outnumbered his soldiers three to one. But on the other hand his men were highly trained and armed. Hers, he studied their ranks thoughtfully, useful allies. Had they really materialised out of nowhere, summoned to Elen's aid, according to the murmur in his ear of one of the officers at his side, by the servant of the Christian hermit. It seemed they had.

Back in their private rooms at last he stood looking down into the child's cradle. The baby gazed back at him with wide blue eyes, seemingly examining him. Summing him up. He found himself hoping that she did not find him wanting. He glanced at the child's nurse, who was sitting by the window, her fingers busy with her spindle. She had shown no sign of knowing he was there and indeed as he watched he saw the woman's hands fall into her lap and the spindle itself tumble into the basket at her feet. Her head nodded forward and he heard a gentle snore. He glanced back at the baby, who gave him a complicit smile. It seemed as if at last she had registered approval at her father's presence.

He gave the cradle a gentle push and walked slowly across the room, aware that the sound of his nailed sandals on the mosaic floor had awoken the sleeping woman by the window.

Elen was in the next room, a stylus in her hand, sitting at the table making notes on a wax tablet. Gemma was asleep at her feet. Elen looked up. 'So, the traveller has returned.' The little dog stood up and wagged her tail a little hesitantly. She did not approach him.

He grimaced. 'I am sorry, my dear. I have been remiss. You of all people I wanted to greet alone, not in front of hundreds of men.' He strode across the room and swept her out of her chair and into his arms. Gemma flinched away and ran to hide under a sideboard in the corner of the room. 'There is much to talk about.' He glanced over Elen's head towards the door. 'Come into the courtyard. I need absolute privacy.'

She led him to the bench in the rose bower. The original sparse planting, surrounded by clay pots and statues that afforded only a degree of protection from the chance of being overheard, had been augmented with hundreds of new plants with a peristyle and the garden had quickly evolved into a pleasurable place to take repose. She had employed two freedmen, together with their mother, from the vicus, the township that had grown up over the years outside the walls of the fort, and they had assumed the position of gardeners, similar to those in her father's palace. Their arrival had been satisfyingly effective. She saw him look round approvingly. She demurely seated herself beside him and smoothed out her skirt.

'I've missed you, sweetheart,' he said at last.

'And I you.' She glanced at him sideways. 'It's been too long.' She reached out to touch his hand.

'Tonight,' he said. He winked at her.

A tremor of lust shot through her. She composed herself, aware of watching eyes all around them. 'Your meeting went well, husband?' She had by now perfected the gracious lift of an eyebrow.

He nodded solemnly. 'Your father was there as high king, as were tribal kings from across the land, plus most of the district rulers.' There was a significant pause, then: 'We must be thankful, it appears, that the king of the Ordovices did not see fit to attend.' When she did not reply he went on. 'We sent a further demand to Gratian for reinforcements. The attacks on this island are growing ever more violent and ever more frequent. If we don't hear back from him there needs to be a way forward on our own terms. We cannot keep referring back to a higher authority who ignores us.'

'But he made you *Comes* of the whole island.' She was indignant.

'I still have to beg him for reinforcements from overseas and they never come. The ineffectualness and inefficiency of an administration to which we are expected to bow makes me furious.' He stood up impatiently and paced up and down beside the rectangular pool of water that formed a formal centre for the bower. 'I grow ever more frustrated by our masters in Rome, Elen, and the leaders of this island feel the same. They have made a suggestion that I must consider.'

Elen felt a draught of cold air touch her spine. She waited in silence. 'We have given them one more chance to send the support we need. If it doesn't appear by the feast of Saturnalia, then I shall feel compelled to make a unilateral declaration to sever our links with the empire, withhold all taxes – of which we have a considerable sum stored in the strongroom here – and use whatever means we can find to keep this island safe. Your father agrees with me. If the empire cannot protect us, then we have to protect ourselves.'

'Have you talked this over with Titus?'

Macsen's second in command had still not resumed his duties, but he was as far as she knew on the mend. His unexpected and highly convenient fever had rendered him unable to resume his command of the fort. It had struck him down two days after her visit from the king of the Ordovices and she had seen nothing of him since. Julia had been very protective, saying the military physicians were completely baffled by his illness. He was not to have visitors. Macsen was not so under-standing. It was Julia who told Elen what had happened the next day. She was simmering with fury.

'He just walked in, even though the doctor told him Titus was receiving no visitors, and accused my husband of malin-gering. I can't believe it! The poor man has been so ill. He had a fever. He could hardly stand. Of course he couldn't resume his duties. The general accused him of allowing you to leave the fort without an escort. He said had you been killed it would have been Titus's fault. You have to tell him you deliberately tricked us. You left instructions that you couldn't be disturbed because you were ill. It wasn't Titus who was faking it, it was you.' She gave a sob of rage. 'You deliberately tricked me, and you didn't want me there, your best friend! I should have been a sponsor for your child, not your serving woman. How could you ask Delyth to stand for her when I would have been more than willing!'

Elen had risen to her feet. 'Julia—'

'No!' Weeks of hurt and resentment came flooding out. 'You never really liked me. You used me. I helped you settle in here. You let me think you were my friend and all the time you despised me. I even stopped Valeria having that wretched dog knocked on the head after it stamped all over her best tunic with muddy feet. And I kept her secrets. I made sure you would never find out about her and the general—'

Julia's hand flew to her mouth. 'Sorry. I shouldn't have said any of that. I was just so angry.' She stared round desperately, obviously wishing the ground would swallow her up. 'Forget I said it.'

Elen stared at her. For a moment she couldn't speak. She felt an ice-cold sickness sweep over her. When at last she was able to open her mouth, all she could do was repeat those words. 'What should I not find out about her and the general?'

Julia shook her head mutely.

'I need to know, Julia. Don't make me ask him.'

Julia looked up pleadingly. 'I'm sorry. I was jealous and stupid and cross. Forgive me.'

'Tell me.'

Julia gave up. She perched on the edge of a chair, her hands clasped and began to talk, hesitantly at first, then as the words became easier, in a torrent of bitter recriminations. Elen had resumed her seat. She sat very still.

'It was after Ceindrech died. He was lonely and Valeria is a very beautiful woman. Claudius Valentius was away on manoeuvres. They began to take supper together. To begin with, I think it was just a friendship. She had travelled, like him. They could discuss far-off places and the people they had met. They both felt cut off here in Britannia. It is a cold, unwelcoming country to people who are used to hotter climes. His family come from Hispania and she had been to Gallaecia, where he was born.' She shrugged her shoulders desperately. Elen remained stony-faced. 'I don't know when it became more than friendship. Before he ever met you. It was never going to be more than an affair. She ordered me to keep her secret. She threatened me. She wouldn't listen to me. I stood up for you. I told her how hurt you would be, but she wouldn't listen. She didn't care. She knew he needed to marry again, to make a good alliance.' Her voice trailed away.

'So, that is all I was. A useful alliance.' Elen's voice was flat. 'Of course, I knew that, but I hoped we had become more than mere allies. When I was alone; when I was pregnant; when I had given birth to his daughter. He was with her then.'

Julia nodded reluctantly.

'And she went with him to Eboracum?'

'Yes.' It was a whisper.

'Does Claudius Valentius know about this?'

Another nod.

'Of course he does. Is that how he reached such high rank? Because he knew how to turn a blind eye?'

'It is the way things are, Princess. I'm sorry.'

Both women looked down as Gemma crept up to Elen, sensing an atmosphere. Elen bent and picked up the little dog. 'And she wanted my dog killed?'

'She was angry about the mud on her best tunic. I'm sure she would have regretted it.'

'I'm sure she would.'

There was a long, awkward silence. At last Julia stood up. 'I should go.'

Elen didn't reply and with a frantic glance round the room Julia scuttled towards the door.

Elen did not see her husband for two days. He was, it appeared, busy with some reorganisation of the fort's defences. When at last he appeared it was to join her for a private supper. 'I have decided to send Titus on one final mission to Gratian. It will do him good to have a change of scene and he might be able to gain some traction in our attempt to persuade the emperor to send us supplies of men and weapons. He will take Julia and his household with him.'

Elen inclined her head. 'That seems a good idea. Are you planning to send Claudius Valentius and his wife with them?' Her tone was ice-cold, her fury carefully controlled.

For a long minute they held one another's gaze and in that gaze she saw that he knew what had happened. At last he shook his head. 'No. I have to deal with a further threat in the north and I will be leading an army out to deal with that as soon as possible. Claudius will remain in charge here and his household will stay with him.' There was a long thoughtful pause. 'When we were in Eboracum,' he went on at last, 'your father asked whether you might be persuaded to return to Venta for a visit so he can meet his granddaughter. I think that would be a good idea. You don't want to come up to Caledonia with the army. Spend a few months with your father and then we will meet back here in the spring.'

So that was it. A line was being drawn in the sand. She didn't argue. A visit south couldn't come quickly enough for her. Her heart was broken.

16

Cadi was working outside in the shade of the apple tree, her history books and printouts from the internet strewn around her laptop. As she sat there reading through her notes, her attention kept returning to the one word, almost illegible on the page, Caledfwlch. It was not a word she recognised and idly she had turned to the internet. To her amazement it was there. The sword, presented to Elen by the king of one of the ancient tribes of Britain, was none other than Caliburn – Excalibur. Ynys Enlli, Bardsey Island, off the end of the Lleyn Peninsula, was thought by many to be the real Avalon. The Lleyn Peninsula, just round the corner from the old fort of Dinas Dinlle, which was itself less than five miles from Segontium. She sat back, staring up at the lichen-encrusted boughs of the old tree above her, her head reeling with excitement. It was then she heard the tentative knock at her front door. Reluctantly closing the laptop, she hurried back indoors.

'I hope you don't mind me dropping by.' Charles Ford followed her inside. 'I wanted to do some more dowsing in the meadow, but when I arrived the gate was padlocked. I wondered what had been happening. Have they granted them planning permission?'

Putting all thoughts of magic swords aside, Cadi made coffee and he followed her out into the garden. He had a shabby brief-case with him this time, although she could see his famous hazel twig sticking out of the top. 'Can I put something to you?' He glanced at her quickly as if he didn't quite like to broach the sub-ject. 'I don't know if you have ever come across this technique before but I've been doing some dowsing over a map. Before you say anything, I know it sounds a bit wacky, but it does work.' He was anxious again now, reaching for his mug to cover his confu-sion. 'If we can't go into the meadow anymore, it might help. I'm not sure how, but – let me show you. Do you remember when we met, you very kindly gave me a large whisky?' This time his smile was less tentative, the memory clearly pleasurable.

Cadi nodded. 'You were in quite a state. You had seen some-thing odd in the meadow.'

'Exactly.' He pulled a sheaf of papers out of his briefcase. 'I couldn't get what happened out of my head. It kind of haunted me. I knew I wasn't going to be able to get back at once – pres-sures of work – but I could sit at home with a large-scale map.'

He was spreading out what looked like an old plan of the district. 'I tuned in, in the same way one does in the actual field, and using a pendulum I began to quarter the area.' He glanced up for the first time, taking in her garden and the long hedge down one side of it. 'We were looking for a villa. It is right there, isn't it.' He pointed at the hedge. 'In which case, I think I've found it, and at least some of it is here, in your garden.'

'Before you go on . . .' Trying to control her growing excite-ment, Cadi was leaning forward to see the map more closely. 'I think I told you about my uncle who is a dowser?'

He nodded. 'You mentioned him, yes.'

'Well, after you and I met, it reminded me that I should ask him over to do just as you did. To dowse the field. He managed to get here before they locked the gate, but afterwards he did it over a map as well. I have his findings here, in the house.' With her finger she began to trace the lines he had marked on his map in red ink. 'Oh, Charles.' It was all she said. She felt a shiver run across her back. 'Wait here. I'll fetch it.'

They laid the two maps out on the grass, side by side,

weighed down by stones, and, crouching down on their hands and knees, gazed at them. 'Oh my God!' Cadi whispered after a long silence. 'They are almost identical.' She glanced up. He had gone white. He sat back on his heels and reached for his coffee cup. 'You said he was an expert,' he whispered.

She nodded. 'And so are you, it seems. We have to get hold of that ground radar survey.' She leaned forward again, studying his map. 'Meryn says it was a palace. He thinks it would have been too big to be just an ordinary villa, if there is such a thing.'

'Meryn?' He looked at her sharply. 'Not Meryn Jones, by any chance?'

She nodded. 'You've heard of him?'

'Of course. He's one of my heroes. I've read all his books.' He stared at his map again and set his mug down on the grass beside him. 'I nearly didn't come.' He laughed, obviously relieved. 'I felt a bit of a fool. You know, so many people think this is all rubbish. That's why I wanted to have another go in the actual meadow.'

'I don't think you need to.' Scrambling up, she stood looking down at him. 'You look as though you need another Scotch.'

'No, thank you.' He climbed to his feet. 'I was just so shocked by my own accuracy. So many of these things can never be proved. They could as easily be wishful thinking or guesswork.' He was silent for a moment. 'Did you realise that on both our maps there is a bit of the building, whatever it is, right here in your own garden?'

'Yes, I saw that.' They studied the maps in silence. 'Are you suggesting we dig here?' Cadi grinned. 'Shall I fetch a spade?'

He laughed out loud. 'No. No, no it's not something one can rush into. Neither of us would know what we are doing. One needs an expert, a proper archaeologist with a trowel and paintbrush.'

Her attention was fixed on her lawn. 'I can't see anything. You would expect there to be something there. A shadow, a line of dead grass. I've seen photos of crop marks where ancient sites have shown up after droughts, but we've had a lot of rain and I'm afraid I've been watering that flowerbed. I put some new shrubs in. Wait a minute.' She was back on her knees, poring over the maps. 'Look here.' She pointed at the tiny mark on

Meryn's version of the plan. 'Do you see what my uncle wrote here?'

He leaned forward beside her and their heads touched. Both drew back, embarrassed. 'Sorry.' Charles laughed. 'What am I looking for?'

'There.'

'It says wormhole.'

'And you know what that is?'

He frowned. 'Well, I've heard of them, of course. In science fiction. A place where time and space interlink. I never considered they might be real—' He never finished the sentence. He leaned forward again, running his finger slowly over the paper. 'It's where I saw the strange lights.'

'I saw them too. Or at least, I saw figures. Charles, we can't go there, at least not openly in daylight – and Meryn said not to go near it at all; he thinks it could be dangerous – but I could see it from up on the hill fort. Do you fancy a walk?'

'This is the most beautiful place. I'm so glad I came back,' Charles said cheerfully as they wandered down the street later. They had had lunch together at the mill after a leisurely stroll up the hill where they had seen nothing more unusual than a wary fox. Taking care to lower their voices when they spotted two village gossips at a neighbouring table, they had given Chris a summary of what had been happening.

Charles glanced across at her as they walked. 'Christopher can't quite bring himself to believe any of our theories, can he.'

'To be fair, do we believe it totally ourselves? It still seems far-fetched even to me.' They came to a halt outside Cadi's front door.

Charles glanced at his watch. 'I have to go, I'm afraid, Cadi. I had only planned a short visit to walk the meadow again and see if my findings were consistent.'

He was, she had discovered over lunch, a university lecturer; his partner had died five years before of breast cancer, he lived alone in a flat in Cardiff and although term had ended officially he still had people to see, tutorials to debrief, essays to mark and lectures to prepare for the next semester. 'But,' he went on happily, 'as soon as I've got things organised, I can be here to help in any way I can. If you want me to, that is.'

She nodded. 'You and Meryn should meet.'

'I'd like that very much.' He beamed at her. 'Dowsing has been my secret hobby. I wouldn't like my students to hear about it, but to meet someone else who does it, and such an expert—'

Ten minutes after he left, Sally was at the door. 'So, I hear your admirer has been back.' She smiled.

Cadi let her in. 'I suppose that was the village mafia. I saw Maggie Powell at the mill. She didn't waste any time spreading the news. And for your information, he is not my admirer, he just wanted to know about the meadow. He had hoped to do some more exploring and he found the gate padlocked.' She didn't mention the maps. She glanced across the lawn to where they had left all the papers and books stacked on the table under the apple tree and instead of heading over the grass, she led the way to the two chairs on the terrace outside the French doors.

'So, what brought him here in the first place?' Sally threw herself down. She looked exhausted.

'Actually I did wonder that the first time I met him. I never got round to asking. He lives in Cardiff.'

'Has he got friends round here? Arwel, perhaps?'

Cadi stared at her. 'No. No, surely not. We talked about Arwel. He would have said.'

'Not if he's a spy.'

Cadi gave an uneasy little laugh. 'That hadn't even occurred to me.'

'No. Overwhelmed by his good looks, were you?'

'Sal! What's the matter with you? He's not that good-looking. He's just a nice man who's interested in the fate of the meadow. There's probably stuff online about it and that's why he wanted to see it. He's a historian. He loves early history.'

'All the more likely that he knows Arwel.'

Cadi stood up. 'I'll get us a drink.' She sighed. 'You've worried me now. I did think of him as an ally, certainly. But surely,' she added as she walked into the house, turning back on the doorstep with a frown. 'Surely, if he's a friend of Arwel's, he'd have gone across to see him.'

'Not if he's a spy!' Sally laughed.

Cadi brought out a jug of Chris's home-made lemonade. She had added ice cubes that chinked cheerfully as she put the tray down on the little circular table. 'I remember now, when I first met Charles, he said he had heard about the possibility of there being a villa in the field. I don't think I ever asked him where he had heard about it.' She poured the lemonade, thoroughly unsettled.

'Ask him.'

'I don't know how to get in touch with him.'

Sally shook her head in mock despair. 'Look him up online. You said he's a historian? He must be there somewhere. What's his actual job?'

'He was there, contactable through the university. Reader in Ancient History.'

'That's no use,' Sally sniffed. 'Unless you can sweet-talk someone in the department. Of course, you could go straight to the horse's mouth and ask Arwel.'

'Absolutely not!'

'No, I don't blame you.' Sally leaned back in her chair and closed her eyes against the evening sunshine. 'Ah well, we'll have to live in suspense.' She sighed, and then asked suddenly, 'Do you still hear from Ifan?'

'No.' Cadi was appalled by the question. 'He was the biggest mistake of my life! Even Arwel has had the grace not to mention him in my presence. You know as well as anyone what a vicious shit the man turned out to be! Chris Chatto told me a couple of years ago that he's running some sort of high-powered business in London and he married a rich heiress. Well, good luck to her, I say.'

There was a long silence.

'Not long to go now till the end of term,' Sally put in at last, changing the subject. 'I can't tell you how I'm looking forward to the holidays. I might go away somewhere just so I don't miss Gemma so much.'

Cadi sighed. She could still hear in her head the sharp little bark of recognition Gemma had given in her vision of the meadow as it had looked in the fourth century. It had all been so real, so lifelike, and she and the dog had exchanged a look that had been so profound, it had to have been genuine. But she was not going to mention it again. It had been far too upsetting for Sally. They continued to sit in silence for a while, watching a blackbird pecking around in the flower border, and Cadi found herself wondering whether the bird could sense if there was something there under the soil. She knew in that moment there was no way she could wait for Meryn or Charles or anyone else to turn up before she started digging. As soon as Sally had gone she would find her garden fork and, very gently, begin to probe the edge of the lawn.

The fork went in easily. She took that as being a bad sign and withdrew it, moving a few steps to her right. That was in the absolute centre of where she estimated a wall should be. Still nothing there. Disappointed, she moved on. The light was going. Shadows stretched across the grass and between one moment and the next she realised she could see it, a slight line, sharp and distinct, throwing a shadow on the lawn. There was nothing specific to show why the line was there, no visible change in level or colour of the grass, just a slightly different quality of growth. She felt a sharp pang of excitement and reached for the fork again. Nothing.

'It's probably deeper than a fork can reach.' Meryn was indoors this time when she phoned him and she found she was almost sad at not hearing the usual symphony of mountain birds. 'I'd leave it, Cadi. You don't want to damage the site. And you don't want to let on you have inside information.' He chuckled. 'I could come over the day after tomorrow if you like. Go back to your writing, my dear. Did your Elen come back to the palace? It might be worth asking.'

Asking? Was it that easy? She put the fork away, gathered all her books and papers together and carried them back indoors before the dew-damp of the evening could reach them. There was not a trace now of where she had been poking about in the soil, nothing to betray her failed excavation.

17

This time Elen was given an official escort under the command of a senior centurion. Neither Julia nor Valeria accompanied her. She had seen neither woman again after Julia's revelations, and Julia had left the fort with her husband only a few days later. Valeria was nowhere to be seen and Macsen was out on manoeuvres each day. He reappeared briefly to bid Elen farewell in front of the whole garrison, raising her hand to his lips and bending briefly to kiss his little daughter's forehead, and then Elen was on her way, astride the black colt, the child and her nurse riding with Delyth in a wagon pulled by oxen, little Gemma sitting with them in state, Rhys on a sturdy mountain cob at her side, the other members of her own personal household all travelling with her. In her heart she wondered if she would ever return.

The countryside was in full autumn colour, rowan trees and hawthorns laden with berries, putting on a beautiful display for her as they rode south, following the road around the great mountain range, the land of eagles, travelling slowly, taking the road east towards Canovium and then following the river Conwy to Tomen-y-Mur and on southward through the mountains towards her home.

The high king had had word of their imminent arrival and was waiting for her outside the splendid new portico. 'So, you bring my granddaughter to meet me at last.' He held out his arms and took the child from her. 'See, she is smiling at her old grandfather.' He gave a delighted chuckle. 'She is a little beauty. As is her mother.' He glanced up at his daughter. She had matured since he had seen her last and was if anything more beautiful than before. But there was a hardness there, a bitterness in the line of her mouth, a sad weariness in her eyes. He handed the baby to the nurse who was hovering anxiously at her side. 'Your brother is here, my darling, ready to greet you when you're rested, and your new apartments await you.'

A further wing had been added to the south-east corner of the palace since she had left, a bedchamber which had been set aside for her with a beautiful mosaic floor depicting a cornucopia overflowing with fruit and flowers and sheaves of corn, two further rooms for her daughter and the child's nurses, and a reception room where Elen could take her ease.

'See, Gemma recognises the palace.' Delyth stooped to let the little dog off the leash as they walked into Elen's new chamber. They watched as the dog ran around in delight, her tail wagging.

'She's glad to be out of the wagon at last. As am I.' Elen had finally consented to travel with the other women, stiff after the long days in the saddle, allowing Rhys to lead her mount at the rear of the long train of armed men. She stretched her arms above her head. 'Perhaps I can take Emrys for a ride in the fields before the celebrations I am sure my father will have arranged. Poor horse. He is fed up with walking sedately at the pace of draught oxen. He needs a gallop. Oh, Delyth, I am so glad to be home.'

As it transpired, the ride had to wait for the next day after the expected feast, which lingered long after dark.

'So, you still have your favourite horse, I see.' Leaving the baby with Delyth, Elen was joined by her stepbrother, Conan. He eyed the stallion with its red leather bridle and saddle as they cantered together, followed at a discreet distance by a small detachment of their father's troops. 'And you still insist on riding like a man, I see.'

She laughed. 'I haven't changed, Conan, not one bit.'

'I expected your husband to have claimed him as his own by now.'

'No chance. Emrys is not a cavalry horse. He is wild like me!'

'So says my sister, who is now a Roman matron.'

'A matron! Me?' She leaned across and punched him on the arm.

'You are a mother, Elen!'

'And a good one.' Was she? She wasn't sure.

'And your husband is much acclaimed throughout the province.'

'As he was before I married him.' They had slowed the horses to a walk, the animals' breath steaming in the cold air. The track opened out onto the hillside and they drew up to look down towards the gleam of the distant waters of the estuary. 'I've missed this,' Elen said wistfully. Behind them the great hill fort rose on the next summit, its ramparts and palisade solid in the sunlight with narrow trails of woodsmoke rising from the conical thatched roofs of the township. 'The woods here are gentle and lush and the hills hold back the winds. The Hibernian sea is wild and there's nothing to separate us from the storms. Even my rose garden smells of salt and icy distances.'

'But you are not going to live at Segontium forever,' Conan said quietly.

'No.' She sighed. 'Macsen travels the whole land with his army. I can go with him if I choose, when it is safe to do so, but . . .' her voice trailed away.

After a quick glance towards her, her brother chose to ignore the wistful silence. 'Segontium is safe. I heard about Elen's hosts. They call you Elen Luyddog, Elen of the hosts, did you know? I gather you don't need the cohorts of Rome to protect you. You have armies of your own, ready at your command.'

She smiled. 'I have indeed.'

'And he doesn't mind?'

'Not as long as they obey me and pay lip service to the empire.'

'And you are happy, Sister?' This time he looked across at her, studying her profile with care.

Her hesitation would have been barely noticeable had he not been watching. 'I am content.'

'There were rumours at the meeting of the province leaders. Gossip.' He said cautiously. He had heard the stories when he was there with their father and seen Macsen with another woman.

She grimaced. 'I have been told my expectations were unreasonable. I am there as breeding stock.' She slapped the neck of her horse and he tossed his head impatiently.

'He told you that?' Conan's voice hardened.

'No, not him, and never in so many words. But I think my notions of the love one hears about in the ancient tales were unreasonable. I remember how my parents were together. I think they loved one another. I expected too much. But . . .' She took a deep breath and looked him sternly in the eye. 'He is kind and we get on well when we are together. He has left me my horse and my dog and my child – albeit she is a girl so he has little interest in her. And as you say, I have my followers, who are loyal and remind me of home. I had no expectations when my father told me I had to marry him, and he keeps the lady away from me now. When I return to Segontium, I will not expect to see her again.'

Conan nodded, seemingly satisfied. No one could expect more. It was the way of things.

It was her turn to ask questions. 'And are you happy, Brother?' Conan had married a princess from a neighbouring tribe, based in a hilltop fortress a day's ride from Viriconium.

He too had married for political expedience, as was to be expected, but now he nodded. He and his wife rubbed along without too much aggravation. She was expecting their first child. He was content and, as far as he knew, so was she.

On their return they handed over the horses to be turned out in the paddock in front of the palace and walked side by side through the portico.

Branwen was waiting for her in her sitting room. Elen stopped dead, staring at her in disbelief before running towards her, her arms outstretched. 'I have missed you so much.'

Branwen smiled. 'And I you, Elen, my child. But your father was right. It was time. You have your own destiny to fulfil and it is already underway.'

'You have seen my baby?'

Branwen nodded. 'A beautiful child. You can be proud of her. And there will be more.'

'Boys?' It was an automatic question. Did she really care so much that Macsen should have the sons he craved?

'Boys too.' Branwen turned away as a shadow crossed her face.

'What is it? What do you see?' Elen shivered. Had the thought that Branwen had the ability to see the future in the scrying bowl always terrified her? Or was it just the thought that the woman had knowledge of her sons as yet unborn?

'I see nothing you need fear, Elen. Your children will thrive. Your line, with your Roman husband, will be long.' Branwen smiled. She looked round. 'Order us some refreshment, then you can tell me about your life in the land of the Ordovices. I trained there once, at the college at Dinas Affaraon, with one of the greatest teachers in the land.' She fell silent and Elen saw a wistful sadness in her eyes. She waited for Branwen to continue but the woman said no more.

'You have heard how the local tribesmen came to our rescue; how they have brought their armies to follow Macsen,' Elen went on at last.

'I have heard.' Branwen settled herself into a chair, briskly pulling her heavy mantle around her shoulders. 'They will always follow you, cariad, not your husband, be assured of that.'

The door opened and a slave appeared carrying a tray with a jug of hot spiced wine and several dishes of snacks. Gemma ran in at the woman's feet and rushed across to Elen, her tail wagging.

Branwen drew back sharply. 'Where did that dog come from?'

Elen frowned. 'She's mine. She won't hurt you. She's adorable.'

She bent to pick up Gemma, hugging her closely. 'Look, someone has been brushing her coat while I was out riding.'

Branwen flinched again. 'That dog should go home. She does not belong here. You must send her back.'

'Back?' Elen echoed the word in confusion. 'She was a stray but no one ever claimed her. She loves me.'

'She is from another place, Elen.' Branwen stood up and moved towards her, her face stern. Gemma cowered back in Elen's arms, trembling. 'You must let her go. She doesn't belong with us.' She stretched out her hand as though to touch the little dog then withdrew it sharply. 'She's cold. Can't you feel it? Where did you find her?'

'It was Rhys, he found her in the paddock where the horses are.'

'Then take her back there. Now.' The woman's voice was hard and insistent. 'To keep her will cause misfortune for you and the dog. Come. We will go together.' Her tone softened. 'Elen, my Elen, you want the little thing to be happy? She has a home in another world, somewhere where she is terribly missed and will be cherished.'

'No!' Elen hugged Gemma more closely and kissed her on the top of her head. 'No. I love her. She's mine, I told you. I've looked after her.'

Branwen hesitated, then she shook her head. 'I'm sorry, cariad. You must be strong. If you keep her, she will die. She does not belong in our world. Let me come with you. We will take her outside and you can put her down on the grass. If she stays with you, then well and good, but if she runs away, you must let her go. It is her destiny to go to her true home as much as it is your destiny to stay in this world.'

'She will stay with me. I know she will.'

Branwen pushed away the tray of refreshments and beckoned. 'Let us go and see. Now.'

'Why now? Let's have a drink first.'

'Now, Elen. The tides of time are with us. I can sense it strongly. That is why I'm here.'

Elen stood up. 'She will stay with me,' she repeated desperately.

'Then we will bring her back in here and you can give her titbits.' Branwen turned towards the door.

Elen followed her out through the portico towards the paddock where the horses were grazing quietly in the sunshine. The place was very peaceful. Branwen unlatched the gate and strode out onto the grass. Elen followed, clutching Gemma in her arms.

'Over here.'

She followed Branwen towards the stream, aware of the horses. They had stopped grazing and both had raised their heads, watching intently. Branwen glanced up at the sky. 'It is time. Put her down here.'

Elen glanced round. 'She has run about here before. She knows this field.'

'Then she will come to no harm.'

Crouching down, Elen kissed the dog again then put her down on the grass. Gemma gave herself a shake then turned away and trotted purposefully towards the stream.

Ahead of her the air began to shimmer in the autumn heat.

18

Cadi had been writing obsessively all afternoon. When some-one knocked on the door she stood up, her pen still in her hand, her mind still in the past with Elen.

It was Dai Prosser with a small squirming dog under his arm.

'Oh my God!' Cadi exclaimed. 'Where did you find her?'

'I've knocked on Sally's door but she's out. This is her Gemma, isn't it?' The farmer stepped into Cadi's living room and put the dog down on the carpet. He pulled off his cap, twist-ing it anxiously between his hands. 'I found her in the field as I was collecting up the last of the bales. She seemed a bit disori-entated and scared, but I don't think she's hurt.'

Cadi knelt down and took Gemma in her arms. 'Where have you been?' She looked up. 'Oh Dai, thank you. I can't tell you how happy Sal will be.' The little dog's tail was wagging so hard it was almost invisible.

It was half an hour before Sally came over in response to Cadi's urgent text.

'Hi, Cadi, I've just got back from school. What is it?'

The sound of her voice had an electrifying effect on Gemma. With a yelp of excitement she leapt up into her mistress's arms, covering her face in licks, wriggling frantically to try to get ever closer under her chin.

'Where did you find her?' When Sally could speak at last there were tears pouring down her face.

'Dai Prosser found her in the meadow.'

Sally sat down on the floor, still cuddling the little dog. 'Someone must have taken her. She's been looked after. She's not starved. She's been brushed. She's got a new collar.' Sally frowned, stroking the soft leather. 'That's odd. This is her original tag. So if they kept it, why didn't they phone me?'

Cadi shook her head. 'Perhaps they meant to and then they fell in love with her. That wouldn't be hard to do.' She sat down opposite Sally. 'I can't tell you how pleased I was when Dai brought her over. He said he'd tried your house, obviously.'

Sally was still fingering the dog's collar. 'There is another tag here. Look.' She unhooked it and scrutinised it, then she passed it across.

Cadi held it in the palm of her hand, staring down at it, and a shiver ran through her. 'This is rough; it's handmade. Is it silver? And there's a weird symbol here. A hieroglyph of some sort, and it's cold.' Scrambling to her feet she dropped it onto the table.

'Gemma must have been outside all night.'

'No.' Cadi shook her head. 'No, it was a warm night. That is oddly cold.' She leaned across and fingered Gemma's original identity tag. 'This one isn't.' She shuddered. 'Don't put it back, Sal. There's something odd about it.'

'Throw it away. I don't want it. Whoever put it there had no right to. I'm taking her home.' Sally stood up, still carrying the little dog. 'Thank you, Cadi. Did you feed her?'

Cadi shook her head. 'I gave her a drink. She was very thirsty.'

In all the excitement she had forgotten Meryn was coming. When he appeared next morning, Cadi led him out into the garden with a tray of coffee and biscuits. Telling him the story of Gemma's reappearance, Cadi mentioned the mysterious tag.

'Show me.'

She went indoors to fetch it. She had slipped it into an

envelope and put it on the shelf above the fireplace. Taking it, he peered inside. She saw him frown. 'Interesting sygil.' He had not tried to remove it from the envelope she noticed, shaking it delicately so he could see both sides of the disc without touching it.

'Do you know what it means? When I held it, it was oddly cold.' Cadi shivered at the memory.

'You shouldn't have touched it.'

'We had to. To take it off her collar.'

Dropping the envelope down on the table, he sat back in his chair, thinking. 'It's some kind of spiral. It looks a bit Celtic to me. I would think it's a protective amulet. But the fact that it was cold – that is fascinating.' He glanced round the garden. The day was warming up fast. He watched the bees busy in a clump of catmint near their chairs, their hum soporific in the sunlight edging across the grass towards them, pushing away the shadows. He stared at the lawn in silence and she saw him frown.

'Can you see it?' she whispered. 'My corner of the palace.'

He grinned. 'Almost. Are you going to show me your friend's map?'

He opened it on his knee and looked at it carefully, reaching after a few minutes for his own plan, carefully folded amongst Cadi's notebooks. Side by side the two diagrams were extraordinarily similar. He looked up. 'He's good.'

'He is, isn't he.'

He squinted at the map, studying it more closely. 'No sign of our wormhole on here.'

'No. He said he didn't sense it. But to be fair, he wasn't looking for it.'

'Had he come across the concept before?'

'I think he had heard of it.' She grinned. 'And we think he might have actually glimpsed it.'

He nodded. 'Not everybody's cup of tea, that sort of thing. So,' he sighed, 'do I gather we can't go into the field anymore?'

'We could climb over the gate. What can they do? They could shout at us, but if there's no one there, no one will see.'

'Excellent.' Refolding the map, he levered himself out of the chair. 'Let's go.'

She had forgotten the barbed wire.

Someone had cut back the brambles that lined the alternative route so it was easier now than it had been the day before with Charles, to duck off the lane and thread their way up the steep scrubby path towards the hill fort. Emerging from the trees the sun hit them with its full force as they followed the track up towards the summit, the air full of the scent of baked earth and wild flowers. The shrill ceaseless song of skylarks emphasised the silence as they reached the top and turned to look down at the meadow lying far below them, quietly hazy in the heat. In the distance the water of the Bristol Channel was an intense blue. There wasn't a breath of wind.

'Look.' Meryn's whisper cut through her thoughts. She turned to see him pointing down at the meadow. 'A slight shiver of the light, barely visible. It's coming and going; it's not established. I suspect it's variable at the best of times, dependent on earth energies, perhaps, maybe the weather conditions to a certain extent or the moon. I think that is where your little dog has been.' He had moved a few paces away from her and was staring down at the meadow through half-closed eyes. 'Perhaps she was in our palace,' he said at last, 'as that is what we're all concentrating on.' He shook his head regretfully. 'I wish we could ask the dog. Wherever she went, they gave her a new collar, they carefully kept her dog tag, and they gave her a new one to keep her safe. You tell me she was looked after, fed and groomed. Somebody loved her. Perhaps someone is even now mourning her loss.'

'Elen. It was Elen,' Cadi said at last. 'I wrote it all down; I've made notes on what happened to Gemma in my story. Does that mean it's all true? It's actually happening in some other dimension.' She looked at him pleadingly. 'Is that even possible? I thought I'd made it up.'

'There are at least two possibilities here.' He was thoughtful. 'Perhaps you're writing about what actually happened, or is what you're writing creating the scenario in that other dimension? And where is that other dimension?'

'Elen lived here but she took Gemma to Segontium.'

'And Gemma stayed away until Elen brought her back and the dog found her way home through the tunnel.'

'But in their life months have passed, years even, and here it was only a few weeks.'

'Isn't that what so often happens in fairy stories?' Meryn said thoughtfully. 'Someone goes to sleep under a bush or in a cave or on the moors somewhere, and in a dream the enchanted life goes on in fairyland, so when they wake up and return to the present day sometimes days have passed, sometimes hundreds of years. Remember the story of Thomas the Rhymer? And presumably it can work in both directions.' He grinned happily. 'It's fascinating, isn't it! This has all been documented again and again and no one believes it. Of course they don't. It's impossible.' He moved across and sat down on a boulder which was lying on the dusty earth where a round house had once stood. 'But it's not impossible, is it. In our reductionist age we cannot bring ourselves to believe this sort of stuff, but in the old days when stories and legends and fables were part of the common discourse, people were far more observant. They saw strange things happen and, if they couldn't explain them, they had to turn them into stories. But they believed in magic. And maybe that's why our little dog had an amulet affixed to her collar to keep both her and them safe from the evil eye.' He shoved his hands into his pockets and shook his head sadly. 'You can't tell Sally any of this. Better she assumes someone picked Gemma up, shoved her in their car and then had a fit of conscience and returned her.'

'And in the meantime, is it up to me to write the story down?'

'What else?'

She shook her head slowly. 'Of course, your other theory could be the real one. Someone found her and took her home with them.'

'And that is what we will all believe. At least as far as others are concerned. It seems more likely anyway.' He was still beaming. 'Let's wait and see how the story pans out as you write it down.'

'I wrote about something else that would intrigue you.' She turned to him as they walked back. 'Have you heard of something called Caledfwlch?'

'The Welsh Excalibur?'

Of course he had heard of it. She grinned. 'The king of the Ordovices gave it to Elen. He told her it had been held in trust until one of her children or their descendants needed it to save the land. He told her the metal fell from the stars and the gems set in the hilt came from Eryri.'

'Oh wow.' He stopped and stared at her. 'Fantastic. And, believe it or not, one version of the legend I've read said that Magnus Maximus, of all people, brought the sword back to Britain. I can't remember off hand where he found it. I always thought that was probably rubbish; other countries trying to claim the sword's origin. But maybe there is a hint of truth there, if it surfaced during the time of Macsen. And falling from the stars makes more sense: tradition has the blade made from a meteorite.'

'And it was forged on Ynys Enlli.'

He nodded. 'That makes sense too. Bardsey Island. The Island of Twenty Thousand Saints. The burial place of Merlin. Perhaps the original Avalon. So, what did she do with the sword?'

'She gave it back to him to keep hidden. They talked about the destiny of the sword. How it would one day belong to a great king. King Arthur, presumably.'

'King Arthur who some think was descended if not from Elen herself, then from one of her stepchildren.'

'And therefore from Macsen.' She was silent for a moment, then she started walking again. 'Of course some people think King Arthur didn't exist, or that he was just some sort of war lord. I can't get my head round all this.'

'You don't have to, Cadi. Just wait and see what happens in the story.' He smiled. 'That's the wonderful part about all this. You are an amanuensis, a story spinner, dictated to by history itself as it happens.' He put his arm round her shoulders. 'Why don't we go and visit your lovely mill for lunch. I'm hungry.'

The café wasn't so full this time and to her relief Cadi didn't recognise anyone amongst the other customers. Chris came to join them briefly. 'Dai told me he found Sally's dog. I am so pleased. She's all right, is she?'

'She seems fine.' Cadi nodded.

'And no sign of the invasion of the house builders yet?'

'Not since they were all here with the ground radar stuff going on. Apart from the barbed wire of course. Someone must have done that when we weren't looking.'

Chris nodded. 'I'm looking for someone who does drone photography who could take pictures of the meadow for us. Apparently if we get a bit of drought later in the month and the topsoil dries out more, that's when the outlines of buildings show up much more clearly.'

'That's a good ally you've got there,' Meryn said as he and Cadi walked back through the village later. 'Useful.'

'We don't need drones.'

'No, but it's always nice to have things confirmed so that one can convince the greater public.'

'It must be awful having people constantly looking at you sideways and raising their eyebrows at everything you say.'

'I've got used to it.'

'And they never make you doubt yourself?'

'No.' He laughed. 'No, I suffer from utter conviction that what I see is there. I realise most people don't have that gift and I never thrust it in their faces if I can help it, but I do object when they persist in shouting me down, which I fear is about to happen. Do you see who is walking towards us?'

Arwel stopped several feet away. 'Still looking for a hidden city?' He didn't bother to try to hide his disdain.

Cadi tried for a disarming smile. 'Still looking.'

Meryn stayed silent.

'Are you on your way to the mill? We've just had a very nice lunch there,' Cadi went on. She started walking, trying to pass him but he moved to intercept her.

'I've heard the outline planning application is about to go through.'

'Really?' She failed to keep the shock out of her voice. 'Surely not. Not already.'

'The planning department feels there was no reason for delay. It is a popular plan with local support.'

'But what about the survey? The chap picked up the outline of a building. We were there. We saw it.'

'An old barn.' Arwel couldn't keep the glee out of his voice. 'Dai Prosser told me he remembers it. Sorry to disappoint.' He stood aside at last and with a mock bow in Meryn's direction headed on up the road.

Cadi was speechless. Neither of them moved, until Meryn shook his head and said briskly, 'Come on. Let's go home.'

'Surely it can't be true?' She followed him in through her gate, fumbling in her pocket for her key.

'No, I don't think it is. For one thing it has happened too quickly. I don't think councils move at that speed, even if, as he implied, pressure is being brought to bear. I'm sure your friend Chris will be on the phone immediately. I take it Arwel is on his way up to the mill to tell him the glad tidings. There are always rumours flying round in these sorts of situations, Cadi. Don't worry about it.'

'Can't you ask your pendulum? Won't it know if he's speaking the truth?' They walked into the cool shade of the living room.

'It might, but again my own feelings might influence it. It might start spinning round my head in ever decreasing circles which usually means "Unacceptable fury. Recalibrate."' He laughed out loud. 'Sorry, I know that will go a long way to destroying my credibility.'

She shook her head. 'No, it sounds honest.' She dropped onto the sofa. 'So what can we do?'

'We could go outside and dowse in your garden over your own piece of the palace and maybe, carefully, lift some of your grass, and maybe, carefully take a trowel and gently begin to scrape back the soil, but only' – he raised his hand as she leapt to her feet – 'if my pendulum responds to my enquiry as to how deep below ground level the site may be found. That is a question one can usually answer with the pendulum. If it is too far down, we will have to leave it, at least for now. Agreed?'

* * *

What they found was a fragment of stone wall.

'Right.' Meryn was stern. 'At this point we backfill loosely and replace the turf so there is nothing to see. We don't want anyone else interfering, either for or against the dig, and we don't want to do any damage. I can see enough to give me a theory about what happened to the palace or villa or whatever it was. Look, the sunlight is lighting the stones so we can see them clearly.'

'Black? Fire?'

He nodded. 'It's a possibility. I'll ask my trusty friend.' He had slipped the pendulum into the pocket of his shirt.

She sat under the apple tree with a glass of lemonade while he knelt above their hole, the weight on the end of its chain dangling from his fingers. She had given him a note-pad and every so often he scribbled something down. It was ten minutes before with a groan he levered himself to his feet and, brushing the loose earth from his knees, wandered towards her.

'Right. I have answers. I must emphasise, Cadi, that this is not an exact science. It relies on asking the right questions, and I may have rather anticipated what I suspect happened.'

She poured him a glass of juice and sat back in her chair. 'Go on. Tell me.'

'The villa was burned down and, for whatever reason, it was not worth rebuilding. Perhaps in the time-honoured way, the locals, whoever they were, looted the stones to build their own cottages and houses, probably yours included, so in the fullness of time there was nothing left to see, the grass grew over the site and for the next thousand years or so the ground level gradu-ally rose enough to hide what was left. Perhaps there was just enough of an outline left, a few stones, or even the foundations, for some enterprising ancestor of your husband's to build a barn there. But that too has gone.'

There was a long silence.

'So, there's nothing left to stop them getting planning per-mission,' she said at last.

'Except the mosaics.'

'What mosaics?'

Meryn grinned. 'I just happened to ask and it said yes. Two particularly beautiful ones.'

'Here? In my garden?'

'Alas not. Out there in the field.' He took a sip from his glass. 'I fear none of this would be enough to stop the developers, but it would delay them. And they will be found if they dig trenches before they give planning permission, which they will if they adhere to the rules. They would have to excavate and document the site and even if they moved the mosaics somewhere else, at least they would have been saved. I don't believe a word Arwel said. If he had heard anything it was gossip.'

'You know, I think someone mentioned mosaics when I was in the post office a few weeks ago. That and bones.'

'Bones would be good as well! Even better.'

'And what about the wormhole?'

Meryn grinned. 'If they build over it, it will provide some very interesting experiences for whoever buys that particular house.'

19

'Gemma!' Elen's cry echoed across the field. Her grazing horse threw up his head and after a moment cantered towards her, thrusting his nose into her hands. 'Where has she gone? She's disappeared. You knew that would happen!' She was distraught.

'Don't be upset, my dear.' Branwen put her arm round Elen's shoulders. 'She has gone home. She was not yours to keep. She would not have flourished here, and she has someone waiting for her on the other side, someone who has missed her grievously.'

Elen pushed her horse aside and ran a few steps over the grass. 'But where is she? On the other side of what? The stream? I can't see her!'

Branwen shook her head. 'Gemma lives in another world, my Elen. A world you can never visit.'

'You mean she's dead!'

'No, no, not dead, but gone from us to Annwn, to the land of faery, to—'

Elen spun round. 'You told me my mother had gone to Annwn.'

'No, child, I told you that to comfort you when you were

small. Your mother is in the Christian heaven. Annwn is nearer to this land than that.'

'Can you see it? This place. How do you know where she is?' Her voice was sharp; accusing.

'I know, cariad, because I have learned to read the land, the voice of the wind, the cry of the mountain birds, they all speak of other worlds and other times.'

'But if she belongs somewhere else, how did Gemma get here?'

Branwen glanced towards the spot where Gemma had vanished. The slight haze over the grass had gone, leaving sunlight and shadows. The stallion was staring after the little dog, his eyes huge, his ears laid back, ready to flee. 'Your horse senses it. Horses always know where there are special places, places of transition, where the gods play their games of chance with us humans and with one another. Sometimes there are keepers at the gates, sometimes we see otherworldly beings at a ford, and on the banks of lakes and the great oceans and sometimes, as in this case, there is an unguarded entrance to other worlds where people and animals can cross if they know the way, or sometimes they are lost and enter the kingdoms unaware. Sometimes they never find their way home.'

Elen shivered. But now she was intrigued. 'I want to read the land and hear the voice in the wind. Will you teach me?'

'I'll teach you, cariad, if you have the will to learn, but first you have other destinies to follow. The child you carry in your belly will be the mother of a race of kings. Kings of a nation that doesn't yet exist.'

Branwen patted the horse who had moved closer to them, rubbing his forehead, soothing his fears. 'The destinies of all your children will be special. But, for now, you are the wife of a man who has ambition and strength and a destiny of his own,' she went on, her voice low. She hesitated. 'But one day, my Elen, you will be free to live your own dream. Then I will come to find you.' She gave Elen's shoulder a squeeze.

'And you say I am carrying a child?' It was as if Elen had only heard that last sentence.

'Did you not realise?' Branwen smiled. 'When you return to Segontium you will be accompanied by two children.'

As predicted by Branwen, Elen's second daughter, Sevira, was born barely eleven months after her sister. Elen was still in the south, at Venta Silurum with her father. Only after she had recovered from the birth and the Christmas celebrations had come and gone once more, and at last the roads had opened after the winter snows, did Elen return to Segontium with her two infant daughters. Under Branwen's guidance she had gained at least a little patience and fortitude, learned to read the land and to hear the voice of the wind, to speak to plants and listen to the birds and the trees. There was one thing she did not want to learn and that was to read the water in the scrying bowl, and Branwen did not offer to teach her. By the time she returned north, without Branwen, she had learned that she must be content to remain, at least for now, at Segontium. She had married a soldier; she had known that involved him travelling to different parts of Britannia with the army as pockets of unrest appeared more and more frequently, the result of incursions from tribes from Hibernia and Caledonia, from northern Gaul and Germania. The hardest lesson of all had been to accept that she must live with only a part of the heart of the man she had thought would love her, and that to keep herself and her family safe she must be content to remain at home.

She and Macsen lived together amicably enough, at least outwardly, when he was back at the base at her side, but their relationship had changed. The easy banter had become strained, the reliance she had placed in him had gone, as had any feeling of awe. She was her own mistress now, as Branwen had taught her. And she was the wife of the commander of the fort, who was head of the armies and Comes Britanniarum in official charge of the entire province with, supposedly, the direct ear of the emperor – the emperor who still did not respond to requests for more support. But she was also a princess of her native land, her royal blood descended from the gods of ancient times. Carefully managing the situation, she had at her command untold numbers of native troops, the hosts of Britannia. She was Elen Luyddog.

Scarce more than a year after she re-joined Macsen at Segontium the longed-for son appeared and was named Flavius Victor, like his elder half-brother, and after him came in short order three more boys: Antonius Donatus, Eugenius and Publicius, or so they were named by their father. To her they would always be Anwn, Owain and little Peblig.

Cadi frowned. She knew all this from her research notes. Or did she? She glanced through them again, a muddle of different names and sources, from Wikipedia to the annals of the past. No one seemed to agree on dates, if indeed there were any dates at all, or about how many children Elen and Macsen had had, or when. Or even if Elen had been his first wife or his second. Had he really had two sons called Victor? But yes, apparently that was a Roman thing. One, possibly both, would have been known as something else, a nickname, perhaps. How would she ever know what was the truth about what had happened? On one date however all the sources agreed. In the year of Our Lord 383 there was another meeting of the leaders of the Roman armies of Britannia. It was the occasion when, frustrated and driven beyond endurance by the lack of support or money from Rome and in the face of increasing attacks from barbarians on every side, the troops of the legions of the Province of Britannia elected their leader, Magnus Maximus, to be emperor of the West.

The historians were unable to agree on the character of Magnus Maximus at this point. He was undoubtedly wildly popular with his men and a fine general who had consistently held high office in the army. He was a good and fair administrator. But now some doubt crept in. Was he overly ambitious? Greedy? Reckless? Elen would probably have agreed with all those descriptions.

Within weeks of his election the Roman legions of the British province had assembled behind Magnus's standard and embarked for Gaul to confront Gratian, the recognised legitimate holder of the title Macsen had assumed. Finally, Gratian took notice, furious and ready at last to fight for his title and his supremacy. He had been fighting yet another incursion of the Alamanni peoples into the Roman territories, but now he had no alternative but to confront the man who had so openly challenged him.

Macsen took Elen and their children with him, leaving the grown-up sons of his first marriage, Victor and Constantine, behind to supervise the province with Elen's father and stepbrother. And, if the stories were to be believed, he also invited Cunedda, the king of Strathclyde, married to the daughter of Coel Hen, old king Cole, ruler of Eboracum, to come south with a special mandate to oversee the lands of the Ordovices; Cunedda, who was later claimed as ancestor of the kings of Gwynedd.

Cadi shook her head in confusion. So much of this was legend and spurious history. What was she witnessing? Was it real, or was it some fabrication of her own imagination? Whatever it was she was desperate to find out what happened next. Was she going to follow Elen abroad? See ancient Gaul for herself? She threw down her notebook with its confusion of scribbles and arrows and sticky notes. Only one thing they all agreed on, historians then and now: Magnus took with him the best part of the remaining legions of the Roman army, leaving Britannia open to the invasions she had been fighting for so long – the Hibernian tribes, the Picti from Caledonia, the Angles, the Saxons and after them the Vikings. And his wife and family went with him.

Branwen begged her not to go. Arriving unannounced at Segontium on the eve of their long march south and embarkation for Gaul, she seized Elen's arm. 'This is madness. He can leave you in charge, you would be as competent if not more so than his sons or your brother. No, Elen, you must not set foot in Gaul!'

'Why not? I go as my husband's wife, as empress of the West,' Elen couldn't resist placing emphasis on the title, as yet so new and foreign a term. 'Come with me. Please. I choose my own attendants. Then you can watch over me.'

Branwen shuddered. 'I am not leaving these shores. Nothing but tragedy and death can come from this madness.'

Elen shook her head. 'No. You are wrong. Macsen is strong. He is unbeatable. He has every man, woman and child in Britannia behind him.'

'And of the whole Roman Empire as well?' Branwen was scornful. 'Are you sure?'

Elen scanned the other woman's face. 'What do you know? Have you seen the future?' That was the art she had never mastered and for that she was eternally grateful.

Branwen turned away tight-lipped. 'I see no future for Macsen Wledig at all.'

Elen shivered. 'You lie.'

'If you say so. If your powers of foresight are greater than mine, I bow to your knowledge. You have no more need of me.' Branwen turned and, pulling her hood down over her face, she walked towards the door.

'Wait!' Elen ran after her. 'You can't just say that and go. I haven't dismissed you.' She was learning the language of authority.

Branwen's lip curled. 'You have dismissed me. You ignore my advice. I have no further role to play in your life. Be it on your own head and on the heads of your children.'

Elen was aware of the servants in the room watching the scene, one or two moving forward, hesitating, waiting for her to order them to prevent the woman's departure. She said nothing. Branwen walked steadily towards the double doors that led out into the atrium, and disappeared between the row of columns. Elen walked over to her chair and threw herself down, fighting back tears. 'Bring the children to me,' she commanded, steadying her voice with care. The two nurses scurried forward with their charges, the two youngest babies; the elder children she assumed were outside playing in the gardens. Scooping the little boys into her arms, Elen looked down at their faces, dark-eyed, both with mops of unruly curls, both watching their mother with curious concentration. Owain was eighteen months old now and little Peblig barely six months. Hugging them tightly, she had sent out a silent prayer to Mary, the mother of Jesus, to protect them all.

Branwen did not accompany them to the port at Rutupiae, nor to Gaul. As they travelled east through the forests and fields of Gaul, meeting little or no opposition, Elen, safe in the vanguard of the long lines of troops, began to relax. She had not seen Branwen again after their exchange and slowly the woman's warnings were forgotten.

20

Meryn stayed the night in the end. 'I am curious to see how you write about all this,' he said as they walked back into the house. 'Automatic writing is a wonderful gift, and to channel it in the way you seem to be doing is quite remarkable. Maybe there's more of the old family magic in you than you will allow.' He grinned. 'Don't try and force anything, just go on doing whatever it is that you're doing and we'll read it together in the morning.'

Cadi handed him her file of notes before lunch, retreating outside to pick tomatoes and lettuce from her vegetable patch, concentrating on making a salad, blending oil and balsamic vinegar, grinding pepper, trying not to keep glancing across at him as he sat on the sofa near the open veranda doors, the pages of her typescripts spread out on his knee. Some of it was still a scribble of long hand, the rest neatly ordered and transcribed so that she could read it herself before the weird hieroglyphics became indecipherable. Every now and then he reached for his glass and took a sip of wine, then he went back to reading.

She opened the fridge to find home-cured ham and cheeses from the deli in the village and laid the food on a flowered pottery plate, then at last she brought her own glass over and sat down to face him. 'What do you think?'

'Fascinating.'

'Does it read like a romantic novel?'

He smiled. 'A bit. Maybe.'

She scowled.

'But it also reads like a wild tempestuous race through history, with here and there remarks which could only come from someone who has seen it all, been there, done that.'

'What do you think of Branwen. She isn't a historical figure. Did I make her up?'

There was a drawn-out silence as he took another thoughtful sip from his glass. 'No,' he said at last. 'I don't think you did. I think she's a major driver of this narrative.' He shuffled all the pages back together and slid them onto the table, then leaned back on the cushions and crossed one leg over the other. 'What makes you describe her as a Druid?'

'I'm not sure. I suppose she said she was.'

'She's interesting. I have come across one or two of these strong female characters in the past. I tried to work with one once a long time ago. She was dangerous.'

'Dangerous?' Cadi looked up.

'Oh yes, very dangerous. She had been trained at one of their colleges and her uncle was the archdruid in the time of St Columba. She had learned, amongst other things, to shape shift and to time travel.' He frowned. 'I suppose she was what you would nowadays call a stalker. She was fixated on a charming Scots doctor and his family. She was possessed with some astonishing powers and was viciously jealous of anyone close to him.'

'What happened?' Cadi's eyes had widened.

'I let them all down badly. I was a lot younger then, and inexperienced and a bit gung-ho. I let them think I was much wiser and older than I actually was.' He smiled ruefully.

'Let them think?' Cadi looked at him sceptically.

'OK, yes. A bit of sleight of hand. I thought myself into a wiser and more mature persona. If I had been more experienced, I might never have done what I did. I had the knowledge but I was completely outclassed. If I had had the knowledge I have now, perhaps, but' – he shrugged his shoulders – 'I taught the family what I knew. How to protect themselves. I gave them amulets charged with magic I thought could defeat her. I thought I knew what I was doing. No chance.'

'Oh, Meryn, how awful.'

He gave a grim smile. 'I'll tell you the whole story one day. But for now, let's concentrate on our own situation. I'm genuinely older and wiser, I have mountains of learning and donkey's years of experience, I have been taught by far more powerful adepts than her and her family.' He stretched over and tapped the pile of papers. 'You said it was Branwen who told Elen to send Gemma back to us.'

Cadi shook her head slowly. 'In my story, yes. But I assumed I had made up that bit. I doubt Gemma is a time traveller.'

'Why?'

She frowned. 'Oh, come on. I needed to put her in the story, and I needed to make up a reason for her disappearance, but surely it's far more likely that someone picked her up and put her in their car and then had a crisis of conscience. You don't really think she ran away down our famous wormhole and spent the last few weeks in a Roman villa in the fourth century?'

'I thought you were on board with all this, Cadi.' Meryn was frowning.

'I was. I am. But— How do we know Branwen isn't frightening and evil like your horrible Druidess?'

'Because I'm pretty sure that Branwen is one of the good guys.' He smiled cheerfully.

Cadi stood up and walked over towards the kitchen worktop, smacked it with the flat of her hand, a sign of her sheer frustration, with herself and with him, and went to open the fridge. She withdrew the bottle of wine and brought it back to him, topping up his glass with such vigour it slopped over his hand. He licked his fist without comment.

'I want to believe it. I want to so much.'

'Really? It's a terrifying concept if one considers it for any length of time. And you have to be sure. Belief, Cadi, is not always something you can will for yourself. If deep down in your heart you can't believe something, it's better not to try. It can't be forced. Walk away.'

'Have you always believed in this stuff?'

'Oh yes. I have certainty because I've seen things, heard them, been there, if you like. But maybe, even for me, that was not quite enough. You could say my academic life is my attempt to rationalise a belief in the things I had experienced since I was a child, to bring in real scientific proof, and that is where one could and does come unstuck. They are not the same thing. Belief is one step up from faith. I think you will find the definition of faith has an element of blindness in it, whereas belief comes from certainty where there is still no absolute proof, but nevertheless one's inner knowledge is strong enough to make it unshakeable. This is the marshy ground where your friend Arwel and I cannot and never will, agree. I aim to prove something I have already accepted with my heart and soul, but a scientist heads out into the wild blue yonder with no preconceived ideas and hopes to find incontrovertible truth.'

'But Arwel does have preconceived ideas. He thinks it's all baloney!' She took a gulp from her glass.

Meryn sighed. 'You have seen people dowsing. You know it works. Why it works doesn't matter. Not now. Not for us. We know this meadow of yours has a certain amount of history and legend attached to it, which was enough to go on at the start. We want to find enough proof to make it eligible for some kind of archaeological exploration and we have become involved in an aspect of its past. We are curious. We want to know what happened. You want to follow your dream of discovering Elen's story via poetic inspiration. You will never claim it to be authentic history. Your readers will love it; your poetry, with Rachel's lovely paintings, will transport them into that past, just as the original Mabinogion did for countless generations of enthralled listeners by the hearths of their houses on long winter nights. Leave the scepticism to Arwel. Leave the technical battle-planning to your friend Chris the miller. Don't get involved. If the land is destined to be built on, then there is nothing you can do. If you don't like the resulting noise next door, you can grow your hedge higher or even sell your house.'

'No!'

He folded his arms. 'So, you can't be Zen about all this?'

She laughed. 'Isn't that rather a mixed metaphor for you?'

'A mixed spirituality, perhaps.' He watched as she stood up again and went to lay the table.

After a minute he followed her and sat down as she fetched the rest of the food from the fridge. 'I can't bear the thought of my meadow not being there anymore, Meryn. It means too much to me. I know I'm beyond lucky to have a place like that next door where I can walk at any time of day or night – or at least I could. But it has become part of me. It inspires my work. It has wormed its way deep into my soul. It's what makes me the person, the poet if you like, that I am.' She was fighting back tears. She changed the subject abruptly. 'So why don't you tell me more about the dangerous Druidess you met.' She pushed a bowl of coleslaw towards him. 'How did you even get involved if you were so inexperienced?'

He had been studying her face with an expression of overwhelming sympathy. Now he looked away. 'I didn't intend to set out as adviser on these matters. I lived alone in a cottage in the mountains, much like the one I live in now. I was studying. Meditating. I suppose people came to realise I could help them when it came to dealing with ghosts. Stuff like that. I got to know this lovely local family and they asked my advice. But, well. It's not always that easy. I wish it were.' He sat back in his chair. 'That case certainly wasn't. But enough about her. Nowadays most people seem to think I'm a herbalist and a healer. I am more often than not asked for sleeping draughts from my garden, thank goodness, although there was an interesting case, just before I went back to California, right on my doorstep.' He stopped. 'No, enough of all that! You and I have a problem here which needs to be addressed and it's an interesting one for me, as my dowsing skills are seldom called on and apart from your midnight marchers there doesn't seem to be a ghostly element at all.'

'Just time travel and a wandering dog.'

'I would like to meet the dog.' Meryn helped himself to potato salad. 'From the way you describe it, Branwen could sense that Gemma came from a different world. I would like to see if I can sense that the animal has been elsewhere.'

'If we go and see them tomorrow, for goodness' sake don't talk about this in front of Sally,' Cadi put in sharply. 'As far as she is concerned Gemma was kidnapped in this world and the furthest she has been was about twenty miles!'

Cadi woke with a jolt, staring at the ceiling in the dark. The house was completely silent. Sliding out of bed she went over to the window and, pushing it open, she leaned out. The road was empty, a slight breeze stirring the trees in the hedge opposite; moon shadows danced across the tarmac. She opened her door and listened. There was a light showing under Meryn's door. She crept back into her room and carefully closed her own door before tiptoeing over to the chest in the far corner of the room and reaching for her notepad and pencils. Climbing back into bed she propped herself up on her pillows and began to write.

The town of Caesarodunum was bustling as the legions began to march in. There had been no opposition for some time now to the arrival in Gaul of Macsen and his armies. As they marched into the province of Lugdunensis they had, on the whole, been welcomed, or at worst ignored by the local population. The fortress opened its gates to them and the resident officials ushered them in. The market was functioning as normal. The people went on busily about their lives.

The housekeeper in charge of the officers' residence, flustered and far from ready for so illustrious a visitor, had no idea how to greet an empress. Elen graciously forgave her. She had still formed no idea herself of what her rank and position in the world merited. Her husband had taken the title of emperor of the West. There was another emperor of the West – Gratian himself, brother-in-law of the Emperor Theodosius, based in Constantinopolis– but so far neither man had appeared. There were no armies massed on the horizon to challenge them.

Elen, exhausted from the miles of dusty roads, everywhere greeting would-be clients of the new regime, found her way to the women's chambers with her entourage of maids and nurses and the six children. She reassured the housekeeper, gave orders to her steward, Carwyn, and left everything to him. Within minutes the room where she had settled on a shabby couch was silent. The older children had rushed off to explore. The grizzling babies had been borne away by their nanny, leaving her blessedly alone. She had no idea where her husband was, nor his senior officers. Nor did she know where the officers' wives and families were quartered. Somewhere amongst them presumably were Julia Cassia and Valeria Valentina. So far they had always kept scrupulously out of her way. With a sigh she closed her eyes. In too short a time Delyth would appear, servants would bring warm water and towels and refreshments, and the next round of imperial duties would begin.

For Elen this particular stop on their journey to confront Gratian was special for one reason only. This town was the seat of Bishop Martin, one of the greatest and most famous of the Christian teachers, healers and miracle workers in the western world. Macsen had showed no interest. She had never questioned him about his worship of Mithras. She had merely demanded an oratory of her own at Segontium and he had eventually allowed her to have it constructed within the walls of the fort. She had her own chaplain there and all her children save two had now been baptised. Owain and little Peblig, the youngest of her boys, were not yet Christened and she had set her heart on asking Bishop Martin to perform the rite.

Macsen refused to accompany her on her visit to the bishop. When she approached her husband about it, he was as always surrounded by his officers and advisers, the men in intense discussion. They looked worried. Rising to his feet, he drew her aside. 'Finally Gratian heads towards us with a large army,' he said quietly. 'It appears our run of good luck has expired and he has at last grown the balls to confront me. We will have to fight him soon.'

She met his gaze with a frown. 'Surely you knew this must happen.'

He nodded. 'We have come so far into Gaul with no opposition, I suppose I had hoped to avoid it.'

'You thought Gratian would give in without a fight?'

'So my advisers assured me.' Macsen glanced over his shoulder at the table. The tribune Claudius Valentius was there with Andragathius, the master of Macsen's horse, Macsen's brother, Marcellinus and Titus Octavius, his second in command from Segontium. 'Gratian is unpopular. He relies on auxiliary German troops to enforce his rule. His policies are bad. That is why we have come so far unopposed. The people of Gaul want me as their emperor.'

Elen saw first one then another of the men glance across at her. She gave them a gracious smile. 'Then I will leave you to plan your next step and, in the meantime, I will go and talk with the man of God. If he is with us, then we cannot fail.'

The Bishop of Caesarodunum was not at home. The bishop's residence, a complex of administrative buildings near the church, in an angle of the amphitheatre wall, was bustling with clergy and administrators, but the bishop himself, it appeared, had withdrawn to find peace at his retreat across the river. His chaplain, who had introduced himself as Brother James, drew Elen into a side office. The man was clearly flustered. 'My lady empress, the bishop had no idea you were coming or he would have made sure to be here to give you an audience. That is, he would have been here to appear in audience before you.' The man blushed crimson and stumbled over his words. 'He would have been horrified to know that he had ignored the wife of so great a man as the general. As the emperor.'

Elen smiled. 'Please, brother, do not be alarmed. I am here as a supplicant like everyone else. Is it possible for me to go to his place of retreat?'

The young man hesitated, clearly unsure how to respond. 'He has given orders that no one follow him. He goes there to be alone, to pray. Unless it's an emergency—'

'It is an emergency. My youngest sons need to be baptised, and my husband is a follower of Mithras.'

There was an appalled silence. The young man opened and shut his mouth like a fish out of water. 'The bishop preaches against all pagans, madam. He would want your husband and your children to be brought to God.' He crossed himself.

'So, can you take me to his place of retreat?'

Elen's escort and the episcopal officers fell away from the two of them as they crossed the bridge over the river and turned alongside the cliff base, Elen riding a borrowed palfrey, the young priest on a mule. The men of the escort had obviously been told not to approach the lonely improvised monastery with its string of caves, each one the cell of a monk, one of which belonged to Martin himself. Nearby, on the bank of the river Elen could see a chapel and another building which Brother James told her was the refectory for the group of hermits who followed Martin into solitude. The only difference was that he frequently had to leave the silence and beauty of his retreat for the busy life he was expected to lead as the leader of his episcopacy in the town, or his missionary travels further afield, leaving them to commune with God without him.

She expected him to be angry at her interruption of his quiet life, but he waved her to the only seat in his cave, a three-legged stool, and sat down cross-legged on the floor himself. He was a tall bony man in his mid-sixties, with a thin face, tanned by the sun and wind of his many journeys across the countryside, dressed in a simple brown robe with a wooden cross hanging from his girdle.

Neither of them realised that this would be the first of many such meetings, or that Macsen himself would accompany her on the third, that her husband would come again several times on his own and that when at last a date was set for the baptism of Owain and little Peblig, Macsen, won over by the man's simple sincerity and passion, and perhaps by a more cynical sense of expedience, would also present himself to be admitted to the Christian faith.

It was early August when Macsen gave orders for his men to set off at last to meet Gratian head on. The legions followed the well-marked road and marched north-east into the province of the Parisii as Gratian moved west with his own troops, who were largely foreign auxiliaries. They met at last near Lutetia where, after skirmishing for several days, Macsen's army won a decisive victory, with much of Gratian's army defecting to his standard. Gratian fled the field, pursued by Andragathius, and was finally cornered and killed at Lugdunum on 25 August.

It was the end of the battle at least for the time being. Victory was declared. Macsen with his empress by his side set up his base at the great Roman city and capital of the Western Empire, Augusta Treverorum.

Gratian's heir was his brother Valentinian, a twelve-year-old boy.

21

At breakfast next day Cadi glanced through the scribbled pages
with an exclamation of disgust. 'It's happened again. I've read
most of this in my history books. I'm repeating what I already
know of Macsen's career.' She had made scrambled eggs for
them both, the eggs from Dai Prosser's farm, mixed with parsley
and dill from her own garden. Meryn was in charge of making
the toast – bread he had fetched still warm from the mill. After
he put a slice on each plate he reached over and pulled her
notepad towards him. 'This is always a risk,' he said. 'You're
running your research in tandem with the automatic writing.
Resist reading any more background stuff, Cadi. Trust your
pen. And, next time, I want you to do something for me. When
you're in the writing mood, I want you to focus on Branwen.
According to you, she didn't go with them. She belonged round
here, her people came from that great hill fort that looms over
there above our meadow. She is a local and it's her story we
want. We want to know what happened here when the armies
of Rome rallied round Macsen's standard and left the country unguarded. Even I remember enough of the history of this
country to know Macsen was partly blamed by historians for

leaving Britain open to the attack of barbarian hordes. It was the dawn in Britain of what became known as the Dark Ages.'

'But the Roman armies left in AD 410. I remember that date from school.' Cadi put the coffee pot on the table and sat down opposite him. 'They needed all the legions back in Rome to save the city from the invading Hun. Macsen took his army away in the year 383.'

'So we want to know what happened in the intervening years and Branwen will tell us.'

'But we know what happened to Macsen—'

'No!' Meryn held up his hand. 'I don't want to know what Wikipedia says. Nor history from books. Forget what you have read. The people on that hill fort didn't know what was going to happen. All they knew was that the legions had marched away, and yes, presumably you're right, Elen went with them and her children with her. And presumably it's a historical fact that, as you say here, they met up with Bishop Martin of Tours who would not have been canonised in his lifetime but later became known as St Martin. And presumably you're right, Macsen gave up worship of the soldiers' god, Mithras, to follow Jesus Christ though that sounds a bit odd to me, to be honest, if he was a true initiate, but he might have just been a realistic soldier who went with the perceived flow, which was towards Christianity by that time in history. We can check that with your books later if we need to, which we will if you ever decide to publish all this stuff and you need to appease Arwel. But who was left behind? Who lived in the palace at Camp Meadow? Did the invading Irish pirates come back and burn it to the ground? Did the Saxons appear at that date? Were they held at bay, or was this the beginning of the age that turned Albion dark?'

'And you think Branwen will know all this?'

'She seems to be an intelligent woman, educated, strong.'

'You really are very interested in Druids.'

'I met one, don't forget,' he said grimly. 'And I'm often described as one myself.' He pushed away the notebook and reached for the coffee pot. 'In history – that is, the recorded opinion of Romans and Greeks – Druids were educated, philosophers, politicians, leaders in their communities and as such posed so much of a threat to the Romans that they, amongst all the various religions and beliefs tolerated through the empire, had to be eradicated. But even after the massacre of their head-quarters on Anglesey they carried on being the learned people of their world. They ran what we would think of as universi-ties, and their students studied for years, decades even, women as well as men. After the coming of Christianity they probably survived as wise men and women, teachers, judges, poets, with an enormous store of oral history and wisdom, and they were believed to be alchemists, so, yes, they do fascinate me, perhaps because they know – knew – about all the things that I want to know. And, in this context, I suspect your Branwen can sense, or see, or understand the reality of the wormhole down which little Gemma scampered with such carefree abandon.'

'I scarcely paid any attention to Branwen. My interest is in Elen.'

'And it can go back to Elen. Just to appease my curiosity, please, concentrate on Branwen, if only for one session.'

'You make it sound so easy.' Cadi reached for their empty plates and took them over to the sink. 'Shall I make some more toast?'

He nodded. 'Have you seen your neighbour since Gemma came home?'

'Sally? Not much. She's busy with preparations for the end of term.'

'After breakfast, assuming she's at home as it's a Saturday, can we pay a quick call? I would like to check Gemma over.'

Sally welcomed them in, but there was no excited bark. 'Gemma's asleep. She's been very tired since she came back to me. I took her to the vet for a check-up and Hannah said she thought she's been well looked after, except that she had fleas.'

'Fascinating.' Meryn followed Sally's pointing finger and walked across to the dog, curled up in her basket. He sniffed. 'You've bathed her.'

'Too right. I'm not having fleas in my house!'

Gemma woke up as they approached her and, climbing out of her basket gave Cadi's hand a desultory lick, her tail wagging.

She glanced at Meryn and then ran past him; jumping onto Sally's lap she huddled against her, giving the visitors a baleful look.

'She's not her usual self, is she,' Cadi said quietly.

'Hannah thought she was still a bit traumatised. I've to keep her calm and only walk her quietly on the lead.'

They didn't hang about. Leaving Sally cuddling her dog, Meryn and Cadi returned to her cottage. 'I bet you wish you could have laid your hands on a Roman flea!' Cadi said as she pushed her gate open.

Meryn laughed. 'You can read me like a book! Just think! To be honest, I was hoping I could do a quick survey of Gemma's energy field, but I didn't want to upset her further, and anyway she has had a bath or two since her big adventure. It worries me though.' He stood back to let Cadi go in first. 'I wonder if she has aged prematurely. You told me she lived for several months or even years in that other world. How old is she in this one, do you know?'

Cadi stared at him. 'Oh God! That's awful. I can remember her as a tiny puppy when Sal got her. It must be about five years ago now. Surely if she had aged, the vet would have noticed.'

'She noticed she was traumatised. I doubt if she would have been looking for signs of premature ageing. Anyway with a dog, in my somewhat limited experience, the animal is either youngish and full of beans or old. There is no middle age.'

'You don't think she's going to die, do you? Oh, Meryn, that would be dreadful. Perhaps something terrible has happened to her organs.'

'I'm sure the vet – Hannah, is she called? – would have listened to her heart. Vets are like doctors, aren't they, with a stethoscope always at hand?'

Cadi shrugged. 'I don't have any pets. But I'm sure you're right.'

'Then let's hope for the best, and in the meantime I want you to go away and sit quietly, and contact Branwen.'

Cadi stared at him. 'What, just like that? Now?'

'Just like that. This is your part of the experiment.'

'And I should ask her about the dog?'

'You could try. Or just be your usual receptive self. See what happens. I'm going out for a walk. Shall I meet you at the mill later for a quick drink?'

Meryn had obviously braved the queue at the post office. He was sitting at a corner table reading a newspaper when Cadi arrived. He had ordered two glasses of elderflower cordial.

'So, any luck?' He folded the paper and looked at her expectantly.

'None at all. Except I wrote the next verse of my poem ready to send to Rachel.' She grabbed her glass and took several sips. 'I tried. I really did.'

'Too hard probably.' He didn't seem too fazed by her failure. 'In the meantime I've wandered round the village, chatted to various people and established that our arch enemy Arwel has gone away for a few days. Chris has some news too. That survey showed up some relatively recent activity in your meadow. They think they've found the site of a human burial. Everything is on hold. Nothing can happen until an excavation of that particular area has been done. I gather the police and the coroner have been informed.'

Cadi stared at him, shocked. 'But your map didn't show a body.'

'Oh, come on, Cadi, I wasn't looking for one.'

'My goodness! You don't think someone's buried Arwel, do you?'

Meryn smiled. 'If so I would be the first suspect. Surely it can't be that recent or someone would have been able to see it on the surface. Your farmer friend would have noticed when he was mowing the hay.'

They looked at each other. 'Wow.' Cadi had gone pale. 'I don't suppose we can sneak in and have a look before the police arrive, can we?' She put down her glass.

The police were already there. The gate into the field was standing open, two cars and a van were parked in the field and a digger was already at work tearing up the grass. A cordon of police tape had been erected round the site towards the far corner of the meadow where the brook bent at a slight angle away from the village. It lay in the shadow of the trees.

'Exciting, isn't it!' As they stood in the gateway watching, someone had walked up behind them. Cadi turned. It was Maggie Powell. 'I told them they found Roman bones buried here sometime just before the war and then they were reburied and forgotten, but they weren't interested,' the woman said with a sniff. 'The man I spoke to said this was probably much more recent than Roman and if so it could be a crime scene.' Her eyes were gleaming. 'They'll want to question you,' she addressed Cadi, 'what with you living next door to the meadow, and your family owning it.'

'In which case,' Meryn murmured as the woman pulled out her phone and started avidly taking pictures of all the activity, 'I think we're entitled to go over to speak to them.'

'If it hadn't been her it would have been someone else,' Cadi said quietly as they walked towards the digger. 'This will be the most exciting thing that's happened in this village for near on two thousand years.'

Meryn grinned. 'I shall resist bringing out my pendulum in front of the assembled grave diggers. This is a completely unexpected development. My Druidic skills have been blind-sided.'

They recognised the site manager from the last time they had seen the archaeologist in the field. He came over to greet them. His name was Peter Williams. 'I'm beginning to think this place is jinxed,' he said, shaking his head. 'The grave is not all that recent. I was expecting it to be Roman, but I gather from local gossip the bones were exposed and reburied in the 1930s. The police wouldn't normally have been interested but they have a list of missing persons in the general area going back quite a long time; once they've established the approximate date of the deceased they'll leave us alone unless it matches up with one of them. I gather it's not very deep.' He turned back gloomily to look over his shoulder at the lone constable who was standing nearby scribbling in his notebook.

'I never saw a thing.' Dai Prosser was striding across the grass towards them. He looked distraught. 'I told the chap over there, when I took the hay there was no sign of any disturbance. Not a thing. I'd have seen it.'

'There was no sign on the surface, apparently,' Cadi put in. She was fond of Dai and his anguish was distressing. 'There was nothing you could have seen.'

At that moment the digger fell silent and they saw the driver leap out of his cab and run round to the front of the machine. 'He's found something.' Dai led the way as they all moved forward.

Stained as they were to a dull ochre, the sight of the bones was startling against the fresh red-brown of the earth. One of the onlookers ducked under the tape and knelt next to the exposed soil. He was holding a trowel and was obviously the archaeologist in charge. There was total silence; it was as if everyone was holding their breath as he gently scooped away the soil, exposing more and more of a complete skeleton. He glanced up at the policeman behind him. 'Well, I can confirm it's human; and it's not recent. The fact that it's skeletal tells me that much. But he's lying face down, which is odd.'

'But not recent enough to be of interest to us, you reckon, Steve?' The policeman squatted down and peered into the grave. The two men obviously knew each other.

'I would say not.' Steve brushed away some more of the soil. He had reached the skull. Cautiously he began to dig away the impacted soil from around it with a palette knife, until it was almost completely exposed. He reached in to lift it gently free of the earth and caught his breath as he turned it over. 'Oh my God! Take back all I said.' He flicked a lump of earth away with delicate fingers. 'Look! He's been shot.' He carefully probed various holes and indentations in the cranium. 'Shotgun, by the look of it. Yes, look. Pellets.' He raked his fingers through the soil left inside the bone cavity, then in the soil and around the spot where the skull had lain.

'Suicide or murder?' The constable reached for his notebook again.

'I doubt he would have done it to himself.' Steve shook his head. 'Besides, someone buried him. And it was a hasty burial, I would guess. See how the bones are folded into the grave?

I'd say someone dug it in a hurry, then forced the body into the hole. I was wondering why it was so close under the surface and so roughly dug.' He put the skull back gently and levered himself to his feet. 'Better not touch anything else. From the context, I'd have sworn this was going to be Roman, and in some ways it looks Roman, but an Ancient Roman wouldn't have been shot in the head.' He stared down for a minute or two. 'I gather there's a record of a body or bodies being found in this meadow as war broke out. I believe the excavation was shut down and any bones were hastily reinterred. But if that story is correct, I don't think we're looking at the same burial. Look, mate,' he addressed the policeman. 'Even if this was murder, I doubt the person who did this is still around to arrest. It may not be Roman but it was buried long ago. That is certain. If you agree, I'll apply for a Home Office licence to excavate the bones here and now. They'll probably give it to me straight away. We need to get the poor chap up out of the ground to stop further contamination now he's been exposed to the air. I'll photograph the site and bag the bones. Get him back to the lab. We'll need to carbon-date him and come back, especially if there's a chance there are other burials in the area.'

'You said "him". You are certain it's a man?' Peter Williams had ducked under the tape to join them.

'As opposed to a woman, you mean? Almost. From the shape of this piece of the skull. It will be easier to check in the lab when we put the skeleton back together.'

'There's something sticking out of the earth over there.' Peter squatted down to get a closer look. 'I don't think that's a bone. Looks like a piece of metal. Farm machinery, perhaps?'

Steve moved back to scrape away the soil from the rusty oblong which had been exposed as a clod of earth fell out of the side of the grave. He gave it a gentle tug and it rattled as he pulled it free.

'Oh boy!' the words were no more than a whisper.

'What is it?' The policeman edged closer to him.

'You're not going to believe this.'

'Not unless you show us!' The policeman impatiently raised his voice.

'I think it's a sword. I reckon we might have found our Roman evidence. Perhaps our victim here was doing his own quiet bit of excavation and whoever shot him caught him at it.'

The policeman stood up. 'I'd better call this in. I've no idea how we deal with this. Have you informed the coroner? I expect I'll have to stay here at least for a while. If people get wind of swords and Roman bodies, you'll have dozens of them up here with spades. We need to keep this under our hats for now.'

'Too late.' It was Meryn. Glancing round he had noticed that Maggie Powell had followed them across the field and was now close behind them, her phone in her hand, snapping the grave, the sword, the people clustered around the scene. Ignoring her, Meryn took the opportunity to step closer to the grave, squatting down and peering in at the bones while everyone else was distracted. 'There's something else in here,' he called out. 'The body was lying on it. See.' He pointed down between the exposed ribs. 'It looks like a belt buckle.'

The other two men joined him, leaning down to scrutinise the bones. The policeman shook his head and turned to face Maggie Powell. 'Right, that's it. Can you leave, please, madam.' He rounded on the woman who was reaching over his shoulder with her phone. 'This is a crime scene. If you don't go, I will have to arrest you.'

'But it was me told you about the bones in the first place!' she replied indignantly. 'I remembered from when I was a girl.'

He looked taken aback. It was Peter Williams who stepped in. 'Thank you, Mrs Powell. I expect the police will want a statement from you later.'

She hesitated, obviously tempted to argue. Then she nodded and turned away.

There was little more any of them could do. Everyone, it seemed, had to consult with a higher authority. Cadi wondered if she and Meryn would be threatened with arrest as well, but it seemed that the other people present all knew who she was. Being the next-door neighbour gave her some sort of protected status, and Meryn had been identified by someone as 'an expert'. In what no one specified but it amused them as they walked back across the field to wonder how he would be described in the various reports which would undoubtedly already be on their way to everyone from the head of the county council to the coroner's office and the relevant police commissioner.

'I would have given a great deal to lay my hands on that sword,' Meryn murmured as they walked into the cottage. 'It had a strong force field.'

Cadi grinned. 'I hope you don't say that if they ask for your learned opinion.'

'Give me some credit – of course not, but I doubt they will ask us. We were just witnesses who happened to be there. Interesting though. I think it had been used to kill.' He forestalled whatever response she was about to make by glancing at his watch. 'Cadi, my love, much as it grieves me, I've got to go. I've arranged to meet someone later this evening in Brecon. And nobody has told me not to leave the village, like they do in films when the police list their suspects!' He winked at her. 'Keep me posted. I'm going to try and sort out my diary and give myself a bit of space to return if you need me. Not that I can really do anything meaningful. I think you have to leave all this to the powers that be from now on. Your job is to keep writing.'

The house felt horribly empty after he had driven away. Cadi stood at her table looking down at the piles of books and notes, a jigsaw waiting to be assembled into a meaningful picture. Then in spite of herself she smiled. Who would have thought that Meryn, a man of mysterious psychic powers, would even have a diary. Or that he watched police dramas.

22

The green silence of the trees enfolded Branwen as she followed the river north and west. In one of the two panniers on her trusty mule, Pedr, were her most treasured possessions, the scrying bowl, various scrolled books, writing materials. She had folded a spare tunic and a stole and a blanket with her extra sturdy walking sandals into the second pannier and for the time being she walked at the animal's head. She carried a staff on which were engraved various symbols to protect her and her four-footed companion from the dangers of the road. Anyone who thought about robbing her would almost certainly recognise the staff with its signs of her calling and realise that it would be wise to leave her severely alone.

Pedr's hooves padded almost soundlessly through the soft earth of the path, the branches of the trees brushing his flanks. Over her shoulder Branwen wore a satchel into which one of the servants of the headman had packed a linen napkin wrapped around a loaf of bread with a wedge of local cheese and a bottle stoppered with wax.

To begin with she had been alert for noises behind her. She knew no one from the oppidum would dare follow her, but woods were traditionally the lair of robbers and outlaws. There were none there, however, to bother her today and her journey was tranquil. Any eyes watching from the shadows were benign.

She followed the ancient trackways of her people. Some had been made good by the Romans with their admitted engineering skills to make the roadways solid, with good drainage ditches on either side where they were needed. Elsewhere she followed the age-old paths angled to the solstice lines, all leading without deviation to her destination, Dinas Affaraon, scarce half a day's walk south of Caer Seiont, or Segontium, as the Romans called it. The man she sought had been her teacher years before at the college in the grove of oaks beside the hill. He would be her teacher still.

But it was not to be.

King Brennius was standing on the clifftop near Dinas Dinlle staring out to sea as he leaned on his staff. 'Your teacher tarried for you as long as he could, Branwen, both at Dinas Affaraon and then here, in the place of his birth. But he was old in years and longed to go to his gods. He left messages for you, though, in case you ever came back to find him. He trusted you. He told me you had learned all he could teach and that you had passed the learning on where it was needed. But even so, you come in good time, sister.' He turned to look down at Branwen, his dark eyes gentle. 'There is trouble in the air, for our empress and for her children. I can feel it.'

'You acknowledge her as empress?' Branwen met his glance with a slight raise of the eyebrow.

He nodded. 'She won't use that title when she returns here, as she surely will, but she will always be a queen to us here in the western kingdoms. Her blood is royal, she is the descendant of the gods of this land.' He turned back to gaze across the angry grey sea. The tide was high and it crashed against the cliffs below the ramparts, throwing spray high in the air. 'I hear Macsen has had success after success after he was accepted by Britannia and then by Gaul and Hispania and Africa as emperor of the West. His capital at Augusta Treverorum is a rich and peaceful place, I understand, and his rule is successful as he and our queen live in Gratian's palace surrounded by Gratian's riches. Macsen has coins minted with the image of his head upon silver and gold.

He has in many ways achieved all the success he dreamed of, but now word is he has turned greedy eyes towards the city of Roma herself. He covets the entire empire, east as well as west, and on top of that he has offended the gods he worshipped. He has broken his sacred oath to his god Mithras and to his fellow initiates in their temple.'

Branwen grimaced dismissively. 'A Roman god; a god of blood; the soldiers' god.'

'Indeed. And one very easily angered. Our queen follows the men of Christ and she has succeeded in luring Macsen to their cause. I hear he wins these victories under the banner of their cross as did the old Emperor Constantine.' He looked down at her again. 'You knew?'

'I knew she was a Christian and her children are baptised in that faith. It is a gentle faith, one of love and brotherhood, and through the Roman sentence of death, their Christ hung from a tree like one of our gods.' She was amazed at how much he knew, this elderly man who ruled this isolated land with its islands and its mountains and its green strip of flat countryside bordering the vast ocean to the west. It might all ostensibly be part of the Roman Empire now, but she suspected below the surface he had command of far more men than the legions that had been based in the Roman forts before Macsen led them away, could ever guess, men who had vowed allegiance to Elen as their queen and who would do so again if she ever returned. For now it suited him to bide his time and watch.

'Do you follow the Jesus god?' He turned to her again. Below them the inexorable waves thundered against the cliffs, showering them with spray.

Branwen shook her head. 'No, I am faithful to the forest ways I was born into, but I will not kill to preserve the old ways as the followers of Mithras do and I can accept Elen's Christ as another of our woodland gods. But, how can these men threaten Macsen with all his legions round him? He has thousands of men under arms.'

He nodded gloomily. 'I hear Mithras still has very strong magic. The flow of blood releases so much power and I'm told they released it here recently in the ultimate sacrifice of a white bull.'

She looked shocked. Then she shrugged her shoulders. 'Our own people once made sacrifices, don't forget, long ago.' She cocked her head towards the sea. 'Out there. On Môn.' The sacred isle, along the wild coast and across the narrow strait, was lost now in the clouds of sleeting rain as were the mountains behind the fortress where they stood. 'But I've been told the followers of Mithras no longer make sacrifices to their god. If they ever did. Are their gods not up there in the constellations with the sun and moon?'

He snorted. 'Perhaps we're all learning gentleness from the Christ. I understand his followers use wine to represent his blood, but the fact remains that Macsen has broken the sacred vow he took, here in Segontium, to be a follower of Mithras. And by breaking that vow he has opened himself to the ultimate penalty, and he has doomed his sons after him unless they return to worship here in the temple where he first made his vows.'

'He first made his vows far away in North Africa,' Branwen retorted. 'Not here. He brought the god with him.'

'You know that for certain?'

She gave a slight nod of the head. 'I am told it was generally known in the fort. His senior officers were all initiates.'

'So.' The king nodded slowly. 'It was not so secret, and never was. Nevertheless, someone else less inclined to change, has stepped into his shoes at Segontium.'

'There are always people eager to step into another man's shoes,' Branwen muttered under her breath. 'It is the way of men.'

'But not women?'

'Women wait in the dark, then they pounce!'

There was a moment's silence then he laughed companionably. 'Will you stay at Segontium?' he asked as they began slowly to walk back along the top of the rampart.

She shook her head. 'With your permission I will stay with you here at the oppidum. I have plans to make. For now, as is the way of women, I will wait in the dark before I pounce.'

* * *

Mithras! So, Branwen had been prepared to tell her side of the story, and it was the story of the temple of Mithras. Cadi shivered. The name even today had connotations of dark caves swimming with the blood of sacrificial bulls, sinister places full of shadows.

She walked over to the door into the garden and pulled it open, stepping out into the darkness.

Steve, the archaeologist and two assistants had returned that afternoon and painstakingly removed the bones from the ground after taking dozens of photographs, leaving the empty grave under a small tent. Presumably they would come back another day to make a more intensive search of the area.

As she stared through the hedge towards the meadow an owl flew low over the grass, distracting her from her thoughts of the dead for only a second with its echoing call. For a moment she couldn't move, then slowly she extricated herself from the clinging branches. Ghosts. That was all. Her story was about ghosts. Echoes. Meryn had barely given any thought at all to her descriptions of the armed men marching up the road, along Sarn Elen. He had thought the whole thing so unremarkable as to be unworthy of comment. She could almost hear him ridiculing the creeping chill which had run down her back. 'Don't be frightened, Cadi, for goodness' sake. Don't worry about it. It's only an echo. And even if it isn't, even if it's a warning, they're on our side. Enjoy the fact that you can hear them. Most people can't. Cultivate your sensitivity. You're blessed with a talent many would give their eye teeth for.'

A warning. But what was she being warned about? Her story? The fate of Elen and her children, or was it a danger nearer to home? A danger lurking in the meadow.

23

The knock on her door was tentative. She glanced at her wrist-watch. It was only just after eight.

'Is it too early? I can come back later – or not at all, if you're busy.' It was Charles Ford.

'Of course it's not too early. Come in.' She was genuinely pleased to see him, Cadi realised. She beckoned him over to the breakfast table and rummaged for another mug. 'Sorry about the mess. I've been a bit preoccupied.' The room was littered with papers and books, but he didn't seem to have noticed.

'I was hoping to nip over the gate and do a bit of dowsing before people were up and about,' he said as he pulled up a chair. 'But, my goodness. What's been happening out there? Police tape!'

'They found a body.' She poured coffee for him and pushed the milk bottle across the table. 'Have you had breakfast? I can make you some toast.' She had been nibbling at a slice while reading over her notes from the night before.

He shook his head. 'I'd been thinking about your meadow so much; I just had to come back to have another look at it. I didn't want to bother you, so I've put myself up at the B & B at the other end of the village for a couple of nights. My landlady, the lovely Annabel, gave me a complete cooked breakfast at seven o'clock this morning when I told her I was going out early. I think I'm going to have to ask her to desist. Far too much, but it was a real treat before getting down to work in the meadow, then I saw the tape. A body, you say? I take it you mean a Roman body?'

She sighed and shook her head. 'They dug up the bones and took them away yesterday; I think the police want to establish that whoever it was isn't on their missing persons list. He. It's a man.'

'It was a man,' he repeated ruefully. 'How awful. And so not a Roman, presumably, if the police hope to find him on their missing persons list?'

She gave a wry grin. 'They expected him to be Roman, of course, but then they found his head riddled with bullet holes.'

'Ah, then I suppose the police would take an interest.' Charles sat back in his chair. He frowned.

'I think they're going to do carbon-14 testing,' she went on. 'The interesting thing was that there was a rusty old sword buried with him and what they think is a Roman belt buckle. Curiouser and curiouser, as Alice said. I think the theory at the moment is that the guy was doing some excavating of his own when someone came up and shot him.' She paused. It had only just sunk in properly that David's family had still owned the field until after the war, that this might have had something to do with them.

'Presumably that will stop the whole planning permission thing for a while?' Charles was silent for a moment. 'Cadi, I hope you don't think I'm interfering – and please tell me if you would rather I disappeared – but the summer vacation is under way and my duties at the uni are on hold for the time being. I couldn't get this place out of my head and I've been doing a bit of digging. Metaphorically, that is. I can't remember if I told you, but Ancient History is my thing and it turns out I know one of the chaps who has been put in charge of surveying this site for planning permission. He is, at least for now, in charge of the archaeology section at your county hall. Naturally I rang him as soon as I realised.' He glanced up. 'You don't look horrified.'

'No. Not at all. This is brilliant. Chris at the mill knows some-one, but I don't know how close he is to the actual planning department. Chris is a bit protective of his source.'

Charles laughed. 'I'm not entirely surprised. If you get a large development going through, or not going through, for whatever technical reasons, I understand everyone gets a bit jumpy. Luckily, my chap, Stephen Graham, isn't in that posi-tion. He produces a report and a recommendation, but that's as far as it goes. Others make the final decisions.'

'I might have met him. The chap digging up the body was called Steve. He seemed very nice and very efficient.'

Charles laughed. 'That sounds like him. It was Steve who told me about this place. Do you remember, when I first met you I had come to check it out with my hazel twig?'

'And will he be digging for the palace?'

'Palace? So, we have definitely decided it was more than a villa.'

'A large villa, but it belonged – that is, we think it belonged – to a king, which makes it a palace. Right?'

He gave a slow nod. 'You "think" it belonged?'

'We dowsed it again. My Uncle Meryn dowsed it. I showed him your plan. I hope you don't mind.' She reached for her coffee.

He laughed. 'Of course not.' He hesitated. 'So, do you want to hear the rest of my discoveries? Nothing to do with dowsing, just fairly competent computer skills delving into information you may already have, but if not, it may be helpful. Steve gave me a nod in the right direction. He's on your side, by the way; he thinks it would be a desecration to build an estate in an idyllic spot like this, but of course he can't say so. And as we all keep saying, they have to put people somewhere.' He paused. 'He has had a look at some of the paperwork behind all this. It was attached by mistake to a file he was sent. The company who spotted a development possibility here seems to have some kind of local connection. It's called Meadow Holdings. They have an area office in Cardiff, although the main company is registered in London. Steve said the original "survey"' – he sketched the quotes in the air with his fingers – 'which was attached to their initial approach to the council, was nothing more than a page of notes plus an assurance that there was nothing here to warrant any further investigations, which is why no one at the planning office here bothered about sending in the archaeologists, at least to start with. They assumed that had already been covered. We mustn't say anything. Steve would get into all kinds of trouble for telling me this and it may not be relevant, but it seems too much of a coincidence. The parent company is a city finance firm. Meadow Holdings find niche areas suitable for very upmarket development but relatively cheap because they haven't got prior planning permission. They gamble on getting the permission; of course the land is far cheaper without it because of the risk involved. The company builds expensive houses. These days that in itself is problematic because people need affordable housing not the other kind, but I expect they'll get round that by sketching in a little terrace of houses on the edge of the development which, sadly, if the past is anything to go by, will end up being abandoned because, too late to do anything about it, they find water or subsidence or something else to get in the way.' He tapped his nose. 'By then of course the rest of the houses will be well under way, so they'll make an undertaking to put the affordable housing elsewhere or arrange a donation towards some green cause or other, and there you are: a beautiful, very expensive cluster of desirable houses on the edge of a pretty village with no cheap little houses as neighbours.'

'That's dreadful!'

'Cynical. Greedy and unprincipled, to my mind, but there you are. It's the way of the world.' He sighed. 'What we need to do is find enough archaeology to put paid to the entire development and send them packing. And it sounds as though we might have done just that.'

'You said there was a local connection?'

'To the parent company, yes. Steve was a bit suspicious. He said the detail as to why they didn't need to do any surveys was very thorough for an initial approach. He thought it showed insider knowledge.'

'So it's someone who knows the village?'

'Oh yes.'

'Who?'

'It's a company: John Davies Associates.'

Cadi frowned. 'Arwel is a Davies. But surely he would have said.'

'Not if he had any sense. Not if the feeling in the village is anything to go by. Most people are dead against it according to my landlady.'

'Everyone is related to everyone round here.' Cadi pulled a face. 'It could be some relative of Arwel's. He's never mentioned a John, unless – oh my God!' She shivered.

Charles raised an eyebrow. 'Unless?'

'Arwel's son, Ifan. That's Welsh for John.' She stood up abruptly, her stomach clenched in real fear. 'It couldn't be him, could it? He ran some kind of tech company, then I heard he had switched into investments. And,' she took a deep breath, 'he hated me.'

Charles studied her face anxiously. 'I can't believe anyone would hate you, Cadi.'

'Oh believe me, he did. We had a . . .' she hesitated, 'a fairly passionate affair.' She glanced across at him, embarrassed. 'It was a couple of years or so after my husband David and I were divorced, and I was feeling a bit low. Ifan turned out to be a vindictive bastard! Coercive, I suppose they call it nowadays. Controlling. Increasingly nasty. When I tried to end it and he realised it was over, he set out to destroy me. He refused to go. He threatened me. He made my life hell.' She wasn't sure why she was telling him all this, but somehow she couldn't stop. 'Eventually, I told him I was going to go to the police and he upped and left for London. He deluged me with vicious emails and letters for a bit. I blocked the emails and burned the letters, and they did stop in the end. I heard later he had married a beautiful rich woman. Of course he did.' She gave a little snort of derision. 'I never heard anything again. It could be him. He knew full well how much I love this cottage and the meadow. It would have been just like him to try to do something to ruin it for me. But why would he do that now? Why start the vendetta again?' She shook her head resolutely. 'No, it can't be him. It just can't.'

Charles frowned. He had seen the panic in her eyes, just for a second, before she sat down again and reached for the coffee pot. Her hands were shaking. He felt a wave of anger, mixed with enormous compassion. 'With all due respect, Cadi, I can't imagine anyone would go to this much trouble to get his own back for a failed love affair! Think how much organisation it would take.'

She shook her head slowly. 'He might. As I said, it would be just like him. And it would be win-win. Make me miserable and make him lots and lots of money. It would have given him so much pleasure to hurt me. Perhaps he hasn't changed.'

Charles let out a long sigh. 'But, as you say, why would he do this after – how long ago did you break up?'

She was chewing her lip. 'I suppose it all stopped four years ago. I've no idea why he'd do it now. Why does anyone do anything?'

He nodded thoughtfully. 'Are you going to mention this to Arwel?' he asked gently.

She shook her head, swallowing hard. 'No. No, of course not. It's only a suspicion. And it seems barely credible. Anyway, as you say, we've got to protect Steve as our source of information. It's some totally different John Davies, I'm sure it is. It's a common enough name. I couldn't bear it if it was Ifan and he was still after me. It's unimaginable that he might have been here spying on the meadow. And on me.' She shuddered.

Charles glanced up at her then looked away quickly, realising she probably hadn't intended to reveal so much of her private life to him. 'OK, let's change the subject and go back to thinking about our masterplan to save the field.'

She smiled. 'Yes, let's. So, does Steve approve of dowsing?'

'Yes and no. I have talked to him about it, over several beers, in the past. The trouble is nowadays they have machines and cunning devices that can do the job far more reliably. That's his view. If you can do it by radar, why resort to mumbo jumbo, basically.'

She laughed. 'Which I suppose is fair enough. It must have been one of his colleagues who came to do the radar stuff in the field. That wasn't Steve. I gather it showed up some walls and a general outline of a big building which he thought was a barn, and it was then they must have spotted the outline of a grave, because they went straight for it. Surely the planners will agree to a proper dig now. It may look like a barn, but we know it was a palace. We just have to convince them. The trouble is, the palace was burned to the ground, probably in the fourth century.'

He frowned. 'How do you know that?'

She hesitated. 'Dowsing.' She reached for her coffee cup again and he saw her hand was still shaking. 'You know all about dowsing. Can you accept ghosts, visions, automatic writing?'

He stifled a laugh, then he stared at her. 'You're not joking.'

'Of course I'm not joking. I'm Meryn's niece.'

'OK. Fair enough.' He sounded doubtful. 'Ghosts I can understand. And dowsing, obviously. But visions? Automatic writing?'

'Visions are easy. We've both seen horses. Flickering lights, all that stuff.'

'And automatic writing?'

'Ah, that's me,' she acknowledged, embarrassed. 'I seem to be doing it. Writing a story about the past which links to the meadow. I don't understand it myself, but Meryn says I should go on doing it. See where it leads. To be fair, I'm only just beginning to accept all this myself. Meryn has been very stern with me.' A thought struck her. 'You knew about Meryn's books, didn't you.'

He laughed. 'Of course. I told you. I'm a fan. I love his style. His angle is what I like to think of as metaphysical history. Not my official course subject, obviously. But nevertheless it all fascinates me. Why do you ask?'

There was a slight pause before she answered. 'Arwel made a huge deal out of the stuff he writes not being proper history or science or whatever. Woo-woo, he calls it.'

'And why does it matter what Arwel thinks?'

Cadi smiled. 'It doesn't. Of course it doesn't. But, Charles, supposing it is Ifan? Supposing Ifan has offered his father shares or something and they see Meryn as a danger to the deal going through? No.' She shook her head. 'I don't want to even think about that.' She scrambled to her feet. 'Come on, shall we go and see who, if anyone, is in the meadow. Bring your hazel twig.'

'Charles,' Cadi turned her back on the view, 'can you do some dowsing up here. This was still a township at the time the palace was flourishing down in the meadow below us. I saw it in my . . .' she hesitated, unable to put a name to her experience.

'Vision?' Charles put in helpfully. The padlock on the gate had not been replaced and they had spent twenty minutes or so wandering round the meadow, then walked up the lane to follow the redirected footpath to the summit of the hill.

'OK. My vision. A woman called Branwen lived up here. Some kind of wise woman.' That was a better word than Druidess. 'When I saw it, saw her, there was a village of round houses, like one sees in Iron Age reconstructions, but we're talking about a much later date, towards the end of the Roman occupation, and what I saw was far from primitive. The houses were furnished with carved furniture and hangings on the walls. I thought they would contrast to the wealthy Romans down below, but they were just as civilised.'

'Ah.' Charles was threading his way through the beds of nettles and bracken. 'Another of our famous mistaken assumptions. I often think we inherited from the Romans as they conquered their empire, our – and by our I mean largely English – tendency to assume all others are inferior. They must be if they allowed us to defeat them.'

'You're talking about the British Empire here?'

'Maybe. It was certainly the approach of a lot of Victorian historians, but I was actually thinking about the Roman attitude to the people they called barbarians. Our friends here, for instance. The thought that your wise woman had retreated from a beautiful Roman villa, probably with running water and mosaics and statues and carefully cultivated gardens, to an Iron Age township, and a round house, which until only recently was assumed, even at this date, to be furnished little better than a pigsty, and to hear that they lived in some comfort and with exotic and beautiful furnishings, that is fascinating. Proof that the Brits weren't as primitive as the Romans wanted people to believe, or at the very least that they were able to learn from their conquerors.'

Cadi laughed. 'Sadly, not proof. That was my vision, Charles. How can I ever prove it?'

'It doesn't matter. Maybe it just proves it to me. I'm happy with our rather wacky method of researching history.' He smiled. 'Opinions in general are actually changing all the time. We are discovering more and more from the archaeological record as our own forensic methods improve, finding out that things were far more civilised than people assume. It all comes down to archaeology and our wretched climate. Rain – damp soils, acidic soils – makes things rot! That doesn't mean we can assume that people in our little godforsaken island up here beyond the North Wind were little better than ape-men! It's just their stuff didn't survive easily. But look at all the wonderful archaeological evidence they are finding at Vindolanda.' He paused. 'Sorry. I'm lecturing. Force of habit, I'm afraid.'

Cadi nodded, 'I enjoyed the lecture.' She smiled, briefly holding his gaze before hurriedly looking away. 'So, until we find a Welsh Vindolanda, let's go back to our own wacky methods. Can you dowse the centre of the township? I've tried but I'm no good at it, but perhaps you can discover something to back up our theory.'

'They didn't have books, did they?' He stopped and looked at her enquiringly. 'Bookshelves in their round house?'

'Had they invented books at that date?' She grinned. 'No, of course. That's your point. We don't know, do we. They would have rotted! No, there weren't any books as we know them. I would have noticed. And not in the villa either. But when Branwen left she took her most precious things on the back of her mule and they included several scrolls. I think they were their equivalent of books. And Elen had a whole trunkful.'

'Yes!' He grinned. 'Excellent! I can feel a thesis coming on.'

'Good.' She found herself liking this man more and more. 'But in the meantime, please can we try dowsing?'

Charles put his hand in his pocket and produced a pendulum, much like hers to look at. 'I prefer working with the twig, it's more traditional, and easier if it's windy, but it's also harder to disguise,' he said with a wink. 'I live in fear of running into Arwel.'

Cadi sat down thoughtfully on an earth bank and watched as he wandered away from her.

'So, what have you discovered?' she asked when at last he came back and sat down beside her.

'I think there were a dozen or so houses up here and, according to my methodology, they were occupied well into the eighth century when I'm afraid it finally succumbed to Viking raids.'

He slipped his pendulum into his pocket and stared round. 'The weather is closing in.' The air was humid and very close. 'It feels as if there's going to be a storm. Shall we go back?' The view of the estuary had disappeared.

'Wait.' Cadi had turned to look back down at the meadow. 'Look. Where the grass is short now, and the ground has dried out a bit, isn't that the outline of a building? You can't see it down there, but from this distance, in this light, it's quite clear. Charles. We can see it!'

'You're right. Oh my goodness!' He reached into his pocket for his phone. 'There is a distinct drought mark. Well spotted. I'll take some pictures. If it's going to rain, the marks may have disappeared by morning.'

The first heavy drops of rain were falling by the time they reached the village and a distant rumble of thunder rolled round the hills as they made their way indoors.

Transferred from their phones to Cadi's laptop the photos showed the clear pale outline of a large building laid out in the meadow. It was rectangular with two distinct wings, one each end of the main body of the structure, identical to the dowsed outline both Meryn and Charles had sketched out.

Cadi was studying it carefully. 'I suppose it could be a barn? Isn't it quite likely that a barn was built over the original footprint? Maybe using some of the old stone.'

He nodded. 'That's probably right. Just think, if we hadn't been up there we would have missed the chance to see the outline in the dry ground.' He glanced towards the window where huge heavy drops were beginning to fall, then checked his watch. 'I'm really sorry, Cadi, I hadn't realised it was so late. I've arranged to meet up with some friends over in Penarth this evening. I think I'd better nip back to my digs to change and pick up my car before the heavens open. Can we follow up on all this tomorrow?'

'Of course.' She felt strangely let down for a moment and quickly pushed away the feeling. After all, he had his own life. 'Do you mind if I email these to Meryn?'

'Not at all. Take care, Cadi.' He hesitated for a second and then he was gone.

She watched as he disappeared down the path then turned back to her laptop. Five minutes later she pressed send, then she gathered up her notebook and pen and retired to the kitchen table. As the sound of the rain outside grew heavier all thoughts of Ifan and of Charles had vanished. She was already back in the past.

24

'I need my empress at my side!' Alone with his wife at last, Macsen, divested of his armour, and dressed only in his tunic, threw himself down on the couch, a goblet of wine in his hand. 'How can you possibly say you want to go back to Britannia now?'

Elen was sitting at a table near the narrow window, a letter unrolled before her. She had weighted it flat with her own goblet and a polished marble paperweight. Her pen-case lay on the table nearby. She had dismissed her scribe and the servants as soon as Macsen had appeared. He looked exhausted. With a sigh she stood up and walked over to him, reaching out to smooth his curly hair back from his forehead. There were streaks of grey there now. 'Running an empire is more tiring than you expected?' She smiled.

He laughed. 'Indeed it is.' Setting his goblet down on a side table, he pulled her to him and settled her on his knee. 'And we have so little time together.'

She still felt that visceral longing when he touched her, but always the thought of Valeria somewhere out there in the officers' quarters came between them. 'Your children miss you,' she said stiffly. She made to move, but he held her still.

'And I them. We will have plenty of time once the world is at peace. So, who is the letter from?' He had noticed her pre-occupation as he came in.

'Branwen. She is at Segontium.'

He nodded slowly. 'And is all well there?'

She hesitated. 'Nothing to bother you.'

'Tell me.'

'She worries that there is local unrest. They have sent for Conan to come and take charge.'

'Conan? Why not someone from Deva?'

Because there is no garrison of any note there anymore. You took them away. She did not say it. 'Branwen does not go into detail. This letter was sent several weeks ago. I am sure all is well by now.'

'My own messengers say Britannia is peaceful. Conan ought to be in Armorica as I ordered. Your father is based at Camulodunum as high king. There should be no unrest.'

She smiled. 'As always you have your hand on every province, my dear. Have no fear. All you need think about is your next campaign. But I would feel more use to you if I returned to Britannia with the children.'

'No!'

'You are forever preparing for war! Can you not be content?' Surely he could feel that her fists were clenched as her voice rose. 'Gratian has gone and your position is unassailable. Theodosius seems happy to allow you the title of co-emperor of the West with Valentinian. Is that not enough? Theodosius rules the eastern half of the empire from Constantinopolis and young Valentinian is happy enough playing emperor in Mediolanum. Sharing with him is no more than a sop to his pride.'

'I intend to take Mediolanum and then Roma itself, to make it once again the centre of the world.' His eyes glittered.

She frowned. 'I've every faith in you. You know that. I'm sure you will vanquish their opposition should they offer any, but surely it makes sense for your family to be removed to safety, at least for a while, until all is truly at peace.'

'I want the children at my side.' He reached over for his wine. 'I'm going to make our eldest son my heir.'

She felt a sudden chill. 'Victor has proved himself in Britannia in your absence. I suppose that makes sense,' she said warily.

'Not Victor Magnus.' It was their nickname for the son of his first marriage. 'I speak of Flavius Victor, our son. I am going to create him co-emperor with me.'

Tearing herself free of his restraining arms, she slid off his knee and stood up, appalled. 'You can't do that! He's a little boy.'

'He is the emperor's son, Nel. Gratian made his brother, Valentinian, co-emperor with him at the age of four and Valentinian, child as he still is, sends messages to Theodosius begging him to help reinstate him in all his brother's lands; lands I have conquered. Theodosius himself made his infant son Arcadius co-emperor with him only last year. I need to do the same to show my commitment to my dynasty and to the future.'

'Then why not make your eldest son your heir?'

Macsen stood up. He walked over to the sideboard and reached for the jug of wine, topping up his goblet. 'Because Big Victor is not your son!' He was getting angry. 'It's your royal blood that makes my imperial line unquestionable. Little Flavius Victor is the descendant of kings. Besides' – he took a gulp of wine – 'Big Victor is fully occupied elsewhere.' The air was heavy with unspoken words. His eldest son had been a disappointment to his father. He was hot-headed. He lacked judgement. His was not considered to be a steady hand. But the fact remained he was a grown man and a soldier. Surely she did not have to remind him that the mother of Victor and Constantine, Ceindrech ferch Reiden, had also been the daughter of a royal line.

'If you do this the Emperor Theodosius will see it as a direct challenge,' she said at last.

'And we can settle our dispute once and for all, in battle if need be. I intend to be emperor of the entire empire, not a mere half of it.'

'So half the known world is not enough for you?' It was a cry of despair. 'You have to have more, always more! You plan to use my son as bait to lure Theodosius to meet you in battle! No, Macsen. I forbid it!'

'*You* forbid *me*!' He turned on her, furious. 'You do as I say, Elen. I am creating our son heir to the empire. That is the end of the matter. And you and the children will stay at my side. You will not return to Britannia. And whatever seditious rubbish that old woman in Segontium has told you, you will ignore it. I forbid you to correspond with her anymore.' He strode across to the table and, seizing the letter, he screwed it up and hurled it to the floor. 'Your place is with me and there you will remain, if I have to chain you to my chariot wheel!'

The shouted words jerked Cadi out of the story. She stared round the room, the quarrel still echoing in her head, the lamp-lit shadows of the great palace at Trier hovering around her in the cottage. She dropped her pen and found that her hands were shaking, the emotion of the story still raw. She stood up and walked over to the kitchen to fill a glass with water, sipping it as she stared out of the window into the darkness of the street. It was still raining and somewhere in the distance she heard the sound of marching feet, ominous, somehow inexorable. With a shiver she leaned across the sink and drew down the blind. An echo. Or ghosts? Hobnailed sandals on Roman stone. An echo, trapped in the foundations beneath the tarmac for millennia, only waiting for someone with the ears to hear it. Marching men of the legion, on their way to do their duty wherever it lay, in fourth-century Gaul or Viking Wales, or here in a twenty-first century meadow threatened by someone whose aim was, for whatever reason, to obliterate history and perhaps to destroy her.

Hurrying to open the front door to the urgent knock next morning and hoping it was Charles, Cadi was surprised to see Rachel on the doorstep. 'Don't tell me you weren't expecting me!' Rachel was not pleased by Cadi's moment of blank confusion. 'Do you ever look at your emails?' She pushed past Cadi into the room and stared round at the mess of papers and books lying over every spare surface. 'Bloody hell! What's been going on?'

Cadi smiled. 'Sorry. No, I didn't see your email. When did

you send it?' Automatically she headed for the kettle. 'It's good to see you, by the way.'

'I should think so.' Rachel laid the portfolio she was carrying under her arm on the table. 'I've brought some sketches to show you. I told you, if you'd bothered to read my message, that I was on my way to meet a potential buyer of some of my paintings in Cardiff and I was going to drop in on the way. What on earth have you been doing?' She walked over to Cadi's desk where one of the large-scale maps was laid out over a heap of notebooks and sketch plans.

'I'm still researching the meadow. All sorts of exciting things have been happening. They found a body.'

'What!' Rachel stared at her. 'A recent body?'

'Not that recent. Well, probably mid twentieth century. They were a bit puzzled by the apparent age and the Roman context. The bones have been sent away for testing.'

'And you saw them?'

Cadi nodded. 'They had the police here and everything.'

Rachel whistled. 'Exciting.' She accepted a cup of coffee and took a sip. 'So, do you want to see what I've done for those last verses you sent me?'

Cadi nodded.

There were several minutes of total silence as Cadi flipped through the dozen or so watercolour sketches in the portfolio. They were pretty, misty, fairy-tale drawings of a lantern-jawed hero and a beautiful princess. She finished and shut the folder, shaking her head. 'They're nothing like the real people. Sorry, Rachel, but they're not.'

'But you said— This is what we discussed.' Rachel stared at her.

'I suppose. But that was before. I've—' She was about to say, I've seen them, but she realised she hadn't. Not really. Not even in dreams. They were just there on paper and inside her head. She glanced up and saw the confusion on Rachel's face. 'Sorry. I know we discussed it and that's exactly what we talked about and they are lovely but, they're just not right.'

'Well, I think they're right. I think they're exactly right! That was why I brought them over.'

'I thought you brought them over to ask me what I think. And I think they're wrong.' Cadi was surprised by the wave of impatience that swept over her. 'They are beautiful and pretty and all that, and fairy tale, but that's just the point. They're not a fairy tale. These are real people in a real world. A world of blood and sweat and tears.'

Rachel sat down with a thump on one of the kitchen chairs. 'Well, you've changed your tune. What happened to fairy-tale castles with medieval castellations in the shadows and heroines in beautiful medieval gowns?'

Cadi shook her head. 'I know. I'm sorry. But I hadn't quite realised how flesh and blood these people really were.'

'But, Cadi, we're not writing history. We're reproducing a version of the story in the Mabinogion. That was medieval! You're writing a modern version of a medieval allegory.' She stood up and moved over to Cadi's desk. 'So, where is the poem? How much more have you actually written since I was here? You sent me two more verses. Where's the rest?' She picked up the map and dropped it on the floor, exposing the drifts of paper on the desk underneath. She rifled through them. 'You haven't done anything, have you. This is all your stupid automatic scribbling! I thought we agreed you were going to do both. You haven't given a thought to the poem.' She found the pile of printed sheets Cadi had transcribed that morning. 'You haven't, have you. You're obsessed with all this stuff that reads like a novel!'

'You knew I was doing them both,' Cadi said indignantly. 'I thought you were fine with it. I didn't know you were coming over today – so soon after you were here last! If I'd known I would have concentrated on the poem.'

'You would have known if you'd bothered to look at your emails. You were too preoccupied with all this stuff to even do that.' Rachel waved her hand over the desk.

'I was preoccupied, you're right. Of course I was.' Cadi knew she looked guilty. 'It's just I haven't had time to do both. There's been a lot going on. It's not just the story. It's the battle to save the meadow, the archaeology, the police. It's distracting. And, yes, it's linked to the story in my head. This was

Elen's home. They've found the outline of the palace where she was born – I've seen the drought marks in the field – and it corresponds to the outline Meryn dowsed, and we know it was threatened by pirates who probably burned it to the ground. I've even seen the blackened stones here in my own garden.'

Rachel shook her head. 'Pirates now!'

'Yes, pirates. From Ireland.'

'And am I supposed to paint them for you, with cutlasses in their teeth and gold rings in their ears? Shamrocks tucked into their head rags?'

'No. They're not in the poem. Of course they're not. I know what I'm going to put in the poem, I just think it would be nice if Elen and Macsen looked a little more realistic. Make them stronger personalities. Macsen is good, but too young, too handsome. He needs to be more like you painted him in that first sketch you did. And Elen,' she hesitated, 'I know what I said, but she's strong, Rachel. A real woman, not a fairy-tale princess!'

Rachel narrowed her eyes. 'I went to a lot of trouble over these. I'm inclined to tell you to stuff your poem!'

She sounded like a child and Cadi was reminded of the quarrels they had had when they were little. Both only children, the cousins were the nearest thing to siblings each had and when they met they hadn't always got on. It was only later they began to forge a closer bond. She scowled. 'You can't do that. Your paintings are what make them so popular. Oh please, Rachel. Try to understand.'

'I do understand. You're bored with the whole concept. Historical fiction is more fun and probably more lucrative.' Rachel turned away from the desk, went over to the kitchen table and slammed her portfolio shut. She picked it up. 'I have to go to Cardiff.'

'Rachel. Please, don't be cross. Those sketches are lovely. And listen! Do you remember when we were doing the last book, the story of Math, the mythical king of Gwynedd, we went to see the site of that Iron Age fortress on the clifftop? Dinas Dinlle. You did some fabulous sketches of it as it is now and as it might have been in the story? With Caer Arianrhod, the magical palace of the goddess, out there in the sea and we couldn't tell whether or not one can still see it because the glare of the sun on the water was so strong and we decided that's perfect for such a special place. Well, Dinas Dinlle has come up again, in this story. Not mentioned in the original, but in my version it was the fort where the local king was based with his tribesmen when Elen gets to Segontium.' She waited for a response from Rachel. None came. 'OK. Tell you what. Let's leave them as they are and I'll send you some more of the poem. I promise. Soon. You did say you had other things going on, and you've obviously got other customers or you wouldn't be rushing off all the way to Cardiff to meet someone.' She bent to gather up the map, then stopped, frowning as a thought hit her. 'You always used to say, if they won't come to see you in your studio by the sea, then they aren't going to understand your paintings enough to buy them,' she said softly. 'What's changed?'

Rachel scowled. 'I haven't got the choice anymore. I need the money.'

'I thought you were doing OK.'

Rachel shook her head. 'I've lived and worked in my beautiful studio by the sea for years without a thought for the future, but now my landlord has said he needs to sell.' She sighed. 'He's being very fair. He's given me some time to try to get the money together, but it's a huge amount, Cadi.'

'I didn't realise you didn't own it.' Cadi sat down heavily next to her. 'Oh, my dear. I am so sorry.'

'These things happen. Everyone needs money these days. He wouldn't be doing it if he didn't have to. It's all one godawful knock-on effect. Someone is pushing him so he has to push me, and I expect someone else is pushing that person and so on up the chain.'

'And your mum can't help?'

'No, of course she can't help.' Rachel's mum, Cadi's aunt, lived in Wrexham. Rachel's father, apart from donating his name and a fairly hefty artistic gene to his talented daughter, had never featured in her mother's life and therefore never in hers. As far as Rachel knew, he had 'buggered off to who knew where', as her mother so elegantly put it, before she was born.

'But, Rach, what we get for the book isn't going to go far; not enough to buy a house.'

'I know.' Rachel sat glumly silent for a few seconds, then she climbed to her feet. 'All the more reason to get to Cardiff asap. Sorry to be grumpy. I'll be in touch.'

'And I will work on the poem, I promise. I'll email it to you bit by bit so you can get on with the sketches. And you're right. They're perfect for what we're doing. It's a completely different animal from the other weird stuff I'm producing. I wasn't thinking straight.' Cadi put her arm round Rachel's shoulders as they walked over to the front door. 'Keep your chin up. Something will turn up.'

Charles knocked on the door an hour later. 'I saw the car outside, so I walked on past and went to hang over the gate into the meadow until your visitor had gone. There is absolutely nothing happening out there. Steve said it would take a while before they got round to testing the bones, and when I asked if he was being chivvied by the owners of the field he went all po-faced and said I should know him better than thinking anyone could chivvy him.' He chuckled. 'The longer the better, I say. Can I take you to lunch?'

It dawned on her that she had been afraid he might have changed his mind about coming back, as almost without realising it, she launched into an explanation of Rachel's situation. They were sitting at a corner table in the café. 'It's such an awful thing to happen out of the blue. She must have been there at least fifteen years and it never occurred to her she had no security of tenure. She's spent her own money on doing the place up and creating her studio. It's the most idyllic place up on a cliff looking out to sea.' There she was, once again confiding in him as if he were an old friend.

'Is she sure she hasn't got any rights?'

Cadi nodded. 'She said she had consulted a lawyer. He's a neighbour who has a holiday home in the village. And her landlord is a friend. She doesn't want to go to war with him. It sounds as though she's stuffed.'

'Could she take out a loan?'

The trouble was, she was finding him increasingly easy to talk to. 'I doubt it. What collateral would she have?' She sighed and sat thinking, her eyes fixed on her plate. She had ordered quiche with salad and Charles had chosen a ploughman's. 'Poor Rach. What a complete disaster. But, it's not our problem.' She looked up at him with a watery smile. 'I'll talk to her again in a day or two to find out how she got on with her buyer in Cardiff. In the meantime, she wasn't pleased to see how much time I was spending on my prose-writing about Elen.' She gave another heartfelt sigh. 'And I can understand why. I'm not pleased either. I'm supposed to be working on my version of "The Dream of Macsen Wledig", not invoking my own dream. And the only thing I can do to help her is to produce it as soon as possible so we can give the completed manuscript to the publisher and collect some money. We won't get a huge advance. Far from it, but it's better than nothing for two ladies neither of whom have a proper day job.'

Charles laughed.

'Do you think I'm mad?' Cadi glanced up at him. 'To pursue this whole Elen business. Beyond the poem, that is.'

'You're asking me, an ancient historian!'

'Not so ancient.'

'OK. I've heard that one before.' He grinned amiably. 'I'm fascinated by the whole process that's going on here. How could I not be? I don't understand it and I find it quite creepy, if I'm honest,' he held her gaze, 'but I'm ready to go with the flow. I'm as anxious to see what happens as you are. I've looked up the history, of course I have, to remind myself of this point towards the end of the empire. Your Macsen – Magnus Maximus – has a fairly well documented, if rather brief, place in what I would call proper history. His wife less so. She immediately tips into legend. I have colleagues in the Celtic Studies department who would be far better placed to talk to you about her, but I don't feel that would be of much help to you. Or not yet. So, let's see what happens in your version.'

'Meryn wants me to concentrate on one of the lesser characters in the story. A Druidess. A wise woman who seems to be able to see into the future.'

'In other words an avatar of you.'

'Me!'

'Yes, you. You can see into the future as far as your characters are concerned. You know what's going to happen. Can I read it?'

'No.' It was an automatic response and she was shocked by the force with which she had replied. 'No,' she repeated. 'Sorry. Perhaps at some point, but not now. Not yet. Do you mind? It's nothing personal, it's just that I don't want to do anything that might switch it all off. Your reaction might be enough to put me off completely. When Meryn told me it read like a romantic novel I was gutted.'

'So, he's read it.'

'Some of it. I'm not showing him the rest.' She could feel herself going red with embarrassment. 'I guess I'm not confident in what I'm doing, Charles. I feel a complete fraud. And a fool. This automatic writing is something I used to do when I was a child and a teenager. I shouldn't have even mentioned it to you. I wouldn't have if I wasn't so wrapped up in it, but now with all this going on, the body and everything, I'm not sure anymore. It's all crazy. The man was shot! This is not romantic nonsense. This is real.'

'And exciting.' His smile was sympathetic. 'I can see why you would want to go on with the story.'

'It's like reading someone else's novel. A thriller. The sort of thing you find yourself reading late into the night because you can't put it down.'

'It sounds as though you're a novelist manqué,' he commented thoughtfully. 'And a poet, of course, but surely you can be both?'

'I have to be both. For Rachel's sake.'

'A great many other people read your poetry apart from Rachel,' he put in gently. 'It seems to me you don't have much confidence in yourself, Cadi. I looked you up.' He raised his hands in mock surrender. 'I know. I should have heard of you.

214

I'm sorry. I'm a historian without an ounce of poetry in my soul, but I loved your stuff. I found a volume of your collected work in my local bookshop and one of your Mabinogion books. They are very beautiful.'

She could feel the heat in her cheeks, deepening them to scarlet. 'Oh, please!'

'Sorry. I shouldn't embarrass you. But it needs to be said. I suspect your nasty neighbour hasn't encouraged your confidence, and nor did his unpleasant son.'

'No.' She shook her head. If he only knew. Sally's voice echoed in her head. The virgin poetess!

'Right.' Charles stood up. 'Wait there. I'm going to go and buy us each a coffee while you compose yourself.'

She watched him thread his way between the tables to the counter, order the coffees, point to two pastries in the display shelf and proffer his card. As he waited for the coffee he glanced down at his phone and returned it to his pocket.

By the time he returned with a loaded tray she was calm again. 'I'm sorry. I'm an idiot.'

'Subject closed.' He had chosen two chocolate eclairs. 'I've just had a message from Steve. We should know the date of the bones and their possible provenance within a couple of days.'

'And what about the mosaics? Surely the ground testing stuff would have shown them up?'

'Apparently he's been told there's no possibility of them surviving the deep ploughing so it wasn't worth surveying the whole meadow or putting any trenches across.'

'What deep ploughing?'

He pushed a plate towards her and handed her a fork. 'Presumably the farmer—'

'No. That's ancient meadow. No one has ever ploughed it. Dai has taken hay off it once or twice a year ever since I've lived here, and put his sheep to graze there, but it's never been ploughed.'

He frowned. 'Not even in the war? Are you sure? I wonder who told him otherwise.' He raised an eyebrow. 'Hold on. Let me ask him.' He pulled out his phone and began tapping out a brief message.

'We can guess, can't we,' Cadi put in. She speared her eclair and sucked some chocolate and cream off the fork.

The reply was pinged back within seconds. He held out the phone so she could read the screen.

Orders from above. Will investigate further. Watch this space.

'Who told you about the mosaics, or was it part of our paranormal experience?' he asked. He was concentrating on his pastry and didn't look up.

'It was Maggie Powell,' she said, amused. 'Nothing paranormal about her. She was talking about riding in the meadow when she was a child. She's probably in her eighties. She might be worth talking to.'

'Are you sure she's that old?' He was fiddling with his phone again. 'She's pretty social-media-savvy for an eighty-year-old. She's put all her pictures of the dig on Facebook.'

Cadi laughed. 'I'm sorry. I shouldn't judge other people by my own failings. I'm the one who's not all that media-savvy round here! It hadn't occurred to me to look.'

'Hang on.' He was tapping away again and handed her his phone. 'Don't forget as a lecturer my life is constantly interacting with my students so I've got to try and keep up with them a bit.'

Cadi squinted at the photos scrolling down the screen. 'She's a good photographer, isn't she. But her comments are pretty barbed. I wonder what Peter Williams thinks about it. His employer can't be too impressed, whoever it is.'

'Perhaps he doesn't know. Are you up for going and asking her about the pavements?'

25

It was after three by the time they walked down through the village to Maggie Powell's cottage beside the pub. She was in the garden pruning back the wildly rampant rose bushes in her front borders.

'Bloody rude, that policeman, wasn't he!' was her first comment as she saw Cadi at her gate. 'Throwing his weight about. Who are you then? Another of them archaeologists?' she addressed Charles as she tore off her gardening gloves.

He gave her what he hoped was a friendly smile. 'Local historian.'

'Not another one!' She was not impressed. 'It's bad enough being stuck with that Arwel trying to tell us all about our own village.'

So, not a fan. Cadi tucked that information away for future use. 'You mentioned that a mosaic pavement had been dug up some time before the war, Mrs Powell, and I was wondering if you had any idea whereabouts in the field it was?'

'Can't they find it with all their fancy equipment?'

'No. Apparently not.'

'And you think they're hiding it.' The woman's bright blue eyes were piercingly shrewd as she stared into Cadi's face.

'I don't know. To be honest, I don't think it would make much difference. They would dig it up and put it somewhere safe if they found it. But it does seem odd that they're not surveying the whole field, especially if there is a local story that there's something special there.'

'That would cost money,' Maggie said with exaggerated cynicism. 'But on the other hand, after finding that skeleton you'd think the police would insist. Especially when we told them there were other bodies there. But then again, perhaps they only want to find out about the modern one. Have they spoken to Joyce yet?' She tucked her gloves under her arm and groped for a tissue in her apron pocket, mopping her nose with vigour.

'Joyce?' Cadi frowned.

'Joyce Blackdon. She was brought up in your cottage. Her grandfather was a gamekeeper on the Caradoc estate.'

Cadi frowned. 'I didn't know that. I thought the family who lived there were called Harris.'

'They were. She married Jo Blackdon. He was the farrier; died about twenty years ago now. She lives in the almshouses, if you want to speak to her. I doubt if she'd remember what happened when they found the mosaic – that would have been before she was born, but you'd think the family would have talked about it. It was right next door to their allotment.'

'Shall we go now?' Cadi and Charles had walked away from Mrs Powell's house with a mutual sense of excitement.

'Oh yes. I think so! Strike while the iron's hot.' Charles was smiling. 'This is fascinating.'

'You don't mind being dragged around on a wild goose chase?'

'I love wild goose chases. I'm glad she didn't pretend to know things which she obviously didn't. She struck me as being someone who likes to know everything.'

Cadi nodded. 'I expect she'll know what Joyce Blackdon says before we do, even so. The almshouses are down here.' She led the way down a cobbled lane behind the church.

Joyce seemed overjoyed to see them. Cadi suspected she was lonely, but the tea and home-made shortbread she produced were surprisingly welcome considering they had only recently had lunch.

'I knew your grandfather,' she announced to Cadi.

Cadi looked blank at this, then realisation dawned. 'Ah, you mean my husband's grandfather. He was Harri Caradoc.'

Joyce nodded. 'Of course. Nice man. His father died in the war like my uncle George who was a keeper on the estate, like his father before him.' She glanced up at a black-and-white photograph hanging over the fireplace which depicted a line of serious-looking men very obviously in their Sunday best.

'I wanted to ask you something about the cottage your family used to live in. Sarnelen.'

Joyce nodded. She took a sip of tea. 'They were kind to let my family stay on after the war. Tied cottage it was though, so they didn't need to after my *tad* and my *taid* – that's my grand-dad – died. When I married Jo they took the cottage back. My mam was too old to live there on her own anymore. I heard they gave it to you and young David when you got married.'

Cadi glanced at Charles, who appeared rapt. 'I live there by myself now,' she said. 'David and I were divorced.'

Joyce gave a sad thoughtful nod and fell silent; Cadi had the distinct impression that the woman was updating the databank in her head.

'I hope you don't mind, but I was wanting to ask you about the old days when your family lived in the cottage. You'll have heard about the plans for Camp Meadow.'

Joyce's face froze. She put down her cup abruptly. 'What about them?'

'They're planning some excavations in the meadow to see if there are any Roman remains there which they need to check out before they build houses on the site. I expect you heard they had found a body there.'

'No. I can't talk about that!'

Cadi opened her mouth and then closed it again. Joyce had gone white.

Charles sat forward on his chair. 'We didn't want to talk about the body, Mrs Blackdon,' he said gently. 'Mrs Powell thought you might remember something about a mosaic pavement which she thinks was dug up sometime before the war. Long before you were born, obviously.' The woman didn't look much over seventy, if that. 'We were hoping someone in your family might have mentioned it to you. It must have been exciting at the time. The trouble is, no one can remember where it was exactly or when they dug it up. We've heard it was covered over again at some point and forgotten until now.'

Joyce shook her head. 'I'm sorry. I thought . . .' She gave a little sigh and picked up her cup again, stirring the tea with the silver teaspoon lying in the saucer. Her hand was shaking and the spoon rattled against the china.

Cadi bit her lip. 'I'm sorry, I didn't mean to upset you, talking about the meadow.'

'No. It was just such a shock after all this time.' Joyce gave a rueful smile. 'But I knew it would happen one day. It was bound to.'

'What was bound to?' Charles's quiet voice was obviously more reassuring than Cadi's.

Their hostess put down her cup and saucer again. 'I suppose it would be a relief to tell someone. My mother told me the story and swore me to secrecy with my hand on the Bible. She was near the end and she said it was important someone knew. I think it was a sort of confession. To get it off her chest, like. Just in case. It was an accident, you see. She was only fourteen. Her brother George had had his call up papers, and he was off the next day.' She glanced up at the photograph again. 'He took the gun out to see if he could get a rabbit for the larder. My granddad was too ill to go out anymore and things were hard for everyone.' She gave a stifled sob.

Charles glanced at Cadi. Her eyes were fixed on the woman's face. 'She heard the shot,' Joyce went on at last. 'Quite close it was. Then George came back a bit later. He was white as a sheet, she said. And shaking. Said he'd aimed at a rabbit but all of a sudden there was a man in front of him and the shot got him full in the face. He hadn't meant to do it. There was no one else out there. There was no one in the field. No one. He was aiming at a rabbit,' she repeated. Her eyes were pleading. 'He said it again and again and then he was crying. She said he didn't know what to do, but they knew no one would believe him. That it was an accident. So he decided to bury the man. The ground was soft after all the rain and he was going off to the army the next day. *Tad* couldn't have borne it if his son had been had up for murder. And my mam was so young. There was no one else in the house and her *taid* was bedridden upstairs. George waited until dark, took a couple of spades out of the shed and made her go with him. She told me the man's face was all bloody. George made her help him dig a great big hole and pushed him in. George was frantic, she said. Angry and frightened. He piled the earth over the body and made her jump up and down on it. He said if she ever told anyone he would say it was all her fault and she would be hanged!' Her voice broke. 'He thought the man must have been digging for treasure in the field. He was dressed funny and he had a sword with him. All shiny it was. George hadn't aimed at him. He hadn't seen him. He insisted he shot at a rabbit. The man came out of nowhere – there was nothing he could do. It was too late. The shot had gone off.' There were tears running down her face. 'My mam lived with that secret all her life. George had gone by next morning, before dawn, without saying goodbye to anyone, and the same day the Germans started bombing Cardiff docks, so no one thought about the meadow after that. No one came looking for the dead man. The grass grew. No one noticed the grave.' There was a long silence. 'George never came home,' she said at last. 'He was killed in 1942 and my *taid* died later the same year. My mam kept silent all those years . . . and now they've found the body.'

She slumped back in her chair. Charles stood up and gently took the cup and saucer out of her hand. He put it down on the tray.

'You'll need to tell the police,' Joyce said at last through her tears. 'It had to happen one day. The man's family need to know what became of him, it's only right.'

'You want us to tell the police?' Cadi repeated at last.

Joyce nodded. 'Will I be in trouble?'

'I doubt it.' Charles walked over to the fireplace and gazed up at the photograph. 'It was all a long time ago. Your mother and brother are dead and the police may not find any relatives of the man who was shot – assuming they can identify him at all after so long.' He and Cadi exchanged glances. 'I think they will want to come and talk to you, but all you have to do is tell them what you've told us. You've done nothing wrong.'

'I hope that's right,' Cadi said as they walked back to Sarnelen Cottage. 'Perhaps she should have told them before her mother died.'

Charles grimaced. 'What good would that have done?' He stopped in his tracks. 'Did you notice what she said about the man being dressed funny and the sword? Shiny.'

'Not when we saw it. If that was what we saw. It was corroded. But he hadn't dug it up, had he.' She was trying to make sense of the scenario in her head. 'We think he was in the field for some reason, this Roman guy.' She glanced at him. 'That is what we think, isn't it? That he ran down the time tunnel brandishing a sword and popped out in 1939 in front of the gamekeeper who had just at that second aimed his shotgun at a rabbit.' They walked on. 'So, we'll tell them what she said and no more.'

'There's nothing more we can say. Not without being certified.'

'Even if it explains why the man wasn't there and then he was, intercepting shotgun pellets that had already been fired? If we believe that.'

'We'll talk, cautiously, to Steve when he's had a chance to work on the bones.' Charles looked at her sideways, then burst out laughing. 'I knew coming over to have another look at the meadow would be interesting. I never guessed it would be this interesting. Are you going to tell Meryn?'

Of course she was.

She rang him later that evening after Charles had gone back to his B & B. She was standing in her garden, staring out through the hedge towards the tent, which was still there in the meadow, over the site of the grave.

'Have you told the police yet?'

'No. We thought we'd go into town tomorrow and explain what Joyce told us. Ask them to go easy on her. She's pretty vulnerable. I can't believe they would charge her with any-thing. Isn't there a statute of limitations?'

'Not on murder. At least, I don't think so. But I don't think they'll be interested in a murder dating back eighty years or so. Obviously no one would still be alive to charge. My guess is they'll take a statement from this lady and then they'll wait to see what the lab comes up with. If anything. We'll all be inter-ested to see what the lab comes up with.'

'Did you manage to clear your diary?' She found she was smiling at the hedge as she asked.

'Almost. I'll come over as soon as I can. Just one or two things to sort out here first.'

Meryn hadn't asked about Branwen, she noticed as she switched off her phone and slipped it into her pocket. But he would when she next saw him. She shivered. She wanted so badly to dive back into 'the novel', as she was now thinking of it. But she needed to do some more writing for Rachel so that when she next spoke to her she could in all honesty say she had written some more verses. She stood watching a couple of bats swooping across the garden. If only she could keep her mind fixed in poetic mode. The way to do that was of course to go back to the Mabinogion. As she walked into the house she saw a light come on at the back of Sally's cottage and moments later she heard a cheerful bark. She smiled. That was at least one time traveller who seemed to have come to no harm.

26

Branwen was standing in the shadows, only half sheltered from the rain by the spreading branches of a rowan tree, heavy with blood-red berries. She could hear, above the patter of the raindrops, the shouts of acclamation from the entrance to the temple where the followers of Mithras met for their rites. Brennius had warned her this was about to happen. The German cohort still based at Segontium had been ordered out to join the forces of the high king after further raids from the northern Picts. A new initiate was to be admitted to their number and the senior officer had decided to conduct the ceremony before they left. There was no time to wait until the feast of Sol Invictus when like as not the ground would be thick with snow and icy winds would be screaming in across the Hibernian sea. The relief cohort would leave within days. A bull had been ritually slaughtered, so Branwen had heard, not in or near the temple, but by one of the slaughtermen from the vicus, its blood collected in a chalice and its entrails preserved to be burned on a ritual fire. And now, the mysteries completed, a feast was in progress within the inner sanctum of the temple. Some two dozen men had made their way quietly in procession out of the fort down the short path to the bottom of the shallow marshy valley to take part in this most secret celebration, following the road without light, their robes blowing round their legs. Only at the entrance to the narthex did each man briefly walk into the light of the torch pushed into a bracket in the wall and then plunge once more into the darkness of a passage heading down towards the temple itself which was lit by flickering lamps. She could smell the aroma of roasting meat on the air. As the last man passed the torch he took it out of its bracket, dowsed it with a hiss in a bucket of water and carried it with him into the utter darkness, leaving the night to the stars.

Branwen shivered. She made the sign against the evil eye and, to be doubly sure, the sign of the cross as she knew Elen would have done. Leaving the safety of the blessed rowan, she tiptoed closer to the entrance to the temple. Just in time, she spotted a man outside, leaning against the wall, his outline barely visible in the starlight. So, they had left a guard even though they must realise that the fearsome reputation enjoyed by the followers of Mithras would ensure that no one would dare spy on their ceremonies. No one that is except a woman protected by her own gods. She withdrew silently into the shadows. She had no need to see more and she had accomplished her mission, which was to identify the men who were members of this most fearsome cult, men who, according to her informer, had vowed to kill the high king, men who Macsen had trusted to guard the northern shore of this land, men who once they had murdered the high king had vowed to hunt down the emperor himself.

Back in the great round house at Dinas Dinlle, she sat before the blazing fire with the king of the Ordovices. She declined with a shudder a portion of the cawl made with meat, and accepted only a vegetable broth, warming her hands on the bowl. 'I have no way of knowing if the information is true,' she said, her eyes on the men and women she could see through the doorway, sitting in groups out of the rain under the overhanging eaves of the large building. They were talking and laughing quietly amongst themselves and somewhere in the shadows someone was playing a harp, the sound almost drowned in the rattle of the waves crashing on the shingle below the cliff as the tide came in. 'But I hear the men of the garrison guard the roads so no messengers can get through to the high king?'

The old man grimaced. 'That is, after all, their job. They do as they are bid.'

'And where is Eudaf now?'

Some weeks after Macsen had sailed for Gaul, the high king had left with his followers for a meeting with his son Conan. Without the backup and structure of the Roman legions and the regional officers, and the more recent and efficient but brief rule of Macsen himself, the countryside had lain unprotected as it basked in the summer sunshine. The local chieftains and kings needed oversight and the high king and his stepson were the men to impose it. Time had passed and the autumn gales threatened to make the roads impassable.

'He is down south somewhere. It is not the high king they plan to murder, or not yet. They will start with Conan, who has returned from Armorica and is temporarily based at Eboracum. The word is that the emperor plans to send his second son back to Britannia to rule with Conan. Constantine, so they tell me, is a proven leader, unlike his elder brother who is an unsteady hand for any tiller. Both young men have adopted Christ as their god, like their father.'

'So the followers of Mithras have vowed to kill them all?'

The old man nodded, his eyes fixed on the flames. 'I am too old to go to warn them and I don't know who I can trust to take a message across the country to Eboracum.'

'Except me.' She smiled quietly.

'You know the old ways of travelling without being seen as you slip through the forests with the protection of the woodland gods. But even so,' he looked directly at her at last, 'it is a large thing to ask of a woman alone.'

'But you know I will go.'

'You and your sure-footed mule.'

She laughed. 'Pedr has carried me across the land without putting a foot wrong. I am sure he can take me out of the mountains here to find my king. And the good thing is both the high king and Conan know me, and have known me since our empress was a child. They will trust what I tell them.' She did not add that the high king at least would probably be too afraid of her to do anything else.

The old man nodded, satisfied. He leaned forward and put his hand on hers as they sat opposite one another near the fire. 'Your teacher would have been proud of you, Branwen. You, of all our elders, carry his learning and his courage with grace and strength.'

She returned to the fort next morning after witnessing the early muster in the parade ground. All the senior officers were missing and her casual enquiry as to where they were was greeted by the house steward in the praetorium with a snort of derision. 'Important meeting of the lodge,' he said as he put breakfast food on the table before her. 'Followed by a feast for the initiates. Much wine would have been consumed.'

Shocked at his candour she looked at him and held his gaze. 'Initiates?'

He shook his head and tightened his lips. 'A word to the wise, *domina*. Don't ask. They will all be back on duty by high noon.'

She nodded. 'Then that is a shame. I shall have no chance to make my goodbyes. I leave straight after breaking my fast. I've sent for my mule and my saddlebags are packed.'

He did not ask where she was going and she was not followed. Pedr set off at a brisk trot along the road towards Canovium and she found herself greeting imperial messengers, merchants, pedlars, and family groups on their way to visit friends and relatives, all friendly. The old man had been right. Thus far it had been safe for a woman alone to travel the roads, but she could not be certain it would remain so. She might if she were lucky be able to join a family group and with them find lodging in a caupona or a taberna on the road. Or she might be directed to a house of holy women and beg their hospitality, but it was more likely she would have to divert into the gentle safety of the woods and forests with, as the old man had predicted, the protection of her gods. She knew what Pedr would prefer. A warm stable and a net of good hay. She slapped his neck affectionately and he nodded his head in acknowledgement.

It took ten days to reach Eboracum and find the lodging of the king. Conan recognised her with astonishment as she found her way into his presence. He was even more surprised when she insisted on speaking to him alone.

'I would expect a personal messenger from the Empress Elen to be attended with waiting ladies and slaves and a guard of honour,' he said wryly. 'She is a very great lady now.'

'Indeed, and would probably have given me such attendants had she known I was coming. I haven't come from the imperial court. I was in Segontium.' She glanced over her shoulder to make sure they were alone.

He noticed her caution and led her out into the atrium of the villa he used as his headquarters in the north when he wasn't with the army. The silence was broken only by the sound of water splashing into the basins of the line of marble fountains. 'No one can hear us here.'

'I come from the king of the Ordovices. He gave me a warning for you and I have seen with my own eyes that he speaks the truth. In spite of the law of the Emperor Constantine that Christianity be observed throughout the empire without hindrance, there are many places where his decree has never held sway. Segontium is such a place.' She was choosing her words with care. 'I know the Emperor Macsen is your brother-in-law and you respect him, so I know I can speak freely. He himself was a follower of Mithras and wore the ruby ring of the most senior initiate when he was here, but he has forsworn Mithras and turned to Christ.' She was studying his face. 'The officers at Segontium maintain the temple to Mithras outside the fort; they still worship there and they have sworn to destroy any leaders of this land, be they officers of the legions or the officials of the empire or the emperor himself who have accepted Christian baptism. Your name and the name of your father the high king, have been mentioned, though I don't know if either of you were ever followers of Mithras or have become Christian . . .' His expression remained inscrutable. 'And the elder sons of the Emperor Macsen were mentioned specifically as well,' she went on, 'for being traitors to the sun god, having broken their oaths of allegiance. They too must therefore die.

This is not a battle such as the legions carry out in the open, man to man and sword to sword. This is a secret and horrific oath pledged by men vowed to a bloody and unforgiving rule by the worshippers of the Unconquered Sun.'

Conan walked a few paces away from her and stood, arms folded, staring down into the water of the central fountain. 'This is not entirely news to me,' he said at last. 'Though I had no idea of exactly where the danger would come from. There are Mithraea all over the land and there have been no orders to close them, just as there have been no orders to close other places of worship. The emperor – both emperors – all the emperors' – he gave a wan smile – 'understand that it is often more effective to win people over by persuasion than force, and such is the teaching of the Christ, I believe. Although I have also heard that our emperor,' he added wryly, 'is more forceful. Since he was baptised by Bishop Martin he has become more zealous than the bishop himself, I gather. He has sentenced men to death for apostasy in spite of the pleas by the more merciful bishop. Maybe that is why now we have a threat of retribution and it is the initiates of Mithras who feel that my brother-in-law is the apostate. He is the only one of us, as far as I know, who was an initiate, so as he has betrayed those vows, in their eyes he deserves death. But the rest of his family as well?' He let out a groan of frustration. 'At least we know now what to expect. Have you sent a warning to him?'

She shook her head. 'There was no one I could trust at Segontium. I assumed you would have imperial messengers who can carry correspondence to his court at speed.'

'Speed yes. But confidential? I'm not so sure. Their messenger bags are locked, but . . .' He made a hopeless gesture with his hands.

'So, I should be the one to go?'

'If you were to go with my messengers, they would keep you safe and nothing need be written down. You can be at his imperial palace in fifteen days.'

'Not on poor old Pedr, I couldn't. He is exhausted after our journey from Caer Seiont.'

'Pedr?'

'My faithful mule.'

Conan laughed. 'My sister's horse, Emrys, who is no cavalry steed, has a home here while she is away. We will keep your mule safe with him for your return. He will have a holiday, fed on the choicest oats. You have my word.'

She held his gaze. 'I hope you mean that.'

To his intense surprise he felt the power of her gaze and shivered. 'You have my word,' he repeated and this time he meant it.

The journey to Augusta Treverorum was made in the company of one of the imperial messengers, using relays of fast, well-fed horses, following Ermine Street to Londinium and then on to Rutupiae, stopping briefly for food and short overnight breaks at the army mansiones on the route, lucky enough to catch a fast trading vessel when a brisk wind was blowing in the right direction for once and riding on, following the well-marked roads across Armorica and Gaul towards the royal palace of the Emperor Magnus Maximus Augustus.

He refused to see Branwen and forbade her from seeing his wife. Stunned by her reception, exhausted and angry after the stress of her journey, Branwen was in no mood to be rejected. She stared at the emperor's aide as he conveyed the message, at first cocky, then merely insistent, and at last quailing under her furious ice-cold glare. She walked out of the reception room without a backward glance and he was left standing, staring after her, unsure what to do. She had no interest now in speaking to Macsen. She walked down the corridor, oblivious to her mud-splashed clothing and the untidy hair beneath her veil, approached the first reasonably senior-looking woman she saw and informed her that she needed to speak to the empress at once. The woman did not see any reason to question her and led the way to the empress's quarters. Later she did not even remember the encounter.

'Branwen?' Elen saw the figure in the doorway as she was in conference with her secretary, another member of the household she found recently that she could not do without. She jumped to her feet and ran across the salon which she used as her office to hug her visitor, much to the surprise of the staff scattered round the room. Within a few minutes they had served wine and refreshments to the visitor, and the room was cleared of people.

'What is it? What's wrong?' Elen had given Branwen one look and grown cold with dread.

Branwen looked round to ensure they were alone and, her voice no more than a whisper, leaned closer.

'I was at Segontium less than a month ago and before that a guest of the king at Dinas Dinlle. He warned me of a plot against your husband the emperor, and the men of his family. Your family.'

It did not take long to relay the detail of what Branwen had been told, and what she herself had seen on that windy night outside the temple of Mithras. 'King Conan will warn everyone who needs to know in Britannia,' she concluded at last. 'We judged it best I came in person to warn the emperor, lest anyone try and prevent him receiving the news. It appears he is his own worst enemy. He refused to see me.'

Elen gave a wry smile. 'That is because he would not have realised that you were the bearer of such serious information,' she said gently, 'and also because he is suspicious of anyone from my own peoples. He knows how much I long to go home and he has forbidden me from leaving his side. No' – she raised her hand to forestall the indignant comment she saw coming – 'it is his right, I suppose.' She slumped forward, chin on her hand, elbow on the table, deep in thought. 'In fact, perhaps it is as well you've told me first. We can decide what should be done.' She gave a weary smile. 'Bishop Martin was here recently. He came to try and dissuade Macsen from sentencing some men who have been accused of heresy. Macsen was determined they should die. Bishop Martin says this is not what Christ would have wanted. They quarrelled. Martin is as fiery a character as my husband when crossed.' She gave a reluctant smile. 'If Macsen knows that the men who follow Mithras are after him he will want to slaughter every one of them and tear down their temples across the empire. These men are high ranking officers, legionaries, he can't afford to alienate them all.'

Branwen nodded. She allowed herself a sip of wine. 'But the fact that they are embedded within the legions means they can come close to the emperor. Very close.'

Elen nodded gloomily. 'Bishop Martin feels the right approach to the many cults and religions of the empire, and even among Christians themselves, is to convert by gentle methods, let them see the love of Christ in action. Win them over rather than terrorise them with torture and death. But that is so often not the way of men. They prefer the language of the sword. It is quick and it is final.'

Branwen shuddered. It was as if a black shadow had fallen across the room as Elen's words dropped into the silence.

27

'So, how do you feel that went?' Charles and Cadi had visited the police station the next morning and spent a good
half hour in consultation with a young detective constable.
Afterwards, they headed into a coffee shop and sat down with
something like relief. 'Do you think he understood anything
we said?'

Cadi shook her head slowly. 'Poor lamb. He had no concept
of ages past. He couldn't get his head round the dates of the
Second World War, never mind three generations of a family
and a murder that had happened deep in the countryside
eighty or so years ago, which no one had even noticed.'

'You think he will follow it up?'

'I expect he'll run it past someone a bit more senior. They
will at least liaise with the council archaeologists; perhaps Steve.
Do you think you should warn him?'

Charles nodded. 'I tried ringing him this morning but he
was out of the office and I didn't want to leave a message.' He
grinned. 'I'll certainly keep him updated. After all, it explains
how the shotgun pellets got into the grave and solves his dating
problem.'

'Not if the bones test as Roman it won't.'

They looked at each other and both smiled. 'What an interesting conundrum we've set ourselves,' Charles said at last.

It became even more interesting the following afternoon when Cadi was sitting at her desk copying out some rough verses. Charles had to prepare for a Zoom call with one of his students to discuss next term's curriculum and had elected to do both preparation and call in the quiet of the room his landlady called her visitors' parlour. Cadi was, if she was honest, quite relieved. They had spent a lot of time together in the last couple of days and she enjoyed his company. But did she enjoy it too much? They had fallen into an easy friendship, facilitated by the strange circumstances in which they found themselves, but she didn't want to risk letting it develop further.

She knew why. She had had enough time to think about it. Her relationship with Ifan had deteriorated so fast and so disastrously that her life had been left in shreds. To find herself the target of such venom in the wake of his departure had destroyed her trust in men. Destroyed it so completely she had resisted even the most tentative approaches from anyone else since. She replayed Sally's humorous comment in her head. 'The virgin poetess' more or less covered it! And it had all been brought back by the horrific suspicion she kept on trying so hard to dismiss that Ifan might be John Davies, the man who now owned Camp Meadow. The more she thought about it, the more likely it seemed.

The knock at her door made her start. She dropped her pencil and spun round in her chair to stare at it, half expecting Ifan to be there on her doorstep. Forcing herself to stand up, she went towards the door and put her hand on the latch, then she stopped.

'Who is it?' She couldn't believe she was asking.

'Detective Sergeant Idris James. I wonder if I could have a quick word with you, Mrs Caradoc. I'll put my ID through the letterbox.'

She pulled open the door. 'No need. Sorry, I was half expecting someone I wasn't too keen to see again.' She tried to soften the words with a smile. 'I'm Cadi Jones now. My husband and

I were divorced and I've gone back to my maiden name. What can I do for you?'

'I understand it was you who spoke to my colleague yesterday about your conversation with Mrs Joyce Blackdon?' He was a tall young man and had to stoop to come in through the cottage doorway. She led him over to the kitchen table so they could sit down. 'I've just spoken to her and taken a statement,' he went on. 'I very much doubt there will be any comeback on the old lady. She was very nervous that she would be penalised for keeping her mother's secret so long.' He paused to take out his notebook. 'I understand from her that this is the house where her family lived at the time of the incident but that it actually belonged to your – or your former husband's – family?'

Cadi nodded. 'The Caradocs owned a lot of land round here before the war, but afterwards they sold most of it. In the end this cottage was the only thing left. My husband inherited it as a holiday home, and he gave it to me as part of our divorce settlement. Joyce's grandfather, I think it was, appears to have been a gamekeeper on the estate and Joyce said his son George was training to succeed him. I'm not sure of the actual dates, but I gather George had been called up at the beginning of the war. The shooting occurred the day before he left and he never came home.'

'No, he was killed in action. We checked.' Sergeant James opened his notebook. 'There is just one thing I need to clear up. The murder weapon. Mrs Blackdon doesn't recall ever seeing or hearing of a shotgun. She has no idea what would have happened to it. Presumably as the men were keepers on the estate, the guns were tools of their trade and that was why they had one or more on the premises.' He glanced up at her. 'I would assume the guns might have been requisitioned by the home guard and that Mrs Blackdon's family might have claimed them back at some stage, or perhaps technically they belonged to their employer and were returned to him. I just need to check whether you or your husband— your ex-husband' – he corrected himself quickly – 'found any guns on the premises when you inherited the cottage? Perhaps in an old gun cabinet, or in the garage or shed or somewhere? People often keep them as antiques or mementoes of the war.' He glanced at the fireplace which was, she realised, just the sort of place where an old gun might have been hung as decoration.

She shook her head. 'The place was pretty much derelict when we took it over. There is no garage and we put in the shed ourselves for gardening tools.'

'Are you and your husband on good terms?' He looked up from his notebook again.

She nodded and then, catching his expression, laughed. 'Oh, my unwelcome visitor? No, that's not David. A rather unpleasant ex-boyfriend who, please God, will never darken my doors again. I've only just heard he might be back in the area.' She realised she was clenching her fists and forced herself to relax them.

'Well, remember there is action you can take if he's stalking you.' Sergeant James stood up. 'And if you are talking to your former husband, perhaps you can ask him if he can remember any stories from the family that might help. I won't take any more of your time, Mrs – Miss – Jones, but please let me know if you hear anything that might help with our investigation. We can't find any record of anyone missing in the area at that time, and it is more difficult, keeping in mind that there was a war on, so we might never be able to identify the victim; he could have been a poacher, a member of a travelling community, just some itinerant passing through, but villages have long memories. People might start to remember things.' He pocketed his notebook. 'And if you're worried about that unpleasant ex, feel free to let me know.' He smiled.

He had extraordinarily blue eyes, she realised.

To Charles's surprise the gate into the meadow was open. His Zoom call finished, he had decided to walk up to the hill fort again. There was a car outside Cadi's cottage. He had wondered anyway if he might have overstayed his welcome there for a bit. He hoped not, but he was getting mixed signals from her. Friendly, even warm, but then a reservation would appear. Perhaps that wasn't surprising, after what she had told him about

Ifan Davies. Whatever the reason, perhaps they both needed a breather from one another's company.

There were two cars parked inside the meadow, close to the hedge, and he could see a couple of men in the distance walking across the grass. They had clipboards and didn't seem to him much like archaeologists. They looked up as he approached. 'Can I help you?' The shorter of the two men was younger, obviously aggressive, and glanced at him impatiently. Why was it when people asked if they can help they so often meant the reverse? Charles grinned at him amiably.

'I presume you're part of Steve's team? I was wondering how things were going with the forensic tests.'

The man frowned. It was his colleague who said, 'He's talking about the bones, Tim.'

Charles nodded. 'Sorry. Aren't you from the council archaeology team?'

The man addressed as Tim shook his head. 'We work for the owner of the field. All this archaeology is a damned nuisance, if you ask me. Hopefully it will be resolved within the next week. My boss has been putting pressure on them. It was all supposed to go through seamlessly. A word in the right ear, and all that.' He tapped the end of his nose. 'Once planning gets involved with council red tape the whole schedule becomes a nightmare.'

Charles nodded understandingly. 'Tell me about it. So, you work for John Davies?'

They both nodded.

'Of course he used to live round here, didn't he.' Charles thought it was worth a guess. 'Has he been up to look at the site since they found the bones?'

Tim nodded. 'A couple of times. He's pretty livid about it. But I suppose one can't blame some poor sod for getting murdered and buried in the middle of our building site.'

Charles gave a wry grin. 'I don't suppose the poor guy was too pleased about ending up here himself. I saw the bones. I know Steve, the archaeologist, that's why I was interested.'

'John reckons someone's stalling,' the second man put in.

Charles shook his head. 'I don't think so. Tests like that take a while to come through. I believe you have to pay extra to speed up the results and the council isn't going to cough up extra, if I know anything about councils. And of course the police are involved as it was obviously a murder. They'll take their time as well.'

'Surely not,' Tim said with a smirk. 'I heard it happened a thousand years ago.'

'Hardly. The man was shot.' Charles was enjoying himself and intrigued to see that the two men had obviously not heard that particular detail. They both looked shocked.

'Does John know about that?' Tim asked his colleague.

'It's pretty common knowledge in the village,' Charles went on comfortably. 'You know, obviously, how unpopular the idea of the development is. No skin off my nose. I don't live round here, but it does seem a shame to build here, doesn't it. Such a pretty spot.'

'They're all pretty spots.' Tim gave a cynical laugh. 'Otherwise we wouldn't be interested and nor would our punters.'

Charles managed a wise nod. 'John coming back any time soon?'

'He's staying here now. In the village.' Tim's colleague scowled. 'Wants to keep an eye on things in person.'

Charles kept his face as bland as he could. 'Moved in with his dad, has he?'

Tim shook his head. 'Na, I understand they don't get on.' He didn't seem curious as to how Charles knew so much about his employer. 'He's staying with some former girlfriend right here in the village. I think she's got shares in the company so he knows she's on board. Ear to the ground and all that. Crafty operator, our John.'

Charles was astonished and for a moment he was afraid he had given himself away. To his relief neither man seemed to have noticed his change of expression. But it was time to go. He had all the information he needed. A couple of further cheery comments and he set off back across the field and headed on towards the hill. No way did he want the men seeing him going back towards the village.

* * *

'They were unbelievably indiscreet,' he said to Cadi as he threw himself down on the sofa. 'I wouldn't want business partners like that. You won't believe what they told me.'

She listened without comment. 'So, it is Ifan. Who on earth is he staying with?' Her mouth had gone dry.

'I didn't dare ask any more questions. They were bloody naïve giving so much away to a stranger, but I couldn't push my luck. It's a small village. Surely it can't be hard to find out where he is. I'll ask my landlady. She knows everyone.'

'I thought I knew everyone,' Cadi whispered. 'I've lived here a long time and no one has said anything. You would think I of all people would know if he had another girlfriend around here. Anyway, I thought he was married.' She was feeling sick; this was her worst nightmare come true. She swallowed hard. 'I wonder if Arwel even knows he's here. If those men knew he and Ifan don't get on, that implies they never made up.'

'You can't ask him?'

She had gone pale, he noticed. He wondered if he should have told her what he'd discovered. But surely it was better she knew.

'No. I can't.' She shuddered. 'I don't want to have anything to do with Arwel. I can't bear the idea that Ifan is actually here, so close. This is deliberate. He knows how much it will hurt me to develop the meadow. He might be watching this house at this very moment. And who the hell is this girlfriend?'

It didn't take long to find out. It was only an hour later that Chris Chatto knocked at the door. 'Do you know who the developer is?' He had a bottle of wine in his hand and he was bursting with the news. 'One of his men came into the mill. My God! It's only Arwel's son. He's a multimillionaire now and a property developer and he's back, staying in the village. I can't believe it.'

The only thing he hadn't been aware of was that Cadi and Ifan had once had an affair. John as he was now known, at least professionally, was, it appeared, staying with Madelaine Bristow; her beautiful Georgian house on the edge of the village was in effect her second home, based as she was in London where she ran a globally acclaimed fashion business. As far as

Chris knew she was away on one of her regular trips to Italy and had lent Ifan the use of her house.

'Jesus Christ!' Cadi stared at Chis in shock. 'He's gone up in the world since he and I were together!'

Charles had found some glasses. He opened the bottle and poured what he described as a restorative dose each. 'So, Cadi,' he asked gently, 'do you know her?'

'I've met her but we move in different circles.'

'Sounds just as well.' Chris felt in his pocket for his phone. He chewed his lip as he scrolled through a clutch of photographs. 'You need to see this.' He passed Cadi the phone.

She stared at it for several seconds, enlarging a corner of what looked like a plan. 'What is this?'

'The latest outline planning application.'

'But it's—' She turned the phone upside down.

'Much larger than the original one. The houses are more tightly packed and one street is right up against your hedge and overlooks your garden. Don't worry. Even if they allowed the development, I doubt they would accept that bit, but it does rather prove how personal this is.'

Cadi leaned back in her chair. She was as white as a sheet. 'I can't believe it. Where did you get this from, Chris?'

'It was your friend Steve, Charles. He sent it to us at the anti-development committee. I didn't ask how he got hold of it. He seems a far better source of information than my own contact at the council.' Chris retrieved the phone from Cadi and passed it to Charles. He grabbed the bottle off the table and refilled her glass. 'Ifan Davies is obviously an A-grade bastard. If this is about you, Cadi, what on earth did you do to him to deserve such an extraordinary revenge?'

Cadi grimaced. 'I dumped him. That was enough. He persecuted me for a long time after we split up, but I thought, I hoped, he had forgotten all about me. But this has his signature all over it. Complicated, subtle, and vicious. He must have been planning this for months, if not years.' She bit back a sob. Charles and Chris glanced at each other uncomfortably. 'I think I can guess why he's homed in on the meadow.' She took a deep breath and steadied her voice. 'When we finally fell out properly it was because he wanted us to move to London. He said he hated the village and the countryside. He had been brought up here of course. He wanted me to sell Sarnelen Cottage. Naturally I refused and, thinking back, it did rather become an "either the house goes or I do" sort of duel. If I had really loved him there might not have been a problem, but I had realised by then that our relationship was not going to work. I had seen so many signs that he wasn't the nice person I thought he was. He had a vicious streak even then and once I said I wanted to end it, he went ballistic. I was really scared of him for a while. I did wonder if he might burn the house down. He blamed it for our break-up. Thought I loved it more than I loved him. Which was true.' She gave a shaky grin. 'But eventually he went away and his threats faded out. At some point he'd got married. You told me that Chris. I thought he had forgotten about me. So why now? Why, after all this time?'

Chris and Charles exchanged glances again. 'I think the only possible upside of this is that if he's planned such an intricate revenge, maybe he won't want to spoil it by knocking on the door and threatening you in person,' Chris said thoughtfully. 'He wants to ruin Sarnelen Cottage for you; he doesn't want to hurt you physically.'

'I wish I had your confidence.' Cadi shuddered again. The palms of her hands were sweating. 'I'm not going to feel safe here anymore, am I.'

'But you wouldn't go away?'

'No, of course I wouldn't.' She gritted her teeth. 'That would be letting the bastard win.'

'You need someone staying here with you,' Chris went on.

'My uncle Meryn,' Cadi put in hastily, afraid Charles was going to volunteer. 'It's already arranged. He's coming for a while to help with the historical side of all this.' She gave Charles a quick glance.

'Good.' Chris seemed satisfied. 'I have no idea where we go from here. I suppose we have to see who makes the next move. If the council refuse permission because of the archaeology, no doubt he will be very angry and presumably he will appeal.

And if they allow it, we will be absolutely furious and we will appeal.'

They sat in silence for a while after Chris left. Eventually Charles sighed. 'Oh, Cadi. I'm so sorry.'

She shrugged her shoulders. 'I'm glad you found out. I'd been suspicious for a while. The meadow was where I escaped from him. I've always loved it out there. It's my special place.' She sighed. 'Charles, would you mind very much if I asked you to go. I need to be alone for a bit. I need to think. Sorry.' She was terrified she was going to cry.

'Of course.' He stood up. 'I ought to go back to the B & B anyway. I need to make some notes on the call I made this afternoon.' He waited, but when she made no response he continued, 'And I'll have a better chance of running into my hostess if I go back early. I can quiz her about our friend and the exotic Madelaine Bristow.' He hesitated. 'You will be OK on your own until Meryn comes?'

She nodded silently.

'Ring me if you want me to come back.' He waited for her to say something, but she didn't reply.

As he walked up the narrow street into the heart of the village he thought he could feel eyes boring into his back. He did not look round.

28

'I want that woman out of my court!' Macsen had walked into his wife's bedchamber that evening, dismissed her ladies and servants and slammed the door after them. 'How dare you ask her here after I told you not to communicate with her.'

Elen sighed. 'I did not invite her here, she arrived. And she arrived to warn you of an impending assassination attempt. If you had bothered to talk to her she could have told you herself.' She rose from her couch and pulled her stole more closely round her shoulders. The wind off the river was somehow finding its way into the palace, shaking the leaves from the pots of plants in the atrium. Exhausted after her long race across Gaul with the imperial messenger, Branwen had begged to be allowed to go and sleep at last.

Elen folded her arms. 'So, do you at least want to know where the threat comes from?'

'Mithras.' He tightened his lips.

'So, you already knew?'

'I didn't know specifically about Segontium, but the threat has been made in several centres. In Roma itself. Bishop Martin and I discussed it.'

'And yet you sent the bishop away, both of you in a rage.'

'He feels I should be more lenient with men who diverge from the Christian faith. He is wrong. It is important to show strength and resolution. And that will be my response to the initiates of Mithras as well if they prove implacable. If necessary they must die.'

'Which is exactly what they have said about you.' Her blood was up and she was prepared to stand her ground. 'Except that you cannot deny breaking your vows to their god. You stopped wearing your Mithraic ring as soon as you became a Christian, but you must do more; you must break with them openly and officially.'

'I must do nothing of the sort. Bishop Martin baptised me. That is all the proof I need that I am forsworn against other gods and other ways of worship.' His eyes narrowed. 'Has Branwen forsworn her forest gods?'

Elen fell silent. 'I do not ask other people's beliefs,' she said at last.

'No,' he said drily. 'Well, I suggest you do. I will expect her to accept baptism if she remains in this court for even a day longer.'

After a formal meeting with his advisers and officers he was wearing his imperial toga and she saw him draw the heavy purple folds over his shoulder as he faced her. He too was feeling the cold breath of the wind on his back. She shuddered. There was danger in the room. She studied his face and changed the subject abruptly. 'Were decisions made this afternoon?'

He nodded. 'It is invidious that I continue to recognise Valentinian as some kind of distant co-emperor. I have a co-emperor of my own in my son. I have no need to abide by some vague agreement I made with that stripling. There will be no more delays. I have decided to move my capital to Roma as soon as possible. The court will go with me.' He held her gaze.

'By the court, you mean you expect me to be at your side?' She refused to quail at his words.

He nodded. 'And the children. You will follow well behind the army.' He relented a little. 'There will be no danger. There has been none yet. The peoples of the empire welcome me. They recognise that my rule is strong and efficient. They see in me the true worth of the imperial power, and besides,' he smiled, 'I have the royal blood of Britannia at my side and flowing through my children's veins. Their next emperor will be descended from the gods.'

'Who you don't recognise,' she retorted sharply.

'They take their places as servants of Christ, as his saints and angels,' he said piously. 'That's close enough.' He grinned again and, stepping forward, swept his arm around her. 'Without you I would be a lesser man, Nel.'

She fought free of the heavy folds of the entangling toga. 'I'm glad you recognise the fact.' In spite of herself she felt herself succumbing to the attraction she still always felt in his presence, however much they quarrelled. Minutes later he had lifted her up and carried her through into her bedchamber. The attendants, alert to any sounds behind the doors of the empress's chamber, glanced at one another knowingly, and melted back into the shadowed passage that led towards their own quarters. It was unlikely they would be needed again tonight.

In one of the guest chambers of the palace, Branwen stirred in her sleep. She was back in the forests that clothed the lower slopes of Yr Wyddfa. The air was cold, the trees and grasses bending before the west wind, a golden eagle riding the clouds with the rain in its feathers. And there in the shelter of a stand of pine trees she could see the horsemen waiting near the road. The tribesmen from Dinas Dinlle, mounted on their sturdy mountain ponies, carrying shields and armed with spears. Who were they waiting for? The usual enemies came from the sea, fighting the waves and the vicious tides as they beat in towards the shore. In the past the invaders had been pirates, but more often now, their crews were intent on more than a quick snatch-and-grab raid, instead eyeing the richer lands to the east of their own, hoping to chase the remnants of Roman order from the mainland of Britannia. But these Ordovician men were not facing the sea. They were watching over one of the main routes from Segontium, not towards Deva and Eboracum but south through the mountains to Tomen-y-Mur, and the party they were waiting for would be bound, almost certainly, for Viriconium and the road some call Watling Street, the fastest route to Dubris and the coastal crossings that would take them with the greatest speed to the continent, to Gaul and to the emperor's base at Augusta Treverorum.

Had the Mithraean party, hand-picked assassins, left the fort yet? Branwen struggled to see back along the road towards Segontium, but there was no sign of them in the whirling mists. Was it possible they had gone another way? The paths through these wild mountains, far from the recognised roads with their beaten surfaces and regular military stations, were steep and secret, following hidden passes between high crags and wild river beds. A small party of highly trained men could travel unseen even by the most alert of locals if they too had expert guides, men who had forsaken their local gods for the more glamorous worship of the Parthian Sol Invictus. In her dream, Branwen reached out to pull at the sleeve of one of the king's scouts, but he felt nothing but the tug of the wind, and the catch of a bramble to his cloak and brushed her away.

Cadi read through the last sentence she had written and gave a shaky smile. She had sat still for a long time after Charles had left and then, at last, stood up and walked over to her desk. She needed to take her mind off the latest revelations about Ifan. What better way than picking up her pen and fixing her mind on the past. She liked the description of Branwen's dream. Macsen was luckier than he knew to have her on his side. She let out a sigh and frowned. She reached for the folio of Rachel's illustrations and leafed back through them to the earliest sketches of Macsen in his sexy shirt, and with glowing eyes, and yes, there it was. On his right hand he was wearing a large ruby ring, the ring of the highest-grade initiate of the temple of Mithras. How on earth had Rachel known about that? She shivered and glanced towards the window. The sun had set into the black horizon beyond the distant Bannau in a dramatic flourish of crimson and gold; she could just see it through her kitchen window. In seconds it would have gone. She tensed. Was that a face looking in? She stood up so suddenly her chair fell backwards onto the rug. Peering out of the window she couldn't see anyone. She grabbed at the cord and closed the blind to find that she was shaking all over. Ifan. Was it Ifan? She swallowed hard, clinging to the rim of the sink, trying to steady herself. Hell and damnation! She was not going to allow him to terrorise her again. She walked across to the front door and pulled it open, standing on the doorstep to look up and down the street. There was no one in sight. The last line of light in the sky had gone and darkness was on its way in. Stepping back inside, she closed the door with a bang and pulled the bolt across, astonished by the wave of fury that swept over her. How dare he appear in her life again like this. To threaten an entire community in order to victimise her was beyond the pale. The bastard! She reached for the bottle of wine that was still standing on the table and poured herself another glass. She might have topped it up again had her phone not rung. It was Meryn. 'I sense all is not well in the meadowlands of South Wales. I'm sorry it's taken longer than I expected to get away. I was planning to come tomorrow but I can set off now if you like.'

She managed to laugh. 'I think I can contain the situation for another few hours. Bless you. I shall expect you at coffee time tomorrow.'

In the event it was Sally who arrived first next morning with Gemma close at her heels. 'Chris told me about Ifan.' She reached for Cadi's cafetiere, still half full amongst the remnants of her uneaten breakfast and she shook it experimentally. She found a mug on the draining board. 'Do you mind? Gem and I have been for a walk up the lane and I could do with something hot. There's no one in the meadow right now, but that tent is still there over the gravesite. Chris and Melissa thought I should know what's happened as I'm next door. She rang me last night. I'm so sorry, Cadi. I remember so well what that bastard did to you after you broke up. You were a nervous wreck.'

'I was not!' Finally Cadi managed to get a word in. 'I hope they haven't gone round telling everyone in the village. That would be a disaster.'

'No, no. They know we can't tell anyone.' Sally tapped the side of her nose. 'Don't worry. Watch and listen is the way forward for the time being. Does Charles know?' She couldn't contain the cheeky grin.

'He was here when Chris came over yesterday. He was the one who found out about Ifan through his mate in the archaeology team.'

'And that nasty creep Ifan is reborn as John Davies the ultra-respectable and very rich businessman who just happens to have discovered a nice little development possibility in the heart of the countryside. Have you seen him?'

Cadi hesitated. 'I did wonder last night. I thought I saw someone peering in through my kitchen widow.'

Both women turned to look at it. 'Shit!' Sally said.

'I was really scared, then I got angry. But it might have been nothing. A trick of the light. It might have been anyone. I must learn to shut the blind when I have the lights on. I forget that people can walk down the street and see in. It's so quiet here normally.' She sighed.

'You shouldn't be alone, Cadi.'

'I won't be. Uncle Meryn is coming to stay and he'll be here soon. I spoke to him last night.' When he had psychically realised he was needed at once. She didn't say it out loud. 'He's going to help with the history. I think he and Charles will get on rather well.'

Sally managed to keep a straight face. 'Good. I hope between them they can outwit the bastard developer. I gather he's staying with Madelaine.'

'Apparently. Except that she's not there. She's off on one of her Italian trips.'

'She ought to be careful or he might sell half her garden for a nice little profit before she gets back. Can I make some more coffee? This is cold.' Sally glanced down at Gemma, who had curled up under the table. 'She's not herself, Cadi.'

Cadi slid off her chair and sat down on the floor next to the dog, fondling her gently as she slept. 'Have you seen the vet again?'

'I spoke to her on the phone. She says Gem is probably still traumatised by whatever happened to her. Can you ask Meryn to have a look at her when he arrives? I know he's not a vet, but he seems to be so good with animals and he has an amazing instinct about things.'

Cadi glanced up at her. 'Of course I will.' Sally had no idea just how astute Meryn's instincts were but then she had no idea either how traumatising Gemma's adventure must have been.

He arrived about an hour after Sally had finally gone home. The morning had warmed up and he and Cadi sat in the garden while she filled him in with all the details of everything that had happened.

'Forgive me, Cadi,' he said at last, 'but are you sure about this developer's identity? It seems to me that no one has actually seen him yet.'

She nodded ruefully. 'Well, I'm not going to go and knock on his door, am I.'

'Perhaps not, but your friend Chris could arrange an interview. He would be within his rights as the organiser of the village opposition to the development.'

'I suppose so. But we know he's Arwel's son. It's Ifan. There's no doubt. And he must know I would find out eventually. After all, the whole point would be to upset me as much as possible.' She steadied her voice with an effort. 'I don't think I'm being paranoid. He had a real vindictive streak. I just can't work out why he should revive the vendetta after all this time.'

They found out at lunchtime. Charles had phoned and suggested they all meet at the mill. 'I went to see Maggie Powell, to thank her for the introduction to Joyce,' he said after he and Meryn had shaken hands. He grinned. 'I guessed she might be a source of more information so I accepted her offer of a cup of tea and a flapjack. She knows all about our Ifan and she knows it's him.' He lowered his voice with a glance round the café. There was almost no one there, so he had beckoned Chris over to join them. 'She doesn't like him. I'm not sure if she knew you had a history with him, Cadi, but she knew his father and he had a massive row way back. She thinks he might have given or at least promised Arwel a stake in the development to try and lure his way back into favour. But that's not the most chilling bit. She says he's come home because he and his wife have split up and she's done a runner, accusing him of abuse and all sorts.

I'm not sure how she knows all this, but as far as I can see this village is an echo chamber of gossip and secrets. I had no idea I missed so much, living in the city.' He looked at Cadi. 'It gives us something to go on, though. Might explain a lot, no? Memories of being rejected. Maybe he hoped he could move in with his dad, though from what I hear that would be a vain hope, or so Maggie thinks. She's not sure how he knows Madelaine, but she reckons all rich people "from off", as they say round here, know each other anyway. And she thinks if Madelaine is rich, maybe she's an investor.'

'She's probably right about that,' Chris commented. He stood up. 'The place is filling up. I'll chase up your food, folks. A lot to think about there, Charles. Did you ever work for MI5? If not why not?'

'I was wondering that too,' Cadi put in with a smile.

29

In her bed in the guest chamber in the palace of Augusta Treverorum Branwen groaned and turned over, her dream growing ever more real. How could a bowl of water hold so many flames? She swirled the water gently and watched as the walls crumbled, the roof fell in and one by one the well-loved landmarks turned to ash. They were still there, the men who had fired the palace, shouting with glee, dancing in the glow of the embers as darkness fell, raking through the ash for anything that might have survived. She saw one, with a yell of triumph, point towards a figure emerging from the ruins. A guard from the villa, a retired legionary, sword in hand, had ducked out of the smoky shadows and was running for his life towards the shelter of the trees and the safety of darkness. The invaders spotted him and with shouts of rage began to give chase as he ran, ducking across the meadow where the horses had grazed. He didn't notice the pale flickering lights spiralling in the deeper shadow down by the stream, he was too intent on escaping the pursuers behind him. In moments he had run into the strangely uneasy silence of the spiralling lights and in an instant he was lost to sight, leaving his pursuers milling in confusion in an empty field. They all heard the one clear report echoing through the trees, the sound of a shotgun being fired in another age.

So Branwen had foreseen what was going to happen. She had even heard the shot. Cadi put down her pen and stared unseeing at the page before her. It was several long minutes before she picked up the pen again to see what happened next.

Still in her dream, Branwen put down the scrying bowl. Ducking out of the round house with its woven hangings and carved oak furnishings, she hurried across the roadway towards the gatehouse with its high lookout tower. Climbing the steps, she was relieved to see that the palace was untouched. It looked normal. Sleepy.

She screwed up her eyes in the bright sunlight and now she could see signs of life. There were men in the fields cutting the barley and others working in the vegetable gardens. There were vines in rows in the south-facing vineyard and the hay had been safely stooked and most of it brought into barns against the wet weather that would surely come. All looked peaceful and secure, but if she shifted her gaze across the tinder-dry countryside to the glitter of water that was the estuary of the great river Sabrina, she could see a distant cluster of black dots approaching from the sea.

She shivered. She did not have to see them more clearly to know that this heralded another incursion of pirates and there was no one to protect the palace. She had already seen what was going to happen.

'You have seen them as well?' The elderly man behind her had been standing there for several moments before she noticed him. He was leaning heavily on his staff. Behind them the villagers, seeing their concentration on the distant river, began to climb the steep flight of steps to gather around them, staring out across the forest.

'You must warn them,' Branwen said to him quietly.

'I'll send messengers down to speak to the steward. He will have to inform everyone so they can hide what they can and bring the people and stock up to us. They will be safe here.' The old man glanced round at the ramparts of the hill fort. Rising hundreds of feet above the forest even the most determined invader would baulk at trying to storm their defensive earthen walls and intervening ditches.

'I wish I could be here with you, grandfather,' Branwen said. 'But I have no fear for our town. It is the palace below that will burn. It is undefended and will be rich pickings. If only the pirates could see its potential and settle here to work the land. One day they will, but not this time. You must send messages to the high king, but whatever he does it will be too late to save it.'

'You saw it burn in the bowl?'

She nodded. 'Hurry. They still have time to save themselves. And the animals and crops.'

Only one man would die, that one guard who was to travel inadvertently through the corridors of time to an unlooked-for death in a distant and unwelcoming age.

'And you?' The old man looked at Branwen sharply. 'Where will you be?' He knew he too was dreaming. He knew he must soon wake up.

'I am going to come back to Albion and then I will go north into the mountains. I have to prepare to receive Elen's children.'

He frowned. 'But they are with her in Gaul.'

Branwen smiled. 'And she is already regretting it. They have a destiny to fulfil in Albion and it's written that they will come home.'

He scanned her face intently and nodded. 'Then go with the gods, my child, and with my blessings. Have no fear. I will heed your warning. We will save the people from the palace.'

Alerted by the old man's dream the duty guard rang the great alarm bell that hung by the watchtower. As its bronze note rang a warning across the hills and the forests into the dawn, the people of the fort streamed down to help their neighbours in the palace and the remaining servants and slaves frantically gathered their belongings, rounded up the stock and loaded hay and harvested crops and as much foodstuff as they could carry onto carts to drag up to safety even before the fleet of ships were visible in the estuary. No one queried the warning of a dream. Such messages were sent by the gods.

Cadi sighed. So, the palace had burned at the hands of the Irish pirates, towards the end of the fourth century, in Elen's lifetime, and just as they had guessed a fleeing guard had escaped through the wormhole to be killed by a man with a shotgun some fifteen hundred years later. Quietly opening the back door she walked out into the night, and across the wet grass to stand on the place where they had exposed the piece of burnt stone walling here in her own garden. It had stopped raining and the sky had cleared. Meryn had gone up early and she reminded herself that he was not a young man. He had come to be with her here, but he was still busy, working on his own book. The night was dark and very silent. She stepped nearer to the hedge. There was a quick rustle of leaves as some small animal took exception to her presence. She stepped closer and reached out towards the closely knit branches of hazel and dogwood and yew and found she could peer through a gap into the starlit meadow beyond. The tent was still there and the fluttering police tape, almost luminous against the dark hedgerow beyond it.

She was starting to untangle herself from the wet embrace of the hedge when she paused. She caught her breath. She could hear it now, the steady march of feet out in the lane beyond the gate, the steady crunch of hobnails on stone and, frighteningly clear, a barked command as the file of men turned into the field and came to a halt before the smoking ruins. Somehow she knew they had come from Isca. Paralysed with fear, she watched. She could see them clearly, helmets, swords, spears, shields, a standard carried by the man at their head.

'Too late,' she heard the words distinctly. And then they were gone. She pulled back out of the hedge and stood for a moment, feeling her heart thudding in her chest. She was shaking all over. Slowly she tiptoed back towards the house, then as the shock subsided she started to run, diving through the door, locking it behind her with shaking hands. Hugging herself she took several deep breaths. It was still there in her nose, the smell of burning, the sour ashes that were to lie in the field for sixteen hundred years. The field where the repercussions of that night were still being played out in the echoes of the past. Echoes that she could hear again and again in the street outside as men came to the rescue too late.

Too late. The words echoed in her head. They were the words Elen had heard when she had tried to see the future as Branwen did. The results of that fateful night had terrified her so much she never attempted it again.

It seemed like hours before Cadi was able to walk over to the sink to reach for the kettle, an automatic action, filled with normality, reassuringly ordinary. While she waited for it to boil she went back to double-check the lock on the veranda doors, then the back door, then returned to pull down the blind. The window was dark, the last hint of daylight gone. Glancing out as she reached up for the cord, she froze. Was that a figure in the front garden? She stood paralysed, unable to move, staring out past her own reflection. A man. A soldier? Ifan? Ifan was in the garden. He had been staring in at her while she had been oblivious to anything but her own frozen terror. In a moment of instant, uncontrollable fury she found herself scrabbling with the latch and before she knew what she was doing she was out on the front path. 'What the hell are you doing here, spying on me!' she yelled.

She was calling into the empty night. Whoever had been there had gone. Only the gate, swinging in the wind, showed where someone had hurriedly left. The road was deserted. Arwel's house was in darkness.

30

Meryn helped himself to some more coffee. They had been sitting over breakfast for some time. Charles had phoned early to say he was driving back to Cardiff for a departmental meeting. When the call ended, Cadi had fallen silent, staring down at the phone in her hand. Had he sounded a bit strained? She hoped he hadn't been put off by everything that was happening and decided to give up on the meadow. On her. Meryn glanced at her. She was looking exhausted, and he had heard the drop in her voice as she wished Charles a safe journey.

She had told him about her experiences the night before, including her sighting of someone in her front garden. 'Of course, it might have been my imagination.' She sighed.

'You should have called me. I wasn't asleep.'

'I know. I saw your light under the door. I just had so much to think about and I didn't want to have to deal with Ifan as well. I had finally seen the marching soldiers and understood where they were going, why they were here. And before that I had been dreaming or watching or imagining Branwen who was dreaming or watching or imagining what was happening at home in Wales when she was somewhere in Germany – or France, I'm not even sure where – and she was trying to warn

Macsen about the men who vowed to assassinate him. But I know they don't succeed because I know what happens to him in history and I can't bear it.' She broke off, unable to go on. 'Why, Meryn? Why can I see all this if I can't change history? Branwen can't change history. It's all an echo. A pointless echo.' She shook her head, shocked to find herself near to tears.

Meryn sat back in his chair. He looked thoughtful as he sipped his coffee. 'I can't answer your questions, Cadi. I can only assume that there are no reasons we should pick up the echoes of the past, except that of course the past is there. On all sorts of levels it is still with us. Some people are aware of it and some are not. The echoes are there, but perhaps they're no more meaningful than the voice that comes back from the darkness in a cave when we shout up into the unseen shadows. And if we accept the premise that there are many parallel options in the present as to the way the future will pan out before us, perhaps we can learn—'

'Can we?' she interrupted.

He smiled. 'Oh yes, I think we can assume that.'

'So we have a choice?'

'No, Cadi, that's not what I mean. I think it's perhaps easier to see time as a bagatelle board. There's no knowing where the ball will fall with each pull of the spring. We can't judge which energies and forces will come into play at any particular second. I think we can – some people can – influence the fall of the dice, to mix my board games, but even then there are too many options, too many possibilities ever to predict the future.'

'And yet Branwen can do it. For her the future has already happened. And her present is our past.'

He grinned. 'It's all relative, Cadi. Look, you're worn out. It's too early in the morning for this level of philosophy. Let's leave it at that for now, shall we?'

She nodded with a rueful smile. 'I suppose we have to. But Ifan is in the present. Perhaps I should concentrate on him.'

'Indeed. Simple precautions there, I think. Keep your kitchen blind drawn, even in the daytime.' They both glanced at the window where they could see the climbing rose flowering gloriously outside the window; as they watched a car flashed past and disappeared down the road. The rainclouds had vanished in the night and sunshine was pouring in, lighting up the kitchen, sending patches of warmth across the floor. He got up and went over to the window, pulling the cord. The room became shady. 'And don't wander around at night on your own.'

'Even in my own garden?'

'Even in your own garden. Anyone could walk through your side gate or push through that hedge if they wanted to.'

'You don't think . . . You don't actually think that Ifan is a threat to my safety?'

'I've no idea. Although, I suppose everything is a possibility. Did you mention his name to the police sergeant who came to interview you?'

She shook her head. 'Ifan owns the field. Or at least his company does, as far as I can gather, so they know he exists, but I don't think anyone has actually seen him round here except his own employees. I can't even be sure that I really saw him at the window last night. I'm probably the only person who knows, or guesses, that there might be a personal element in all this, apart from Chris and Mel. And Sally.' And Charles. Who had gone.

'So the police need to know about him. I'm sure they've clocked him as being around, because he's involved in the development plan, but you must make sure he's on the police radar. After all, you're being stalked, Cadi. Did you report him after you broke up with him?'

She shook her head. 'I was just so relieved he'd gone. But you're right. The police could at least question him. Why not? It might rattle his cage.' She gave a grim smile. 'And if the gossip Charles picked up is true, his wife has left him because he was violent towards her.'

'Then what are you waiting for?' Meryn stood up. He wandered over to the desk and picked up her last batch of notes. 'I think I might take these upstairs. Meditate with our friend Branwen. See if she's amenable to two-way transmissions.'

Cadi stared at him. 'You're serious?'

He winked. 'It's worth a try. And meanwhile, why don't you pop up to the mill and get some of their delicious pastries for our lunch. It would be good for you to stretch your legs; you'll be perfectly safe in daylight and you might pick up some more gossip from Chris. Then when you come back you might feel like doing some more writing.'

In seconds Meryn had disappeared upstairs.

'You have to come back to Britannia with me.' Branwen was sitting with Elen in one of the courtyards of the palace at Augusta Treverorum. The nurses had brought the children outside to play. Sevira and Maxima were busy with their dolls, earnestly taking off their clothing and re-dressing them in their night-shifts before tucking them up side by side in a beautifully carved miniature cradle made for them by one of Macsen's army carpenters. Anwn was drawing with a stylus on a wax tablet and Owain and Peblig were throwing a ball for two puppies, smuggled into the palace by one of their nurses, while Flavius Victor had climbed onto his mother's lap. He was sucking his thumb, watching his brothers with wistful concentration. 'Why don't you go and play with the others?' Elen gave him a gentle push. He resisted, putting his arms around her neck. She sighed. 'Macsen has been too hard on him. He's only a baby and yet since he was made the imperial heir he is expected to sit in on council meetings and watch the men parade.'

Branwen nodded, tight-lipped. 'All the more reason to come away. You have to bring the children. If he doesn't give you permission, then we should go without it.'

'And how far would I get without his permission?' Elen buried her face in the little boy's hair. 'He would send half the army after us.'

'Only half?' Branwen sneered. 'He might try but he would never find us if we go alone and secretly. I traversed the forests and hills of Gaul with the imperial messenger. I kept my wits about me and my eyes open. I made contact with the men of the trees and the gods of the country and they will protect us if I ask. No one will catch us. We have to get those children away.' She was watching Elen with her son, her expression one of such sorrow that Elen felt a shiver of apprehension.

They were interrupted by the tutor Macsen had appointed to Flavius Victor. He walked up to them and bowed as the boy scrambled hastily off his mother's lap. 'I was sent to find the little emperor,' he said stiffly, addressing the air somewhere above Elen's head. He stooped and picked up the toy sword lying on the floor at their feet, handing it to his charge. The other children had all stopped playing and were staring at him nervously. Behind him, the two nurses approached cautiously, obviously expecting some kind of reprimand and Elen realised that he had assumed an authority over the nurseries she knew nothing about. She rose to her feet. 'I will send the prince to you when we have finished here. You may wait for him outside.'

She saw the flash of anger in his eyes, but he said nothing, bowing meekly and withdrawing without argument. She bent and took the sword out of Victor's hand. 'Is it time for your lessons?' she asked quietly. He nodded. 'Then you may go. Leave the sword with me.'

She and Branwen watched as the boy reluctantly made his way out of the room.

Elen tightened her lips. 'I suppose the eldest has to have special treatment.'

'But surely, he isn't the eldest,' Branwen put in.

Elen gave a grim smile. 'No. But apparently Ceindrech's sons don't count. Macsen already has plans for my two girls. Their husbands are chosen. I have been told their names.'

'Told!' Branwen's voice shot up with indignation.

Elen smiled. 'I have his agreement that will not happen until they are of age. He is emperor, Branwen. His children have value, just as I had to my father. I had no choice in my husband. You of all people know that. His only concession was that they cannot go until I say that they are old enough, and with that I have to be content.'

'All the more reason to go away now. With the children. All the children,' Branwen added. 'You know there is danger. The followers of Mithras—'

'Have no quarrel with children. Children are not initiates. Even if the men you saw in the temple escaped the ambush of the warrior tribes of the hills of the west, the fortress here is guarded, and if they try to reach the emperor they will be cut down without mercy. The children are safe.' She walked across the room, spun on her heel and walked back, tense with anger. 'No, Branwen. You have done your duty and warned us of what the men from Segontium plan, but that is all you needed to do. Thank you for your services. You have done enough. I want you to go home now. Back to the palace of my father and the oppidum where you were born. That is where you are needed.'

'Needed!' Branwen turned to face her. 'I am needed here with you. I see what is going to happen in the future. It is too late for your father's palace.'

'Too late? What do you mean, too late?' Elen stopped in her tracks, the words reverberating round in her head.

'It is burned to the ground. Surely your husband's messengers told you.'

She stared at Branwen, rigid with disbelief. 'Burned?'

'Yes, burned.'

'And Macsen knew this? He didn't tell me.' She fell silent. 'And my people?' she whispered. 'The women who served me?' All but a chosen few had been sent back home when the armies were readied to cross into Gaul and Elen finally accepted the fact that she had to follow her husband and his imperial ambitions into the heart of the empire. She had wanted to keep them safe.

'All safe as far as I know.' Branwen relented a little. 'They had word that the raiders were coming and fled up to the oppidum where the men would make sure they were safe until your brother came to clear the countryside of raiders. But the palace itself is destroyed.'

Elen went to stand in the doorway, looking out into the garden. Behind her the nurses gathered the children up and with a look at her rigid shoulders and clenched fists ushered them away to the nurseries.

'It was you who warned them the raiders were coming, with your magic scrying bowl.' Elen said quietly. She shuddered as fragments of memory surfaced then sank back into the shadows. 'You saved them. You are always trying to save us.'

Branwen didn't answer. Behind her Elen turned and went to sit on one of the couches. 'What do you see for my children? Tell me.'

'I see them back safely in the lands of their fathers, of the Silurian peoples and of the Ordovices.' Branwen shook her head sadly. 'All save your little boy Victor. For him I can see nothing and that is why I want to take him, above all of them, back to Albion where he will be safe.'

Elen bit her lip. 'Tell me what you see for my girls and their destiny?'

Branwen sighed. 'Your daughter Sevira and her husband will be the progenitors of a line of kings stretching far into the future.' She gave an enigmatic smile.

Elen sighed. 'Macsen has promised Sevira to his general, Prince Vortigern.' Macsen had great plans for Vortigern, in whom he saw much promise. That much she knew. He had sent the young man back to Britannia where he had been entrusted with overseeing a vast swathe of the province under the over-lordship of her father.

'So, who has he chosen for Maxima?' Branwen's gaze was implacable.

'She is promised to another of his generals, Ennodius. Both are men grown. Both are respected and trustworthy, but my girls are still children.' A tear rolled down Elen's cheek.

'And the thing now is to keep them safe until they are of an age to marry,' Branwen put in gently. 'I see Maxima as travelling to distant lands. But she will thrive. You need have no fear for her. So, my Elen, if they have a future written in the stars, then it is up to us to make sure they live safely to fulfil their destiny.'

Elen wiped away her tears. 'And my babies, Anwn, Owain and Peblig?'

Branwen smiled. 'I see no disaster for them. They will thrive. Anwn and Owain will be kings; their sons will be kings.'

'And Peblig?'

Branwen shrugged her shoulders. 'He too will live to be famous through history.'

'And me?'

Branwen nodded. 'You too will live, my Elen, and your name will live after you. For ever.'

Elen shook her head with a sad smile. 'That I doubt.' She was silent for a moment, then she went on in a whisper, 'And Macsen?'

'He is the author of his own destiny. My powers do not see that far. He has been warned of his immediate danger. I can do no more to advise him.' Branwen's expression had become implacable.

Elen studied her face, aware of the icy chill spreading through her bones, and slowly she nodded her head. 'I will speak to him, although it is hard to get near him alone these days.'

'Indeed.' Branwen gave her a speculative look.

Elen blushed. 'Indeed,' she repeated. 'Go home, Branwen, please. Take my blessings and my love to the mountains of home. I shall not forget them and if it is at all possible I will return.'

Alone in her bedchamber Branwen began to pack her few belongings into her satchel. By dawn she would be gone. Even without Elen and her children she planned to go home via the byways, through the forests, living off the land and the friendship of the tribal peoples of the unseen places. She had no wish to see Macsen again or the men of his entourage. Their future was no longer her concern.

With a sigh she sat down on the bed. Night was coming and the guest chamber was lit by lamps, filling the air with the scent of olive oil and of something else. She sniffed cautiously. Surely she could smell the scrying herbs of home.

'Branwen.'

The voice came from the shadows from undreamt of distances.

31

Cadi glanced up as Meryn slowly descended the stairs, bringing with him a faint scent of burning herbs, mugwort and
vervain and sandalwood. 'So, did you manage to contact
Branwen?'

He walked across the room and threw himself down onto
the sofa by the back window. 'Yes and no.'

Cadi smiled. 'Always the enigma.'

'Indeed. I saw her, in a small shadowy room, lit by oil lamps.
She was sitting on a narrow bed with a pack of some kind beside
her. I think she heard me, but she made a sign against the evil
eye and the air around her shimmered and dissolved and the
sighting faded away.'

'She had your number.'

'It appears so. I will try again. Next time you write about her,
can you write into your record that I'm a good guy and only
want to help.'

'You really think that's worth a try?'

'Why not?'

Cadi hadn't expected Rachel to call in again later that morning.
'Are you here to solve the crime of the Roman in the grave with

a bullet in his head like Sherlock Holmes, Uncle Meryn?' Rachel did her best to grin.

'I wish I was.' Meryn greeted her with a hug.

'How did the trip to Cardiff go?' Cadi closed the door behind her.

'Good and bad. That's why I wanted to call in on my way home. To discuss it with you, Cadi.' Rachel dived into her bucket-sized shoulder bag and produced a bottle of champagne. 'Can we stick this in your freezer for a few minutes. It's got a bit warm in the car.'

'Champagne usually means good.' Cadi glanced at her. 'Why don't we have lunch outside on the terrace? I'll lay everything out while the bottle chills.'

'You may not want to drink to anything but my perdition when I tell you what my news is,' Rachel put in as they opened the doors into the garden and made their way outside. Last night's rain had dried up and the air smelt of grass and roses and jasmine.

'I think you'd better tell us instead of dropping dark hints,' Cadi said when at last they were sitting in front of the food. She had brought ham and pâté and some salmon and asparagus quiche and miniature pasties from the deli, together with Chris's sourdough bread and local cheese. 'So, what happened?'

Rachel took a deep breath. 'I had a meeting with the potential buyer's agent. His boss has seen my work online and at some local gallery. He likes my work so much he wants to give me a one-woman exhibition in Cardiff.'

'But that's wonderful!' Cadi exclaimed.

'Except I haven't enough work for a single-hander and he wants me to give up all my other commitments for the next few months to concentrate on producing enough larger paintings.' She gave Cadi an anguished look. 'It's like a dream come true.'

There was a moment of intense silence, then Cadi shook her head. 'You have to go for it. Of course you must. Macsen will wait.'

'But our contract?'

'I'm sure the publisher will understand. After all, a big exhibition will make you even more famous and desirable as an illustrator.' Cadi smiled.

Rachel looked even more unhappy. 'Apparently he doesn't think our little books of poems are quite the right look. He said I might have to stop doing that.'

'Oh, surely he can't do that. How can he dictate what you do?' Cadi was incredulous. 'There's no hurry. We can wait for the poems, but to forbid you from working with me—' She broke off. 'Who is this person?'

Rachel shook her head. 'An American.'

'Are you sure?

'Why?'

Cadi shook her head. 'Just a paranoid suspicion. Don't worry. You must do what you think best. But I don't see how he can hold you to a contract like that. He's buying your pictures, not you, for goodness' sake.'

'He's not buying me, but he said he's prepared to buy my cottage to give me somewhere secure to work.'

Cadi stared at her.

'The guy said he loves my seascapes, my Welsh countryside scenes, all the things I love painting. My home would be safe, Cadi. I wouldn't have to move.'

Silently Meryn stood up. He made his way indoors, reappearing a few moments later with the champagne bottle and three glasses. 'I think we should drink to Rachel's success,' he said softly. The others were watching as he wrestled the cork out of the bottle. Cadi held out a glass.

'Cadi, you can still write your poetry, and this will give you the chance to work on your story about Elen and her Macsen as historical characters. Discuss it with your publisher,' Meryn went on thoughtfully as he filled their glasses. 'All I suggest is that you don't sign anything, Rachel, until you have had a solicitor look at the contract.'

There followed a moment of electric silence.

'You've already signed it, haven't you?' Cadi said at last. Her voice was flat.

Rachel nodded miserably. 'I had to. They said otherwise he would look for someone else to sponsor.'

* * *

'You thought it might be Ifan, didn't you,' Meryn said when Rachel had at last gone home.

Cadi nodded. 'It's the kind of thing he might do. He hated Rachel. He was intensely jealous of anyone close to me and she was very much in the firing line for a time. Literally. He threatened to burn down her house and he despised our "little books", as he called them. The phrase jumped out at me when she mentioned it.'

They had both looked at Rachel's copy of the contract and it was drawn up for someone with an address in New York. None of them had recognised his name but when they checked online he appeared to have sponsored several one-man exhibitions in the past, two in Scotland, two in northern England and one in London.

'I think you have to accept that he's genuine,' Meryn said. 'Your Ifan could not be that devious. Or if he is, he didn't think of this one. It would have taken a lot of organising. Darling girl, I think you've got to try and look on the bright side. This lets you off the hook. You can follow up our story here, as far as it goes, and you can still write your poems so they're ready for Rachel when she's fulfilled her side of the contract. And the bonus is, she keeps her home.'

'For now.' Cadi was still determined to be worried. 'What happens when she's finished this man's paintings? Is he still going to keep the cottage for her? After all, he'll own it.'

'We'll have to wait and see. I'm sure she thought of that when she signed the contract.'

'And if all her paintings belong to him, she's not going to make any money out of the sales, is she.'

'She shares a percentage with him.' Meryn leaned forward and put his hand over hers. 'You didn't read it properly, Cadi. That contract was OK.'

She laughed. 'So, you're not only working with Charles for MI5. You're a solicitor now.'

He tapped his nose. 'As good as. No. It's just that I read it more carefully than you did. So, let's forget Rachel for now and concentrate on your story. I will try and link up with Branwen again, but in the meantime you seem able to do it effortlessly. So, let's see what she does next?'

'You want me to do it now?'

He glanced at her. 'No. You're exhausted. I don't want you to do anything until you want to or it happens spontaneously. What we need to do is have a quiet evening.'

Once again he went up to his room early, saying he was tired, but when she went up herself a couple of hours later she could still see the line of light under his door and hear the soft strains of a Chopin nocturne drifting across the landing. She let herself into her own bedroom and closed the door softly behind her, then made her way across to the window without turning on the light. Looking out she saw a figure standing in the moon shadows on the far side of the narrow street.

Tiptoeing downstairs she eased the front door open and peered out. There was no one there. She walked soundlessly to the gate and pulled it open. Was that a figure in the distance, walking up the road away from the village towards the meadow? She ran a few steps after it.

'Cadi!' The voice came from close behind her.

She let out a little scream of fright. 'Charles! What on earth are you doing?'

'Sssh!' He put his finger to his lips. 'The same as you, presumably. Trying to see where he's going.'

'Where's who going?'

'It's John Davies. I followed him all the way from his digs. He's been spying on you for about half an hour, and seemed quite pissed off he couldn't see through your blinds. He was up close, trying to peer through the corner of the kitchen window. He went to your side gate and spent some time staring over it, then he came back to the front window. He gave up in the end and he's headed on up the road. I thought I would see where he's going at this time of night.'

'You mustn't, Charles. Supposing he saw you.'

'If he saw me I would ask him what he thought he was doing.' Charles stopped and stood facing her. 'I'm sorry, Cadi – I don't want to interfere, but I'm scared for you. That man is stalking you. There's no question about it and you walked out of the house alone in the dark! Did you know he was there?'

'I thought I saw someone—'

'And you came out to see?' He sounded utterly incredulous.

'Uncle Meryn is here.'

'Standing guard over you with a gun?'

'Well, no. He's upstairs listening to Chopin.'

For a moment they stood looking at each other in the half-light of the moon then both burst into smothered laughter. 'Come back indoors,' she said quietly, 'and have a drink and then you can tell me how you got on in Cardiff. Let Ifan walk on in the dark, if that's what he wants to do. Good riddance.'

In his guest bedroom Meryn heard the quiet laughter from downstairs and nodded. Almost reluctantly he turned down his music. Time for him to leave. Metaphorically speaking, of course. He was pretty sure that Branwen was home. From his window which faced across the back garden, he could see the tall silhouette of the hillside beyond the meadow, topped by the oppidum of the Silures tribe. There were cooking fires up there tonight, and the glow from the burning logs silhouetted the cone-shaped roofs of the houses. If he opened his window a crack he could smell the roasting venison and hear the sound of music carried on the wind, some kind of pipe and now and then the gentle more melodious sound of a harp or perhaps a crwth drifting in and out over the trees. They were happy up there and secure, while below, the cold ashes of what was once a magnificent Roman-style villa sank into the mud. He frowned, trying to see the ruins more closely. There were crumbling walls there, hard to see in the dark, and the remnants of pillars. A coloured floor caught a stray flash of moonlight and he glimpsed the outline of a broken column, half hidden in the tangled grasses.

And then he saw her; Branwen. She was standing up there on the earthen ramparts of the hill fort looking down across the trees towards the ruins, just as he was. Her eyes were narrowed as she sensed him watching and she crossed her fingers in the sign against the evil eye.

'I am your friend. Elen's friend,' he whispered. 'I am Cadi's teacher.'

He saw the confusion in her face and felt a cold wall between himself and the woman coalesce and thicken. She did not want to communicate with him. She wasn't afraid, though. She had her own protections against the liminal worlds. Even as he watched she was fading and the hillside was disappearing into the drifting mist.

He smudged the room with the fragrant smoke of incense, whispered a blessing on the souls of the men and women from the past, even now still wandering the field in lonely, lost confusion and opened his window wide before climbing at last into bed. From downstairs he could hear the murmur of conversation and the occasional subdued laughter. He considered Charles for a moment, surprised by his own almost paternal feelings about Cadi. She was such an independent soul, but he thought, at heart, lonely. He hoped Charles would be good for her.

32

News of the slaughter of twelve men from the garrison at Segontium, twelve men out on manoeuvre in the mountains, twelve men who just happened to be initiates of the Mithraean temple, and the supposed consignment of their bodies to the icy depths of Llyn Llydaw on the slopes of Yr Wyddfa, reached Elen before her husband heard the news. His response was a raised eyebrow, hers a quiet thank you to Branwen, wherever she now was.

Macsen was distracted by other more pressing events.

His decision to march south towards Italia and Roma was made. However popular, efficient and unopposed Macsen's rule over Britannia, Gaul, Hispania, and North Africa had been, he was not content with half the empire. He wanted more. And his spies had told him that Valentinian was at last about to make a stand. The boy, with Theodosius's support, was ready to fight him the moment he reached Italia.

Macsen told Elen the evening he first received details of his rival's decision. He had put his army on notice of imminent departure and only then did he tell his wife what the future held. She had already heard the gossip of course; the news had flown round the fortress at Treverorum as soon as the

271

commanders of the army and his ruling generals had left the imperial audience chamber. When he arrived in their private apartments Elen was waiting for him, tight-lipped. 'So, finally you come to tell me.'

He seemed surprised that she already knew.

'The entire town knows, down to the lowliest slave,' she retorted, simmering with anger. 'It appears I am the only person you forgot to tell. Well, I have news for you. This is the moment when I return to Britannia and to my own kingdom and my children will return with me.'

'No.' He was in no mood for opposition. 'You will accompany me at the front line of my forces and my children will all be with us. Flavius Victor will ride at my side. Not in actual battle, of course, if there is one,' it was a small enough concession, 'but until then my men will see that my son and heir is with me.'

'He's a little boy!'

'He is my co-emperor, I have given him the title Augustus.' He was implacable. 'Valentinian is a boy too. He is sixteen years old. He will not fight. Not when it comes to it.'

She knew there was no point in arguing. White to the lips, she turned away from him, arms folded into her shawl as she walked away from him. They were alone. She knew that her servants and her ladies were huddled in the next room as near the door as possible, already knowing what was to happen, already knowing her arguments would be fruitless. The smaller children were safe in their nurseries with their own attendants, but they too had probably picked up on the general atmosphere. She wasn't sure where Victor was. His tutor had collected him from his schoolroom earlier saying the emperor had sent for him. No doubt the little boy already knew he was to ride his beautiful chestnut pony beside his father at the head of the entire army, not for a parade, but to take possession of Urbs Aeterna, the rightful capital of the greatest empire there had ever been. He would be proud, a little nervous but knowing he mustn't show it. He wouldn't look back for his mother or the nursemaids or the cuddly woollen rabbit he secretly hugged at night. He was a prince, a royal child, son of the emperor and of the royal line of Britannia and he would one day be sole emperor of the whole of the Roman Empire. He was born to lead.

'No!'

It wasn't Elen speaking, it was Cadi as she threw down her pen. She looked at her watch. It was 1.30 a.m. Charles had left a couple of hours before to walk back through the silent village. They had talked for a long time, companionably, at first in the quiet dark of the garden, then as the grass became cold and damp with dew, indoors, where Cadi lit the fire, and they sat together with glasses of wine, staring into the flames. 'Do you think Ifan was in the meadow?' she asked him.

'I think it's unlikely. He wouldn't want to risk being questioned if there was anyone around. It may be his land but he obviously doesn't want people to know about his connection to you or he would have mentioned it by now. I should think he wants to keep a low profile at the moment.'

'But he was willing to risk walking up here and hanging around my house.'

'I doubt if that was a rational decision.'

'You think he couldn't help himself?' she smiled. She took a sip from her glass and then bent forward to throw another log on the fire. 'What a mess.'

He wasn't sure if she was referring to Ifan or the body in the field, or the whole development debacle.

The room filled with the scent of the apple branch burning, fragrant and spicy in the dim light of the single lamp on the desk. They sat in silence for a while.

'Did Steve give you any clue as to when they will have the results of the carbon tests?' she asked at last. While he was in Cardiff, Charles had dropped in at the lab and Steve had shown him the bones. The two men had bent over the table studying the skeleton, which was accompanied now by an assortment of other bones from deeper in the grave. Steve had pointed to various slight differences in colour and consistency. The original skeleton had been dated to the modern era. The 1930s fitted. The others appeared to be Roman. The confusion had arisen from the extra bones that had found their way into the original dig and from the accumulation of artefacts, some fourth century, including the shoes that it had been assumed were worn by the man shot by George Harris.

They looked at each other and Cadi shook her head. 'Are they going to do the tests again?'

'What else can they do? They brought in an osteoarchaeologist. The theory is that this was a Roman-period burial pit. By good or bad luck, Harris dug a hole in the middle of it and buried his victim there without ever realising there were other bodies there already, probably not much further down. If there are any anomalies with our bones, owing to their possible weird origins, it would in those circumstances be very hard to prove. Which is probably just as well.' He grinned.

'They'll never work it out, will they.' Cadi took another sip from her glass. 'Is Steve coming back to work on the grave?'

'He certainly wants to.' Charles gave a wry smile. 'But I doubt anyone, even Meryn, is going to suggest the scenario we suspect as an option.' He downed his last drop of wine and stood up. 'I must go. It's very late. Cadi,' his voice took on an awkward note, 'is it all right if I come back in the morning? I don't want to intrude. I don't want you to feel I've imposed myself on this situation. Please say if I make you feel uncomfortable.'

She looked up at him, horrified. 'You're not intruding. Of course you must come back.' She stood up and reached for his hand. 'I'm sorry if I've been a bit touchy. This whole business with Ifan is . . . It's hard. I'd like you to be here.' She smiled. 'You're part of the team.'

He grinned. 'Good. Then I'll see you in the morning.' Gently, he withdrew his hand. 'And we can decide if there's anything we can or should do? All three of us.' He turned towards the door.

'You will be careful, Charles, won't you. If Ifan thought you and I are . . .' she trailed off, embarrassed. 'That we are friends. He is – or he was – an insanely jealous man. I keep remembering how scary he was, and how awful those last months with him were. If he's out there somewhere—'

'Don't worry about me.' Charles grinned. 'Lock the door

behind me. Among my hidden talents – in fact, one of my few hidden talents – is that I have a black belt in karate. I know it's hard to believe, and it was a comparatively long time ago, but I think if your Ifan jumped me he would be in for quite a shock.' He winked.

She closed the door silently after him, slid the bolt and quickly checked the back door in the pantry for the umpteenth time before going over to the fire, where she stood for a while looking down at the burning embers. When she returned to her desk and picked up the pen, she was hardly aware that she had done it.

Elen rode with her children, all except Victor, amongst the army followers. She refused to go to the head of the long columns of the massed cohorts and Macsen didn't insist. As the men marched out of the fortress the sound of their hobnailed sandals echoed round the city of Treverorum. They were bound south-eastwards, destined to confront the young Emperor Valentinian in his base at Mediolanum.

The legions made camp at last outside the city of Lugdunum, which Macsen designated their temporary staging post. He took over the old palace buildings on the heights of the hill for himself and his entourage. Elen found herself in the imperial apartments with the children. They were now on the very edge of Gaul and still miles from their target ensconced at Mediolanum. Valentinian knew they were coming but their messengers had already informed them that he had no intention of fleeing. He was, they were told, strutting up and down the walls of his city shaking his fists in defiance at anyone who would dare to threaten him. Macsen gave a grim smile when he heard the boy's response to his approach. 'Stupid child! He will change his mind when we get closer. But for now I will let him sweat while we rest and allow our troops some time to train and replenish their stores. Then we will march on to Mediolanum.' He put his arm around Elen's shoulders. 'Are you not pleased I made you come? The children are enjoying themselves. Our boy trains with the men. He is an excellent rider. And the little ones are thriving.' He turned his head slightly towards the long passage which led to the children's quarters. Shrill shouts and laughter echoed towards them, followed by the distant sounds of a remonstration from an impatient adult voice.

Elen smiled. 'They do sound happy. They're tired after the long days on the road. They'll enjoy staying in one place for a time.'

The door opened and Marcellinus joined them to discuss the state banquets for the city dignitaries they were to host once they were settled in. The city dignitaries in question had no doubt been summarily displaced from their homes by Macsen's outriders to allow room for the emperor and his family and his generals to make themselves comfortable in the old palace and the beautiful townhouses of the city. Macsen settled into his office with his scribes and contented himself with sending off yet another letter to the young emperor, demanding that he amend the agreement they had made three years before and recognise him as sole emperor of the West with his son as co-emperor. Then he sat back to wait for an answer. It was a respite. For a few weeks his young family settled into something resembling a routine. Elen saw little of Macsen and, she realised, she didn't much care. Life was too stressed and uneasy when he was there. His endless energy was exhausting, and his constant demands on poor little Victor made her feel helplessly angry for the child, though the little boy was doing his best to imitate his father and learn his duty, a duty that made him arrogant and hard to control and a nightmare for his older sisters. The three smaller boys he ignored. They were too young to be rivals and he barely noticed them at all. Only Elen saw the softer, frightened child still there beneath the braggadocio and because of that he avoided her whenever he could, only crawling onto her couch, his thumb in his mouth, when life became too much for him, snuggling into her arms, hiding his tears and trying to pretend he wasn't there.

No answer came to the emperor's letter and the date for leaving Lugdunum was set. The soothsayer came four days before they were due to leave the city and march eastwards towards Mediolanum, the centre of Valentinian's resistance.

The man had, it appeared, demanded to see the emperor. His demand was refused, so he turned his attention to the empress. Autumn had come early to the palace and the wind whistled through the corridors and huge pillared chambers. Elen was huddling by a brazier in one of the reception rooms, talking to the children's tutor. It wasn't only young Victor who was learning now, all the others were being given lessons, even little Peblig. The tutor bowed and retired after giving the visitor a haughty look, unable to believe that the empress had allowed the stranger to approach her. The long white beard declared him a non-Roman and his robe, though clean and far from ragged, was roughly woven and without decoration. He carried a staff and wore a pouch on a long ornate leather strap over one shoulder. That at least declared him a man of means. Elen guessed he might be a Druid, but did not show any recognition. Instead she waved her attendants back to the far end of the chamber and demanded his name.

'I am Cador.' His gaze swept over her and his eyes narrowed. 'You recognise my calling, I suspect. And will not be surprised to learn that I bring warnings. The emperor will not listen to me so I come to you. We are kin in blood, you and I. I come from Albion; my father was a chieftain among the Silures, your own people.' She waited, her attention fully on him though she sensed the restlessness amongst some of the crowd at the far end of the room. They could not have heard his words, but they were suspicious.

'Greetings, my friend,' she said it very quietly. 'What do you have to tell me?'

'My dreams tell me the future.'

She looked at him uneasily. 'And what do you see?'

'Your husband. If he does not turn back now, he will never return to the west. And neither will your eldest son.'

She felt a clutch at her throat. 'He does not plan to return to the west, my friend. He is set on reaching the eternal city.'

'Theodosius will not allow it.'

'Theodosius is far away.'

'Valentinian will flee from Italia, and that will encourage Macsen in his dreams, but they are fruitless. At least save your children, lady. They are blameless and they are of the blood of Albion, the sacred isle. They are destined to breed a line of kings such as the land will never see again.' He was staring into the distance, his gaze fixed on some distant vision.

She had grown cold all over. 'My husband will not listen to me. Warnings have been given before and he refused to listen. Besides' – she reminded herself – 'magic and thus foretelling the future is forbidden by the teaching of Christ.'

He drew himself up to his full height with an air of wounded dignity. 'I do not read the entrails of animals or ritually slaughter fellow men, as you should know, lady. I merely dream of the future and god, your god or perhaps my gods, give me messages so that disaster can be averted. I have listened and passed on the information. The rest is up to you.' He turned away slowly.

'Stop!' The word rang out loudly before she could stop herself. She stepped back, her hand to her mouth, as everyone in the room turned towards them. 'I am sorry. I should not have accused you. I believe your messages, but my husband' – she shrugged her shoulders in despair – 'will not.'

'I have done my part.' He half turned towards her, then he shook his head slowly. 'I can do no more.'

33

'And neither can I.' Cadi found she was whispering to herself. 'I know what is going to happen. I have to stop it.'

Daylight was filtering into the room around the blinds. She glanced at her watch. It was morning. Her head cushioned on her arms, she had fallen asleep over her notebook. Wearily she staggered to her feet and went over to the kitchen, pulling up the blind. The tiny front garden was full of sunlight, the puddles on the road beyond the gate sending glittering reflections into the hedges. Having filled the kettle, she watched it while it boiled.

'Good morning, Cadi.' Meryn had come downstairs without her hearing him. 'Any spare coffee going?'

She nodded. 'I fell asleep at my desk. Too much going on in the story.'

He nodded without comment.

'She was warned by a soothsayer that the end would be bad. But she doesn't take any notice. Or at least she knows that Macsen won't.'

'Macsen can't.' Meryn watched as she reached for the coffee jar and spooned ground coffee into the jug. 'It's not in his nature. Besides, what kind of emperor would he be if he turned tail.'

'Julius Caesar didn't, did he, and look where that led.' Cadi gave a rueful smile. 'And it wasn't Branwen this time. It was an old man with a long white beard.'

'Splendid.' Meryn reached out for the mug she had poured for him. 'I was beginning to think that all the soothsayers and wise people of old were women.'

'She thought he was a Druid.' Cadi picked up her own mug and went over to her desk. Sitting down, she flipped back through the pages of scribbled writing. 'See, here. I describe him. He had a white beard and a long staff and a satchel-type bag over his shoulder.'

'Of course Druids had a fantastic reputation in those days and amongst other things they were known as fortune tellers.' Meryn took a gulp of coffee. 'Once they had managed to convince the Romans they didn't do human sacrifice, or eat each other, they were perfectly acceptable, even welcome. Rich when you think about it, when the Romans themselves had thought up the most barbaric ways of putting people to death ever invented by man.'

'I don't think Macsen trusted the Druids.'

'It sounds as if he didn't trust anyone who tried to come between him and his ambition.'

'So he wouldn't even listen to their warnings.'

'All the more reason. Male logic, I'm afraid.' He grinned.

She sighed and stood up. 'I'm glad you said that and not me. I'm going to go up and have a shower to wake me up properly.'

'Can I look at your notes while you're upstairs?'

'Of course. If you can read them. I'll print them up later.'

Walking over to the bathroom window to grab her toothbrush from the glass on the sill, she glanced down into the street. There was someone out there, walking away from the house. A man. She felt a prickle of alarm. He was too far away to see clearly, but there was something about the way he walked she recognised. It was Ifan, she was sure of it.

When she went back downstairs she found Charles had arrived. The men had made fresh coffee and were engaged in deep conversation.

'Ifan has been out and about this morning,' Charles said

without preamble. 'I followed him down the road. He hung around outside here for a while, went to look at Meryn's car, obviously suspicious about who was staying here, and then he walked on up the road to the meadow gate. He didn't go in. He stood looking over it for a while then he turned back and I had to duck in to someone's front garden and hide behind their hedge till he had gone by.' He laughed. 'If there are any reports of sinister goings on in the village, that will be my part in the activities, I'm afraid, though I don't think anyone saw me. I think it's one of the holiday homes and there's no one there right now. There was no car there, anyway. Thank God!'

Cadi sat down at the table with them and reached for the coffee pot. 'What am I going to do about him?'

'Nothing yet. We were discussing it just now,' Meryn said. 'You were going to contact the police. Did you do it in the end?'

She shook her head. 'I wasn't sure it was him then.'

'Well, you need to be very careful, but he hasn't done anything actually threatening to you, has he.' Meryn took a sip of coffee. 'I think you were right to hold back and I think we want to find out a bit more about what his motives are.'

'And is that your official Druidic verdict?' She gave a faint smile.

'It is.' He winked at her.

'Right.' Charles sat forward, his elbows on the table. 'We should decide what to do next. I was wondering if we might go to the local museum. Anything interesting from a Roman site will be there, or it should be. We might find stuff from this village.'

They did. To Cadi's amazement there were a great many finds, dug up in the village gardens over the years, some from the farm, one from the mill, and some from 'the Roman marching camp' in the meadow. There were even several from 'the gamekeeper's cottage'. She stared down at the exhibits in the glass case in amazement. 'Do you think that's my house?' There were several blue pottery beads, various iron nails, some coins, a hair pin and a twisted metal brooch. She glanced at Meryn. 'I wish I could touch them. I don't suppose they would let me.'

He shook his head. 'Too much hassle to ask them, Cadi. Have you never found anything yourself?'

She shook her head. 'I've found lots of bits of broken clay pipes but, to be honest, I'm not sure I would even have noticed a bit of iron or a blackened coin all covered in mud.'

'Perhaps we should borrow a metal detector,' Charles put in, 'especially as you have a fragment of the villa actually in your garden.'

'There's nothing here about a mosaic floor,' Cadi pointed out when they had finished touring the museum. It was in the corner of the local library, about four miles from the village and consisted of one small room dominated by a few glass-fronted wall cupboards and a dusty mannequin of a woman dressed in a betgwn with apron, shawl and tall black hat. Beside her stood the ubiquitous spinning wheel.

Cadi stopped at another display case. 'Look, this is from the oppidum. "Iron Age Fort on Bryndinas Hill. Partially excavated in 1938." I didn't realise anyone had ever found anything at those old hill forts. More beads, this time faded ochre in colour. No nails, in spite of it being Iron Age. Arrowheads, bits of decorated pottery. Such tiny reminders of a once-thriving town.'

The lady in charge of the library didn't know anything about the museum. 'It's been here for years,' she said ruefully. 'Hardly anyone comes to look at it. Sorry I can't tell you more than that.'

'Not very helpful,' Charles said as they walked back down the road to the car. 'When and if we find out more about the meadow site I think we should make a point of trying to improve things in there, especially for the local children. It was not overwhelmingly exciting.'

'It was for me.' Cadi grinned.

'Then perhaps you can do something to convey some of that excitement locally. Maybe give a talk to the children one day.' He laughed out loud at the expression of horror on her face. 'Well, at least have a word with Sally. Isn't she the head teacher there?'

Cadi shook her head. 'Different village, different school.

But I agree it must be worth talking to her about it. She's bound to know someone.'

She didn't. 'It might be a bit uncomfortable to rush in criticising someone else's patch,' she pointed out when they asked her over that evening. 'I will keep it in mind though, and if I think of a way of broaching the subject, I will. I might suggest I take my kids over to the museum when we're discussing the meadow next term, assuming there are exciting Roman finds there. All the kids know about the skeleton. They were hugely excited when they heard about it. While you were all gallivanting round the museum I was at school, of course. Thank goodness it was the last day of term. Blessed holidays now. And I wanted to give you my spare key, Cadi. Please can you keep an eye on my house. I'll be away for a couple of weeks or so with my sister in France.'

'I expect you'll be glad to get away for a bit.' Meryn was pouring out the wine. He passed her a glass. Gemma was asleep beside her on the sofa and he went to perch on the arm next to the little dog. He put out his hand to stroke her gently. Gemma looked up and wagged her tail.

Sally was looking expectantly round the room. 'Is Charles joining us?'

Cadi shook her head. 'He's had to go to another meeting at the university. His professor is planning a reorganisation of the department, hence all these meetings in the vacation.' Out of the corner of her eye she saw Meryn run his hand gently over Gemma's back. The dog looked up briefly, and then settled back to sleep. He left his hand resting lightly over her shoulders as Cadi and Sally chatted about Sally's forthcoming trip and Cadi endured a few gentle jibes about Charles's attentions.

'So did you feel anything?' After Sally had gone home, Cadi turned to Meryn eagerly.

'Her energy field is very depleted, but I couldn't sense anything particularly odd, I'm glad to say.' He reached for the wine bottle and tipped the remaining dregs into Cadi's glass. 'I gave her some healing which will, I hope, help, but I suspect the best tonic of all will be going away for a bit and having Sally to herself.' He threw himself down on the sofa. 'Cadi, I want you to tell me honestly. Am I de trop here? Would you rather I went back home tomorrow?'

'De trop?' She looked at him, confused.

'Would you rather be alone with Charles? I take it there's something going on.'

'No! No, there isn't.' Cadi gave an embarrassed laugh. 'Don't take any notice of Sal and her innuendoes. She's been teasing me about him since the first time I met him. I've only known him a few weeks. We met in the meadow that time when he was dowsing and we have, I suppose, become friends almost without realising it, because of the circumstances, and everything that's going on, but it's nothing more than that. Absolutely not. No, you must stay. I need you. Please.'

'Fair enough.'

Charles appeared later that evening. 'While I was in Cardiff I dropped in at the lab again and Steve gave me a copy of the report.'

Cadi and Meryn looked at each other and then waited in silence.

'To be exact,' he reached into his pocket and produced a sheaf of folded papers, 'they retested various samples from his skull, pelvis, femur and footbones and separately tested scraps of leather from what it was assumed were his shoes. Basically, most of him was 1930s. Pre 1950s is important, apparently, because for ten years or so they were doing atomic testing and it lingered in the atmosphere. Shotgun pellets are inorganic, of course, and no one knows the exact age and provenance of the shotgun so there was no point sending them for analysis. The shoe leather from both shoes was, interestingly, dated at CE 300–400 and appeared to have been on his feet. The foot bones have been sent for retesting. They don't seem to be consistent. They seem to match the shoes rather than the leg bones they were assumed to have been attached to. The other extra bones are also from around the years 300–400 and are almost certainly from the Roman burial pit, so a theory is being posited that there must have been some cross-contamination as far as the feet go. But the osteoarchaeologist seems to think that would be impossible. Not within a single bone.'

He sat back on the sofa and looked at them expectantly.

'Steve knows our theory, I presume?' Meryn asked.

Charles nodded. 'We talked it over. We had to really. I made sure I came over as a bit sceptical in the way I discussed what we suspected, as you can imagine. "I know this sounds crazy" and all that guff. I have my academic reputation to think of.'

'And his reaction to the results?'

'We went for a beer. He started quoting Shakespeare at me. "There are more things in heaven and earth, Horatio" – that sort of thing. Oh, yes, and "knowledge is limited, imagination encircles the world". I don't know who said that.'

'Einstein.' Meryn filled in for him. 'I think that's right. We can and must sidestep science here. We must agree there are times when only poets and philosophers can answer these questions.' He glanced across at Cadi. 'I'm glad to say we have one of each present. I would class myself as halfway to being a philosopher and Cadi is definitely a poet. And you, my friend, are a historian, a perfect member for our triumvirate and possibly the only sane one amongst us, so, between us we ought to be able to provide some plausible theory as to what happened here.'

'Not one that will satisfy the police,' Charles put in.

'Why not? They will surely be happy with the science lab theory that the victim was buried in a pre-existing grave. Once all the bones have been tested and none are found to be modern enough to be of interest to them, my guess is they'll shelve it. As for how our poor victim happened to pop up in front of a man who had taken aim at a rabbit, I have no idea how these things work. I've been looking this up and I gather the carbon-14 tests will date the samples from the moment of burial, so where the specimen actually originated won't show up.'

'I suppose we could suggest the vet takes blood and tissue samples from the little dog,' Charles suggested. 'That might be interesting. But I don't think Sally would go for that, do you?'

'No way,' Cadi spluttered. She glanced a Meryn, who shook his head. 'Anyway, she and Gemma are off to France, so whatever happens next they will be safely out of the way.'

The next step was revealed when Charles received a text message from Steve the next morning as he sat at breakfast in Annabel's dining room.

> My team and I have been asked to do a thorough forensic dig. Starting with the grave site. Looking for the Roman burial pit initially. Starting today. I'm already here. I'll leave your name at the gate so you can come in as a consultant.

Charles called in at Sarnelen Cottage on his way to the meadow. 'I'm sure I can get Meryn in by uttering the magic word "professor".'

'I'm beginning to regret not pursuing an academic career,' Cadi put in ruefully, 'it seems to get you in everywhere, but for now I'm quite happy to stay at home and write. I'm sure you two will fill me in if anything exciting happens.'

It was only an hour later that there was a knock at the front door. Cadi threw down her pen and hurried over to open it, expecting to see Meryn or Charles or both of them. 'Have they found something—'

She broke off in horror. Ifan was standing on the doorstep. She tried to push the door closed but he stepped forward and was inside before she could stop him. 'So, Cadi, how are you?' He was dressed in a formal business suit, and had a leather portfolio under his arm. 'I thought it only polite to call in as we are to be neighbours.'

He hadn't changed much over the years, she realised. He was still a good-looking man, straight-backed and athletic, but his hair was greying and his face more lined. 'You've heard about the unfortunate discovery of a body in the meadow, I take it? It's a damn nuisance. The police seem to be completely baffled, but what can you expect from woodentops in the depths of the countryside? I'm glad to say they've concluded the whole thing is a problem for the archaeologists rather than the coroner. The council have brought in forensic teams to check if there are any other bodies lying about and that will also dispense with this stupid theory that there is a

Roman villa there. I don't suppose it was you who started that rumour?'

'No. I didn't.' She kept her reply short. She folded her arms. 'You look well, Ifan.'

He gave a little bow. 'As do you, although I see you're still not bothered as to what you wear.' She was wearing jeans and a T-shirt, her hair, still damp from the shower, tied back with a green scarf. She opened her mouth to retort, but already he was glancing round the room and she saw his gaze linger over her desk where the lamp floodlit her notebook and pen and various open textbooks. 'Still writing your little poems, I hear.'

'Indeed.' She spoke through clenched teeth.

'Nothing seems to have changed in here.'

'There is no reason why it should.'

'No ambition. That was always one of your problems. I would've expected you to achieve far more with your life.'

'Ifan, if you've come here to insult me, I see no point in this visit lasting another moment. Would you please leave.' She turned towards the front door.

'Aren't you going to offer me a cup of coffee?'

'No.'

'You never guessed I bought that meadow, did you. It was four years ago now, soon after I left your charming abode.' He glanced disdainfully round the room. The shock in her face was obvious and he smiled. 'I offered them a price they couldn't refuse. I told them it was a gift for my girlfriend, so they let me have it in the end. It made no difference to the people who owned it. It was just another field on the edge of their property.' He was watching her closely for her reaction. 'Of course it could have been a gift. But you chose otherwise. Just think, Cadi. You could have owned it. But no. You wanted nothing to do with me. It gave me so much pleasure to think how upset you'd be if you knew it was mine, down to the last blade of grass.' He folded his arms, studying her face. 'I have enjoyed wondering what to do with it. For a while it was a bit of a white elephant in my portfolio, then of course the answer became obvious. It gave me an idea. I've bought several more such sites over the years. Sleepers, I call them. All of them ripe for development.

And now your turn has come.' He paused, waiting for a reaction, then he went on, 'I thought it was time I showed you the plans I have for Meadow Heights. That's what I'm calling the development, by the way. Suitably bland and unpoetic. They're going to impinge on you and your pathetic little life very closely.' He gave her a cold smile.

'I believe I know about the plans you have for the meadow,' Cadi retorted. She took a deep breath, determined not to show any reaction to his obvious glee. 'This village is not so lost in rural ineptitude that we can't use the internet. And there are people who are very competently keeping an eye on what you are trying to do.'

'Ah yes, Christopher Chatto and his village committee. I suppose you're a member of that cabal?'

'I know what they're doing, of course I do. Chris keeps me informed.'

'He's an interfering little man, isn't he. I gather he runs the Mill Café. There's always someone like him in a village, itching to take over and stick their nose in where it isn't wanted.'

'Which is just as well, if you ask me. Otherwise interlopers would get away with far more than they do. And for the record, Chris is not a little man. He can give you a few inches any day.' She managed a scathing glance which ran from his head down to his feet and was rewarded by the fleeting look of discomfort that crossed Ifan's face. She managed to keep her voice steady. 'So tell me, Ifan, have you seen much of your father while you've been here? I expect he's one of your investors. I would've thought you'd have been staying with him.'

'You really have forgotten a lot about me,' he snapped back. 'My father and I never got on. But then no one gets on with my father. He's a grumpy old goat and we cordially loathe each other. No, he isn't one of my investors. He has enough money already and I wouldn't dream of allowing him to make another penny out of me.'

'Watch out, Ifan, your vicious streak is beginning to show.' Cadi opened the front door. 'I would like you to leave, please.'

'What, no farewell kiss?'

She didn't bother to reply, and to her relief he turned towards the door and went out. She watched him stride down the path and out into the road where he turned right towards the meadow. He left her gate wide open.

She closed the door and walked back to her desk. It was only when she was sitting down that she realised she was shaking. She banged her fist on her notebook. 'The bastard,' she cried out loud. 'The utter bastard!' Unable to concentrate anymore she stood up. Perhaps she should ring Charles and warn him and Meryn that Ifan was on his way. But it was already too late. He would be there by now. It was no use trying to write, she was far too agitated. There was only one thing she could do. While the complete and utter bastard was in the meadow, she would walk down to the village and talk to Chris.

Arwel was standing outside his front door. 'I saw him go into your house.'

Cadi stopped. 'Indeed.'

'You know he's the one behind the meadow development.'

'I do. Yes.'

'I hear he's staying with that fashion designer woman the other end of the village.'

'I believe so. But I don't think she's there. I heard she's in Italy at the moment.'

'Women can never resist him.' Arwel managed to get the maximum of unpleasant innuendo into the phrase. 'I cannot imagine what they see in him.'

'For once I agree with you,' she said. 'I can't think why I tolerated him for a single minute. Thank goodness I managed to see sense in the end. I pity the poor woman he married.'

'Be careful, Chris, he has you in his sights,' she said as he filled her bag with goodies for lunch. 'You're obviously his chief opponent in the village. I wouldn't trust him further than I can throw him.'

Chris gave her a cheerful grin. 'I've met far worse than him before now,' he retorted. 'Don't you worry about me and Mel. For a few miserable years in the dim and distant past she and I ran a pub in a disreputable part of London, and if we could deal with the clientele there, believe me, we can deal with Mr Davies.'

'Yes, but he's not the sort of customer you need to throw out physically. He's a subtle schemer. He bought that meadow four years ago!' That last sentence came out as a cry of pain.

'Even better.' Chris gave her back her card and pushed the bag over the counter to her. 'I like a challenge. Subtle schemers are not going to present insurmountable mysteries as far as I'm concerned. But it's good to know he's declared himself. I shall be ready.'

'Many a true word is spoken in jest.' Mcryn liked the term 'insurmountable mysteries'. She had told them what had happened. Neither man seemed all that surprised by the news that Ifan had owned the meadow all along. She was the one who was shattered by the revelation, just as he had intended. He had appeared in the meadow, but one of his minions, a man who had been watching the careful initial cuts into the turf near the grave, had headed over to speak to him and he had walked away without coming over to the dig.

'So, how is the dig going?' Cadi was concentrating on setting out the food on the table.

'Carefully.' Charles had picked up a bottle of wine at the deli on his way down that morning. He poured out three glasses then he glanced at Meryn. 'While the experts were distracted, your uncle and I had a bit of a wander around the meadow.'

'Charles has been doing some dowsing for the pavement,' Meryn added. 'And I think he's remarkably good at it. We've found it.'

'Or we think we have,' Charles put in quickly. He put his hand in his pocket. 'I filched a bit of evidence. I can't take any credit. It was a rabbit.'

'A rabbit?' Cadi put the salad bowl on the table and wiped her hands on a dishcloth. 'Show me.'

It was a small square of dull blue stone with a faint sheen on one side.

'A tessera.' Charles dropped it into her palm. 'Just lying there in a scrape of earth.'

'A scrape of earth we walked straight up to, thanks to Charles's efforts over a sketch map last night.' Meryn grinned. 'As I said, he's good at this.'

'And the rest of it is still there?'

'Who knows. There's no sign of it and of course we can't make any trial digs for it ourselves, but we can suggest one of the exploratory trenches heads that way.'

'Did you show it to Steve?' Cadi closed her fist over the fragment and shut her eyes.

'Not yet. But we will. We needed to do exactly that first.'

She opened her eyes again. 'Exactly what?'

Meryn had been watching her. 'Feel its vibe. Tell me.'

She frowned, then closed her eyes again.

'Don't take time to think about it,' he commanded. 'Just speak.'

'Someone is running across it. As fast as they can. Fear. Panic. Oh!' She dropped it on the table.

'See. You can do it.' Meryn looked extraordinarily pleased with himself. 'I knew you could.'

'Impressive. Between us we could go far,' Charles commented. He handed Cadi a wine glass.

She shivered. 'That was my imagination, yes?'

'Probably.' Meryn glanced at the kitchen window. 'Uh-oh. I think we have a visitor.'

As he spoke there was a brisk knock at the door. It was Charles who opened it.

'Who the hell are you?' Ifan walked in, pushing him out of the way with a sharp thrust into the chest. He didn't wait for an answer as he transferred his attention to Meryn. 'I might have known you would be here, interfering as usual. Are you still casting your pathetic little spells over Cadi, putting her off me, telling her lies about me, trying to destroy my life?'

'Whoa! What are you talking about?' It was Cadi who interrupted him as the two men stared at him in astonishment. She was overwhelmed with rage. 'How dare you push your way back in here like this?'

'I saw you both in the meadow, poking about, trying to find things to interfere with the planning applications.'

'We were just looking for clues,' Charles put in mildly.

Ifan sneered at him. 'Oh yes, I'm sure you were. And who are you, Sherlock Holmes or the latest boyfriend?'

'Ifan. Leave. Now.' Cadi lowered her voice threateningly.

He walked over to the table and sat down. 'I don't think so.'

'Call the police,' Meryn put in quietly.

'Don't even think about it.' Ifan folded his arms.

'Are you going to stop me?' Cadi was fizzing with anger. She could barely contain the urge to smack him in the mouth, and he could see it, she realised, recognising the smug expression on his face. She walked past him and pulled the front door open. 'You have two minutes.'

'Don't worry, Cadi,' Charles said quietly. 'I've already called them.' He had his phone in his hand.

Ifan stood up. 'Don't bother them. I'll go. But don't think you've heard the last of me. You'll be sorry that you crossed me, Cadi – very sorry. And you.' That last remark was addressed to Charles.

They watched as he strode out of the house and out to the gate. He came to a brief halt, looked up the road, then half turned. 'The police don't seem to be in any hurry,' he called, then strode off.

Cadi slammed the door behind him. 'Did you really call them?'

Charles shook his head.

Steve dropped in before he drove home that evening. 'As you know, the police have officially given us the all-clear to go ahead with a dig and we've already found some interesting Roman artefacts below the level of the more recently disturbed soils. There are quite a few silver coins. They look black and are very small, so wouldn't have caught the attention of anyone in a hurry, and there were some more black lumps of what may have been leather. Possibly the coins were in a bag. And we found a few buckles, possibly from some aspects of a uniform. I've sent it all back to the lab with one of my assistants. Nothing from the twentieth century that I've seen.'

Charles walked over to the table and picked up the square

tessera which Cadi had placed in a little bowl to keep it safe. 'Take a look at this.'

Steve held it in his palm and squinted at it. 'Where did you find it?' He groped in his pocket for a magnifying lens.

'About ten metres from your tent. Just the far side of Cadi's hedge.'

'You know what it is, of course.' Steve glanced up.

Charles nodded. 'It was lying on the surface, in a rabbit scrape.'

'Rabbits are great excavators!' Steve put the little piece back in the bowl. 'Most pavements in the UK were made of local stone and I'm pretty well up on our own most usual varieties. This is Lias limestone, I'm fairly sure. They got it from the Severn Valley. Show me where it was tomorrow and we'll get some technology over to see if the rest of the floor is around there. If so, the villa extended much further east than we originally thought. We've all been too distracted by the barn theory and then finding the bones.' He put the bowl back on the table. 'One piece of good news – at least, I assume it's good. That wretched man John Davies called in this afternoon. He cast an evil eye over the proceedings, then he announced he was going back to London. He'll send a minion down to keep an eye on things and in the meantime his site manager, Pete Williams, is going to be here. Davies is obviously bored and impatient in equal measure at the pace at which this is all going.'

'I can't say we're sorry,' Charles said after a few moments' silence. 'Unpleasant man. Not keen on the niceties.'

Steve nodded. Declining the offer of refreshment, he headed for the door. 'I'll be back tomorrow. The forecast is good. See you in the meadow.'

Charles followed him out a few minutes later. 'I have reading to catch up on and I might just take a stroll past the said John Davies's lair. Annabel has told me where it is. I'll see if his car has really gone. I'll see you both in the field tomorrow.'

Cadi rebolted the door after him. 'I won't feel safe until we're sure he's really gone.'

Meryn nodded. 'Now at last we can talk.' He walked across to the garden door and looked out. The sun had gone round and the shadows were growing longer. 'Tell me what you felt when you held that little bit of stone.'

'I think I know where it came from. Elen's bedroom. There was a lovely blue floor in the new wing of the villa when she came back from Segontium. I think it showed an urn of some sort, laden with fruit and flowers, with a swirling border and little waves. The room was warm and she was so pleased they had extended the hypocaust. Would they have put a floor like that over a hypocaust?'

Meryn shrugged his shoulders. 'Not my area of expertise.' He screwed up his eyes as he stared across the grass, seeing walls that were no longer there, flower beds and formal avenues of trees. Pale figures flitted in and out of the shadows and he could hear the faintest sounds of life going on as if there had been no interlude; no span of more than a thousand years. No fire. He gave himself a slight shake. 'We will no doubt find out tomorrow whether there is anything left to see,' he said at last.

34

Valentinian fled from Mediolanum before they arrived. Macsen's troops marched unopposed into the great city with its high walls and many watchtowers, its magnificent amphitheatre and basilicas, and within days the court was ensconced in the imperial palace, Macsen now the undisputed emperor in Northern Italia.

Messages arrived from Britannia. Vortigern sent a bag full of reports, including pleas for Macsen to send reinforcements to the meagre forces that had remained when he left. The encroaching tribes, a threat always to the northern boundaries of the empire, were again targeting its most distant western borders. And it was not only the threat from the Déisi and the Scoti from Hibernia that the rulers of Britannia had to manage; the Picts were once more on the march from Caledonia. He confirmed the sad news that Elen's father's palace in the land of the Silures had been burned to the ground and the remaining occupants had withdrawn to Venta Silurum, to the high king's town house there. The livestock had been left to the tribal peoples in their great hill fort that still towered above the former glory of the old king, and as the ruins were looted and dismantled and the fences removed, the meadow reverted to a grazing ground for sheep and horses, while the wild boar and the great white cattle roamed through the woods and forests as they had always done. In a special message for Elen he said Conan had left Emrys and three of the best mares at Eboracum and they were all safe and well. Conan himself had returned to Armorica as Macsen had ordered.

'Was there word from Branwen?' Elen had read through the pile of scrolls and note tablets her husband had passed on to her. A considerable number, she noticed he had put aside to take to his office.

'Nothing.' He barely raised his eyes from the scroll he was reading. 'I doubt you will hear from her again.'

'Why?' She fixed him with a steely gaze.

'Because she has finally accepted that her interference in the imperial household was unwelcome and is unnecessary.'

She did not bother to reply.

'Vortigern thinks I should send him reinforcements. The wild neighbours are raiding Britannia again.'

'And will you send them?'

'I left him enough manpower.' He grimaced. 'I can spare him no one at the moment.'

'You left almost none, as I recall, save for my native troops.'

'Which my armies trained. If he is any kind of a general, with your father's oversight and Conan's support, he will have more than adequate forces to hold an island nation moated by the sea. I left a token garrison at Segontium, but that it appears was a mistake. They turned out to be a seditious group of heathen rebels.' He threw down the scroll and stood up. 'I need to go to the office. We have to reinforce our own borders in northern Gaul and we still don't know what Valentinian is up to. His silence perplexes me. My guess is he will try to chase me out of Italia. But maybe he needs to grow up a bit first. My spies tell me he is at present hiding in Thessalonica.'

Elen shook her head in despair. 'Don't underestimate him.'

'I don't. We had an agreement to share the Western Empire but it was no longer viable. I informed him of my decision and he must take the consequences. And until he decides what to do, we will enjoy the hospitality of the imperial palace here and

I shall get on with ruling my large and expanding empire. It is nearly Christmas, Elen. Bishop Ambrose is to celebrate in the basilica. Forget that godforsaken misty isle of yours and enjoy the climate of Italy. One thing my predecessor got right was to make his capitol here. And here we shall stay until I make my move on Roma.'

When Macsen's spies brought further news of Valentinian he chose not to tell Elen. It appeared his cousin was at last comfortably ensconced at the court of Theodosius and was busy pleading with his brother-in-law to join him in confronting his enemy and destroying him and his claims to the empire for good. Theodosius, Macsen was told, was listening. Macsen filed the reports. They would not change his plans, but in any case nothing would happen until the spring.

His mother, Flavia, joined them for Christmas. She had made the long trek from Hispania with her household now that her ambitious son seemed to have settled down at last. She had no time for her nephew, Theodosius, and young Valentinian. As far as she was concerned her son was the only true and unquestionable emperor. Her worries about her warring family seemed to have left her youthful looks unscathed. She was a tall, slim woman of immense dignity, her Spanish colouring and aquiline nose proclaiming her aristocratic descent. Her hair was still ebony without a trace of grey, her face relatively unwrinkled, with only the laughter lines around her mouth and the radiating crows' feet at the corner of her eyes betraying her age and her years in the hot suns of Hispania. The children adored her and with their popular uncle Marcellinus there as well for the Christmas festival the palace rang to the sound of excited laughter and the thunder of children's feet. It was all their nursery staff could do to keep them in the private wing of the enormous building. Only Victor seemed withdrawn, muddled and confused by his dual role as miniature emperor and little boy at play with his siblings. He spent a lot of time with his mother. In her company he could relax and giggle and cuddle the children's puppies and kick a ball around the family's private garden. He was in awe of his grandmother; her mock reverence to the little emperor confused him. All he wanted was the gentle secure base of the nursery, but it was not to be. He had his sworn role and there would be no let-up in the relentless lessons, weapon training and horseback riding. His father had cemented his son's position as Augustus by having coins minted in the boy's name. The head on the coin was that of a young man, not a child, but Victor was crowing with pride as he showed them off to his brothers and sisters.

The weather was growing colder now, winter setting in. The city, far from being the warm haven they had anticipated, was enveloped in cold damp fog, made worse by the smoke from thousands of fires and braziers and ovens. Macsen's mother and Elen huddled in the empress's apartments swathed in furs with the senior ladies of the court, entertained by local musicians and storytellers and games with the children.

There had been no more babies after Peblig. This last little boy was the only child to inherit her colouring, her pale skin, his dark curls growing progressively more fair. Only thirteen months younger than Owain, the two were as inseparable as twins and both mischievous, constantly plaguing their bigger sisters. Anwn was the quiet one of the family, sitting in corners on his own, building endless towers out of bricks, drawing on old scraps of parchment or on his own carefully treasured wax tablets. When Victor was with his tutors, the little boy would creep in and listen to his brother's lessons without a sound. The two teachers privately agreed the boy was far more intelligent than the elder son and had huge potential for scholarship. This was tactfully and quietly mentioned to his mother, who made sure he had all the tablets he needed. She correctly guessed his younger son's academic potential would not be of any interest to her husband.

The letter she had been waiting for had arrived in mid-December. The detailed account of her trip home and what had happened since must have taken Branwen a long time to write, but it was worth waiting for. Elen waited until the palace was asleep to lift the seal and unfold it.

There had been no sign of Macsen in her bedchamber for several weeks and she wondered occasionally where he was. She tolerated his visits, as was her duty, and her love for him still persisted deep down, but the shock of realising he was not faithful had changed it forever. It was no more than usual behaviour, she realised, for men of high rank. Women would always be throwing themselves at him and he had the right to take what was offered should he wish it. Now she made her own position clear. Six children in barely more than as many years was her duty performed. She wanted to go home. He had refused her that right, but the least he could do was make her life as easy now as possible. Another baby would be unconscionable.

She was content with her own hand-picked companions and her trusted British household. The two wives from Segontium, Julia Cassia and Valeria Valentina, were at least nominally both part of that household. Valeria and her husband, the tribune, had an apartment in one of the great townhouses requisitioned by the army and Elen saw little of her. Julia and her husband were in the officers' quarters. Julia still came regularly to the imperial suite as one of Elen's companions. Neither woman had young children. Julia's had grown and left home before they had left Britannia, and as far as Elen knew Valeria had none. The atmosphere of the court was too intense, too public, too crowded, to allow for much privacy and for that at least Elen was thankful. She had no idea if Macsen was still sleeping with Valeria, and she would, she realised, rather not know, although she was fairly sure Macsen's affair with her had ended soon after their move to Gaul. If he had mistresses, she assumed they would be younger and more beautiful than the tribune's wife.

The empty bedchamber was very peaceful. Taking a spill, she lit a second oil lamp and sat down at the table to read. The light was weak and flickered in the draught, but Branwen's writing was neat and her ink colour strong.

Dearest lady,

I am home in the land of the Silures and back in my own warm corner of my grandfather's house on the hill I am told the seas are increasingly rough now as winter draws close and we should be safe for the next few months against the raiders who destroyed your father's beautiful palace. Only one man is presumed to have died; his body was never found. It was Marius. The others fled up to the oppidum with all the beasts and those who wished to leave have now settled safely in Venta.

I look daily into the scrying bowl to see if there is news of you. A man pesters me in the bowl, and he scares me. He knows the way to see through the shadows, but he is not from our time. I fear he seeks to find you and you are in danger, my empress. I see it every day.

Please beg the emperor to allow you to come home. You could rule the entire province for him – your father grows old now and although he is still high king, come next season when the attacks commence again on every side, I fear he will not be strong enough to fight. He is much loved and supported, but the tribes need a leader who is in the fullness of youth and you, the carrier of the royal blood would win their instant obedience as would your children in due time.

I write this knowing it will be read by others, but it is for you to put it to your imperial master and husband . . .

Elen dropped the letter and turned to the wrapping she had dropped on the floor. The seal had not been broken and redone or replaced as far as she could see; it was unmarked other than by the quick slit of her own knife which had lifted the wax whole from the parchment. She looked at it thoughtfully. Branwen would have chosen a trustworthy messenger to bring her the missive, but she was right, it could have been intercepted at any point, and if it had, it would most likely have happened here in the palace. In which case she should take it to Macsen as soon as possible. She stood up but then after a moment's thought she sat down again. Time enough in the morning. She did not want to risk demanding entry to his bedchamber and being refused by a slave, or worse still, being granted access to find he was not alone.

She picked up the letter again and held it to her breast. It was as though Branwen were there in the room with her, the woman who had taught her to read and write, painstakingly helping the little girl to trace her letters with a stylus onto a wax tablet. Elen had copied sentences and then longer extracts; she had borrowed scrolls from her father's library and Branwen had helped her read them. When she was old enough she had been taught by Conan's tutor, who was grateful for the reason to stay on with the household after his pupil had graduated to learning philosophy and geometry with another instructor. Elen was a bright little girl and a ferociously clever student. Branwen had taught her further skills later, but without the help of books and ancient texts. The learning she taught came from her own people, and when Elen was at her father's palace awaiting the birth of her second child she had taught her the secrets of the forests, and to recite by heart, to hone her memory and to respect the fact that some of what she heard orally was for her ears only. Elen treasured that learning. One day, she felt sure, it would stand her in good stead.

She read the letter again. She had skimmed over Branwen's reference to her scrying bowl. It made her uncomfortable to think the woman could be watching her from afar, but who was this man she mentioned? Hadn't she spoken of him before when she was with them at court. It was someone who worried her; a persistent spy. Someone tracking her through the secret ways.

She stood up again. No matter that it was late, she had to speak to Macsen. She rang her bell for her maid, pulled her shawl more closely around her shoulders and set off after a lantern boy through the long corridors towards the emperor's apartments.

35

'Meryn!' Cadi knocked on his bedroom door. 'Are you busy?'

'Come in.' He was sitting at the small table, his laptop in front of him. She saw he had moved the oval dressing-table mirror to the floor to make room for a slew of books and papers.

'You needn't come and work up here. You can always use the kitchen table.' For a moment she forgot why she had come up to speak to him so urgently.

He sat back with a sigh. 'I know. But we both need quiet to work. It's easier up here.' He swivelled round to face her. 'In fact, I'm going to have to go home again, Cadi. I'm sorry. I thought I could stay longer, and I hoped I could, but I really have a lot of work to catch up with. My book is nearing completion and I must concentrate; and I need access to libraries in London and Aberystwyth and possibly even Paris. Most I can get online, but some sources aren't there yet. Just now I was contemplating a trip to Dublin as well.'

Cadi sat down on the end of his bed. 'I'm sorry. I was so wrapped up in the meadow and Ifan, I forgot how busy you are.' She knew she sounded crestfallen, but she couldn't help it.

'I'll be back.' He smiled. 'I will miss being here, but for now

302

I do need to go. I'm worried about abandoning you, but I know I can trust Charles to keep an eye on you.'

She stood up. 'No one needs to keep an eye on me! Anyway, Ifan's gone back to London. Don't you worry about me. Chris and Mel are on the case, and even Arwel seems less than enchanted by his son. And if by any chance Ifan does come back, there are always the police. If I'm worried I will get in touch with them. That young sergeant said I could contact them at any time.' She gave a rueful grin. 'I will keep you posted about what's going on, I promise.' She sighed. 'If you go to Paris will you call in on Dad?'

'Your dad does not live in Paris, Cadi. And I doubt if he would want anyone dropping in, as you well know.'

She shook her head. 'You're right, as always.' She gave a rueful smile.

He nodded. 'As always. But for now, Cadi love, it's late and you came in full of urgency. What did you want to ask me about?'

'Not ask. Tell. Ironically, Branwen thinks you're spying. On her. She doesn't like it.' She had run upstairs, her notebook in her hand. She folded it back and passed it to him. 'Can you read what I've written? It's my transcription of a letter Branwen sent to Elen.'

Taking it over to the bed he held it under the bedside light. He read it and then read it again, then he looked up. 'I am sorry I'm scaring her. She sees me as a stalker. I'll stop. I was so anxious to make contact I didn't think what her reaction would be.' He frowned. 'There is something else here. She names the man who died, whose body was never found. If that was our man, our poor dead Roman, shot as he came through the wormhole, then he needs to be given his name. We should tell someone.'

Meryn left next morning after breakfast, just as the cars of the various archaeology team members were arriving, parked along the lane, their offside wheels up on the bank. Cadi waved him away then stood leaning on her gate watching as the various arrivals walked towards the meadow. There was still no sign of Charles and for a moment she considered ringing him, but she thought better of it and turned back into the house. She did not want to seem too needy, but he was the one she should talk to about Marius. He would know how to tell Steve. The living room did seem very quiet, though. With a sigh she gathered up the breakfast dishes and put them in the sink, then she went over to the desk and began to sort through her papers, trying to bring some kind of order to the heaps of notebooks and sketch pads. Not only was the house empty without Meryn but she was very aware of the silence from next door. Sally had left in the early hours with an excited Gemma uttering one short bark as they drove off, heading for the south coast and the ferry to France.

By mid-morning Cadi was beginning to worry. There was still no word from Charles and his phone had gone to voicemail. She had typed up her latest session, editing it as she went to make it more readable and noting the places where she felt she could check facts and dates as a way to make it more authentic. Adding the printed pages to her pile, she stood up and went to the door.

There seemed to be no control over who came into the meadow and she walked across the grass unchallenged. Steve was there with two people she didn't recognise, one of them on their knees beside the grave, trowel in hand. Steve greeted her cheerfully. 'On your own today?'

'Looks like it.' She smiled at him. 'Have you been looking for our mosaic pavement?'

He shook his head. 'One thing at a time. I'm afraid it will have to wait its turn. We need to be systematic.'

'So, have you found anything exciting this morning?'

'Indeed. More bodies. Several bodies, I suspect, and some the victims of a fire.'

Cadi shivered. Poor people. 'Did Charles happen to say where he was going today?' she asked. It was silly to be worried, but she couldn't help it. The last time she had seen Charles, he was setting off up the road about twenty minutes after Ifan had stormed out.

Steve's only response was a shake of his head.

* * *

It was two hours later that Cadi had a visit from Mel Chatto. A tall, slim, elegant figure, most often seen in the background behind the counter at the mill when she would be swathed in a floury apron, Mel followed Cadi into her living room and perched on the edge of the sofa. 'We knew you would be worried. Charles is OK. He said he'd come and see you this afternoon. Someone vandalised his car in the night. Properly trashed it, then while he was outside early this morning with his landlady looking at what had happened, someone nipped into the house through the open kitchen door at the back, ransacked his bedroom and smashed up his laptop, phone, phone charger, camera, everything. The police have been there all morning.'

Cadi sat down opposite her. She felt sick. 'Was it Ifan?'

Mel gave a non-committal shrug. 'I gather when they asked if anyone had a grudge against him, Ifan was the only one he could think of. But apparently Ifan had told everyone in his team he was driving back to London last night. There's a crime scene investigator fingerprinting the car and the doors to Annabel's house and Charles's bedroom, and Chris suggested they go and talk to Arwel. Poor Charles. He's devastated. Whoever did it was out of there so fast. There was absolutely no sign of anyone around.'

'Shall I come and talk to him?'

Mel shook her head. 'I should wait. I told him I'd pop in and tell you what's happening. He's going to come and see you once the police have gone. The village is heaving with cops.' She gave a wry smile. 'Annabel is a friend of mine. She rang and asked me if I'd take over a couple of coffees for her and Charles because she can't use her kitchen until the police have finished in there.' She stood up. 'Typical Annabel. She always thinks about her guests' stomachs, bless her! The whole thing is a nightmare! I must go.'

Cadi stood in her doorway staring down the street after Mel left. This end of the village seemed deserted and the quiet digging in the meadow seemed to be continuing undisturbed.

It was nearly three o'clock when Charles finally appeared. He looked exhausted.

'I am so sorry. This is all my fault!' Cadi led him in and sat him down at the kitchen table. 'It was Ifan, wasn't it.'

'They don't know. Maybe not. He was seen driving out of the village last night. I gather the police are going to consult their ANPR to check if and when it shows his car was on the road to London. The trouble is if he doubled back on little country lanes, they won't know. Thanks.' He reached out for the mug of tea she offered him. 'Everyone has been so kind.'

'Mel said he destroyed your laptop and your phone as well as the car.'

He gave a grimace. 'He did a really good job on me, that's for sure.' He sighed. 'Whoever it was made it clear it was personal. Annabel's laptop was in the kitchen, albeit half buried under cookery books, but he ignored that. It was me he was after.' He took a sip of tea. The colour was returning to his cheeks. 'The police were asking about my relationship with you. I am afraid, as far as the village is concerned, you and I are an item.' He grinned.

Embarrassed, Cadi gave a nervous laugh. 'I'm sorry. You must wish you'd never met me!'

'Not at all. I'm very pleased I met you. You know, if I hadn't dropped in that day to ask you about the ghosts in your meadow, and we had never met, I would have spent this summer holidays pottering around, maybe doing a bit of hill-walking, maybe visiting my mother for a few days by the sea in Devon and working on next year's syllabus. And instead . . .' He gestured round the room.

'Instead, you're knee-deep in crime, have had your laptop destroyed, your car is a write-off, you have spent hours digging human bones out of a field and everything you ever knew about the space-time continuum has been thrown up in the air!'

He laughed. 'And I've made some wonderful new friends.' He held her gaze and she felt herself blushing. 'Please don't blame yourself for any of this, Cadi. I'm fully insured and I haven't lost any work as it was all backed up. But what I'm worried about is you. If Ifan is that vindictive, perhaps you're in danger.'

Cadi sat down opposite him. 'Did you mention his visit yesterday to the police?'

Charles nodded. 'I had to. I'm sorry.'

'No, don't be. I'm glad they know. I don't think he would hurt me. It's you and Meryn I'm worried about. After all, he had no idea who you were and at once leapt to conclusions about our relationship, which was enough to whip him into a frenzy. He didn't target me. At least I don't think he did. I haven't checked my car. It's parked a bit further up the road. He would have known which one is mine; it's the same old thing I had when he and I were together. I'd be far more worried about Meryn. He sounded as though he really hates Meryn. I don't remember Meryn interfering in our lives. I don't think I remember them even meeting, but I suppose they must have done.'

'Where is Meryn?' Charles glanced towards the stairs.

'He left this morning before we knew what had happened. He had to go home.'

'You'd better warn him to keep his door locked. In fact, do you think we ought to tell the police we think he might be at risk?'

They did. It was only an hour later that a young detective constable came to take Cadi's statement about her relationship with Ifan and his visit to her house the day before. 'Do you think he's the one who vandalised Charles' stuff?' Cadi asked as the three of them sat at the kitchen table.

The young man shrugged his shoulders. 'We're just trying to get a picture of all the individuals involved in the case.'

'And how did he know where I was staying?' Charles put in.

'Everyone in the village would have known,' Cadi said. 'Everyone knows everything round here.'

'Or I suppose he might have been lying in wait for me to see where I went. I only left about half an hour after him yesterday. He was in a pretty foul mood.' Charles shifted uncomfortably in his seat. 'I can't think of anyone else I might have offended, but if it was a passing thief, he would have stolen my phone and my laptop, not smashed them with a hammer.'

'We can't be sure it was a hammer,' the policeman said cautiously.

'Well, it was something heavy and hard. Your colleagues couldn't find anything that had been moved that he might have used, so he must've brought it with him.'

'Fingerprinting will tell us if anything else was touched,' the young man said, 'but Mrs Roach looked in the drawers in her kitchen and all her cooking equipment seemed to be in place. And her late husband's tools were all still in the garage which was locked.'

'Have you been up to the excavation site?' Charles asked. 'I doubt if they leave any spades and things lying around, but it might be worth checking.'

'They've already been warned about leaving anything up there,' the policeman went on. 'The archaeologists confirmed they take everything away with them each time they finish. And I gather the landowner's agent has organised security guards to patrol the site at night in case of nighthawks. Apparently it's very common for people to try to dig up archaeological sites if anything interesting has been found, in case there's treasure there.' The young constable stood up. 'Ironic that the landowner is the same man you suspect.' He gave a cheery smile. 'I'll let you know if there are any developments, and in the meantime, I'm sure I don't have to remind you to keep your doors locked, Miss Jones. And if you see or hear anyone in the meadow at night it will be the guard doing a patrol – but if you are at all worried, call us.'

The moment he had gone, Cadi reached for her phone. 'I'll ring Meryn and warn him.'

Meryn had arrived home by ten o'clock that morning. He drove the car around the back of his cottage and climbed out stiffly, drawing in lungfuls of the glorious mountain air. Much as he loved Cadi, he was used to being on his own and the events of the last few days had worn him out. The sun was beating down, barely shrouded now and then by fair-weather cloud, and he stood squinting up to see if his birds were around. A pair of buzzards nested in the high woods on the far slopes of the next valley and he was used to seeing them riding the thermals overhead. At this time of year they were usually joined by their new family. They had reared three young this season and the parents spent hours teaching their kids to revel in the soaring air currents that spiralled over the high tops.

He heard the croak of a raven nearby and frowned. The ravens and the buzzards were age-old enemies, sparring in dramatic stand-offs overhead, but this one was sitting in one of the thorn trees in the paddock behind the cottage. That was unusual. 'Do you have a message for me, old friend?' He was glad there was no one around to hear him talk to the bird. None of his human friends would be surprised, but in a village like Cadi's it would have been easy to be caught out. He wandered over to the gate and leaned on it. The great black bird preened itself for a few seconds then hopped onto a closer branch and croaked again, the raucous sound somehow deeper and more anxious than usual. Meryn frowned as the bird took off, circled once then went to sit on the cottage roof. He glanced round. The garden was silent. Even the wind seemed to have dropped and he could hear no birds at all. Where were the skylarks, the stonechats out on the hillside, the pipits, his wheatear?

He groped in his pocket for his keys and walked slowly over to the back door, every sense alert. The cottage was very isolated in spite of its prominent position on the hillside.

He pushed the back door open and peered in. The house felt normal. No one had been in. He went back to the car and collected his bag and his laptop. He raised his hand in acknowledgement to the great bird still sitting on the roof. The raven cocked its head down at him, almost seeming to check that he had got the message, before taking off, circling once and setting off down towards the distant Wye Valley.

Meryn locked his kitchen door after himself. Something he very seldom did. He frowned. The bird had made him uncomfortable and he was aware of it now, a tenseness in the air as he walked into the kitchen. There was a dead mouse lying curled on the worktop by the kettle. Round its neck someone had loosely wound a strand of honeysuckle, interwoven with vervain, the enchanter's herb.

* * *

Branwen smiled. She could see him in the water reflections now. An elderly man with short white hair, a man who knew how to talk to the birds. She watched him pick up the tiny corpse, gently stroking the soft fur with his little finger and carefully unwinding the plant stems. He had such a sad expression on his face she almost warmed to him. It was a warning. Did he understand that? A warning to keep his nose out of her business. She glanced round the room in which he was standing. It was full of jars and pans, there were cups and plates on the shelves, a table in the centre of the room on which there were sheets of script and the stylus with which presumably he wrote. She tensed. Her eyes were growing tired, focusing so intently on him, but she had become aware of danger. Danger to him. She drew back, still watching from the shadows. She could see him listening. He could feel it. He was an adept, of course he could feel it. She saw him put down the little body, with careful respect. Then he walked over to the door and bolted it before he crossed the room to the window and, his back to the wall so he was out of sight, he carefully peered round the curtain and looked out. There was someone there he couldn't see. Nor could Branwen, but she could feel the presence of a malign force out there, in the sunlight.

She stood back thoughtfully. This man interested her. There was more to him than she had realised. He had treated the small creature as a fellow soul. He too should be treated with respect. She bent over the bowl again, sweeping her long hair back with her arm so it didn't dangle in the water, and studied the blue sky, the trees, the carefully tended herbs in his garden. And then she saw him, another man, tall with short hair, wearing a shirt and trousers as all these men seemed to, creeping up the path, close to the house wall. There was a dagger in his hand. Her eyes narrowed. She watched him reach the corner and peer round.

The flash of protective fury she felt surprised even her. She felt the lightning bolt leave her as the water bowl shattered, showering the ground with pottery shards.

* * *

Meryn heard the bang. It was as if a shotgun had gone off close at hand. He waited several seconds then cautiously he opened the back door and looked out. Ifan was lying on the ground, obviously unconscious. There was a vicious-looking burn running down his face into his shoulder. Gazing up at the sky, Meryn frowned. He hadn't noticed the thundercloud earlier, but there it was, hovering over the top of the mountain.

When the air ambulance arrived, he was able to tell them the man's name. He had met Ifan in South Wales the night before, he told them, but hadn't realised he was planning on calling in. He was able to give them the name of the man's next of kin: Arwel Davies.

Lightning strikes in the mountains, especially in sudden summer storms, were not unknown.

When Harry Smith, one of the local policemen from Hay, came up to take a statement from him about the incident, it was almost no surprise to hear that there was a warning out about Meryn's safety. Turning his phone back on at last he listened to Cadi's message with care, then turned back to the table and, rummaging amongst his books, produced the corroded dagger. 'I found this after the paramedics took him away,' he said as he handed it over. 'I wouldn't be surprised if it was Roman.'

'You mean he was the nighthawk they were talking about all along?' Constable Smith stared at him and then at the dagger.

Meryn shook his head. 'No idea. It would hardly have been worth stealing.'

'But it is possible he was planning to use it on you?' Smith stared at him. 'I suppose I could take it for fingerprinting. This is a weapon, so we're not talking about stalking or threatening behaviour here, we're talking about possibly planning to commit murder.'

Meryn shook his head. 'I don't think we can possibly know what he was planning, Constable.' He sighed. 'Just keep him in hospital for as long as you can.'

When at last he was alone again he walked back into the kitchen. The room felt different somehow. The dagger was still lying on the table. He and the constable had agreed there was no point in fingerprinting it if Meryn had tried to wipe off the rust and then handled it himself. He went over to the kettle and, remembering, looked round for the body of the little mouse. There was no sign of it. He walked over to the back door and pulled it open, staring up at the sky. The buzzards were back. He looked up for several minutes watching them, then at last he smiled. 'Thank you, Branwen,' he whispered. 'I owe you my life. Take care of the little one.'

The only answer came from a rustling of leaves in the trees.

He was sufficiently worried to ring Dai Vaughan. Dai was the son of one of his neighbours and a policeman. He left a message, asking him to pop in when he could. 'It's not urgent,' he added as he switched off his phone.

Dai 'popped in' that evening.

'I was coming up to see Dad anyway,' he said as they sat on the terrace in front of the cottage. The entire vista of mountains was bathed in evening light, with the Wye Valley laid out as a vast patchwork of fields and hedges, a carpet of shifting shadows, and beyond that the further ranges of the Radnor Forest; in the far distance the mountains were slowly being shrouded by mist. 'So, I haven't heard anything from "the mad wizard on the hill" for a long time.' It was the nickname, according to Dai, by which Meryn was known down in Hay. 'Word was you were in the States,' he went on comfortably. He gave a deep sigh. 'God, I miss this place!'

Meryn cocked an eyebrow. 'Don't you live in Hay anymore?'

Dai shook his head. 'Promotion. I'm DCI Vaughan now and based far away.'

'Ah.' Meryn nodded. 'Congratulations; that means my little chat may not be of interest.'

Dai grinned at him. 'Oh, I think it will. If I remember right, your last consultation with me was fairly spectacular.'

'That's one way of putting it.' Meryn grimaced. 'This is something that worries me, and I need your advice. My niece, Cadi, lives down in rural South Wales. She has a particularly unpleasant ex-boyfriend. They split up years ago and he married someone else and that was that. But recently he reappeared on the scene, engaged in what appears to be a strangely complicated plot to upset and frighten her. He's some sort of developer and has bought the field next to her cottage with plans to put a housing estate on it. The way he went about that in itself seemed vindictive and personal, but since then he's been spying on her and behaving in a threatening manner. She rang me this morning to tell me that someone, no one knows who' – Meryn glanced across at Dai – 'had vandalised the car of the nice chap she's been seeing. They broke into the B & B where he's staying, ransacked his room and smashed up his laptop. The local bobbies have looked for fingerprints, but without success, I gather. Ifan Davies's alibi will be that he is supposed to have left the village the evening before to go back to London and so wasn't around.'

Dai frowned. 'So this is a South Wales Police matter?'

Meryn nodded. 'It was. Until today. Did you hear about the freak thunderstorm up here this afternoon? A man was struck by lightning.'

Dai tried to suppress a smile. 'No, I hadn't heard.'

'It happened outside my cottage.' Meryn sighed. 'The air ambulance came and took him away. He'll live,' he added as an afterthought. 'It was him.'

'Ah.' Dai finally reached for the bottle of beer Meryn had dug out for him from his fridge.

'He was very threatening to me when we met briefly yesterday. It appears he blames me for his and Cadi's break-up four years ago, even though neither of us recall my ever meeting him, and I was almost certainly in the States when they split up.'

'Sounds nasty. I don't like stalkers, especially when they think they've got a grudge. Does your niece know what's caused him to rekindle this war of attrition?'

Meryn shook his head. 'Although we've heard he has recently separated from his wife.'

'That could be important.'

'There is something else.' Meryn stood up. 'Let me show you.'

He went indoors and reappeared a few moments later holding the dagger. 'I found this after they took him away. I assume he meant to stab me with it.'

Dai reached out for the knife and examined it with a frown. 'Not exactly new, is it?'

Meryn grinned. 'My bet is it's Roman. It might be evidence. I offered it to your local bobby but we decided it wasn't worth fingerprinting as I'd wiped the dirt off it to try to work out how old it was.' He sat down again and gave Dai a quizzical glance. 'This knife probably came from the excavation in the field he wants to develop next to my niece's house. A purely vindictive choice of site, I think it's fair to say. The archaeologists have dug up a grave there.'

Dai looked at him hard. 'A body?'

Meryn shrugged. He reached for his own drink at last. 'Bones. A skeleton. A twentieth-century chap, shot by a game-keeper just before the last war. The local police have dealt with that, as far as it goes. But there were other bones.' He paused. 'And artefacts. And shoes.'

'And?'

'You're not going to like my theory about it, but I may as well tell you. No one else is going to believe me.' Meryn shrugged his shoulders.

'Go on.' Dai took another swig from his bottle.

'We think he was a ghost, or at least not a ghost as such but a traveller from a distant time.'

'You're right, no one is going to believe you.' Dai grinned. 'So, let's concentrate on our villain. Name and address?' He reached into his pocket for his notebook.

'I'm afraid I don't know his address. I don't think Cadi does either. They separated years ago. He's based in London.'

'How badly hurt was he, do you know?'

'He was unconscious when they took him away. I rang the hospital to ask, but they wouldn't tell me anything.'

Far away in the valley, car headlights were beginning to appear as little strings of bright beads, following a winding road in and out of the shadows.

Dai sighed. 'If he lives in London I expect the Met are already involved in this. And I'll contact South Wales and see what they've got on him so far. What you're saying is that he was threatening to kill you? I think we can ignore the exact provenance of the knife for now. The point is that he had one. I'll take it with me, if you don't mind. And, Meryn old friend, I know you may well be right about there being ghostly involvement, and I remember only too well how much you know about all this sort of stuff, but keep it under your hat for now, OK? For your own sake.'

36

Macsen had summoned his wife to his private office. Winter had come and gone, and spring was giving way to summer. As Elen entered the room he walked across and closed the door behind her. 'At last, we have news of Theodosius.' He spoke in a whisper. 'He has marched out of his encampment. My spies tell me he has a huge army under his command. He has decided to try to oust me as emperor, to reinstate Valentinian in the west.' He clenched his jaw as he walked back to his desk and threw himself down in the seat. A narrow ray of sunshine lay across the floor, bringing a welcome warmth to the dull chill of the room. 'So, at last, we know what he plans!' She could see anger in his face, and excitement. He had been chafing at the bit for months, waiting to see what Theodosius would do, postponing his plans to march on Roma itself, waiting endlessly for news, watching the men train, sending out spies in every direction to keep his network of informants intact, planning fresh campaigns with his senior generals, then abandoning them for yet more ambitious ideas. But at last there was proper news. Decisions had been made and now he had no alternative but to meet Valentinian at a place of Theodosius's choosing.

Elen felt cold fear in the pit of her stomach. She took a deep breath. She was an empress. She did not show fear. 'So, the moment is coming. When you defeat him, you will be ruler of the world.' The alternative was not to be countenanced. Even so, she tried one last time. 'If I take the children back to Britannia, they will be safe and you will not need to have the extra distraction of women in the baggage train.'

'There are always women in a baggage train,' he snapped back at her. 'And British women know how to fight. You have always told me so. You can have a sword and wear a cuirass or mail if you wish.' He gave a bitter smile. 'You will look magnificent, my Elen. With you and my children at my side they will see I have royal heirs to my dynasty and that I have no fear of defeat. The smaller children can ride in the baggage train,' he conceded, 'but Flavius Victor Augustus will be at my side.'

But Victor is still a child! She wanted to cry it out loud, but she knew there was no point. Her husband was emperor. His word was law.

That night in her lonely bed Elen found her thoughts going back yet again to her homeland, the mist-shrouded mountains, the thick forests with their scents of oak trees and pine, and the crashing waves of the wild western seas. Branwen was there. Branwen had foreseen the outcome of this campaign. Branwen who from the start had tried so hard to persuade her that Macsen's ambitions had little to do with Britannia and the tribes of Elen's ancestors and only served his greater ambition. Branwen had begged her to grab her children and run. Branwen had predicted disaster and every bone in her body told Elen that the time for disaster had come.

Macsen's mother, Flavia, refused to leave when her son told her it was time for her to return to Hispania. She planned to ride alongside her son into battle if such a gesture was called for. Nothing would deter her. Elen admired the old woman and was enormously impressed by her stubborn courage. After a spasmodic relationship over the last years while Flavia was still based at the family home in Cauca in Gallaecia, she had made several visits to them at Treverorum and now at last to Mediolanum where she had remained. The two had formed a firm friendship in those last months and Flavia, after growing to know and love her young grandchildren, supported Elen in her desire to keep them safe, but not Victor Augustus. There she drew the line. The boy was the heir. He was co-emperor. He must step up, however young he was, and be ready to fight at his father's side.

The long winding formation of fighting men set off at the end of June, the massed infantry cohorts and cavalry of Macsen's army stretching out along the road south to join the Via Postumia and on eastward to Cremona and Verona and then towards Aquileia to meet their destiny.

Elen saw nothing of her husband for days on end. He rode far away at the head of his troops with his brother Marcellinus on one side of him and Andragathius, his master of horse, on the other. The men were all in good heart despite the summer heat, which had grown intense. Lagging behind with the baggage and the chariots and the wagons that contained the children and their attendants there was an atmosphere of holiday cheer about the excursion. There were plenty of stopping places to water the draught animals and the horses and for the men to rest and eat. Macsen was an experienced general. He wanted his men fit and rested for the battle which would inevitably come. Theodosius, backed by his powerful and experienced general in the East, Richomeres, had reinforced his troops with auxiliaries from Richomeres' own cohorts of Franks, and men from all over the empire. His army was vast.

Macsen's army crossed into Dalmatia. His spies informed him that Theodosius's force was moving northwards towards him at a steady rate. When he appeared at the doorway of Elen's tent she took one look at his face and dismissed the few ladies who had been attending her. The children were all in their mobile nursery, a large canvas shelter which had become their home for the summer wherever they camped.

Macsen looked fit, bronzed by the fierce sun. With her pale skin she avoided it where possible, shading her head with a broad-brimmed hat and a veil, but his Hispanic colouring seemed to flourish in the burning rays of this midsummer heatwave. 'You are well, my Elen?' It seemed a strange, almost distant greeting. He sat down on the edge of the camp bed and looked down at his clasped hands in thoughtful silence. 'The time has come,' he said at last, 'to think how I am going to deploy my troops. The vast baggage train slows us up. I am going to send it back to Aquileia and I want you and the children to go with it. I know you would have wished to fight at my side, in a knife-wheeled chariot as is the habit of your people's women, but I need you to take charge of the household.' He glanced up at her and there was a gleam of the old humour in his eyes. 'I know you would rather fight, my Silurian queen, but on this campaign, I think it would be more expedient for you to remain behind the lines.'

Just as I have been saying for months. As often happened, she did not utter the words out loud. She came to sit down beside him and for a short moment they touched hands. 'You don't need to meet him, Macsen.' She meant Theodosius. 'You can demand to go back to the discussion table.'

He shook his head. 'Our agreement left me as emperor of the West and I'm the one who has broken that agreement. I have crossed a border. He sees my ambition. Yes, Valentinian refused to meet me to discuss the agreement, but it was never going to work. This divided empire can never hold strong against the barbarian hordes. It has to be one entity again, however vast, united under an experienced, powerful general. I have the same royal blood in my veins as Theodosius, but Valentinian is a weak boy, and Theodosius has made a mistake in supporting him. The centre of his strength is Constantinopolis. That will not protect that greater empire of the west.' He paused, as though thinking over his last few words, then nodded, satisfied. 'Wait for me in Aquileia while I chase them back to the Bosporus, then we'll celebrate our united empire together.' He stood up. 'I am sending Flavius Victor Augustus back to Aquileia with you and the other children. It seems to me that, brave as he is, his presence with me would only be a hindrance at this stage in the proceedings.' There was a moment of silence between them. 'His army seems to be somewhat larger than mine, Nel,' he said quietly, 'but we're vastly better trained and experienced. We can trounce them.'

She stared after him as he ducked out of the tent, sitting for a long time without moving. After her initial relief and joy at the thought of having Victor back with her, only one part of what he had said stuck in her mind. *His army seems to be somewhat larger than mine.* Something had made him change his plan of attack. She closed her eyes and breathed a silent prayer.

Cadi stared unseeing at the wall in front of her desk. Poor Elen. It must have been appalling to have foreknowledge of what would happen, especially via Branwen and her terrifying gift of second sight. Cadi put down her pen with an exhausted sigh. Writing endlessly as she was, fast, without stopping, she was putting herself in Elen's shoes, under her skin even. She could feel her every emotion, her every sick lurch of fear, her determined bravery and her agonised terror for her eldest boy. Just how old was Victor? Six? Seven at most. In one source she had read he was referred to as an infant. Reading the accounts of Elen's life, the historical comments about the family, the information was so sparse, guesswork at best, the historians knew less than she did. Much less.

She stood up and went over to the kettle. Charles had gone back to his B & B. She had insisted he go back if only for Annabel's sake. The poor woman must have been devastated by the whole experience. His car had been taken away on a low loader and a new laptop and a phone were being couriered to him this evening. He had seemed remarkably resilient. She gave a sad little smile. She was, she realised, becoming increasingly fond of Charles and it would have been reassuring to have him stay with her. He had suggested it but she refused. She was not going to allow herself to rely on anyone else, however much she wanted him there. He would undoubtedly have made her feel safer. He was tall and he was well built, and good grief, he had even admitted to having a black belt in something or other! She glanced at the door, carefully bolted, and felt a pang of regret for the carefree life swept away by Ifan's appearance.

Meryn rang later that night. She listened in silence to his

account of what had happened since he arrived home, then she groaned. 'I am so sorry.'

'No harm done. Except to Ifan. Dai rang the hospital and of course they gave him information they wouldn't give me.' She heard him sigh. 'Ifan came round in the ambulance apparently and seemed OK. He had a burn down his face and the length of his arm, but it wasn't too serious. They said he had been extraordinarily lucky. People are killed by lightning every year.'

'Zeus's aim was obviously a bit off!' Cadi said grimly.

'Ouch.' She could hear Meryn's smile. 'Anyway, he was still waiting to go up to the ward when he sat up, climbed off the trolley, swore at the nurse who tried to keep him there and left. They said they couldn't keep him by force if he was well enough to leave and they had no reason to detain him; as far as they knew, there had been no police involvement at that point. Dai has been in touch with your police down in South Wales, and they said they already had a warrant out for him on suspicion of committing various offences including threatening behaviour, and now they've added the knife to the equation, but by the time they all spoke to each other he had already vanished. Dai managed to keep a straight face when I told him about our time travellers and only just managed to tolerate the dagger being Roman when I showed it to him. Unfortunately, he took it away with him, but you might tell Steve tomorrow that it's possible it came from the site. I took a photo of it, so if you can get hold of Steve's email address I'll send it to him. Oh, and they're going to keep a special eye on you, so if you see any lurking policemen be nice to them. And keep your doors locked.'

So Ifan was free. No one knew where he was. She felt a surge of terror. Meryn hadn't mentioned coming back. Cadi put down the phone and walked over to the kitchen. The blind was already closed even though there was still light in the sky. After a moment's hesitation she rechecked all the downstairs doors were locked and bolted, then she ran upstairs and checked all the windows again. Meryn's bedroom still smelt faintly of incense. She sat down on the bed. 'Branwen?' she said softly. 'Please don't be cross with my uncle for trying to contact you. And if you did save him with a thunderbolt, thank you.' She shivered.

Once more downstairs she sat down at her desk and, opening her laptop, she googled the Celtic god of thunder and lightning: Taranis. Had Branwen called on him to deal with Ifan? She would have felt safer if Ifan was still safely in hospital; he would probably blame Meryn for the thunderbolt. But the thought did not displease her. She studied the pictures of Taranis in the article. He appeared to be an athletic young man with a wheel in one hand and yes, a thunderbolt in the other which he was about to hurl like a javelin. She sat back in the chair thinking. Branwen paid allegiance to older, more secret gods, probably the goddess Branwen among them, after whom she must have been named. She was a woman of the woods and forests, the mountains and the mists, and obviously she knew how to make the secret magic work.

Cadi picked up her pen; the blank page was in front of her but, she realised, she was reluctant to go back to Elen's story. Elen and her children were far too real for her to be able to face their fate. She threw down the pen.

But surely what she was doing was no different to watching a thriller on TV. She was involved, yes, and she knew she would be holding her breath as the story grew more frightening and that she was emotionally so entangled with it that it hurt, but it was all in the past. The people she was watching were all beyond feeling pain. Nothing could change what happened to them. And she could switch off at any time. She stood up, pacing up and down the room. She needed to be outside. It was outrageous that she should be imprisoned like this in her own home. Besides, Ifan would hardly be in a fit state to drive back here tonight, wherever he had gone after leaving the hospital. Meryn hadn't even mentioned which hospital he was at. She walked over to the garden doors and after a second's hesitation she turned the key in the lock and pulled them open.

The darkness in the garden was warm and soft as she stepped outside. She walked slowly across the grass towards the apple tree, breathing the sweet smell of the grass from the meadow and the wild mountain greenery that surrounded the hill fort. It was almost disappointing not to smell the smoke from the cooking fires of the round houses which had been clustered inside the ramparts or hear the faint sound of distant music or children's voices. Everything was completely silent. Gratefully she felt herself relax. Seconds later she heard the soft click of the latch on the side gate.

She froze, straining her eyes in the darkness. She had left the door open and the lights from the house spilled out across the terrace. Silently she tiptoed further into the shadows, hiding behind the apple tree. The old trunk was rough under her fingers as she peered round. She groped in her pocket and was relieved to feel her phone. Hardly daring to breathe she took it out.

Her mouth had gone dry. Holding her breath she waited. A gust of wind stirred the leaves of the tree above her head and she heard the gate rattle again. It was the wind; the garden was empty. There was no one there.

When Cadi finally went to bed that night she found it impossible to sleep. The moment she closed her eyes she was back in the dark garden, her heart thudding with fright, and then she was running, running down the road with the sound of footsteps close behind her. Her eyes flew open each time she was on the verge of dozing off, her pulse racing. Reaching out she turned on the little bedside lamp so that she wouldn't have to lie in the dark.

When at last her eyes closed again, she found herself listening to the sound of shouts.

The sound of swords clashing.

The heartbroken crying of children.

The terrified screaming of a horse.

The reverberation of hoofbeats and then, outside the tramp of hobnailed boots, coming to the rescue. But too late . . .

Even a cold shower had failed to wake her up properly and at first, still half lost in the nightmare of war, she could only stare at Charles as he stood on the doorstep next morning. He followed her into the kitchen and set about making them coffee while he updated her on what had been happening overnight.

'Ifan is back in hospital. They picked him up in London late last night. Meryn couldn't get an answer from your phone so he rang me first thing. He knows someone senior with Dyfed-Powys police and they've kept him informed. Things have become much more complicated. Ifan's wife has been found badly injured at their home in London. It seems that after he discharged himself yesterday he sweet-talked a young nurse into finding him details of a local taxi company. She said he had his phone and a wallet on him with presumably his cards and some cash. The man is obviously not short of money. He took the taxi all the way from the hospital in Wales back to his house in London, and it appears that his wife was there. Someone in the local CID has interviewed the cab driver, who said Ifan slept most of the way back to London and didn't talk much. He didn't look well. They're used to collecting people from the hospital so he didn't make anything of it. Ifan tipped him generously and the man didn't wait to see him go into the house. A neighbour heard shouting and called the police. Ifan ran for it when the police showed up and it seems he was either still suffering from the lightning bolt or he tripped and fell. Either way, he knocked himself out and they've taken him to hospital in London. I think he's under arrest. His wife is badly hurt. They're not sure if she will live.'

'Oh no.' Cadi sat down abruptly.

'Meryn thinks it's possible that whatever has been happening between them over the past months might have triggered this whole episode of trying to contact you.' He held her gaze. 'I'm so sorry, Cadi. This must all be a complete nightmare for you.'

She flinched. The word nightmare had been hovering at the back of her mind since she woke up.

Nightmare. It was only a nightmare.

'The thing is,' he went on. 'You have nothing to be afraid of now. Ifan is in custody and will stay there at least for the time being.' He brought the coffee pot over. 'Try and drink something. You'll feel better.'

She nodded, and reached for her phone. 'Meryn hasn't left a message.'

'No. He was worried when he couldn't reach you.' He sat down opposite her. 'I've had a text from Steve as well. They have been told to suspend all the excavations indefinitely. None of his guys are being allowed back on site.'

'But why?'

'He doesn't know. He's pretty pissed off. I suppose it might be something to do with the dagger Ifan threatened Meryn with.' He sighed.

'So we can't go into the meadow either?' It felt like the last straw.

'I'm afraid not.' He cleared his throat. 'Cadi, I need to go home this morning. I'm sorry. I feel bad leaving you, but with Ifan back in hospital you've nothing to worry about, at least for now. I've got to look out insurance documents for my car and my stuff. They brought me a new phone and laptop last night, and the hire car was delivered this morning, so I must get it all sorted quickly.'

'Of course.' With the horror of what was going on all round her, she was forgetting the scale of his predicament. She felt suddenly awkward, 'I'm so sorry, Charles, all this is my fault. It's wrecked your life!'

'Hardly that,' he returned with a smile. 'I'm just so pleased I was here to support you. You know where I am, so if you want me for anything at all, please get in touch. Cardiff is less than an hour away if you need me.'

But I do need you. I want you to stay.

She nearly said it. She might have said it had there not been a knock on the door. A woman was standing on the doorstep. Dressed in a formal skirt and blouse, she showed them a police ID. 'Is this a good moment for us to have a quick chat?' She followed Cadi in and gave Charles a friendly smile.

'Perfect timing,' he responded with a little bow. 'I was just leaving. Your colleagues have my details if you need anything else from me.' He turned to Cadi and gave her a quick kiss on the cheek. 'I'll ring you later to see how things are going, if I may.' And with that he was gone.

Cadi stared after him with an overwhelming sense of loss. He hadn't said a word about coming back.

'Nice man.' Detective Inspector Gwen Pugh accepted her offer of a cup of tea and sat down opposite her at the little kitchen table. She was an attractive woman in her mid-forties with whom Cadi felt immediately safe. 'Now, I've been in touch with the Met in London and, as I expect you know, Ifan Davies is in hospital and he's got a burly policeman watching over him so you've no need to worry that he's going to walk out again, not for a while anyway. We're holding him on various charges now, one of which is on suspicion that he attacked his wife.' She took another sip of tea. 'Did you ever meet her?'

Cadi shook her head. 'Until recently, I hadn't seen him for several years.'

'And was he ever violent towards you?'

She nodded. 'Mainly his unpleasantness was more subtle than that. Watching me, criticising, following me when I went out, threatening my friends so they stopped coming over and I felt more and more isolated, and when we quarrelled he would shout at me and get verbally nasty. But . . .'

'But?'

'There was always that sense of underlying controlled threat, I have to say, I was frightened of him at the end. We weren't married, so I felt entitled to ask him to leave as it was my house – and that really, really infuriated him. That was when he hit me and I told him I was going to call the police. At that point he finally left. He bombarded me with unpleasant emails and threatening letters for months, then overnight it all stopped. I was incredibly relieved when he disappeared from my life. I heard later he had met someone else, and that took a huge weight off my shoulders.'

'You didn't worry about her?'

Cadi grimaced. 'I'm afraid not. I assumed his aggression towards me was because I had asked him to leave. He couldn't take rejection.'

'Ah, and now his wife has in her turn tried to leave him.' Gwen nodded slowly. 'Did you ever see him violent to anyone else?'

There was a brief pause. 'If I'm honest, I'd have to say he had a short fuse. He would shout at people, other drivers, you know the sort of thing. But I never saw him actually hit anyone.'

'You don't need to feel you're being disloyal, you know.'

Cadi laughed. 'It does feel a bit like that. But it's true. Although I never saw him actually carry out any threats until that last time, I was very scared of him towards the end. I did think he could be capable of serious violence if he was pushed too far. Is his wife going to be OK, do you know?'

'As far as I know, she's still unconscious. Did you never think of reporting his attack on you to the police?'

Cadi shook her head again. 'He would have denied it. It would have been my word against his. Besides, I just wanted to be shot of him. I never wanted to see him again.'

Gwen sighed. 'Which brings me to the threat he made to your uncle. My colleague Dai Vaughan from Dyfed-Powys has been in touch. He's been telling me all about Professor Meryn Jones.'

'Oh.' Cadi didn't know what else to say.

Gwen laughed. 'Oh, indeed. Don't worry. I gather they've known each other for a long time. He's a family friend of theirs, it seems.' She leaned back in her chair and sipped her tea. She hadn't produced a notebook, somewhat to Cadi's relief. 'We seem to have Ifan Davies walking round your uncle's property in a furious temper, possibly in possession of a knife from the Roman dig, which he might have picked up in the meadow next door to you, possibly intending grievous bodily harm or even murder. At which point he was, I gather, stopped in his tracks by a thunderbolt, hurled by a Druidess who lived some sixteen hundred years ago. Have I got that right?'

Cadi laughed. 'I take it my uncle put that theory to your colleague in complete confidence.'

Gwen gave a slow nod.

'And you've come to ask me if my uncle is off his rocker?'

'No. Far from it. Between ourselves, my granny had second sight. Not that that means I can believe any of this in my official capacity, you understand.' Gwen grinned. 'But it might make me less inclined to look elsewhere for a perpetrator. Incidentally, I understand that my colleagues are still somewhat puzzled by the identity of the body in the grave.'

'Ifan's not guilty of that murder. We know who did that; it was Joyce Blackden's uncle.'

'But there were, I understand, other remains?'

'Ah.' Cadi stood up and went to switch on the kettle. 'More than one body, I think. Very much older bodies from a burial pit that doesn't seem to have much connection with the murder apart from a sad coincidence. That is, I gather, one theory from the archaeology department trying to make sense of the incomprehensible. Beyond that, I couldn't possibly comment.'

'Fair enough.' Gwen sighed. 'It's a bit of a tangle, isn't it.'

'Do you buy the theory that dowsing works?' Cadi's voice was almost drowned by the sound of the kettle coming to the boil.

Gwen nodded. 'For underground water, anyway. I won't have any more tea, thank you, I'd better go.' She stood up. 'Thank you for your help. I might need to come and speak to you again, if I may. I think for now we're all waiting to see if this poor lady in London wakes up. Then we'll know a lot more about what has happened and Ifan's state of mind.'

'Have you spoken to Ifan's father?' Cadi asked as an afterthought as she showed Gwen to the door.

'I didn't know he had a father.' Gwen frowned. 'At least, not round here. No one mentioned him to me.'

'He lives just across the road. I gather they don't get on, but he might know a bit more about Ifan's state of mind.'

Cadi stood in the doorway, watching as Gwen walked towards Arwel's house, then she turned back indoors. There was a missed message on her phone. Although she didn't recognise the number, Ifan's voice, though husky, was easily recognisable. 'Don't think this is the end of it.' That was it. Nothing else.

Cadi turned and ran back to her gate just as Gwen walked back towards her car. 'Mr Davies isn't in. I'll ring him later and make an appointment to come and interview him another time,' she called. 'What is it?' she asked, realising that Cadi was waving her phone in the air. She listened to the message and frowned. 'OK, he's obviously regained consciousness. That was sent within the last half hour. I'll send someone over to the hospital and we'll make sure the phone is removed and the constable there is reminded he's not allowed to have one. He really is a nasty piece of work, isn't he.' She gave Cadi a reassuring smile. 'Try not to worry.'

37

The two armies met at Siscia in Pannonia. Elen listened to the breathless messenger, her fists clenched with fear, the sight of his face enough to tell her the news was bad. They had been back in Aquileia for barely a week. Theodosius must have turned his vast army round and marched it directly towards a confrontation with Macsen's troops, taking him by surprise before his forces had united and reformed. 'It was a disaster,' the messenger said, shaking his head as though he couldn't believe his news himself. The man's clothes were bloodstained and his arm was in a sling. He looked near to collapse. 'Andragathius, our emperor's master of horse, was in command. He had to retreat; he ordered his men to scatter and regroup so they could join the main body of the army. Andragathius was humiliated. There was nothing for it but to take his own life.'

Elen tried to steady her breathing. 'He fell on his sword?'

'He threw himself into the river.' The man stifled a sob. 'He could not face our leader, not after letting him down so badly.' He took a deep shuddering breath. 'Our emperor sent me to make sure you and his lady mother and the children were all safe here. He bid me greet you from him and to tell you that he had high hopes of absolute victory when the two armies next meet. The Emperor Theodosius wasn't leading the army at Siscia himself. Richomeres, his Frankish general of the eastern army was in overall charge of the men. Richomeres is known to be a phenomenal general.' He paused to draw breath. Elen saw the man's face and read real fear there. 'The emperor of the East has called for a brief cessation in hostilities to amalgamate his armies,' he stammered at last, 'and our leaders will take the chance to do the same.'

'Then there will be a final battle,' Elen said softly.

He looked up and met her gaze squarely. 'Then there will be a final battle.'

Elen had ordered their party into the city of Aquileia itself, basing the family in the imperial palace there. For several days there was no news and they breathed again. Elen oversaw the children's lessons, trying to establish a feeling of normality, but when she was alone, or with Macsen's mother, she could not hide her anxiety. 'Magnus will win.' Flavia took Elen's hand and clasped it tightly. Elen nodded grimly. She still had Branwen's letter in her correspondence box.

'I have something I intended to give Magnus to keep him safe.' Flavia came into Elen's room two days later, carrying a small intricately-carved wooden casket. 'When he sent us back here, I had no time to fetch it from my luggage to give it to him.' She gestured sharply at their attendants, who bowed and withdrew. 'I wanted to be alone with you to give you this. You must pass it on to him if—' She corrected herself: 'When you see him next.' She sat down opposite Elen and set the casket on her knee. She felt for the fine gold chain around her neck and produced a tiny golden key.

Elen moved forward slightly in her chair. 'What is it?'

Flavia pushed back the lid of the box. Inside, cushioned in a bed of lambswool, lay a tiny clay dish. 'When the Virgin Mother of God appeared to her nephew John after he brought the story of the Christ to Hispania, she gave him this little bowl, which had been used to catch a few drops of Our Lord's blood as he hung dying on the cross. John was not having much success converting the people of my country to become followers of Christ and he was dispirited. Just holding this gave him the strength he needed to continue with his mission.'

Elen stared at the little bowl. She reached out her hand and then withdrew it quickly, not daring to touch such a sacred object. 'How did you come to have it?' she breathed.

'It was given by a holy man to my father, the Count Theodosius.' She sat in silence for a long time then heaved a sigh. Slowly she shut the lid and relocked it. 'There was no chance to give it to Magnus. He came late to the Christian faith and perhaps he was not meant to have it. Perhaps it is for your little Victor to own it in due course. I give it into your care, my child. You have been faithful to Magnus. You have carried his children and you have always been a follower of Christ. I am old and I realise I may never go back to Hispania. I may never see my sons again. No' – she raised her hand as Elen started to protest – 'I am a realist. Magnus is ambitious. He's a fine general and he made a fine emperor, but he was not the true heir and his supporters, though they represent a goodly portion of the western empire, are not going to be strong enough to win this war, especially now that, as Marcellinus told me, the Franks have invaded northern Gaul and our armies there are not going to be able to join his legions in time to reinforce them here. No one can fight on two fronts at once.' She sat staring down at the little box on her knee. 'May God go with them. But this is for you, to use as you see fit, my dear.' She reached up to the chain around her neck and unfastened it. She handed the little key to Elen and then the casket itself. 'A gift freely given should be as freely accepted.'

Cadi sat staring at the wall behind her desk then she looked down again at the words she had just written. It couldn't be, could it? A little bowl, used to catch a few drops of Our Lord's blood. Was this the actual Holy Grail? She had always pictured the grail as something studded with gems. A chalice, not a tiny clay dish. And it was a legend. Another Arthurian legend like the legend of the famous sword, the sword the Welsh called Caledfwlch. But here was another version of the story, linked, however tenuously, with the Emperor Magnus Maximus. And this one, as she had written down its origin with the daughter of Count Theodosius, this little bowl was a Spanish legend. She pictured it as she had just described it in Elen's hands. A dull reddish-grey clay. Had there been a stain in the bottom of the bowl, a bloodstain? She didn't think so, and anyway even if there had originally been a few drops of blood, surely the blood wouldn't have still been there after so long. If Christ died in about year 33, the year 388 was three hundred and fifty years later. The bowl was already ancient. No, she was being seduced by the story as people always were. She stood up and restlessly began to pace up and down the room. If only Meryn were here. Or the vicar! She had enjoyed the company of their elderly former vicar even though she wasn't a member of his congregation and not strictly speaking a believer – an agnostic, perhaps – but he had retired and his replacement was never around as far as she could see. The woman seemed to be in charge of about ten parishes. Cadi wasn't even sure she would recognise her; she was certainly not someone she would feel comfortable turning to with stories of ghosts and wormholes and a possible sighting of the Holy Grail. And if this was the Grail, then what about Excalibur? Caledfwlch? What had happened to the sacred sword hidden by the king of the Ordovices? But then of course the old man had made it clear that had never been intended for Macsen either, as he battled far away from Albion. The sword was one of the Hallows of this sacred isle.

'Hello? Cadi? How are things?' It was Meryn! She wandered out into the garden with her phone, checked the gate was still closed and now firmly chained and padlocked, and went over to sit under the apple tree.

'I gather Ifan is back in hospital and under guard.' She was reassuring herself as much as him. She told him about her visit from DI Gwen Pugh, then launched into her story about the Holy Grail. Meryn listened without comment. 'Do you think it's real?' she said at last.

'Unless it apports through the wormhole and we can see and touch it ourselves I don't see how we will ever know,' he commented at last. 'Besides, its provenance is tricky. You say it came from Spain, via what was even then an apparition of the Virgin Mary, and Macsen's mother has brought it with her to Aquileia, which I see is near Venice. Now Elen has it. What we need to find out is, where does it go next? What did she do with it?'

'We are very close to the time when all record of Elen stops,' Cadi said sadly.

'But that doesn't apply to us, does it. You have a direct line to history.' She could hear the smile in his voice.

Not only to history, it seemed. Almost as soon as Meryn finished the call with a promise to come back as soon as he could be spared from his writing and an assurance that he would come instantly if she needed him urgently, she heard a knock at the front door. Her blood ran cold. She hurried inside, locking the French doors behind her and paused for a moment to summon up her courage before opening the front door. It should after all be safe with Ifan in hospital again. On the doorstep was a woman in a dog collar, presumably the famed local vicar. Cadi stared at her in astonishment.

'Sorry, are you very busy? If so, I'll buzz off, but I thought you might like a bit of moral support.'

'I would, but I'm afraid I'm not a member of your congregation.' Cadi found she was hanging on to the door handle as if she were on the point of collapse.

Her visitor gave a rueful grin. 'My congregations are not so huge that I don't realise that. I'm Kate, by the way.

'Come in.' Cadi stepped back and indicated the sofa by the window. 'I'm sorry if I seemed a bit gobsmacked when I saw it was you. I was just thinking about you. Or not you personally, but the need to consult a vicar.'

'Ah. Well, that's me. The emergency hotline.' Kate smiled. She was slim and pretty with short curly hair and a bright blue blouse which framed her dog collar. The blouse matched her eyes. 'As I've been stalked myself, I know how you might be feeling. It's unutterably scary, and it must be worse if it's someone you once had feelings for. When I first went to my previous benefice I was so full of optimism. But,' she sighed, 'a gay woman priest who had just come out. What could possibly go wrong? Though most of my congregation were very supportive, I have to say, there was someone there, someone who liked me but refused to recognise that I didn't like him. And never would; or could. It all turned rather horrid for a while. I managed to convince him in the end, and anyway he was never violent. In your case everything seems to be far more scary, and it's anchored around here, so you must feel totally trapped. Gwen mentioned that you were up against it and maybe you could do with a bit of company.' She paused. 'Sorry, am I gabbling? Just say if you would rather I left.'

'Gwen?' Cadi picked up on the name.

'Ah, maybe I should have said. She and I are a couple.' She gave Cadi a quick glance as though trying to judge how the news would be received. 'Gwen Pugh? The police inspector? In case you're thinking she broke some kind of confidence, like the confessional, your circumstances are pretty much general knowledge in the village, I'm afraid. I brought the matter up, not her, and I only asked her if she thought it would be all right if I called in.'

'Yes of course it's all right. Sorry. I've only met her recently when I was a bit stressed, so I didn't register her name. I'm grateful for the company.' Cadi relented. 'The stalker's in hospital under guard at the moment, but he managed to leave once before so I'm still a bit scared. He's violent and malicious and he has vandalised the car of a friend of mine, and the police seem to think he might have attacked his wife.' She shivered.

Kate nodded. 'Men can get very possessive,' she said sadly.

'When you and Gwen were talking, did she mention my uncle Meryn?' Cadi stood up again and went over to the kitchen. She reached for the coffee jar.

'No. I told you, she's very discreet. But Arwel has. Several times.' Kate stood up and followed her.

Cadi looked up from the coffee to see she was smiling. 'Ah.'

'I won't say I believe all of it, but I have looked your uncle up online and he seems a very interesting guy.'

'I expect you think he's on the side of the devil.'

'Certainly not! I don't believe in the devil. Evil yes, but I don't see Meryn Jones as evil. Far from it. If anything, he's obviously on the side of the angels. We may differ in our approach to all things spiritual, but at least we agree that there are such things, which is rare enough in itself these days.' Kate gave a hearty sniff. 'That coffee smells good. I get the real thing all too seldom. Once in a while I give myself a treat and go and see Chris and Mel in the mill. I have several parishes, as you probably gather, so I'm most often on the road with a thermos.' Taking the mug Cadi proffered, she went back to the sofa and sat down. 'I sense there are a lot of unhappy energies in this village,' she said thoughtfully. 'I'm on my way to the church to light some candles and pray. I'm afraid I've been neglecting my duties here. A service once a month hasn't been enough.'

'When you talk about energies you sound like Meryn.' Cadi sat down opposite her. 'He prays.' She put her head on one side. 'But I'm not entirely sure who to.'

Kate threw back her head and laughed. 'I'm sure the message gets through to the right department.' She sobered abruptly. 'Do you ever pray?'

'Only when I was little. God bless Mummy and Daddy, that sort of thing. It didn't work Mummy died.'

'Ah. Tough.'

'Didn't seem any point after that.'

'No.'

'I've never told anyone that before. You must be a good vicar.'

'No. I'm a good listener, that's all.' Kate put down her mug and sat forward, elbows on knees. 'Cadi, I want to go into that meadow next door to your house and say some prayers. Will you come with me? If you're embarrassed, you can wander off and pretend you don't know what I'm doing.'

'You're going to pray for the poor man who was shot? Of course, I'll come.'

'And I'll pray for peace as well for all the poor souls who seem to have suffered so much there. I heard there were the remains of several people. A burial pit.'

Cadi nodded thoughtfully, then suddenly she made up her

mind. 'Before we go, can I tell you something. It was what I was thinking about before you arrived. A story. It might interest you. It's about the Holy Grail.'

After Cadi had finished, Kate sat for a long time without speaking.

'It's a bit far-fetched, isn't it,' Cadi said at last.

Kate frowned. 'Traditionally the Holy Grail was the cup used at the Last Supper. At least I believe it was in the Arthurian legends.'

Cadi nodded. 'I thought that too. But as I have gone on writing Elen's story, it's checked out as far as is possible. Martin of Tours. He was a real man, a bishop and a saint. Macsen is real in his alter ego as Magnus Maximus. The Theodosius family were real in Roman history, even if historians don't seem to be sure where Macsen fitted into it. But here we have his mother. In Spain. A devout Christian. Arriving at her son's court with a holy relic. Arwel would say I had been at the magic mushrooms. For goodness' sake don't tell him any of this! I'm trusting you as though this really was the confessional.'

'Don't worry. My lips are sealed. Gosh, this is exciting. So what happened to it? That's the exciting bit. How did it come back to Britain?'

Cadi gave a rueful smile. 'I haven't written that bit yet.'

'So, will you tell me what happens next.' Kate finished her coffee and stood up. 'Come on. In the meantime, let's go into your meadow.'

'We'll probably have to climb over the gate.'

'It doesn't matter. And if the police or security guards are there, I'll just show them this.' Kate touched her dog collar. 'I find this gets me into most places.'

In the event the whole area was empty. No police, no archaeologists and no cars. The gate was still padlocked and they had to scramble over it, but having done that the meadow was its old peaceful self, apart from the tent still in place over the lonely grave; the police tape had gone and the only sound came from a skylark hovering high overhead.

337

Cadi glanced at her companion. She half expected her to hold out her hands as Meryn had done in order to sense where the areas of unrest were. She had never seen a Christian in action before in these circumstances. She was about to ask whether Kate was in the business of exorcism when she turned. 'Do you know where they found the body?'

'The excavated body was under the tent. That is regarded as an archaeological site. I don't think anyone has thought of giving a blessing. They bagged him up and took him away for forensic examination with a whole lot of other bones. Although,' she hesitated, 'Meryn might have blessed them in his own way.'

Kate smiled. 'All blessings are valid, Cadi. Show me.'

Cadi set off towards the tent. Halfway there she stopped. 'Kate, what happens to bones after all the scientific stuff is done, do you know?'

'You mean how are they disposed of?'

Cadi nodded.

'There are strict rules. If they're from a Christian burial they're re-interred in sanctified ground.'

'And if they're older? Much older?'

'Roman, you mean? Funnily enough I had to deal with that situation at my previous parish. It was decided that as the bones dated to the early fifth century, which was post the Council of Nicaea, I think it was, when the whole Roman Empire became Christian, he could be buried in a Christian cemetery. That was what my parishioners wanted. They felt very protective towards him.'

'As we do towards our body. His name was Marius.'

Kate's eyebrow shot up. 'I'm not sure I want to know how you know that.'

Cadi smiled. 'Let's say an ancient document.'

Kate nodded. 'Then I shall pray for Marius by name. Shall we go to the site of the grave?' She took a few steps forward, following the path which was still just visible in the grass and Cadi grabbed her arm.

'Kate!' she called. 'Stop.'

Kate froze. She turned round. 'Am I going the wrong way?'

Cadi hesitated, then she nodded. She pointed towards the tent. Kate moved forward, more slowly this time and coming to a standstill just outside it. It was full of shadows. She bent her head and stood in silence for several minutes. The lark stopped singing and Cadi looked up. Had it flown away or was it sensing the power of the prayer. She could feel it herself, a gentle warmth, a caring loving energy that seemed to engulf the place. She bent her own head and whispered the blessing Meryn had taught her when she was little. Strangely she had never forgotten it.

> Deep peace of the quiet earth to you,
> Deep peace of the shining stars to you . . .

When she opened her eyes, she found Kate was watching her. 'This is a very special place, isn't it,' Kate said. 'Wherever the bones of the dead end up, I trust their souls found comfort here as they left this world.'

Cadi nodded. 'I was reciting the Celtic blessing Meryn taught me. My family were never churchgoers, but I've always felt he's very spiritual in the broadest of senses.'

Kate nodded. 'I'm beginning to realise that.' She walked back to stand beside Cadi. 'When you called me back just now, you sounded as though you were afraid of something. Something near the path?' She scrutinised Cadi's face. 'I felt it. Something beckoning, almost compelling me to go forward. Not evil, more a form of vertigo as though, if I went on, I would pitch over a cliff face.'

Cadi stared at her incredulously, then she found herself nodding. 'That's it exactly. I'm not sure how to describe it to you. Several people have felt it. People, horses, dogs' – she paused, thinking of little Gemma – 'have been enticed through it. It's a hole in the fabric of time.' She waited for Kate to laugh and instead, to her astonishment, saw her grow visibly pale. 'You believe me?'

'I don't know what to believe.' Kate turned to face out into the meadow. 'There's nothing to see, but I could feel it. No question.' She shook her head slowly. 'No, it's not possible.'

'That's why we don't really talk about it. Especially to the coroner, or the police' – Cadi cast a meaningful glance in Kate's direction – 'or anyone with a solid rational mindset.'

'Which luckily clergy people often don't have, or so people suspect.' Kate had recovered herself enough to laugh. She shivered. 'Can we leave now.' She looked round a little wildly as if wondering which way was safe.

Cadi headed back across the grass towards the gate. 'Your prayers keep you safe, don't they?'

'To be honest, I'm not sure. If this is a physical thing . . . And I'm not sure if that's what you're describing. Is it a geological occurrence like an earthquake or a whirlwind, or is it an opening up of the pathway between heaven and hell? If the former, no, prayers won't help unless God feels a need to intervene, which sadly it appears he seldom does. But if it is the latter, then . . .' Her voice trailed away.

'But aren't heaven and hell a concept for humans?' Cadi put in. 'You can't tell me that a horse or a dog are so evil they would go to hell.'

'Not everyone believes they go to heaven either,' Kate replied softly.

'Oh, surely!'

They both laughed. 'Much as I'm enjoying this discussion,' Kate said with renewed determination, 'I need to go and see someone later and I want to call in at the church here first, so can I come back another day to go on with our conversation?'

They exchanged a quick hug outside Cadi's gate and Cadi waved goodbye to Kate as she turned indoors with the comforting thought that she had found an unexpected new friend and the overwhelming feeling, that stayed with her as she wandered through the house and out into the back garden, that, if Kate felt the wormhole, if she knew it was there, it couldn't be her and Meryn's and Charles's imagination.

Meryn agreed when she rang him later. 'She sounds like a good ally. Very few men and women of her calling are as bigoted and closed as you fear, Cadi, as you will find as life goes on. Far from it. But these things can be problematic for them. That goes without saying. She's obviously sensitive. And she sounds very sincere. You're lucky that you seem to have some very good support down there, but always remember, I can be with you in a couple of hours if you need me.'

And she needed him now. She switched off her phone and looked down at her desk. In the story Elen was there in Aquileia. She was looking down at the box that contained the clay dish and she was consumed by fear. The end of the story was near. Elen knew it and Cadi knew it. And there was nothing either of them could do about it. It was written in the stars.

38

The messenger was drenched with blood. His knuckles were bruised and cut and his shoulder wound barely staunched by a wad of gory wool. He fell on his knees before Elen, his face streaked with tears. He was shaking all over. 'It is over, lady. All over. Our army is defeated. We met the enemy at Poetovio. The emperor was captured.' He gulped, unable to go on.

Elen stood up, clutching her wrap around her. The only sounds in the room came from the splash of the fountains in the atrium outside and then she heard it, the distant shouts of men, the thud of marching feet, all drawing closer and then, too close, the banging of doors.

'And the emperor? Where is he now?' Elen's throat was tight with fear.

'He is dead.' The man's voice was inaudible.

'What did you say?' She stepped forward, an ice-cold clamp over her heart.

'Dead, lady. Captured and executed. He begged for his life, but the emperor, our other emperor, our true emperor,' the man stammered over the words, 'he did not listen. He gave the order and it was done at once. His brother Marcellinus died earlier, at his side, fighting bravely to the end. Our legions surrendered.

Their officers, any that still lived, were also executed. The battle is over. We are lost.' His voice faded and as she watched, slowly he crumpled to the floor.

Elen stood looking down at his body as slaves rushed forward to drag it away. 'Wait!' her voice was sharp. 'At least make sure the poor man is dead. Maybe he can be saved.'

She could see it was useless. One of the servants knelt before him and put his ear to the man's chest, listening. He looked up and shook his head. Flavia made her way in, clutching a tasselled silk shawl around her shoulders as the body was carried away. She stood before Elen, her face tightly controlled. 'So. That is it. Both my sons are dead. Magnus's cause is lost.'

The two women looked at each other in silence, conscious of the huddle of silent figures at the far end of the room, their numbers increasing every moment as the news spread and more and more of the household servants and slaves crowded in.

'Where are the children?' Elen's throat was dry.

There was a long silence, then someone stepped forward. 'They are in the nursery, with their attendants.'

'Is there a hidden way out of here?' Elen looked round almost wildly.

The man shook his head. It was her own household steward, Carwyn, his face ashen. 'We are surrounded. The enemy are already in the palace. The emperor is here.'

They all knew it was not their emperor he spoke of and it was barely a few moments before the sound of marching boots and the rattle of swords announced his arrival at the head of a group of fully-armed men.

Theodosius strode up the long room and came to a halt in front of the two women in Macsen's life, his mother and his wife. He was of middle height, strongly built with even features. Younger than Macsen by some years, or so it seemed to Elen, his expression was grim.

'So, greetings to my aunt Flavia, and you must be Magnus's British queen.' He gave Elen a speculative look. 'You have heard the news, I take it. The traitor is dead. I have commanded that the senate pass a decree of Damnatio Memoriae against him which will wipe his memory from the face of the earth.'

Neither woman moved a muscle. Elen clenched her fists, hidden in the folds of her tunic.

'It is therefore within my rights to condemn you, his wife and his mother, and his children to death.' He paused, his gaze fixed on Elen's face.

'My children are only here at their father's wish. If it is your command that we all die, so be it. I only ask you to spare the children pain.' She managed to keep her voice steady. She sensed Flavia straightening her shoulders. The family of Magnus Maximus would die proudly and bravely.

He moved towards her and took the chair in which only moments before, or so it seemed, she had been seated in all confidence in anticipation of the evening meal with her children. Leaning back, he folded his arms.

'If I spare your life, what will you do?' He looked up at her.

'I will go back to my father, the high king of Britannia.'

'And you, Aunt?' He glanced at Flavia.

'I shall go back to Gallaecia. My campaigning days are over.' Flavia managed to remain upright, her head carried proudly on rigid shoulders.

The emperor sat back, his chin in his hand, in a careful pose of thoughtfulness. 'Send for the children,' he ordered.

The air seemed to freeze. Even the men who had followed him in and who stood in serried ranks along the walls of the room held their breath. Elen could do nothing except nod at the servants who stood huddled at the back. They disappeared, their shuffled steps audible as they made their way down the long corridor towards the children's quarters at the far corner of the palace.

Somehow Elen remained upright. She did not dare look at her mother-in-law. She fixed her eyes on the fresco on the wall at the back of the room. It showed the lagoon which in real life lay beyond the walls of the city. In this version its blue waters were full of fat happy fish and pretty, draped green and red weeds. She was finding it hard to breathe.

The children came in in a huddled group, four boys and two

girls. The girls were holding hands and she could see they had been crying. Had someone told them of their father's death? Her gaze passed over the faces of the boys: Victor trying hard to look tall and brave, as if even now he wanted his father to be proud of him. Then came Anwn, his chin set in an attempt at defiance. Owain and little Peblig too had faces streaked by tears.

Theodosius's gaze sharpened. 'I had heard they were older than this. One was in charge of the province of Armorica.'

Elen shook her head. 'My husband had a first wife. Their children were grown. Mine are babies.' Her voice threatened to break.

He remained unmoving, his gaze wandering over the small group, and his expression stayed thoughtful. 'I will allow the two women to return to their homelands on condition they never return to Gaul or any other part of the mainland empire. You,' he turned his attention to Elen, 'may take your daughters with you. As to the boys . . .' Again he appeared to ponder. 'The smallest are of no interest to me. You may take them on condition they too remain forever at the farthest reaches of the empire. But you' – he turned his gaze to Victor – 'you who feature on the coins and who have been made Augustus . . .'

Elen saw Victor sway slightly. He was trying so hard to remain brave, but she could see that he too was almost crying.

'My son is only seven!' she cried, unable to contain her terror. 'He had no part in his father's ambitions. He will renounce anything, everything, you wish. I will take him with the others to my distant lands and you will hear no more of any of us. You have my word.' She was dimly aware that Sevira and Maxima had put their arms around their little brother, trying to shield him, their eyes wide with panic.

Slowly Theodosius stood up. 'I have made my decision. The lady Flavia is to be escorted back to her home in Galicia. I am informed that her son left a division of men there; if they do not surrender at once to my forces she will pay the price of their insurrection. As long as they acknowledge the rule of my co-emperor, Valentinian, who I now reinstate as rightful ruler of the Western Empire, she may stay there in peace to live out her days. You, Arbogastes,' he turned to his most trusted commander who was standing attentively at his side, 'will take a further division of men and escort the daughter of the high king of Britannia to Augusta Treverorum and from thence send her back to her father with her children and servants. If she wishes to call herself queen in that faraway land, so be it. It would mean nothing to me. I expect to see none of them again.' He turned towards the general, who was watching the scene with flinty eyes. 'See to it. You will have further orders before you leave.'

It was the third time there was a knock at the door. Lost in the past, Cadi hadn't registered the sound. Dropping her pen, she pushed back the chair and walked across to reach for the switch to the outside light. She hadn't realised how long she had been writing and dusk had fallen over the garden outside the windows. 'Who is it?'

There was no reply.

She felt a sharp prick of anxiety. 'Who is it?' she called again.

Again there was no reply.

She waited tensely, immediately behind the door, her eyes on the door latch. It didn't move. 'I'm sorry, I'm not opening the door unless you tell me who is there,' she called, trying to keep her voice steady. She tiptoed over to the kitchen window, but it was too dark to see anything outside and she reached quickly for the blind, pulling it down as she realised someone could have been standing there for hours watching her, without her realising they were there.

'I'm calling the police,' she shouted. Not for the first time she was desperately wishing Sally was at home. Gemma would have barked if there was someone poking around in the garden. She ran towards the pantry, terrified she hadn't locked the back door when she came in. She had. And the veranda doors too. Her mouth dry, she picked up her phone. Surely the police would have called her if Ifan had escaped from hospital. They would have warned her, wouldn't they? She made herself put the phone down and, trying to steady her nerves, she walked over to the kettle. It was as she was running the tap to refill it that the knocking came again and suddenly she was angry. She had had enough of this; she was not going to allow herself to become a victim. Not giving herself time to think, she stormed over to the door and, pulling back the bolt, she turned the key.

There was no one there. She stepped out and looked both ways up and down the street. There was enough light left in the north-western sky to show that the place was deserted. And then she heard it. The distant tramp of marching feet.

She barely slept that night, huddled against the pillows. Charles hadn't been in touch, although she had been half expecting him to come back later in the evening. Twice she picked up her phone to ring him, then she put it down again. He had probably had more than enough of her and her problems.

Daylight crept slowly in through the curtains and she found herself watching the shadowy details of the bedroom appear one by one, as outside a song thrush uttered the first tentative notes of its morning song. She forced herself to stay in bed until it was light enough to go downstairs and make coffee. Her head was thumping, and she longed to go outside into the garden, to feel the cool morning air. Had there been anyone here last night banging on her door or was it her imagination, just as the sound of marching was probably her imagination.

When at last she plucked up the courage it was lovely outside. There had been a heavy dew and the grass was icy under her bare feet. She retreated to the terrace, sipping her coffee. The sun was throwing a silhouette of the house roof onto the lawn and she could see a rabbit sitting out there under the apple tree, nibbling at the daisies. The sight comforted her. If the rabbit was there without a care in the world, there was obviously no one else out there. She glanced towards the hedge. The meadow beyond seemed to be deserted and she realised that for the first time in her life she felt too scared to go over there on her own, just as she had been almost too frightened to open the door and come out into her own garden. She turned back to the door, keys in hand. Behind her the rabbit vanished.

Back inside, the door once again locked, she went to stand at her desk, looking down at the rough pages of notes piled haphazardly in front of her. How long had she been writing last night? She gave a deep sigh, picking up the top sheet to read the last of the tangled web of words. 'You will have further orders before you leave.' And then a dash where she had finally registered the knocking at the door and dropped her pen.

This was it. This was the moment Elen disappeared from recorded history, if she was ever there. The surviving accounts of what happened, none of them contemporary, seemed to agree that Theodosius spared Macsen's mother and his wife and his daughters after Macsen's surrender and swift execution, but his wife was never named. There was no clue as to who she was. Cadi put down the page ripped from her notebook and stared into the distance, fighting unexpected tears. Macsen had been a hard man, in her version, powerful, ambitious, probably a good emperor as far as it went, certainly popular amongst his own legions, but dismissed from history as an interloper, a pretender, a fraud who had lasted only five years before his inevitable defeat. The only place his wife was mentioned by name was in the legends and myths of Wales. Cadi would never have known anything about the story at all were it not for her and her cousin's somewhat arbitrary decision to write books of poems based on the stories from the Mabinogion.

'Rachel? How are you?' She needed to speak to someone, someone who knew nothing of the latest developments in her meadow. 'How's the painting going?'

It was easy to imagine she could hear the sea in the background as Rachel put down her brush and walked out onto the rudimentary terrace at the front of her cottage. On the far side of the lane that ran along the clifftop there was a narrow strip of grass and then the tumbling cliff began its plunge into the rocks. 'It's going well, Cadi. I'm so pleased you didn't mind me shelving our little book for the time being. Are you still working on your novel?'

Cadi gave a wry grin. So much for stepping back from her own nightmares. 'I am. I'm nearly there. The story must end soon.'

She had a sudden memory of the look the Emperor Theodosius had given his general. She knew what happened next. The little boy would die and she could do nothing to stop it. That child, an innocent, unwilling participant in his father's scheme of things, Elen's precious eldest son, the little boy who loved his brothers and sisters and their pets and played like any small child completely oblivious to the fact that someone could calmly order his death, that he would be killed by the man Elen thought was taking them to safety.

'Cadi, are you still there?' Rachel was standing staring out to sea. Somewhere out there, to the west, hidden in the mists, beyond the drowned forests of Cantre'r Gwaelod, Ireland – Hibernia – the land of winter, was sleeping under the unaccustomed heat haze.

'Yes. Sorry. I got distracted. I just wanted to make sure all was OK. Perhaps I'll come over to see you one of these days.'

'That would be great!' Rachel sounded as though she meant it. 'You know I can hardly believe I'm safe here now. I'm going to get a tenancy agreement, something I never had before.' There was a pause. 'At least, I hope I am. I've asked my solicitor to chase it up and she says she's not getting any reply.'

'This is the chap who's laying on your exhibition, yes?'

'Yes. He's gone back to New York.'

'But surely you expected that. You told me he was American.'

'I know, but his solicitor was English and Caro, that's my solicitor, says she can't make contact. It's a real firm, she checked,' she added, 'it's just, the chap who's supposed to be handling the deal has taken leave of absence through illness and he hasn't been there for months.'

'Oh, Rachel.'

'I spoke to one of the other partners and he said he would look into it for me. Oh, Cadi, supposing it's a con.'

'But why should it be?' Cadi felt a cold shiver run down her back. It could be, if Ifan had had anything to do with it. 'What about the guy who owns your house? Has he heard anything? Presumably the deal is with him initially.'

'I haven't dared ask. I don't want to sound as though I'm worried. Surely if they had any doubts, they'd have contacted me, or Caro.'

'I'm sure they would.' Cadi tried to inject some certainty in her reply. 'I should stop worrying and leave it to Caro. You concentrate on what you do best, which is painting.'

She hadn't expected Gwen to answer her phone so quickly. 'Cadi? Is everything all right?'

'Yes. Sorry. I expected to have to leave a message. It's not urgent. I just wanted to check that Ifan is still in hospital. Someone came round last night, knocking at the door, but when I looked there was no one there. I got a bit spooked. And now, well, has he managed to get access to a phone again, do you think?'

'He shouldn't have. I'll check. Why, has he been ringing you?'

'No. But someone is messing with my cousin's head, and I suspect— that is, I wonder, whether he might have set up a scam to get at me through her. A deal to buy her cottage. It's all gone a bit weird.'

'I'll put someone on it.'

'I don't want to worry her so haven't told her of my suspicions. She was so excited when someone offered her an exhibition in Cardiff – she's a painter – and then said they'd buy her cottage to keep it safe; its current owner was going to put it on the open market and she could never have afforded it. I know it seems unlikely, but I was suspicious from the start. Ifan hated me working with Rachel. He was very jealous because we were close and he threatened to burn down her cottage at one point. And now it turns out the solicitor nominally in charge of the deal hasn't been working for months, so it sounds as though he couldn't have been handling it anyway. There was this strange condition in the agreement that she sign it at once without anything being checked, and then give up working with me on my books.'

'Ah, now that does sound suspicious.' There was a short pause. 'So you think we can add fraud to the list of charges against this man. You may have to confide in your cousin, Cadi.

But in the meantime, I'll check about the phone. Try not to worry. And be careful about who you open your door to. We don't know if he has any accomplices.'

'Before you go' – Cadi had the sense that Gwen was about to switch off – 'I just wanted to say Kate came to see me. I'm so pleased she did. Thank you for suggesting it.'

She put down her phone and wandered back to her desk. It was still there, the last page of her manuscript, the dash from when someone knocked on the door, the knowledge that she didn't want to know what happened next, the knowledge that she did know what happened next and nothing she could do would change it.

Unless.

39

Branwen was sitting under the oak tree in the forest near the lake in the great circle of mountains. The oak's trunk was scarred and hollowed out with age, disfigured with a thousand years of battle against the elements. Swathed now with a gentle patchwork of moss and lichen, it was an old friend, wise with the wisdom of the ages. The silence was full of the sound of running water, and around her a thick carpet of mosses was almost luminous in the shady cwm. She had collected water from the falls in her crystal dish. This was where the gods came to slake their thirst; this was where past and future ran together, and when she looked into the immeasurable depths cupped in her two hands she could see Elen and her children as the baggage train rode into the city of Treverorum. Elen's husband's mother had left Aquileia under escort for Galicia that same day after a hurried farewell to Elen and her grandchildren, but old friends were there with them as the horses clattered over the cobbled road between high stone walls; Delyth and Sian and Nia were still with Elen, as was Rhys, an old man now, hobbling along, leaning heavily on a hazel staff. She hadn't known he had accompanied Elen to her destiny. There too were Valeria and Julia, from Segontium, both widowed in that last battle, united with her in their grief. The water began to cloud and Branwen breathed on it gently. It cleared. They were entering the great arched gateway of the palace, the children running ahead towards the rooms that had been their home for so long. They were happy, chattering, laughing, seemingly forgetting that their father had died on the bloody battlefield far away in Pannonia, and that to all intents and purposes they were the prisoners of the stone-faced man at the head of the cohort that had escorted them back into Gaul. Crowds had come out to watch them ride through the busy streets, some pleased to see them, remembering the bounty Elen had distributed to the people as empress, some silent, anxious, unsure of their own destiny now that news of the death of Magnus Maximus Augustus had spread like a summer fire across the states of the Western Empire. They fell silent as Arbogastes rode past, his standard bearer at his side, instinctively afraid, then dispersed back into the narrow streets and marketplaces to resume their lives, knowing what went on in the palace would not concern them.

It appeared they would not be spending long in Treverorum. Their journey onwards was already arranged. The cohort would spend only one night in the barracks before leaving to march back to the emperor's base.

'Your escort is ready to leave tomorrow. You will no longer be the responsibility of the bodyguard of the emperor. I have assigned you ten men who were about to retire from active service. They are fully trained and armed and will see you on your way. When you reach the coast you will wait there until the high king or one of his minions' – the sneer in the man's voice was undisguised as he addressed Elen – 'send someone to fetch you. It will then be up to the men whether or not they decide to enter your service or take up their pensions in Gaul.'

He hesitated as though about to say something else, then with a salute he turned on his heel and left Elen's presence. She stared after him and shivered.

It was in the early hours of the morning that Arbogastes stalked alone and silent through the long corridors of the palace towards the children's quarters. He walked past the room where the two girls slept with a slave to wait on them should they need any-thing in the night. The three youngest boys slept in the next room with their tutor and one attendant. Victor slept alone as befitted the eldest son and an Augustus, with his own tutor on a pallet bed in the far corner of the room. No one had told him he no longer had the title of Augustus or a position of prece-dence, and when his tutor was called away, silently, an hour before, there was no one to see that the young man had not returned to his post. The door opened slowly and Arbogastes stepped quietly into the room. He stood for a moment looking down at the sleeping boy by the flickering light of the oil lamp on the stand in the corner. The child was handsome, his hair tousled, carefree in sleep, looking forward to his journey back to Britannia to see his grandfather. For a moment the general considered overlooking the secret order from Theodosius. Who would know if the boy lived or died? The mother would hide him and keep him at her side. But then there was always the chance he would remember his past and one day grow up to try to further his father's treacherous ambitions. Better to end it now. Quietly he reached into the folds of his tunic for the looped length of wire.

Branwen, staring down into the bowl of water, let out a gasp. There was nothing she could do. She had warned Elen. If this was the will of the gods, there was no escape from their plans and the child would be reborn to find happiness and love once again. Elen would know nothing until dawn and by then Arbogastes, with his horse's hooves muffled and the hobnailed sandals of the men of his cohort carried in their packs to stop them echoing on the cobbled streets, would be well on the road back into history.

Cadi looked up from her notepad, tears running down her cheeks. She had known it must happen, but she had so hoped that it could be avoided, that history had been wrong, that the brave little boy had escaped his cruel destiny, that the histori-ans had believed the gossip when the truth might have been more merciful. Why hadn't Branwen done something? Surely she could have rescued the child somehow, when she obviously knew what was going to happen. Branwen, who had watched the night unfold in her scrying bowl.

Standing up, Cadi walked across the room to stand at the window looking out as the sun lowered in the sky behind the village. Now, the clouds were an angry crimson, bringing in the night, and there in the street outside the gate she saw Branwen, standing looking in at her. The woman was tall, thin, her hair almost white now, her cloak a deep plaid, the colour of lichen and heather and blackberries, tightly wrapped over a tunic that reached down to brush the surface of the road; Sarn Elen, Elen's road. Cadi bit her lip. She could see the exhaustion and, was that misery showing in the taut mouth and dark-circled eyes? Branwen had not been able to stop the tragedy; she had tried and Elen had ignored her warnings, and now all she could do for her was make her way once more back down the long road south to the kingdom of Elen's birth to bring news of the return of the king's daughter and wait, here perhaps, up on Bryndinas, for Elen to come home.

As Cadi watched, the colour of the sky faded and so did the shadow of the woman outside her gate. In moments it had gone. Reaching up, she closed the blind. She had been writing all day, with no further word from the police or Charles, or Meryn. They were all busy with their present-day occupations while she had been lost in the past, watching tragedy unfold.

She walked over to the sofa by the garden doors and sat down, exhausted, looking out at the long shadows thrown by her desk lamp through the window and across the lawn. There was no one she could justifiably call. She was alone with her sadness and with the spectre of Ifan in his hospital bed, reaching under his pillow for a hidden phone. If he had escaped, Gwen would have called her, so there was no chance he had been the one knocking on her door last night. She hugged herself miserably. Who had it been outside? Perhaps just someone from the village calling round to wish her well.

She found herself staring over at the desk. What had happened next? She owed it to Elen and perhaps to Branwen too, to write down the rest of the story. It wasn't up to her to mourn.

She was the observer, the unseen diarist, the only witness. The novelist. The story spinner.

Dragging herself to her feet again, she wandered back to stand looking down at the strange spider web of writing in front of her in her notebook. Would she even be able to read the story she had written down? The rest of the narrative had been difficult enough to unravel and transcribe onto her laptop, but this tangle of words was different. It was even more unintelligible. She had been writing more and more quickly, trying to capture the narrative, almost trying to outrun the plans of Theodosius's murderous general, and she had been crying.

When had Elen found out that her precious eldest son was dead?

The first person to see what had happened to Victor was his brother Peblig, running, barefoot, clothed only in his little night tunic to show his brother the toy they had left behind by mistake when they set out on the long march to Italia, those few short months earlier, the missing toy with its soft rabbit-skin fur and its little blue scarf that he had found under his bed. 'Victor! Look! I've found the rabbit you gave me!' The little boy stopped abruptly, clutching the furry animal, gazing down at his brother who was lying as if asleep though his eyes were open, the thin sheet pulled up around his neck. 'Victor? Wake up.' His voice wavered and it was then the slave girl who should have been helping Peblig dress ran in after him and skidded to a stop, staring down at the child's brother with his unnaturally twisted neck and alabaster-white face, gazing up at the ceiling, still registering the terror and disbelief of the moment of his death. The girl grabbed Peblig and dragged him out of the room and it was only then that she screamed.

They found his tutor in the end. The man's throat had been cut and his body concealed in a storeroom behind the kitchens. There had been no one with the boy when Arbogastes had entered his room, for it must have been Arbogastes, Elen was sure of that when Delyth woke her moments later. The general had left in the early hours; the watchmen at the gate and on the walls had seen him go with his cohort of men behind him and seen no reason to be alarmed. The man was in charge, acting under the emperor's direct orders. The fact that he had seen fit to flee the palace under cover of night sealed his guilt in Elen's eyes.

The palace was deserted save for its resident staff and servants. The only escort left for Elen were the men chosen to accompany her west towards the coast, less than a dozen Alamanni mercenaries who might at any moment desert to return to their homes in the north. In the palace too were her own trusted followers, the women and two loyal men, both of whom had followed her from Britannia those five short years before. Somehow Elen had to cope with the agony of loss, the shock and terror of the other children, particularly little Peblig, her fury at the betrayal of the man who was supposed to see them safely on their way, and the realisation that perhaps none of them were safe, that the other boys might yet be the targets of an assassin. As might she.

It was Rhys who had taught the boy to ride, who arranged the swift interment of Flavius Victor Augustus in an orchard to the west of the city walls. Bishop Ambrose was hastily summoned and, shocked into immediate action, came to conduct the service. He poured holy water on the child's body and pretended not to see the furry toy tucked into the shroud by the boy's little brother, then he blessed Elen and her family, consigning them to the Lord's protection.

They left the palace at dawn the next day, heading onto the first of the Roman roads that led towards the coast and the Oceanus Britannicus. For several days they travelled on at a steady rate, stopping at villas, mansiones and cauponae for refreshment and rest. It was on the sixth day that what Elen had feared most happened. Titus Germanicus, the elderly officer in charge of her escort came to her, an expression of such regret on his face she guessed at once what he was going to say. 'I am sorry, lady, but the men and I have been talking and we feel we have to leave you at this point. The general knew we were expecting to return home and this is what we plan to do.' She heard real sadness in the guttural Alammani voice. She knew it was no use trying to dissuade him. She and her small band of followers would be on their own from this point onward. 'Thank you for telling me and not fleeing in the middle of the night like your coward general,' she said sadly. 'I'm afraid I can't pay you. The emperor gave me no money to fund our journey into exile.'

'We have been paid, lady, and we have our pensions.'

She nodded. 'Then I wish you godspeed.'

'And I you and yours.' For a moment she thought he would say more but he turned away. His followers were already drawn up outside the mansio where they had passed the night.

'Where are they going, Mama?' Sevira came and clutched at her mother's hand.

'Back to their homes in the north.'

'Then who will guard us?' The girl glanced at their companions who were gathering round them. They had a cart pulled by a patient plodding ox for the smallest children and their few belongings, otherwise they were walking, a tightly knit group of women, led by Valeria and Julia, with two men, Rhys and Carwyn, who for all their time in Gaul had been Elen's faithful steward. To the remaining household slaves she had given their freedom, though she was not convinced anyone would register the fact. With their freedom came the choice to accompany them into exile. Only the two children's nurses, Flora and Anna, had chosen to do so. 'Will we be safe?' Elen heard the panic in Sevira's voice. Since the death of their father and now their brother, the children's world had fallen apart.

'We will be safe.' Elen tried to sound confident as she surveyed the small group. They relied on her. 'The bill has been paid' – she had seen Titus Germanicus delve into his own pouch to settle the account – 'and we are on our way home.'

She wanted to avoid the towns but she needed money and she had jewellery to sell. Concealed under her tunic she had her own pouch. In it were some of the gifts Macsen had given her. As empress she had been expected to show her finery on every occasion. Theodosius had been quick to have her boxes and chests raided, barely leaving her enough clothes to wear, but she had guessed that might happen and had managed to conceal some of the smallest and least ostentatious gems.

If she could find an honest trader they would have enough for food at least. There were rugs and cushions in the cart and, although late September, it was still warm at night so they could if necessary sleep under the stars. And she had one more ray of hope up her sleeve. Two nights before at a caupona deep in the countryside she had spotted a group of people sitting beneath a tree in the shade. There was something about their quiet dignity, combined with the deep coloured patterns on their clothes that she recognised. She had stood quietly watching them for several moments and, as if recognising an unspoken call, the eldest of the men stood up and walked over to her. 'I sense you are in trouble, lady,' he said gently. 'Can we be of assistance?'

'Could you get a message for me via the secret ways, across country to the coast and beyond, to Britannia?' She held his gaze. There had been no preamble, no stammering excuses. If these people had had any kind of a Druidic education they would know what she was asking. If not, they would look at her and make cuckoo noises, pointing at their heads, the universal sign of madness.

He looked at her hard for several moments, as if searching deep into her soul, then he nodded. 'I will see what I can do. What is your message?'

'The daughter of the high king needs help to return home.'

He raised his eyebrows, then he bowed. 'I will see the message is sent; and I will see that you receive help where you need it on your way.'

She re-joined her companions and when she next looked round the party under the tree had gone. That evening as they camped under the stars in a clearing a little way off the road and out of sight of passing traffic, she saw a slim column of smoke against the sky. It billowed and swirled and seemed to break at times even though there was no wind and she nodded to herself hoping against hope it was the message she hoped for.

Sometimes the messages, if that was what they were, were passed in distant calls echoing across the valleys from hilltop to hilltop, and sometimes by shadowy figures in the undergrowth. Once or twice when they felt threatened by marauding thieves and vagabonds, mysterious groups of woodland folk would materialise out of the trees to follow them, their staves beating a warning on the road. In a small town near a river bridge, a jeweller, when approached by Elen, gave her a more than fair price for her jewellery, and when Julia produced her own almost negligible cache that too was fairly valued and gave them enough to pay for a room overnight when the fine weather finally broke and the rain poured down across northern Gaul.

When they reached the coast at last, a ship was waiting for them, riding at anchor in the harbour mouth. Only once she was safely on board and had found herself a space alone under an awning in the prow did Elen let herself cry. She turned towards the empty shoreline and, raising her arms towards the deserted dunes, she wept again for her lost son, alone in his grave so far away, and then gave thanks to the old gods and their servants who had protected her and her other children on their journey across an empire that was now a hostile land. The second prayer of gratitude to the Christian saints who protected travellers was almost an afterthought.

40

Charles stood up from his desk with a sigh and stretched his arms above his head. He had been sitting at his laptop for what felt like hours attending to the form-filling that persisted after the damage to his car and everything else he had had with him at Annabel's. He looked round the room. It was comfortable and familiar, his own space in his own flat, conveniently near the university, somewhere he had always felt supremely at home.

He had had a partner once, a lovely lady he had adored. They had lived together and planned to marry, to buy a house and have a family. It hadn't seemed so outrageous a dream, but it was not to be. Cancer had taken her only a few months after the first diagnosis and he had been left alone to rebuild his life. Since then he had avoided any close relationships. He was not ready, he told himself, not the marrying type, not even the 'let's live together and see how it goes' type. He had never even considered it until now. And now that he had felt himself drawn to someone, felt himself caring hugely and wanting to protect someone who was obviously in real danger, what had he done? He had fled.

But, he told himself, he had had to come home to see to the insurance.

Rubbish, he thought. Everything was being sorted out online. He didn't really need all those paper files he had carefully lined up on the floor at his feet. He hadn't had to come home.

He walked over to the window and looked out. He was missing Cadi, and worried about her. He took out his phone and scrolled down, looking for missed calls. There were none from her. Two from Steve though. He pressed the number.

'Ah.' Steve's voice rang out loud and clear. 'I wondered where you'd got to. When are you going back?'

Charles gave a rueful smile. Unwittingly, Steve had come straight to the point.

'Not sure,' he replied slowly. 'What's the news over there?'

'You know the police arrested John Davies. He's back in hospital, under guard.'

'Yes, I heard. I hope they've got him chained to the bed.'

There was a moment's silence. 'Not sure about that. Any news from Cadi?'

'Not since I left.'

There was another fractional silence. Enough to be meaningful. 'OK. Well, the news here is that there is an indefinite hold on any planning applications, obviously, but once the police have given us the all-clear over the dagger used to threaten Professor Jones, we're still hoping to dig out the burial pit and a trench or two to establish if there really is a villa there. Have a look for the mosaic floors you mentioned. I'll bring in a team of students to speed things up and carry on until we're told otherwise. Exciting possibilities.'

And what about the wormhole?

Charles almost said it out loud.

'So, when will you be back?' Steve repeated, pointedly waiting for an answer this time.

'I've just got some insurance stuff to be sorted,' Charles replied. 'I'll let you know.'

He stood staring out of the window at the quiet urban street for several minutes after Steve hung up. Deep in thought, he was studying the house across the road with its Edwardian curlicue gables and the pretty rowan tree, its berries beginning to ripen, the solid lines of parked cars, down both sides of the road. Abruptly he turned away and, reaching for his phone again, he scrolled down to Cadi's number, his thumb hovering over the screen. It was several seconds before he pressed it.

'Charles!' He couldn't make out from that one word what her mood was. Pleased to hear from him? Cross? He even wondered if she had been crying.

'How are you, Cadi? Sorry I haven't been in touch. I was knee-deep in this bloody paperwork.'

'That's OK. I've been busy. I've had visitations from the local vicar and from the police. It turns out they're an item.'

He frowned. 'What do you mean?'

She laughed. 'Just that. The vicar and the detective inspector. They've both been very kind and understanding and I feel between them they've got my back. You know Ifan is in hospital again?'

'Yes. Let's hope they can keep him there.'

'He's under arrest, so I suspect I'm safe for the time being.'

'I hear the planning application has been put on hold,' Charles went on after a moment. 'I only hope they don't stop the dig as well. As things are, Steve thinks they can get back on the meadow as soon they get the final OK from the police.'

'That's good.' Cadi sounded more cheerful now. 'Kate, that's the vicar, and I went over there and climbed over the gate so she could bless the site of the grave. It was really rather lovely. Oh, and Charles, she sensed the wormhole.'

'Interesting.'

There was a short pause. 'Will you have time to come back?' she asked at last.

'Would you like me to?'

Another pause. 'You know I would. But I feel so guilty about all the damage he did to your stuff. That was awful.'

'Nothing the insurance couldn't fix.' He had turned back to the window, watching a car trying to back into an impossibly short space. 'I could come back tomorrow if that's OK with you?'

'I'd like that.'

As he switched off the phone, he found he was smiling.

It was a favourite spot with Meryn, a place he came to meditate on the hillside behind his cottage, a place where he was confident no one could find him and yet, with its vast views across the Wye valley towards the Radnor Forest and beyond he could see anyone or anything coming from several miles away. He could feel her probing and that impressed him. She was powerful, of that he was sure, and very skilled.

Turning, he made his way into the natural shelter of the rocks, jumping down below the skyline to where a thorn tree, one of the few trees that grew on these upper slopes, angled over a shadowed corner to form a private space out of the wind. He thought of it as his chapel.

Sitting down on the carpet of dried lichen and drifted leaves, he closed his eyes and waited.

Branwen was watching. He intrigued her, though she was still deeply suspicious. She drifted closer. He was waiting for her, he and the woman from his own time, who in her turn was watching Elen. Could they be spies in the pay of Theodosius? She thought not. They came from a different time, but they were based in the land of the Silures; if they were paid by anyone it would be the sons of Macsen, Constantine and the elder Victor, following the daughter of the high king, testing her loyalty to her dead husband. And she was on her way home, to the palace where she was born, the palace that had been destroyed by the vicious men of Hibernia. Did this man and woman know that the palace had gone? Of course they knew. She had watched them walking in the horse paddock near the spot where the palace had stood. Branwen had seen a man die there. The faithful servant of the old king who had fled from the pirates across the grass and somehow vanished as they reached out to kill him. He had been buried by a young man and a girl and had lain undisturbed until his bones had been dug up and removed without ceremony. In their time there was no palace, no villa, not even a sign of ruins. The grass was sweet and rich, the hay mown, gathered and wrapped up in shiny black bundles.

She knew it was possible to move between worlds. Her teachers had mentioned it; the scholars of past ages had always known it; it was described in the stories of the bards of old, but no one had been able to tell her how. There in the horse paddock was a place where it could be done, and apparently it wasn't a case of knowing the right words, using the right formula of smoke and reflections; there was an actual corridor through which one could pass. She had walked down there in the dark of the evening, picking her way amongst the burnt ruins, trying to find the spot, but as yet it eluded her. Elen's little dog had found it easily, but dogs were clever when it came to scents. She had followed that dog's path later when she was alone, but there had been no trace of where it had gone. She had wondered if it would return but although she had noticed how all the horses avoided that area, however rich the grass, there had been no sign of little Gemma again.

She became aware gradually that the man, Meryn, had turned his attention in her direction. She saw his gaze sharpen and she shrank back, drawing a veil around herself. She feared him and his power almost as much as she was intrigued by his obvious knowledge.

'I know you're there, Branwen,' he said softly. 'We are on the same side, you and I, the side of the truth. The side of peace.'

She stepped back, wondering if he could see the grasses move under her feet. She could understand what he said though they spoke different languages.

'You followed me here, and you know I mean no harm to any of our friends. We have no influence over Elen, we merely want to know the truth of her life, to ensure the poets tell the truth of her story. She holds the history of this land in her hands.'

And perhaps the mystery, he added under his breath.

A breeze swept over the mountainside, bringing with it the scent of gorse and wild thyme and there, always in the background, of sheep dung. She had gone. Had she heard his words of reassurance? He had no way of knowing. Perhaps she had already returned to Elen's side.

41

Elen had found an escort of men awaiting her as they came alongside the wharf at Rutupiae. Sent by her stepson, the elder Victor, they had been watching the fishing boat beat in on the last of the tide as the wind rose and began to swing round towards the west. Their senior officer, Junius Secundus, did not want her to go back to her father's palace. Her stepson, he said, had made it clear that it would break her heart to see her home looted and burned, but she insisted, and thus as the gales of late October lashed the seas behind them she and her party made their way along the road towards the west, their horses' hooves splashing through the puddles, the wind tearing at their hair. The women of the party and the children were accommodated in two wagons, all except Elen herself, who was mounted on a pretty roan mare. Not for the first time she thought about her lovely black horse and wondered what had become of him.

They followed the old roads across the country, the ancient routes, drained, and paved and made safe by the empire. There were still mansiones and cauponae at regular intervals and villas, but the lack of legionary oversight was beginning to tell. The men who had followed Macsen across the sea five years before, had been a good part of the force which kept Britannia safe from invasion and from insurrection. They passed crumbling walls, and burnt-out homesteads, and the lack of military care for the highways was obvious every time one of the carts thumped down into a pothole or stuck halfway across an untended ford.

'Why has everything been allowed to deteriorate like this?' Elen asked Secundus. For all his Roman name he had the wild hair and pale complexion and accent of a native-born Briton. He looked at her in disbelief. 'Because Magnus Maximus Augustus took all the men of the legions with him to conquer his empire, madam,' he said crisply. 'Did you not realise as much? On his orders, Britannia was left virtually undefended. The loyal men who serve your father, the high king, have enough to do without road mending.' He stared down at the broken wheel of the cart that was the latest casualty of their slow progress. 'Even these, the great routes across the land are suffering. Highway robbers and beggars frequent the ways, many of the men who ran the inns have fled with barely the clothes they stood up in. No one travels the roads without an escort. This land is without protection and without leadership.'

It was only a short time later, as if to illustrate his bitter complaint, that a shouting horde of armed men hurled themselves towards them out of a patch of woodland.

The women and children who had been standing round the broken cart scattered, screaming. For a moment Secundus and his men seemed taken by surprise, distracted by his conversation with Elen, as their attackers had obviously realised, but within seconds the scene changed. Three men detached themselves from Secundus's troop and ushered the women and children out of the way as the remaining soldiers, armed, trained and determined, regrouped, rallied, and turned on the attackers. Not expecting any opposition and ill prepared as they were, they fled, but not before one or two of them had dived into the baggage cart, grabbing everything they could carry. In seconds it was all over, two of the robbers dead on the ground, one of Junius Secundus's men wounded, and the two draught oxen that had been pulling the disabled wagon, trotting off loose somewhere in the woodland that bordered the road. 'Follow those robbers,' Elen cried. 'Don't let them get away.'

But they had gone, melting into the shadows.

'Are you all right, my lady?' Junius Secundus turned to Elen at last. He reached up to stroke the mare which was stamping and shuddering under Elen's quiet hands.

'She's obviously not used to battle,' Elen said with a grim smile. 'She will settle.' She turned to the rest of their party. 'Is everyone safe?'

Julia stepped forward, her arm around Sevira's shoulders. The girl was sobbing quietly, her face white. 'We've had a nasty fright, but we're all right. Where did they come from?'

'Out of the wilderness,' Junius Secundus said grimly. 'This is what happens when there's no one to oversee the cutting back of the undergrowth alongside the roads. Robbers can lie in wait and then flee again into the countryside without any warning, so travellers cannot protect themselves.' He walked back to the baggage wagons where the remaining two draught animals were bellowing after their lost companions.

'Or go after their stolen belongings,' Julia said bitterly as she followed him. 'That tall man with the red beard grabbed as many bags as he could carry as well as some of the children's.'

'I don't think he took the time to be selective,' Junius Secundus replied. 'While my men are seeing to the wheel perhaps you can have a look and see exactly what is missing. Not that there will be any chance of recovering it. There's no point in going after them. They've long gone.'

The missing oxen retrieved, the wheel mended, and order restored, the party moved on for some half a dozen miles before turning up the long driveway to the welcoming lights and fires of a homestead owned by a wealthy trader and his wife. They received Elen with due honour, and she and her women and the children were shown to warm, clean chambers in the guest wing of the house. It was then she realised that amongst the stolen bags was her own, containing shawls and tunics, her few cosmetics and brushes and combs, her veils and, she realised with a pang of horror, the silk shawl in which she had carefully wrapped the box that held the little dish given to Macsen's grandmother by the Blessed Virgin Mary herself.

'I'm so sorry.' Delyth had been unpacking her other bag. 'There was so much chaos in the wagon, with all the luggage piled up in a heap and some of the bags coming undone when the wheel came off, I didn't notice.'

Elen gave a sad smile. 'I doubt anyone will find any of it now.' She sighed. 'There was only one thing in there that I treasured before all else, and they will probably throw it away. It will mean nothing without knowing who it had belonged to.'

Delyth glanced at her. In all the time they had been together Elen had seemed so resilient and strong, managing to contain her grief, at least in public, for the sake of the children after the execution of her husband and then again after the murder of poor little Victor, but this, now, so close to the end of her journey, seemed like the final blow. She glanced at Elen as she sat on her bed. 'I'm so sorry. But they were only clothes. See, your other bag is here and the jewel box is safe.'

Elen looked up and there were tears in her eyes. 'It wasn't the clothes. And as for the jewel box, it is empty. There was something else in there, wrapped in my shawl, something very precious my husband's mother gave me.'

Delyth bit her lip. 'I'm so sorry,' she repeated in a whisper. She looked up as the door opened and Maxima came in. The girl was looking frail and her face was blotched with tears. Seeing her mother crying, she let out a sob and ran to her and the two of them clung to each other, rocking to and fro as though their hearts would break. Delyth backed away. 'I will go and see if I can find hot drinks in the kitchens for everyone,' she said quietly, then slipped out of the room, meeting Nia at the door, Nia who had stayed on to supervise the children's nurses and now as an indispensable part of their little household. 'Let them be for now. It will do them both good to have a nice cry,' she whispered practically. 'Can you wait and see no one else comes in.'

Their kind and thoughtful hosts insisted they stay another night as their guests and Elen, too tired and sad to argue, agreed gratefully. Valeria and Julia buried their animosity at least long enough to agree that the household should be kept away from Elen, leaving only Sevira and Maxima with their mother to care for her. Delyth supervised the concocting of soothing drinks, designed to bring sleep, and Nia found a harp in the reception room of their hosts and begged to be allowed to bring it to Elen's chamber.

She slept at last, but it was sleep fractured with nightmares.

Cadi had not expected Rachel to arrive unannounced. One look at her cousin's face led her to expect the worst as she stood back and let her in. 'What's happened?'

'It was your bastard ex-boyfriend. You suspected as much, didn't you. He's pulled out of the deal. Or at least his stooge has. The solicitor was a fake and the American buyer was completely astonished when my solicitor contacted him and told him he had agreed to buy my cottage and set up an exhibition for me. He was very apologetic and all that, but was not prepared to honour anything. And why should he? He knew nothing about it.' She flung her bag and a portfolio on the table. 'Coffee please.'

Cadi nodded and walked over to the kettle. 'I'm so sorry, Rach.'

'So where is he, this mastermind out to destroy you and yours. Have they found him?'

Cadi reached for the jar of coffee beans. 'He's in hospital under police guard. I'm not sure if he's been charged. I gather he hit his head when he fell in the road as he was being chased in London and he got concussion. He might not even be conscious yet, but they've got him. They can add all your stuff to the charges.'

'I doubt it. There's no proof he or anyone else promised me anything. A few letters from a fake address, that's all.'

'But you went to meet them in Cardiff.'

'I met someone in Cardiff.' Rachel pulled out a chair and sat down heavily at the table. She ran her fingers through her hair.

'I don't think he was who he said he was. Oh, Cadi, what am I going to do? Bill – that's my landlord – has said he'll give me three months to sort it out, but then the cottage has to go back on the market. It's really decent of him to wait, but . . .'

Her voice wobbled and her eyes filled with tears.

Cadi turned back to the coffee. For a few seconds the sound of the grinder made it impossible to continue the conversation. By the time she had put the pot on the table, Rachel had managed to regain her composure. 'I'm sorry. I just didn't know who to talk to.'

'I'm glad you came here.' Cadi smiled sadly. 'I wish I could help about the cottage. This is all such a mess. You know, it turns out he bought Camp Meadow years ago, straight after we split up. He told me he would have given it to me as a gift, but because I was nasty to him, he decided to keep it. He enjoyed the thought of being able to do whatever he liked with something he knew I treasured. How vindictive is that! Oh, Rach, how can one man cause so much misery and chaos?'

'You must really have upset him,' Rachel said bitterly.

'And I hadn't given him a thought for years. I assumed, if I thought about him at all, that he'd forgotten about me.'

'He seems to me to be the personification of evil.' Rachel gave a watery grin. She reached across to the folder she had put on the table. 'I did some more sketches for "The Dream of Macsen Wledig". I know we agreed to put it on hold so that you could write your novel, but I hoped you might still finish the poem.'

Opening the folder, Cadi stared at the drawing that confronted her. It was Elen. It was really Elen, the Elen she had seen, the Elen who was telling her story. She gazed at it for several seconds, then turned the page over to look at the next. Macsen himself, with his dark curling hair greying at the temples and his eagle nose and piercing eyes. The ruby ring, she noticed, had gone. It was perfect. She moved on. Elen's father, the high king came next and then—' She looked up in astonishment. 'Who is this?'

'I don't know.' Rachel shrugged. 'I hoped you would tell me.'

It was Branwen.

'She's not in the story. Or at least, not in the Mabinogion.'

'Then where does she appear? I must have seen her somewhere.'

'She has appeared here. In my story.' Cadi couldn't bring herself to refer to it as her novel.

Rachel glanced up at her. 'So, what's her name?'

'Branwen.'

'And she's a witch?'

'Not really a witch, no. A Druid, perhaps.'

'Like Meryn.'

Cadi nodded. 'I think she and Meryn have' – she hesitated over the choice of word – 'interacted, shall I say.'

Rachel screwed up her face. 'That sounds about right. What else would they have done.' She reached for the sketch. 'So, I'd better tear it up then.'

'No!' Cadi put her hand over the sketch to protect it. 'No, don't do that. It's brilliant. It captures her essence, probably better than I ever could in my . . .' Again she hesitated. 'Novel.' She forced herself to utter the word.

Rachel gave her a knowing glance. 'Well done. You said it.'

Cadi grimaced. 'I just don't see myself as a novelist.'

'A historical novelist.'

'Is that better?'

'Of course it is. It sounds more serious. More historical.' Rachel managed a smile.

'It's not coming out that way. There's so much about Elen that no one knows. The mentions of Macsen's wife disappear after Macsen is executed. Somewhere it says Theodosius spared her life and that of Macsen's mother, but the rest is, well, legend. A woman, a queen, called Elen or perhaps Helen, morphs into other people. She is confused with a prehistoric goddess and another empress and a Christian saint. It's only really the Mabinogion that links her to Macsen. So much ties in, but not enough to make it history.'

'Doesn't that give you more scope to invent, if no one can contradict you?' Rachel mused after a moment. 'That's an interesting combination, though. Empress, goddess, saint and presumably, given your own address. Road builder!' Rachel sipped her coffee. 'I'm glad I came. You always distract me from my own miseries.'

'With my dotty ideas?'

Rachel grinned. 'Something like that.'

'Last time I infuriated you.'

'Sorry.'

They both looked up as a knock sounded at the door. Cadi got up and went over to the front window. 'I can almost see who is on the doorstep. Sometimes they stand back enough to get a glimpse – oh, it's Gwen. She's the detective inspector in charge of Ifan's case.'

Gwen sat down with them and Cadi assured her that she could speak freely in front of Rachel. Her face was sombre. 'I have news. Good and bad. The good news is that Ifan's wife has regained consciousness and her pregnancy seems secure. The bad news is she refuses to press charges. She swears Ifan never touched her. She insists she tripped at the top of the stairs and he only grabbed her to try to stop her falling.'

Cadi stared at her in astonishment. 'I had no idea she was pregnant.'

Gwen looked taken aback. 'Oh dear. That was probably confidential information. I took it for granted you knew.'

'No, but I'm glad she's OK. I'm not surprised she's refusing to charge him. He will have messed with her head if my experience is anything to go by. Poor woman. So, what's happening to Ifan?'

'Luckily he's not well enough to leave hospital yet. We're still trying to prove he was responsible for the vandalism to your friend's car and laptop, but there are no fingerprints and it's hard to find any proof as yet. And of course there is absolutely no proof that he had any intention of harming your uncle. The fact that a Roman dagger was found near him proves nothing. He's had a scan of his head and they're not too happy with the results. There is swelling on the brain and they're not going to release him until that has reduced. I'm leaving someone there to keep an eye on him for the time being, but I'm afraid without any further charges we can't really justify the resources to guard him full-time. I know you feel under threat, but we can't prove he's actually done anything.' She sighed. 'I went to see his father just now but there's no one there. I don't suppose you know anyone who would know where he is?'

Cadi shook her head. 'He's not my best friend either, I'm afraid.'

'Nor anyone's, as far as I can tell.' Gwen laughed bitterly. 'What a charming family.'

'And they can't stand each other,' Cadi put in. 'You don't suppose Ifan's murdered him?' Her suggestion wasn't entirely serious but Gwen nodded with a rueful smile. 'It had crossed my mind. So far I'm leaving that one open.' She stood up. 'I must be off. Keep checking your door before you open it, just in case.'

'Nice lady,' Rachel said as Cadi closed the door behind her.

'I don't buy it that his wife has refused to testify against him. If she has, it must be because she's too scared of reprisals.' Cadi sat down again. 'Gwen was telling me they couldn't keep him under arrest, wasn't she. Once his brain has gone back to normal.'

'From what you say, it was never normal,' Rachel said tartly.

'But they won't keep him in prison. His threats to me aren't serious enough. And if they haven't found any fingerprints at Annabel's, and we can't prove anything he's done to you, either, then what can they charge him with?' The two women looked at each other for several seconds without a word.

'Let me take you out to supper,' Rachel suggested. 'I can't bear the idea of us locked up here waiting for another knock at the door. I can stay, can't I? Your secret lover isn't here, is he?'

'No. He's gone.' Cadi hadn't realised what she had said until she saw Rachel's triumphant expression. 'That is, I haven't got a secret lover, as you well know. If you meant Charles, who's just a friend, he's gone back home to sort out the mess that Ifan made of his life. If anything is guaranteed to put you off someone it's a paranoid vicious ex who wrecks your nice peaceful existence.'

'Have you spoken to him?'

'Yes.'

'And?'

'He said he'd probably be coming back tomorrow.'

'And will he be staying here?'

Cadi shook her head. 'He didn't say where he would be staying, but my guess is he'll go back to Annabel, if she'll have him. Of course you can stay here.'

Sitting up in bed, Cadi stared towards the window with a shiver. She held her breath, listening for several seconds, then, plucking up courage, she slid out of bed and crept across to the window to peer out. The street was empty.

She opened her bedroom door as silently as she could and glanced across the landing towards the spare room. There was no light showing under the door. Rachel must be asleep. Turning to the staircase, she tiptoed down and padded over to the front door. She listened carefully for several seconds then quietly drew the bolt and pulled it open. The night was very still. Cautiously she crept out to the gate and stared over it. There was no one around but in the distance she could see a light on in Arwel's house. So, he had come home at last.

42

It was All Hallows' Eve. When they turned at last up the long road towards the high king's palace in the land of the Silures, the small party of travellers were exhausted. There were fewer men in their escort now, having left the injured behind, and the wagon with the mended wheel had been abandoned, all their remaining belongings piled in the one vehicle, which also carried Valeria and Julia and the younger children. The others walked or rode. They had acquired two ponies for the girls, and an extra packhorse. Elen was uneasy. She and Junius Secundus both suspected they were being followed, though there was no sign of anyone even on the straighter stretches of road where they could see for long distances. If there was anyone behind them, they were keeping well out of sight.

They made their way slowly through the village, along the track past the watermill and up towards the palace gates, which hung open and unguarded. High above them on the top of Bryndinas the oppidum was silent, though there were traces of woodsmoke rising above the houses and there was a smell of roasting meat hanging faintly in the air.

The palace with its architrave and pillars, its red roof tiles and its neatly fenced paddocks, had gone, leaving ruined crumbling walls and deserted courtyards smelling even now of burnt plaster and charred wood. Elen drew to a halt with a barely restrained sob of pain. They all fell silent, staring round the desolate scene.

'We have to rebuild it,' Elen said at last, her voice breaking. 'I will not let these pirates win.'

The only sound she recognised, apart from the lonely cry of a buzzard circling high above the oppidum, was the cheerful trickle of water. She slid off her mare and walked slowly towards the sound, picking her way through the wreckage of the place that had once been her home.

The fountain was still intact at the far end of what had once been an enclosed garden. The bench where she had so often sat was still there, and the stone basin. The basin was clogged with debris, but the jet of water spouted high and triumphantly into the air, fed by the stream from the steep hillside, in spate now after all the rain. She stood staring at it, trying to restrain her tears.

'It was so beautiful.' The soft voice behind her startled her.

'Branwen?' She turned and after a moment's hesitation put her arms around her friend.

'I knew you would be here soon.' Branwen gave her a gentle smile. 'I've been waiting. Your stepson told me you had landed and were insisting on travelling back to your father's palace. Then, the commander of your escort sent him a message saying he needed more men because the roads were so dangerous.' She reached out for Elen's hand. 'It is time to leave this sad place and resume your duties.'

'I have no duties. Only to bring my children to safety.' Elen sighed. 'I know now the palace is truly gone but I needed to see for myself. So, I suppose all that is left for me is to go to my father or to Conan.'

She did not notice how Branwen narrowed her eyes. 'And wait for them to tell you what to do?' The woman sounded incredulous.

That made Elen smile at last. 'What else is there for the widow of a disgraced and disinherited family? We were sent away with nothing but the clothes we stood up in.'

'And your lives!' Branwen retorted.

And the Virgin's precious little bowl. The words echoed silently in Elen's head.

She should have known Branwen would pick them up. 'What bowl?'

'Something very special, given to me by Macsen's mother. She meant it for him' – or did she? She tried to remember what Flavia had said. No, she had suspected that it would never reach Macsen as she pressed it into Elen's hands.

. . . this is for you, to use as you see fit, my dear. A gift freely given should be as freely accepted.

Elen sighed again. Her hand went to her throat where she still wore the gold chain with its tiny key. No doubt the robbers had found the box, forced it open and, seeing nothing but the unassuming clay dish, thrown it away in disappointment.

'It was a little bowl, very precious, used by the mother of our Lord Jesus to catch drops of his blood as he hung dying on the Roman cross. It would mean nothing to a robber. It has no value in itself. It was made of clay.'

Branwen shivered.

Elen stood deep in thought for several moments, trying to put the sad memories out of her mind. She had to pull herself together, assume her place at the head of her weary band of followers and decide where, after her visit to her birthplace, she was going to go. Branwen was right. If she went to her father he would once more feel entitled to tell her what to do. He might even arrange another marriage for her to cement some future alliance. And she had no desire to go to Conan, especially if he was now based in Armorica. Besides which, it would put her and her children in danger if she crossed back across the sea to the mainland of the empire. At least in Britannia she thought she would be safe. Theodosius had made it clear that a province at the furthest reaches of the empire was the least of his worries.

She glanced at her companion. It was only then she realised that Branwen was standing immobile, her eyes closed. She seemed far away.

* * *

379

The rain had been drumming on the rough roof of the shelter where the robbers had surveyed their pickings after the robbery. Their leader was disgusted at the haul, which mostly consisted of women's clothes. There was no jewellery. No money. A bundle of blankets. He looked round in fury. 'Who brought the blankets?'

The man who had grabbed the bundle raised a hand half-heartedly. He was nursing a wounded elbow. 'You fool!' his leader roared at him. 'Out of a whole wagonload of treasure you bring me blankets!' He lashed out at his hapless follower. He surveyed the pile of belongings tipped out onto the muddy floor of the hut. 'These at least are better quality. They have some value if we can sell them. And this is silk.' He dived for the shawl at the bottom of one of the heaps of clothing and, grabbing it from the pile, he shook it out. A small box fell on the floor at his feet.

He gave an ugly grin. 'Well, maybe after all I will spare your miserable life.' He picked up the box and, sticking a filthy fingernail under the rim of the lid, he tried to open it. It resisted. He was aware that the group of men around him had fallen silent. They were all watching. He rattled the box. Nothing. With a snarl he reached for the dagger from his belt and, inserting the blade, he threw his whole weight onto the hilt. The blade snapped and the dagger fell to the ground. With a yell of frustration he threw the box down. 'Leave it,' he shouted. 'It's of no value. Go back. We'll follow them.'

He heard the sharp intake of breath from the man nearest him and then a sharp yelp of fear from another standing near the entrance to the shack and he glanced up. They were both staring at the doorway.

A woman had appeared. She was tall, swathed in a black cloak and she was watching them through narrowed eyes. He bared his teeth as she moved closer.

Was this gift freely given?

He wasn't sure where the voice came from. She hadn't seemed to move her lips. She stretched out her hand and drifted closer.

'Get that woman out of here!' The outraged man stepped

back. He reached for the heavy wooden club that someone had dropped beside him in the mud as they scrambled to reach the stolen clothing. He swung the club back and forth a couple of times and then took a firmer grip, slapping it gently against the palm of his free hand. 'One step closer and I take this to your head, hussy!' he said softly.

The woman smiled. 'Give me the box,' she said, 'and I will go.'

He kicked it sharply as it lay at his feet. 'Come and get it.' He tapped his free hand with the club again. He was aware that the men around him were moving back, pressed against the rough walls of the hut. 'I said, come and get it!' he shouted. 'You,' he glanced across at the man who had brought the bundle in, 'you pick it up.'

The man stooped obediently and lifted it out of the mud, the broken dagger blade falling at his feet. He brushed some of the mud off it almost tenderly, wincing at the pain from his elbow as he moved. Blood from the reopened wound was beginning to drip through his tattered sleeve as he glanced from his leader towards the door and then back again.

'That needs to go back to its owner.' The woman's tone was relentless. 'Now.'

'Throw her out, someone,' the enraged man called. 'Or skewer her, if you prefer. With sword or cock' – he gave a suggestive laugh – 'I don't mind which as long as she is out of my sight before I count to two.'

The woman seemed unable to resist a smile. 'So, at least you can count to two! An educated man, no less. You' – her glance flicked sideways to the wounded man holding the box – 'go now. The box will show you the way. Take it to the woman from whom you stole it. Don't come back here. There is honest work out there for honest men.'

For a moment everyone in the shack seemed to hold their breath, then the man turned and fled out of the door, the box clutched against his chest.

The woman waited until the sound of his running footsteps died away then she turned back to the others. 'I advise you all to leave. This man is no leader,' she said, her voice weighted with scorn. Then, before their astonished eyes, she faded from sight, one moment there, her long cloak dragging in the mud of the shack, the next a shadow against the light, and moments later gone. No one moved.

'Well, go after him. Get that box back,' the hoarse whisper rang out in the silence, 'and then we'll find out where those women went. There will be more pickings where that came from.'

In the shadows of the ruined palace the robbers, all but three, had crept close, hidden in the enclosing trees and bushes, before racing through the crumbling walls and columns, brandishing their knives and clubs, letting out wild yells of fury. But they had misjudged the situation. Elen's escort, though quiet and seemingly relaxed, were still armed and, unsettled by the strange atmosphere of the ruins, they had been alert to the possibility that someone had been following them. There were a few minutes of close fierce fighting before the robbers turned and ran.

On Branwen's orders they brought warm water for Elen to wash in, and clean clothes from their headman's wife's own clothes box. Safe under the headman's roof up in the oppidum on Bryndinas, she and Valeria and Julia joined him and his household for an evening meal. It was while they were enjoying a final course of honeyed cream and fruit that Branwen came in and tiptoed towards the table. She was dressed now in a modest tunic of the palest blue with a checked shawl around her shoulders and came to a standstill behind Elen. 'Please, come outside. There is someone there to see you.'

Elen stood up. 'What is it, Branwen? Who—'

Branwen smiled. 'It is someone you will want to see.' Elen made for the doorway, followed by everyone else who had been seated round the table. In the separate kitchen building behind the main hall, the servants and cooks were all standing in a group behind the worktable.

Three men stood in the doorway which led out into the muddy street between the township's houses. The man at the front of the trio was visibly shaking as Branwen appeared, followed by Elen and her companions. He had eyes only for Branwen, Elen noticed, and they were terrified.

Branwen moved a few steps towards him. 'This is our queen. You may return the box to her own hands.'

The man glanced around, almost paralysed with fear, then he stepped forward and held out the box to Branwen. She stepped back sharply. 'I said give it to the queen.'

Elen stared at her and then at the box. Her missing box. The box that contained the clay dish. She stepped forward and held out her hands. The man thrust the box at her. 'I'm sorry I stole it,' he mumbled. 'We've brought all your things back. We weren't part of the attack earlier. We followed behind them to give these back.' He gestured behind him at the two other men who appeared to be carrying various bundles tied up in blankets. They threw them down in the doorway, ducked outside, then all three turned and fled.

'I'll call someone to go after them,' the headman said after a moment of stunned silence.

'No. Leave them,' Elen found her voice at last. 'They brought our things back. That is enough.' She looked round at the assembled men and women. 'What a dramatic end to our evening. I'm not sure what made them change their minds, but I am very thankful that they did.' She was clutching the box against her heart.

Later on when she and Branwen were alone she reached for the key around her neck. She had sent the servants away and Valeria and Julia had retired to bed. Elen looked at her companion with a shrewd smile. 'So, how did you do it?'

Branwen shook her head. 'I don't know what you mean.'

'I saw you. When I first told you about this box, you went away in your head. I spoke to you several times and you didn't hear me. Somehow you went back to find them.'

'Maybe.' Branwen's reply was deliberately vague.. 'Maybe you did it yourself.'

And with that Elen had to be content. 'So, are you interested to see what is in here?'

Branwen shook her head. 'That magic is not for me. I will leave you to pray to your god and I will give thanks to mine.'

Elen nodded. 'You called me queen.' Theodosius too had told her she could call herself a queen. She shuddered.

'You are no longer an empress.'

'No, but I have never been a queen.'

Branwen grinned. 'I think you will find that you are now. You have only to go and find your realm.'

Elen waited until the woman had left the room and then she inserted the key into the lock. The box had been badly marked and scored by the robber's dagger, but the lock turned smoothly and the lid lifted with ease. Inside the lambswool had protected the precious dish and it lay in its bed completely unharmed. She didn't touch it. She just looked at it for a long time then she carefully closed the lid and relocked it. Branwen was right. She needed to pray.

Outside in the heavy rain three men huddled together beyond the oppidum gates, under the trees on the edge of the steep hillside. Below them the track plunged back towards the burnt-out ruins. Only two of the gang had followed Branwen's advice and, grabbing a bundle each from the pile of looted belongings on the floor of the shack, had fled out into the darkness after their companion. Are we going back to him?' one of them said. They all knew who he meant. Their leader and his surviving followers had fled from the fighting in the ruins but they were probably still out there somewhere.

'I don't think so,' the wounded man said, his teeth still gritted against the pain in his arm. 'He will kill us.'

'So, where shall we go?'

'Like that woman said, we could find work, honest work. I vote we head back east, towards Londinium. There are bound to be jobs there. I used to be a craftsman once, till that bastard lured me away with promises of rich pickings on the roads.'

'And I had finished my apprenticeship, but the man who had taught me died,' said the other, 'and I had no place anywhere else.'

The third man looked down at his feet. 'I was a slave. My master gave me my freedom but I didn't know where to go.'

'Right. Then Londinium it is. We can easily give those

bastards the slip. They won't hang around long knowing there's a pack of fearsome natives after them.' He glanced over his shoulder up towards the fort. 'Are we all agreed?'

It was only as they set off down the steep hillside that the wounded man realised his arm had stopped hurting. He paused and rolled back his sleeve. The wound had miraculously healed.

43

Cadi was busy scribbling at her desk when Rachel appeared next morning. 'How long have you been up?' she asked as she made her way across towards the kitchen and reached for the kettle.

Cadi threw down her pen and stretched her arms painfully. 'I'm not sure.'

'You haven't been writing all night?'

'No.'

Rachel put a steaming mug of tea down on the desk in front of her. 'I've been thinking. I'm going home after breakfast. I need to stop panicking and to try to get my life in order.' She sat down on the edge of the chair beside the desk and sighed. 'I've got three months clear to work before the cottage goes on the market, so I'll finish the Macsen sketches as soon as you can send me over the verses, and in the meantime I'll do some smaller, saleable stuff and try to concentrate on producing as much as possible for the galleries I already sell in. I'm not going to let the disappointment derail me.'

'Good for you.' Cadi tried to keep the exhaustion out of her voice. 'And I'll get the last of the verses over to you as I write them. I must be able to multitask. After all, writing a novel and writing poetry is not so different, especially when it's all about the same characters. I'm sorry I've been difficult.'

Rachel leaned forward and gripped her by the wrist. 'You haven't. My God! When I think what you've been going through. If you need me, I'll come. I don't know what I could do to help but I'll be there for you – you know that, don't you. And make sure Charles knows you need him. You're not very good at telling people how you feel.'

Cadi thought about that last sentence later, after Rachel had gone. Her cousin was right. She wasn't good at dealing with people. Ifan had seen to that. But maybe, even if he hadn't, everything would have gone wrong and her relationships would have all foundered anyway on the fact that the life inside her head was more important to her, more real, than the world around her. And this time she had allowed that inner life in until it had become like an all-pervasive coral, creeping across the rocks that were the foundations of her existence, spreading, solidifying, tying her in beautiful intricate knots while she allowed the reality of the actual world to atrophy and die.

She shuddered. What a sinister metaphor.

The immediate cure for impending depression was to do something physical. She had found that out long ago, and the first thing to do was to tidy the place. She glanced round her at the empty mugs and plates, the books and papers scattered across the floor, the chairs misplaced around the room, the dead flowers in the vase on the windowsill. She gave a slight smile as a voice echoed in her head. Not her mother – her mother wouldn't have noticed – but her mother's sister, coming in through the door as though stepping by mistake into dog mess. 'My God, Cadi, what must your neighbours think when they come in here?'

She washed up, dusted and tidied; opened all the windows; she stripped the spare room bed and put on fresh sheets, made a shopping list, did all the boring things she would normally put off as long as possible. Then she walked out into the fresh air and after a moment's hesitation she turned up the road towards the meadow. Nothing had changed in there. The field gate was padlocked again and now she saw a yellow notice about the planning application fluttering dispiritedly in the hedgerow. The little tent had not been removed from its place over the grave, but there were no security guards as far as she could see. With a quick glance over her shoulder to make sure there was no one around, she climbed over the gate and set off across the grass. The meadow was already hot, the sun high. She could hear grasshoppers and the drone of bees; high above her the skylark was pouring out its song into the silence. The scent of the grass was rich and glorious after being indoors all morning. She took a deep breath, reminded suddenly of the joy she used to feel wandering around in here on her own at every time of the year, in the early mornings, or late in the evenings, sometimes with Sally and little Gemma, but more often alone just relishing the quiet. Thinking. Allowing the poetry to flow in. All that had gone of late. This was now a place of violence, of blood and death, of burning buildings and galloping hooves, of mystery and strange unearthly forces. It was as if something weird and dangerous had been unleashed. Had that been Ifan all along? Had his ownership of this piece of land set the air trembling with the echoes of the past? She shivered. Standing still, she looked round and realised with a spike of fear that there was someone standing by the gate.

It was Chris. 'I saw you leave the cottage. I'm sorry. Would you rather be alone?' He had climbed onto the lowest bars of the gate and vaulted over it.

She liked Chris. He was solid; practical; reliable. Exactly the kind of person she needed near her at this moment. Side by side they set off slowly around the perimeter of the field.

'I've just dropped off some cakes and bread at Arwel's. Did you realise he was back?' He glanced across at her.

'I saw his lights on last night.'

Chris nodded. 'He's been in London. He brought Sue back with him.'

'Sue?'

'His daughter-in-law. Ifan's wife.'

Cadi stopped dead. 'Oh my God! The one Ifan is supposed to have beaten up?'

Chris nodded. 'She was in the hall when I knocked and

he had no alternative but to introduce her. I couldn't exactly ask her what had happened and where Ifan was now, so I just handed her the bag of buns and smiled politely.'

'Did she look OK?'

'A bit pale. Very pregnant.'

'And Arwel?'

'High colour. Scowling. Not pregnant.'

Cadi smiled. 'I probably won't call in.'

'Best not, is my guess. I just thought I'd warn you. Ifan is still in hospital?'

'As far as I know.'

'Good.' They reached the gate at last and scrambled back over it.

They parted at her front door. 'Take care, Cadi. Don't let your guard down.'

She watched as he walked away. Behind her a blackbird let out a peal of alarm calls in the garden and she turned to dive into the house. She slammed the door and leaned against it, her heart thudding. 'Breathe deeply and slowly.' She muttered the words to herself sternly. 'There is no one there. You know there isn't.'

She walked over to the garden doors, turned the key and, pushing them open, stepped outside. She glanced cautiously left and right and gasped. A whole section of the hedge had gone, leaving charred twigs and a strong smell of burning. The walls of the villa, ruinous and blackened, spread out onto the lawn, transparent, superimposed on the usual outline of her old apple tree, the boughs heavy with green apples, her round table and the three wooden chairs that stood under it clearly visible, but only half there. For a moment she couldn't move, then slowly the vision faded, the hedge reappeared and the garden returned to normal. Her mouth dry she took a cautious step towards the hedge and then another. There was no trace of the ruin, just the slight signs of the incisions she and Meryn had made in the grass at the edge of the flower bed beneath the hedge. She stood looking down at the place and then backed carefully away.

'Meryn?' Her phone rang at that moment and she groped for it in her pocket, answering without thinking.

'It's me, Charles.' He sounded crestfallen. 'Sorry.'

She spun round and walked back towards the house. 'Charles, I'm so pleased to hear you. Sorry, I was thinking about Uncle Meryn, and you know how he has the knack of responding to random thoughts.' She stepped back inside the house and after a second's thought she pulled the doors closed, turning the key. 'Where are you? Are you still coming?' She hoped she didn't sound too needy.

'I'm up at Annabel's. Can I pop down?'

They took their coffee outside to sit under the apple tree where she told him about the impersonation of the American buyer for Rachel's cottage and her aborted exhibition.

'No proof it was Ifan, of course.'

And, just as Gwen had warned her, no proof, it turned out, that Ifan had been responsible for Charles's vandalism. 'All circumstantial, apparently. No fingerprints. Well, we guessed there wouldn't be. He's far too clever. No evidence to say he was there. The insurance people rang me. My insurance will still pay. I still have a crime number. But there's no proof it was him, no witnesses to anything he may have done or said, just my word against his. He is a very credible, respectable and wealthy man. Why on earth should I suspect him of having any kind of grudge against me?'

Cadi heaved a deep sigh. 'God he's so clever. So plausible!'

Gwen rang later that afternoon. 'I'm so sorry. After his wife withdrew her accusations we had nothing to hold him on. There's no provable evidence against him. It's all hearsay with no witnesses. His last scan was clear so he has been discharged from hospital and we've had to release him.'

'What about everything we've told you?' Cadi heard herself wailing into the phone.

'I'm sorry, Cadi, but it's your word against his. I know as well as you do he's guilty as hell, but without proof we can do nothing. We've been looking into his history. He has no criminal record. He's a well-regarded philanthropist and businessman; and according to him, you're the one who's been harbouring a grudge ever since he had to end the relationship between you because of your impossible behaviour. I know!' She forestalled

Cadi's explosion of denial. 'But there you are. That is what he's claiming. The case put by your uncle has collapsed as well. That too was a malicious accusation, completely without foundation, and the police who went up to his cottage to get a further statement from him yesterday could find no trace of him. A neighbour told them he hadn't seen him for months.'

'What do you mean?' This time Cadi's indignation was so real Gwen listened. 'He has no neighbours; he lives in an isolated cottage in the Black Mountains and Detective Chief Inspector Vaughan went up there to take his evidence after Meryn called the ambulance to Ifan when he was struck by lightning. A helicopter came. Surely the paramedics aren't going to deny seeing Meryn. He's been home for months, except when he came to stay with me here for a few days.'

There was a short pause. 'Ah. There seems to be a gap in the evidence file. Leave it with me, Cadi. And give your uncle a ring. Check he's OK. And, listen. If there is any sign of Ifan anywhere near you – or your uncle, for that matter – ring me on the number I gave you, at once. At once!' she repeated.

Cadi switched off her phone. Charles was watching her.

'You gathered what she told me? They've released him.'

'Friends in high places?' Charles sounded bitter.

'I can't understand it. They know he was responsible for vandalising your car.'

'That was all based on his use of violence against his wife. If she's backed down, then the whole case obviously seems shaky. He's had time to think it all through, calm down and reframe it convincingly. He's a clever bastard!' Charles threw himself down on the sofa and sat, his hands clasped between his knees, staring down at the floor.

'I'll ring Meryn. Maybe he'll know what's going on.' She held on for several minutes, listening to the ringtone, but there was no reply. He had not switched on his answerphone.

'Ring the policeman. Wasn't he an old friend of Meryn's?'

When she finally got on to the correct CID department, all she could do was leave a message for DCI Vaughan to call her back.

'Would you stay here, with me?' Cadi said at last. 'Or maybe you're planning to stay with Annabel again?'

He grinned. 'I was there last night, but I'm sure she would rather I wasn't. Of course I'll stay with you.'

Once he had collected his case, his new laptop, a bag of groceries and the chocolates he had tried to give his former landlady, and which had been firmly redirected by her to Cadi, he drove away to park his car well out of sight behind the house of one of Annabel's friends. As far as they knew, Ifan had no way of knowing what Charles's new car looked like, but they were taking no chances. Once he had been safely ensconced in the spare room, the downstairs windows locked and the kitchen blind pulled down against the low sunlight, Cadi felt safe at last.

It was only then that she told him about her vision of the burnt-out wing of the palace, and after careful scrutiny of the garden, still brightly lit by the evening sun and very obviously empty of intruders, they went outside, drinks in hand, to view the scene where the devastation had occurred, before going to sit under the apple tree.

'Do we gather they never rebuilt it?' Cadi asked as she sipped her drink. He had made them both a Negroni. She was feeling much happier now that he was there, she realised; the shadowy ghost of the ruined building seemed less worrying, less real. 'Elen's first reaction was to say that was what she wanted to do.'

'I expect the archaeologists will be able to tell us that. I'm so pleased they're going to do some investigation.'

'Have the police finished the forensic side of things?' Cadi had found a packet of roasted peanuts in the back of the cupboard and thrown them into a bowl. She picked out one.

'Steve seemed to think so. They're just waiting for an official OK to go back to the site.' He sat back in his chair and sighed. 'You know, I love it here. For all its weirdness and ghostly apparitions, it's a peaceful place.'

She smiled. 'Which of course it won't be any longer if they build houses next door.'

'No. I suppose not.' He sat forward. 'If Ifan has been cleared of any wrong doing, however misguidedly, I imagine the planning application will be reinstated. You do realise that if they give him permission to build here, the dig, even if they find a villa, will only delay the inevitable.'

She nodded. 'I would have to move. Which of course is what Ifan wants.' She reached for the jug with its rapidly melting ice cubes and topped up both their glasses. 'This house, this landscape, made me the writer I am. I've been thinking about it. Ifan couldn't bear that I lived this internal life with people in my head who were strangers to him, people he couldn't get to know and he couldn't control. My thoughts, ideas, the places I could imagine were all inaccessible to him. I could escape from him whenever I wanted to, to a world far away.' She paused thoughtfully. 'It was the same with David, to a certain extent. I couldn't fit into his world either, not really, and to be honest I didn't want to, but he understood. He's a good man; kind. He let me go and we have stayed friends. Ifan never bothered to try.'

'I understand.' Charles said it so softly she wondered if she had imagined it.

'That's because you're a writer too.' It had taken her a while to think of looking him up online after she had first found him on the university website.

He grinned. 'Of two stuffy history books.'

'Well-reviewed history books. So, you know what it's like to live in the past, and besides, you're a dowser. You must be OK.' She sprang to her feet, embarrassed by her own revelations. 'Shall we go in and find something to throw in the pan? I'll make us a stir-fry.'

44

Elen was sitting on a bench staring down at the sad ruins far below them, with the headman and Branwen beside her under the broad overhang of the sheltering thatch. Rain had been dripping steadily into the mud beyond the conical roof with its huge span. 'I need to go before the snows come and close the road,' she said again. They had been discussing it for several days now. She had had messages from her father and from Conan; both had told her she would be welcome to go to them, in Camulodunum or Armorica, to make herself a home. Neither commented on her possible future, wherever she ended up. She was the widow of a defeated soldier, the mother of children, all of whom would need to be settled, married, exonerated from their father's crimes. Theirs was the future; her life was from now on at best unimportant, at worst non-existent; a time of retirement, absolution perhaps for Macsen's ambition, a time to try to cleanse the stain of his name for his children and to forget it for herself.

She stood up abruptly as at last the winter sunlight flickered through the clouds. 'First I will return to Segontium. The legions have gone; there are no more than a handful of men holding the fort. I have friends there; local people who were prepared to give their lives for me, who will support me. I can do good there.'

'And you would be welcomed,' Branwen put in.

'But wait at least until the spring.' The headman stood up too. 'The roads are terrible. They will soon be impassable. Stay here with us until then.'

'The roads are the first thing I will improve,' she retorted. 'No more ambushes. The main routes must be cleared, the holes filled, the countryside, my countryside, opened to scholars and traders and pilgrims so that women like us' – she glanced at Branwen – 'can travel freely and safely throughout the realm. My realm.' She smiled. 'You called me queen. I need to have a realm to leave my sons. You told me I would be the mother of kings. It is up to me to make it so. The tribesmen will follow me, by the grace of God.' She did not see the fleeting look of disbelief in Branwen's eyes. 'We shall be beyond the reach of the empire. Theodosius said as much. He has enough to preoccupy him with invading hordes threatening him on every side, any-where they sense Roma's growing weakness.'

The headman gave her a searching look. 'You intend to make yourself queen of the province of Britain?' He scowled. 'What will your father the high king say to that? Or your stepbrother? Or Macsen's eldest sons? They all live in peace with the empire, albeit tenuously so. You intend to stir up rebellion and pick up Macsen's foolish ambitions where he failed?'

There was a sudden deep silence.

Slowly she shook her head. 'You misunderstand me.' She gave a sad laugh. 'I have an army of eleven men, seven women and my children. But I am descended from the ancient kings, so my blood is royal, and I have the protection of the Mother of Christ. She will tell me what to do to make this land that I love safe. That is nothing to do with Macsen and his legacy. This is mine alone. And it is a legacy of caring and gentleness and prayer.'

She had watched enough of Macsen's soldiers, drafted in to clear and mend the roads as they travelled across Europe, to know how it was done. Everyone agreed that the roads were dangerous and that they wanted to travel safely and with speed where possible. The first route to come to her attention, in the lands of the high king beyond the notice any longer of the Roman Empire, was that which led from the watermill, and the gates of the old palace which had been her birthplace, west towards the main route from Moridunum and then north towards Y Gaer. Then west again towards the sacred mountains and beyond them towards the setting sun of the summer solstice.

With no legionaries to provide the muscle for the roads, the leaders of the tribes along the route they travelled, inspired by her zeal, proved proactive and willing, helping with men and funding extricated from the tightly locked coffers holding taxes collected for Rome but never delivered. Later, much later, the route would be called Sarn Elen, meaning Elen's Causeway.

When at last Elen's small party arrived at Segontium it was to find the remains of a garrison who, disheartened and abandoned by any signs of support from the empire, had developed a loose alliance with the tribesmen of the Ordovices still trying to protect the coast from raiders. Elen and her companions were greeted as if they were uninvited strangers. There were no guards to speak of on the great arched gateways, but the offices in the principia looked as though they were still in use, the barracks and cavalry quarters were occupied. Elen recognised no one in the garrison. The general's house, the praetorium, was untended and shabby, the great reception room obviously used as a mess kitchen for the men, the gardens run to weed. Standing by the clogged fountain that no longer flowed with water from the aqueducts, with Valeria and Julia at her side Elen found herself near tears. She had kept this place warm in her heart, thinking of it as home now that the palace of her birth had gone. Peblig, Owain and Anwn, breaking free of their nurse, ran shouting through the building. They had been promised a home, and Delyth had told them stories of the beauties of the mountains, the painted walls of the nursery, showing the fairies and monsters and exotic animals of her tales, the ponies and puppies which would await them to replace the much-loved animals they had lost, and the boys, fed up with long weeks on the road, were too full of excitement to stand still. The girls came to stand behind their mother and their silence spoke volumes.

Elen sighed. 'So, there is obviously much to do,' she said, her voice steadied once again. 'Delyth, can you recruit servants from the vicus. Presumably the houses there are still occupied with the families of the men of the garrison. Branwen, could you see where our friend from Dinas Dinlle is to be found and explain to him the situation. Rhys?' The old man had followed them in, staring around him in complete astonishment. 'We will need civilian grooms and house staff. And someone please call the officer in command to greet me.' There had been no sign of anyone of any rank in the fort at all. She paused and took a deep breath. 'Valeria and Julia, between us we must make this a home again, and a safe place to live.' She knew Julia would help. Valeria she was not so sure of.

She looked around, trying to hide her despair. If she was to be treated as a queen, she would need the trappings and authority to ensure that she was recognised as such. If she was not to be a queen, what was she, and what place did it hold for her, this far-flung, forgotten corner of a disintegrating empire, not even recognised any longer by an emperor who was anyway her enemy?

'What indeed?' Cadi read through the last of her notes. She chewed her lip thoughtfully. She had reached the end of the story as told in 'The Dream of Macsen Wledig'. In that version Macsen had captured the city of Rome with the aid of his brothers-in-law. A complete fabrication. In her own version she had reached the end of Elen's place in history, sparse as it was. The emperor had spared her life, and the lives of her youngest children. Little Victor had been killed at Treverorum, the German Trier. After that the only mentions of Elen were in the myths and legends, the splendidly detailed but unreliable genealogies of the Welsh royal families and the wonderful inscription on the great Pillar of Eliseg in Valle Crucis, which mentioned Sevira, and Vortigern, names written in stone. But even that was carved after the personalities she was dealing with in her story had been forgotten by authenticated history. Only one indisputable fact remained. These people had left memories. However doubtful and unreliable the memories were, their names and their fame had survived.

She looked up. Had that been a knock at the door? She pushed back her chair and stood up. Charles had retired upstairs an hour or so before, citing some notes he wanted to make for a course he would be running the following term.

She tiptoed across the floor to the door and listened, her ear to the panelling. There was someone out there in the dark. She could hear feet shuffling on the stones on the path.

'Cadi!' The voice came from behind her. Charles was standing at the bottom of the stairs. 'I wondered if you'd heard the knock. I saw her walking down the road from my window. She's alone. I think it must be Arwel's daughter-in-law. I'll make myself scarce, but call me if you need me.' He turned and ran back up the stairs and out of sight.

Drawing back the bolt, Cadi opened the door.

'You probably don't want to talk to me.' Sue waited until she was inside to introduce herself. 'Arwel doesn't know I'm here. He went to bed ages ago. The drive from London yesterday exhausted him. I hope you don't mind me calling, but I felt you and I needed to talk.'

Cadi led the way to the sofa and chairs by the darkened window and sat down opposite the young woman. Chris had been right in his description. She was very pregnant and very pale. He hadn't mentioned that she was also very beautiful.

'The police didn't believe me when I said Ifan hadn't hurt me,' she said after a few seconds hesitation. 'And they were right. He tried to kill me. I thought it was safe going back to the house because he was in Wales, but it wasn't. He told me he had been in hospital. He tried to make me feel sorry for him. He shouted at me and accused me of terrible things. I tried to run away and he hit me and then he pushed me down the stairs.'

Cadi felt her fists clench in her lap.

'I knew if I implicated him he would get even one day, even if he had to wait years. I couldn't risk my baby's life.' She stifled a sob. 'He thinks I've been unfaithful. He thinks the baby isn't his.'

'He told you that?'

'Oh yes. He told me.'

'And is it true?' It seemed a callous question, but then this woman was a complete stranger.

'No, of course it isn't. Arwel came to see me in hospital. He told me a bit about what had been happening to you. He knows his son. He knew I was in danger. The hospital wouldn't let me go home unless I had someone there to look after me and Arwel was the nearest thing I have to family. He offered to bring me back here. He and Ifan don't get on. I expect you knew that.'

Cadi nodded. She sighed. 'Where is he now?'

'Ifan? Still in hospital, I assume.'

'No. They released him. The police decided not to charge him after you – sorry to say this – after you decided not to press charges. After all he's done, and all the things we suspect him of doing, they had to release him. Nothing could be proved. He's like some kind of eel. Nothing sticks to him. He's suspected of all kinds of things but he never leaves a trace, or a finger-print, behind. Oh, Sue, sorry. Are you OK?' she gasped as Sue slumped back in the sofa, her eyes closed.

'Could I have some water, please?'

Cadi handed her a glass. 'Shall I make some tea? That would be more comforting.'

The nod was so slight she barely saw it.

Cadi saw how badly the woman's hands were shaking as she sipped the water. She returned to the kitchen and switched on the kettle. 'The police rang me this afternoon to tell me he had been released. The local DI is very sympathetic,' she said gently. She made two cups and brought them back to the sofa. 'Sue, do you think he's really capable of murder?'

'Yes.' She didn't hesitate.

'But surely you could at least have got some kind of anti-molestation order?'

'I told you, I didn't dare. I just wanted to run and run and run.' Sue's eyes filled with tears.

Leaning forward, Cadi found herself reaching out to put a comforting hand over Sue's clasped fingers. They were ice-cold. 'Do you feel safe with Arwel?'

'As long as Ifan doesn't guess where I've gone. He despises his father, so it's unlikely he'd suspect me of coming to stay with him.'

'Who else knows where you are?'

'Well, the hospital, of course. And our cleaning lady at home. Arwel took me back to fetch my things and some baby stuff. She knows what went on. She was next door and saw us. But she would never tell him.'

Cadi kept her thoughts to herself. Even if the cleaning lady was brave enough to stand up to Ifan, someone at the hospital would tell him without a second's thought who it was who had come to collect his wife.

Arwel agreed. He came over the next morning on his own. 'She's still asleep. We need to talk.' He glared at Cadi and then at Charles. They had been eating breakfast outside and she led him out to the table on the terrace.

Charles sat back in his chair. 'Cadi has put me in the picture, and I have a suggestion to make. My sister lives near me in Cardiff. Supposing I drive Sue over there. I'm pretty sure Margo would welcome her and take care of her. She's on her own now – her husband died a few years ago and there are no children – and best of all she lives only ten minutes from the hospital should the baby put in an appearance early. I won't suggest Sue goes to my flat. I suspect Ifan is probably targeting it for a petrol bomb by now, but Margo would be the perfect refuge for her. If she agrees, I could take Sue as soon as she's ready, settle her in and then come back here this evening.'

The handover was managed with the skill of an army manoeuvre. Arwel drove Sue across the hills to Waitrose in Abergavenny. They wandered round the store for fifteen minutes, throwing baby stuff into the trolley. He then left her and her trolley in the car park, made his way back to his car and set off back home. Two minutes later Charles appeared in his new car, scooped her into the front seat, threw her shopping in the boot and was out of the car park in seconds.

An hour and a half later Arwel phoned Cadi. 'They've arrived safely. Deserted back roads, and as far as they can tell there was no one tailing them.'

Cadi smiled with a sigh of relief. No small talk, no softening of his tone, but at least he must appreciate that she was being helpful. Time to ring the police and tell Gwen what had happened and to find out why Meryn's word had not been sufficient to keep Ifan under arrest.

Gwen rang her back an hour later. 'I'm afraid we've made no progress. The report is correct. Your uncle's house is locked up and there's no one around to verify if they've seen him recently. I'm afraid the local police know nothing about what happened. The young constable who spoke to your uncle has gone on leave and doesn't seem to have felt the event was worth recording.' She gave an irritated groan. 'DCI Vaughan moved on several years ago and I'm still waiting for him to get back to me. Meryn Jones has a slightly unreliable reputation, to put it mildly. The lightning was, shall we say, very localised.' She cleared her throat. 'Even though they got the air ambulance out to the victim and his burns were very real, the mention of Professor Jones's name produced some really sceptical reactions not to say unsympathetic jokes down in Hay. It's unfortunate he shares a name with a film hero action man.'

Cadi sighed. 'I've tried ringing him. He hasn't called me back.'

'I'm sure he'll contact you as soon as he gets your messages.' Gwen's voice softened. 'I'll let you know if we hear anything, I promise.'

Julia and Valeria had left. After a few days in the discomfort of the fort with no goal any longer to pull them forward, they told Elen they were planning to go, taking with them an escort from the already meagre garrison. Julia's sister was married to a senior officer in Deva. They would go there. Elen would not miss Valeria. Her relationship with Macsen would always come between them, but Julia had been one of the nearest people she had to a true friend. They exchanged kisses and Elen and her girls waved them farewell, then they turned back to look down the empty via principalis.

Her only solace was in the emptiness and grandeur of the distant mountains and the return of her beloved Emrys with his mares and two of his offspring, a small family of horses arriving on Conan's orders with their own groom, who, after a stern inspection by Rhys, was admitted to the cavalry barracks. She had been afraid the horse would not recognise her, but he showed every sign of delight when she went to make a fuss of him, whickering with pleasure and rubbing his head against her shoulder. Taking Emrys from the stables and escorted by two or three of the male servants employed by Rhys, it was wonderful to ride again, off the roadway and into the heather and bracken, following deer paths that wound into the woods, exploring the River Seiont and the lonely valleys. Sometimes one or other of the children would accompany her, but mostly she preferred to ride alone, delighting in her own company and that of the wild creatures she saw from horseback, making it clear her escort should lag behind.

From time to time she visited the holy places. Sometimes they were in empty cwms and sheltered passes, sometimes they were deep in the forests on the lower slopes of the great mountain ranges. There she would find small shrines, sometimes still loved, as witnessed by a posy of flowers or a coin or a bent pin tossed into a rock pool, more often abandoned but still redolent with the powerful energies of the earth and there she would pray as Bishop Martin had taught her, feeling nearer to God there than in the little chapel she had resurrected in the fort, leaving the men to watch the horses until she returned from her prayers. Sometimes there were carvings of the old gods, hewn out of the local stone and draped in moss, but once or twice she saw near them a Christian symbol, the chi-rho, or a fish, or a ringed cross and occasionally the figure of a saint with a halo round his head. Where the old gods still ruled she would make the sign of the cross and perhaps leave an offering to a local saint, and several times she vowed that she would rededicate the shrine to Christ and encourage one of the holy men from the local monastery to come as a hermit to offer regular prayers in a place so obviously dedicated to God. She thought often of Bishop Martin, taking refuge from his busy life in the quiet lonely caves beyond the river, of the stories he told of St Antony, alone in the desert, of the examples such men displayed of the holy life a hermit could lead and quietly, in her dreams, she saw that future for herself. When her children were gone and no longer needed her, surely she too could find comfort and the companionship of God in some solitary place where the only sounds were the wind in the heather and the trees, the trickle of holy water from deep in the earth and the calls of the birds.

Each time she headed back to the great fort she would sigh and long to return as soon as was possible to that solitary life of prayer, but for now she was a queen and a mother and her duties lay with her two daughters, now more reliant on her than ever as Julia and Valeria had gone. The only women left at the fort were Delyth, Nia and Sian, washerwomen, servants and slaves and the few wives of the junior officers.

As she stood with the two girls in the garden she had created behind the storerooms in the praetorium the boys burst outside, racing round shouting, kicking a football ahead of them. Elen sighed. Delyth had appeared, shaking something in her fist as she ran after them. Her infuriated shouts went unheeded. 'They need a tutor, Mama,' Sevira commented. 'Owain is becoming a real nuisance!'

Elen gave a rueful smile. 'You are right. I'm going to seek a tutor from Dinas Dinlle.'

'You go there all the time, Mama.' It was Maxima's turn to look disapproving.

'Is it a wonder? I need support.' *I need friends.* The second sentence was unspoken. Branwen had gone ahead of her, preferring the company of the learned men of the Ordovices, who were based there on the edge of the world, to the endless restless, inconsequential chatter of Julia and Valeria. And even now they had gone, she was not prepared to put up with the cold antagonistic looks of the people of the garrison, wives, officers and men alike.

Elen looked thoughtfully at her daughters. The last months of stress and exhaustion, the difficulties of the long overland journey, the loss of their father and their little brother had taken their toll on them as much if not more so than the boys, but now they were showing signs of turning into the beautiful young women they were destined to become. They had been of immeasurable support to her, wise beyond their years, with Delyth filling in the role of nurse and governess and companion to them. It was important they continue to learn to read and write. That was something the Roman Empire had taught their provinces. Elen thought wistfully of the scroll cases with her favourite books, long ago lost with most of her other treasures. The only thing left was that little box, with its precious bowl and that in itself hardly represented the wealth that should surround a queen. Queen of a faraway land. She gave a rueful smile. How apt the throwaway title, bestowed by the emperor of Rome, sounded now that she was here.

She already knew where she was going to hide the Virgin Mary's bowl. It was one of the sacred places of this land, and it held special memories.

She took Maxima and Sevira with her, and Delyth and Rhys. King Brennius provided an armed escort of only four men – she refused to take more and she insisted they waited with the horses at the bottom of the cwm where the spring flowed down the hillside. There was no fear of invaders from Hibernia this time with watchtowers on the shore and lookouts posted on the roads.

The hermit's cave was exactly where she remembered it, on the ledge above the pool with the spring almost invisible behind its curtain of ivy and lichen. Someone had left offerings – whether to the old gods or to the saints there was no way of knowing – but the cave was empty, shrouded with hanging mosses and carpeted with old long-dried bracken, blown in from the hillside.

She stared round sadly. The old man was obviously long gone. While the other three waited outside by the pool Elen made her way into the cave and crept towards the back, where the darkness was heavier, the sound of water muffled. She could hear the restless movements of bats high up above her, disturbed by her presence but not enough to fly out into the sunlight. As her eyes grew used to the dark she glanced up and there on a rocky shelf she saw the old man's meagre treasures: a wheeled cross carved from stone and hung with moss like the wall it leaned against, two scroll cases, the leather mouldy and discoloured, a metal plate and a drinking cup, black and dented. At the very back of the shelf a hidden hollow held a tiny statue of the Blessed Virgin herself, no larger than her thumb. She smiled. Reaching up she pushed the small box to the very back then stood the statue in front of it. Our Lady would keep the bowl that had caught the drops of her son's holy blood safe and guard it until it was needed. She stepped back and bowed her head in prayer.

'Mama?' Maxima and Sevira had followed her on tiptoe.

Turning, Elen stared at the girls, for a moment confused by the pictures that swirled in the darkness. A child, a grandchild, a descendant of someone close to her, would be the one to find the bowl and invoke its power. Not a child of hers, she knew that now, but someone close, someone very close, who would come to retrieve this precious relic and it would be their destiny to give it to a king who would fight to save the country. And until then the tiny chalice would be safe here, guarded by the spirits of the mountain and the saints who served Our Lord. She frowned.

'Mama? Are you all right?' Sevira stepped forward and took her hand.

She bit her lip. 'I was remembering when Maxima was a baby. She was baptised Mair, here and Delyth and Rhys stood as her godparents.'

'So you've left an offering to the saints here. For me.' Maxima moved to stand on the other side of her. 'We saw you leave it on the ledge up there.'

Elen linked arms with the two girls. 'It is to stay there until it's needed. It won't be in my time, or yours, my darlings, but it might be because of one of you that it will come to the aid of whoever comes after us.' The vision had been so fleeting already she could not remember it clearly. In seconds it had gone. She turned to the daylight. 'Come. It will be safe here.'

Cadi stared down at the page in front of her. 'The Holy Grail,' she whispered. 'That is the Holy Grail, and I know where it is.'

'Sorry? What did you say?' Charles had been up to the mill to collect croissants for breakfast and had picked up a newspaper on his way past the post office. He had been buried in the paper, a cup of coffee on the table near him.

'It's the Holy Grail, I'm sure it is. I suspected as much. Listen!' She read out her last paragraph.

Charles stood up and went to pour her a coffee. 'Come and have breakfast while these croissants are still warm. You do know the Holy Grail is a myth.'

'Of course I do. But it's a myth based on a legend based on a reality, the reality I have written here. I have the provenance.'

'The provenance?'

'A vision of the Virgin Mary gave it to a holy man who gave it to Macsen's mother's father who gave it to Macsen's mother. And she gave it to Elen to take home to Wales. She knew it was not for him. It was too late for him.'

'Your provenance is a vision of the Virgin Mary,' Charles repeated solemnly.

'It was a small clay dish used to catch the blood dripping from Jesus's wounds as he hung on the cross.' Cadi sat down at the table. 'OK. Stop looking like that.'

He smiled gently. 'Butter?'

She reached for her knife. 'I always thought the grail was a jewelled chalice made of gold and, if I was imagining it, that's how I would picture it. This was Samian ware.'

'Ah, now that is impressive: a technical description.'

'Red, am I right?'

'Reddish, but not alas with Jesus's blood.'

'No, that was the dried black sediment in the bottom of the bowl.'

He grimaced. 'So, where is it, this grail of yours?'

'In a cave near Caernarfon. At least it was in AD 389 or 390.' She watched as Charles dolloped some honey onto his croissant. 'OK, I grant you it might not still be there.'

He managed to keep a straight face. 'Don't tell me. One of these days you're going to go and look for it.'

'It would get me away from all this. Imagine. This is all to do with King Arthur, isn't it. The grail his knights went searching for.'

'If King Arthur was in any way based on a real person, he would have lived at least a hundred if not a hundred and fifty years later than Elen.' He sighed. 'Oh, Cadi, I'm sorry, but I'm not really buying any of this.'

'Fair enough.' She changed the subject with a rueful smile. 'Has your sister rung you this morning?'

He nodded. 'They're fine. Sue slept well and a friend of Margo's who's a retired midwife is popping round later to give Sue a quick once-over. So' – he peered at her over his spectacles – 'I think we can assume Sue is safe for now.' His face took on a look of concern. 'I don't want to worry you unduly, but if Ifan can't find her, might he turn his attention back to you?'

'I suppose it's always a possibility.' In truth, Cadi hadn't slept at all the night before for worrying about it. 'I was wondering.' She forced a smile. 'I've a vague idea where the cave is; I can tell you how far away it is from Segontium on horseback and I can describe the hillside. Wooded.'

'And there is a sacred spring, you said.'

'There is. Of course it's perfectly possible a magical mist has descended over the hill and it disappeared for a thousand years to keep the grail safe.' She was spreading butter on the warm croissant and managed not to look up, concentrating on the first soft oozing mouthful and then licking her fingers.

For a moment Charles stayed silent, then she heard him clear his throat. 'Only one thousand years? What about the other six hundred or so?' After a moment's reflection, he went on: 'It would be interesting for you to see the fort; help you to place what you're seeing in your head in the landscape of Snowdonia.'

'Eryri.'

'Eryri. Thinking about it, Cadi. I think it's worth taking the idea seriously. It might be a good idea to get away from here for a few days.'

'You think Ifan will come here?'

'I'm sure he will. He'll be looking for Sue. Once he realises Arwel took her out of hospital, his house is the first place he would look. And here you'd be far too close for comfort, given that he already has you in his sights.'

45

Meryn could see for miles. Sitting here on the north-facing slope of the hill he felt safer than he did at home at the moment. A few days earlier he had thrown a few belongings into a holdall, locked up his cottage and set off in his car towards Brecon. From there he planned to follow Sarn Elen as closely as was possible, heading north. He hadn't dowsed the route. There were some perfectly feasible maps on the internet. He gave a rueful smile as he drove. It would spoil his image no end if any of his American students heard that, but there were times when expedience had to take precedence over ideology.

As planned, he had booked himself into a delightful B & B almost within sight of Castell Dinas Emrys, the famous setting of the boy Merlin's fateful meeting with Vortigern – presumably the same Vortigern Cadi had mentioned in her story. The legend of Merlin's confrontation with Vortigern was famous. By then Sevira's husband was a king, and as king he was trying to build a tower on top of the hill. It kept collapsing. The king summoned his Druids to tell him what was wrong and they didn't know, but after some consultation they said Vortigern should sacrifice a boy who had no father. That boy was Merlin, already famous for his powers as a magician. Merlin talked his way out of it, explaining that two dragons were fighting under the foundations of the tower. Digging exposed the dragons, who promptly fought to the death. The red dragon, the dragon of Wales, won; the white dragon of England was killed.

But, and this is what particularly interested Meryn, where had the dragons come from in the first place, and who put them there? Modern archaeology had suggested that an ancient water cistern under the hill had led to the repeated collapse of the walls, but the story went back into the impenetrable depths of Welsh history, long before Vortigern's time. His book, a book that would be an amalgam of a lifetime's research into folklore, magic, religion and science, would be tracing stories such as this back to race memories of earthquakes and volcanic eruptions. Were dragons attempts by the earliest storytellers to rationalise the bones of dinosaurs exposed in the cliffs and crags that were the home of the earliest hominids? Were they ancestral memories of skies lit by volcanic flares, if not in Britain itself, then in distant mountain ranges where volcanos existed to this day? It was an exciting thought. And it linked to his interest in Branwen. Was this not the place where she had learned her art from Druid teachers whose learning was in itself legendary? Branwen would be in his book, if she gave him permission to use her expertise, but first he had to talk with her.

He loved shamanic travelling. It freed him from time and space and allowed him to travel anywhere he wished. Or that was the theory. He could be blocked of course but he had made a certain amount of progress with Branwen. He thought she trusted him now. He could tell she was at the least intrigued by this man who kept appearing in her meditations, just as she kept appearing in his. So, he had often taught those students of his how to contact their spirit guides, and now was his chance to sit quietly here in the beautiful mountains of north Wales, Snowdon, Yr Wyddfa, rising majestically, a sharp volcanic peak in the distance, undisturbed by anyone or anything but the local wildlife, and do it himself. He watched idly as two red kites circled over the hill. The scent of the mountainside was intoxicating, heather and grass and the strong sweet coconut smell of gorse, the wind spiralling up as it carried the great birds on its slowly rising thermals, and from somewhere quite nearby he heard the croak of a raven. For a moment he wondered if it might be a blessed white raven, the raven of the goddess after whom Branwen took her name but no, it was inky black.

And suddenly Branwen was there, sitting on an outcrop of rock several metres away from him. On closer inspection she was older than he had first thought, perhaps in her sixties or seventies, her hair silver. But her skin was smooth and her hands, clasped over her knees, were those of a much younger woman. He could feel her gaze on him intense, focused, her eyes a deep blue, the colour of the sea.

'Greetings.' He whispered the word out loud.

Her reply did not interrupt the soughing of the wind in the grasses, it was deep inside his own mind. She was listening.

'I wish to learn of Elen, to make certain that the future bards and makars of history report her story truthfully. I wish to learn her secrets and her triumphs. I wish to learn your magic and your ways of learning.' He found himself putting his palms together as a plea. 'Too much, you will say, but necessary for Elen's sake. I come from a time far in the future, but still we study her story; her history needs to be told.' He paused, studying the woman's face, unsure whether she understood him. 'Can you show me Elen's future, the life she led when she came back to the land of song and of dreams? Our stories tell us that her children and her children's children became kings in this faraway land. I would know the truth of what happened to her.'

Her gaze hadn't wavered. She appeared to be studying him closely, but she was still apart, unengaged. He waited, wondering if she understood a word he had said. He had made contact, but was that all he had managed to do?

The sky was clouding over, he realised with a shiver. He glanced up. The birds had gone. He looked back at the rock. She had disappeared.

He sat for a while, coming away from his meditation, grounding himself, and at last stood up, stiffly. Had she registered him at all? He wasn't sure.

He drove around Caernarfon later, staring up at the great castle that had been built almost a thousand years after Elen's lifetime, almost certainly using the stones from the fort itself. Another invasion, this time by a king of England, another empire builder intent on making this mineral-rich land a part of his own kingdom. The site of the great fort of Segontium was perched on a high spot above the town; in the past, before the town was built, it must have had an amazing view down to the Strait and across to Anglesey to the north and towards the west across the River Seiont and away towards Castell Dinas Dinlle and the Irish Sea. Behind it, to the south, lay the great ranges of the Eryri mountains, jagged black silhouettes against the sky.

Why was he here? It was because he wanted to help Cadi. He was intrigued by her research, by her experiences, her battle with a talent which she hadn't fully realised and almost certainly didn't want. She was obviously a seer, a sensitive, but her struggle was with herself. It showed in the published versions of her poems, which he always felt were dumbed down in her Mabinogion stories, the magic carefully suppressed, the metaphysics hidden. Then there was the novel which was her way of rationalising the automatic writing. Which in turn, was her way of channelling something she didn't understand or want, and on top of all that she was trying to cope with the anguish of real life which was at the moment a conflict beyond her control, with a man who was obviously a psychopath.

He parked the car in the road, and peered through the railings at what he could see of the great Roman fort's remains between areas of neatly mown grass. The site was closed, the gates locked but he stood staring through the bars, attempting to feel the echoes, hear the clash of swords as the garrison practised their manoeuvres, see the cavalry horses being led round towards the stables. He stood there for a long time before at last turning away with a strange sense of anticlimax and climbing back into his car.

It was not until he returned to the B & B and the evening meal he had requested when he booked in that he thought to charge his phone. It wasn't until next morning as he ate his breakfast that he finally switched it on and saw the missed calls from Cadi and from DCI Vaughan.

He rang Cadi first. Obviously he had been out of touch for

too long. 'I'll ring Dai Vaughan now and put him in the picture. I expect he was ringing to warn me Ifan was on the loose. I find it hard to believe they would let him go without so much as a warning.' There was a pause. 'I came up here to do some background work for my own book, but obviously I can't forget yours. I've been doing some Shamanic stuff as well,' he went on after a moment or two. 'It doesn't matter, obviously, where I am when I do that, but I'd like to stay up here for a few days. I've spoken to Branwen. And I've visited Segontium. I'll go back there tomorrow if it's open and wander around a bit, just to get a feel.'

'You spoke to Branwen?'

'She didn't answer but she listened. I had her attention.'

'Did you ask her about Elen?'

'I did, yes. I tried to explain we wanted to tell the truth about her.'

'And did she understand?'

'I don't know that I described what I wanted very well.'

'I want to know where Elen hid the grail.'

He laughed. 'Ah, so you're sure it is the grail, are you? Can you be certain Branwen was there?'

'No.' He heard the disappointment in her voice. 'I don't think she was. Of course, Branwen wasn't a Christian.'

He sighed. 'I think you'll find at that period there was a huge overlap in beliefs. The important thing was the sense of the sacredness of things. Where pagan gods oversaw the natural world, Christian saints took over, often with similar names. Like Bride or Ffraid who morphed into St Bridget.'

'And Elen. My Elen, seems to have been made a saint. St Helen of Caernarfon.'

'A saint and a road builder.' She could hear his smile.

'Tell me what happens, won't you. And please keep your phone on.'

Meryn's landlady had made him a picnic, vegetarian, he noticed with a grateful smile, and she lent him a local footpath map which showed far more detail than the ancient OS map he had dug out of his own files. He wanted to be off the footpaths, of course, and she seemed to have understood that at once, marking what she thought would be the perfect spot for his meditation with a big red cross.

She was right. As he scrambled up a rocky incline next morning and came to a standstill panting, at the top he found he was looking down on a hidden lake at the bottom of a sheltered valley. Down there out of the wind was a stillness that was magical in its solitary peace.

Branwen appeared to have been waiting for him. Standing some metres away he could see her veil moving in the breeze, strands of her hair breaking free, the sunlight in her eyes, but when she spoke he could not see her lips move. *The man you avoid, the evil one, came to your house again in the night-time. He intended to burn it with dry bracken he piled against the walls. There was no one there to save it.* She was silent for a moment, obviously registering his horror at her words. *So, I chased him away.* Was that a smile? *He was very afraid. He called me ghost and witch and demon, and he was so angry that his fury echoed down the hillside and across the years into the past and into the future. Then he ran away. He won't go back.*

'Thank you with all my heart.' Meryn pressed his hands together and bowed in her direction. 'That house is my home and where I keep my books.' He had a feeling she would know how much that would mean to him.

The shock of her words had almost made him forget what he was going to ask her. 'Did you stay with Elen? Does her spirit linger at Caer Seint?' It seemed somehow more appropriate to call Segontium by its Welsh name.

There was no reply.

'Hers was a fruitful family,' Meryn mused. 'So many descendants, lines of kings, remembered in legend and myth.' He was gazing down towards the little lake. 'But not in history,' he added quietly, almost to himself. 'Never quite remembered in history. And did she care for the roads that the men who came after her called by her name?'

Branwen seemed to smile at that. *The roads were built by Macsen's men. She wanted to travel in safety around the lands that her father said were hers. He did love her in his way, Macsen Wledig. When she came back to us she sent the men of the garrison to keep the old roads clear that lead south to the land of her birth. They called her Elen of the Ways.*

Meryn nodded silently. 'And for that her name will be remembered forever.'

And the woman who writes what you call history, Cadi, she will tell the story?

Meryn stared at her, startled. It seemed incongruous to hear Branwen use Cadi's name. To admit she understood what Cadi was doing. 'Yes. She is writing Elen's story.'

She is in danger. The evil one is close to her now, watching her. Call her here, to the land of snows. She will be safe here.

A cloud drifted across the face of the sun. He narrowed his eyes, trying to keep her in focus as he processed what she had said. 'How do you know? Is that where he went after trying to burn my house last night?' He scrambled anxiously to his feet. There was no reply. As the landscape grew darker she had faded into the greens and browns of the hillside and disappeared.

He grabbed his rucksack and rummaged for his phone. No signal. Turning back the way he had come, he scrambled up the slope and tried again from the top of the rocks.

'Cadi! You're in danger. Is Charles there? Ifan is heading in your direction. Ring the police.'

46

The garrison consisted of a cohort of the remaining auxiliaries from the northern parts of the empire, the parts of the empire that were becoming more and more restless themselves, subject to inroads from barbarian hordes. The news came to her, even here in this distant land in messages from her father and her stepbrother, and from her stepson Constantine and in letters from Julia, happy now with her sister in Deva. She heard no more from Valeria and Julia didn't mention her. The tribal elders at Dinas Dinlle had suggested tutors for the boys and Branwen had interviewed and finally chosen a woman from one of the surviving colleges of the sacred studies of Britannia to progress the girls with their reading and writing. When she took them out into the woods and valleys of the great mountains, Elen sometimes went with them to study the arts of healing with the wild herbs of the countryside, their stories and their astrological attributes, for as Branwen said, even the greatest ruler should be able to direct their household with knowledge that would inspire respect.

Not greatly to her surprise, two faces had appeared from time to time at her small court in Segontium over the course of the last year or so, the two men to whom her daughters had been promised by their father. The first, Ennodius, rode in one summer's day at the turn of the century, laden with gifts and promises for the future. Of senior rank in Valentinian's army, he had somehow cleverly avoided censure for any contact he might have had with Macsen's family. He was bound, it appeared, for a posting in North Africa and wished to take with him as wife the elder daughter of an emperor, even a disgraced emperor, to whom he had been promised. It didn't appear to matter to him that Macsen and his family had been disbarred, and the reason soon became apparent. He had, it seemed, met Maxima several times under her father's supervision, a secret the girl had kept close to her heart. Since their arrival at Segontium the official messengers destined to speak to the commander of the fort had on several occasions had an extra letter addressed to one of the daughters of the former emperor and had willingly acquiesced to being part of the secret tryst. Elen had met Ennodius many times before when, as a senior officer, he had visited the court at Treverorum and then at Mediolanum before Macsen had set off on that final fatal march to Apuleia. Faced with a signed marriage contract and the pleading eyes of her elder daughter, Elen could not bring herself to refuse. Maxima was much the same age as she herself had been when she had been told she was to marry a Roman general. All she could do was give them her blessing and pray for the child's safety and happiness in a country she could only imagine, the country of brilliant skies and hot sands and strange exotic animals, that Valeria had once described for her.

With Maxima gone it was obvious that Sevira would not be far behind. She, the more forceful of the sisters, could also claim a prearranged contract, hers with the British prince Vortigern. For Elen this match was more welcome. Vortigern was someone she knew well. One of the rulers of the province, he had often appeared at their table in Gaul before Macsen had despatched him back to Britannia, the eldest son of a king, and a worthy match for the spirited Sevira. Once Sevira had gone she knew it would only be a matter of time before she left the fort with the boys. There was nothing left for her there now.

* * *

Marcus Quintus, commander of the garrison, gave a perfunctory bow and held out the letter to Elen. 'It came this morning with the general's messenger service.' It had been opened, she noted, although her name was clear on the wrapping.

She rose from her chair in the corner of the reception room and went to the window where the sunlight fell in a narrow beam across the floor. Unfolding the parchment, she began to read. It had been written by her brother Conan and endorsed with an initial at the bottom – her father's. His hand was frail now, and the ink had spattered across the page. 'Why did you open this?' She glanced up. 'It is addressed to me.'

He gave a careless shrug. 'Opened in error. Everything else in the bag was army business.'

She glared at him and went back to the letter. Conan had written this himself. She recognised his writing. Normally he used a scribe.

We hear that Stilicho, Theodosius's most powerful general, is recalling any remaining army divisions from Britain to help the defence of the empire. He is not providing any further wages to pay the garrison at Segontium and orders have been sent to the commanding officer there to pull his men out without delay.

'So, you have obviously read this, and presumably you have received your orders to take the men overseas.'

He nodded. There was a gleam of excitement in his eyes. 'We march out within days.'

'And I presume Stilicho knows that I am here, in this distant land at the furthest corner of the empire? And that has made him think of it particularly. So, what will happen to your men's children? Their families in the vicus? Some of them have been based here for years.'

'They can come with us or stay. Up to them. There will be no more money, as you see, to pay salaries. Most of the women are local peasants anyway, or slaves.' She thought he was going to spit on the floor, but he stopped himself in time. 'They shall all have their right to freedom and to Roman citizenship, but I doubt many of them will want to come with us.'

'And what will happen' – she was not going to give him the satisfaction of hearing her worry about herself – 'to the fort?'

Another shrug. Someone else's problem. After a moment he relented. 'I expect your Britunculli friends will help you. They will probably move in and take it over. King Cunedda will make this one of his bases at least for a time, to keep the pirates at bay. Many of the Hibernian tribespeople have already settled along this coast. They are no longer a threat, preferring to live at peace with their neighbours, so the danger to the western shores is not so great. The danger comes across the Mare Germanicum. The walls and fortifications here are well maintained and the vallum will hold at least for a while. You have no immediate need to leave, if Cunedda agrees.' With a salute and a click of the heels he turned and left the room, not bothering to wait for her to dismiss him.

For a long time she sat in silence, the letter in her hand, as the ray of sunlight through the narrow window moved across the floor and disappeared. Peblig found her sometime later, still staring into space. 'Mama?' Gently he took the letter out of her hand and read it.

'We knew it would happen,' he said at last. 'The king of the Ordovices will help us.'

She sighed. 'That's what the commander said.'

He grinned. 'It will be nicer without the garrison.'

She looked up at him and suddenly she realised he was right. They had lived here for years now and they had not been happy. She missed Macsen and she missed her eldest children enormously. Her heart would always ache for little Victor, trying so hard to be the heir his father had wished. The others who had stayed with her had filled her days with joy and anxiety and exhaustion as did all children, or so she supposed. Finding people to take care of them, to educate them, to entertain them had not been easy but she had managed it and she had loved them all dearly. Maxima had gone now to distant North Africa, and Sevira was married to Prince Vortigern, set to become, perhaps, high king after her father. Anwn was training as a military architect and strategist at the court of King Cunedda, and only Owain and Peblig remained at home. Owain wanted to fight. He couldn't wait to go into the army, anybody's army. Both boys, teenagers now, had inherited their father's ambition, but also their mother's love of their land. Peblig was the gentlest of her sons, studious, anxious to look after his mother. He was intensely conscious of the fact that he had been baptised by the great Bishop Martin and already felt in some deep part of his heart a calling to prayer.

It was Peblig who suggested that they pull down what remained of the Mithracum, wash the floors with holy water and dedicate the site to Christ. The place was shady, and sinister. There was no one there now; it was a long time since it had witnessed any of the mysterious rites that used to go on there, but Elen was sure she could smell the blood of the slaughtered bulls, hear their bellows of fear and pain. Workmen from the vicus and from Dinas Dinlle who had come to help pull it down, stared round with fear in their eyes as they approached the place with sledgehammers and set to work to demolish the already ruined walls.

'Did my father really worship here?' Peblig approached her, covered in dust, his hands cracked and bleeding from pulling down the stones. 'God rest his soul. I hope and pray he was forgiven.'

'Bishop Martin heard his confession. And blessed and baptised him.' Elen looked round uncomfortably. There were still echoes of the old gods here, of Mithras and of the Sol Invictus, the unconquered sun. 'I'm sure your father went to heaven.'

Was she sure? She looked around at the rubble that was all that was left of the temple and thought back to the time she stood almost on this exact spot and heard the singing coming from deep in the ground at her feet. She shivered. Around them the remaining men from the fort stopped work one by one and watched her nervously. It would take only one bird of ill omen flying overhead to panic them into throwing down their tools and fleeing the site. These men were not followers of the Christian faith, but they were not followers of Mithras either. They feared the soldiers' god and the bloody sacrifices that had taken place here.

Peblig stepped forward and raised his hands in prayer. He was a good-looking boy, almost a young man, she corrected herself as she watched him. His hair was fair, fairer than hers now, whereas his brothers were swarthy, dark-haired, their colouring inherited from their father. As they stood together with the men of the Ordovices tribe, watching the dust settling, a stray ray of sunlight pierced the clouds and fell across his face. 'Pray with me, friends,' he cried. 'Pray for a blessing on this place. I want there to be a church here, dedicated to Our Lord, Jesus Christ, and I want it to be a place for holy men to come and pray for peace and joy in this former fortress of war. Let us finish our work by burning the rest of this rubble, by cleansing it with fire.'

Elen closed her eyes. When she opened them she saw a shadow lying across the land, a shadow of high walls and crenelations, towers and battlements and she heard the shouts and screams of fighting men. She shuddered and the vision was gone as quickly as it had appeared. Was this then always to be a place of war? Surely they could stop it, bless it, make this a place of quiet contemplation.

And then she saw the sword, seeming to hang over the site, glittering in the sunlight. The special sword. Caledfwlch. She had given it back to the king of the Ordovices so many years ago, to keep it safe. But now she realised it would be Peblig who would claim it. Not to wield it, he would be a man of peace, but it would be for him to keep it hidden, here in his church. And she knew exactly where. The deep place in the heart of the Mithraeum, where the stone altar had been. Peblig would put the sword there under the stone, once it had been exorcised by fire, and blessed with holy water, and then the place would be walled up until the moment came for it to be used by a future king.

Her mood lifted and she felt her extraordinary happiness reflected slowly in the men around her. They might not be Christian, but they believed in the sacred, they believed in the triumph of good over evil. As their anxiety lifted she saw them return one by one to their work. Peblig put his arm around her shoulders and gave her a squeeze. 'You felt it too?'

She nodded. 'You have been blessed. Your mission here will be remembered forever.' She didn't know yet how or when his moment in history would come, but he was to play a part in the destiny of Albion. It was for him to discover how in due time.

They took Charles's car. As Cadi double-locked the front door she glanced up at the windows and whispered a prayer of protection. Meryn had taught her that. 'Set the wards. Picture an angel at each corner of the house. They will protect it.' It was hard not to believe everything Meryn said, though her logical brain might dig her in the ribs and give a snide giggle, her heart said, *Do it, what is there to lose; it will give you peace of mind.* She threw her bags and her laptop into the back of the car and climbed into the front beside Charles. He put his foot flat in a good imitation of a quick getaway. There was no sign, as she glanced back over her shoulder of any other cars in the street.

'Dai sent the police to check out my cottage.' Meryn met them in a teashop in Caernarfon. 'They found dried bracken stacked against my back door and along under the windows. It hadn't been lit, thank God. There would have been no one to spot it if it had gone up.'

'But Branwen saw what he was up to?'

'She did. And scared him off. I would have given a great deal to witness that moment.' Meryn chuckled. 'I think it best you're away from home until they locate him. I can't imagine how they saw fit to release him. Thank you.' He beamed up at the waitress who had brought them a large pot of tea, and plates of Welsh cakes and bara brith. 'I want to show you the remains of the fort, and I think you should see St Peblig's church.'

Cadi stared at him. 'I was writing about St Peblig. Peblig was one of Elen's sons. He was there as they pulled down the temple to Mithras and he vowed to build a church on the spot. But he can't have. This was too long ago, surely. Before Christianity took hold.'

'Christianity was here in Wales almost from the beginning,'

Meryn corrected her. 'As early as the second if not the first century. A primitive form of Celtic Christianity, I believe. I've been
looking up some of the stories about Elen as St Helen of Caernarfon, and she's credited by some with bringing the idea of
small religious communities to Wales after her meeting with St
Martin. So, this is all part of the legend, but once again it seems
to be well founded in fact. The early Saxon invaders did much
to damage that early tradition, as of course did the Vikings
where they landed in Britain and slaughtered the churchmen.
Hence the period they call the Dark Ages, a term I'm glad to
say is swiftly becoming discredited and going out of fashion.
The next wave of Christianity is attributed to Augustine and to
the Age of the Saints, which was basically a century or so later,
but Christianity was always here. And I mean *here*.' He waved
towards the window. It looked out onto the town square and
beyond it, the great castle looming over the town.

Cadi stared out. 'She saw it,' she whispered. 'Elen saw a
vision of what was to come.'

'The castle was long after her time. Built by Edward I towards
the end of the thirteenth century.' Meryn helped himself to a
Welsh cake.

'And Excalibur. She had a vision of Excalibur. As a magical
sword. Not just the weapon the elders of the tribe had inherited
and hidden. That was a real sword. They planned to hide it in
the church.'

'Excalibur. As well as the holy grail. But you're right. Caernarfon is in the legends as well,' Charles spoke up at last. 'There's
lots about all this in modern guidebooks. They love these stories. Cornwall has had ownership of King Arthur for too long.
Wales has just as good a claim. Better in some ways, though of
course nothing can compete with Tintagel.' He grinned. 'And
then there's Merlin, of course, Merlin who faced up to King
Vortigern and foresaw the battle of the red and white dragons
under the floor at Castell Dinas Emrys.' He pushed the butter
over towards Meryn.

'Vortigern,' Cadi repeated. 'Who married one of Elen's
daughters.'

'Date wise, is that possible?' Meryn asked thoughtfully.

'I guess so. After all, we're not sure when Vortigern lived any more than any of the other protagonists in this story.'

Cadi's phone pinged a message. They all looked at it as it sat on the table between them.

'It's the police,' she whispered. She read the message and looked up with a rueful shrug. 'It's OK. They've checked my house again and there's still no sign of him. Apparently they'll do a drive-by every now and then, but they advise me not to leave the house empty too long.'

'Isn't it safer to stay here?' Charles glanced across at her.

She nodded. 'Now I'm here, I would like to see the fort.' She was silent for a few moments, aware of their eyes on her. 'I've been here so much in my head. Just me and Elen and a garrison of Roman soldiers.' Her smile was hesitant. 'I'm completely torn. I don't know what to do.'

'OK. Why don't we stay here for one night,' Charles said at last. 'Then we can visit Segontium and the church, and we can take a drive out into the mountains this evening to see if we can locate anywhere from Elen's story that you want to see. I'll ring Chris at the mill. No.' He raised his hand as she started to protest. 'He asked me to. I'm going to tell him there won't be anyone in your house tonight and if he or anyone else can keep an eye on it, that would be good. Just the occasional glance down the road. We'll go back tomorrow afternoon. And you know the police will be driving by, whatever that means, so between them and Chris and probably Arwel as well, it will be safe. So, let's forget that wretched man for a while and go and immerse ourselves in ancient Gwynedd.'

47

Marcus Quintus was waiting in the salon, a cup of wine in his hand, staring out of the doorway at the fountain that was once again working in the atrium. As Elen walked in he swung round to face her. 'Who gave you permission to demolish the remains of the temple?' He was seething with anger. He hurled the cup over his shoulder as he confronted her, splashing wine across the floor. 'That place is sacred to the god.'

Elen straightened her shoulders. She was alone. Peblig had followed the horses round to the cavalry stables, talking enthusiastically to Rhys as he went.

'No one but an initiate can enter that place and I hear you have taken in an army of peasant pagans to pull the place apart and fire it. How dare you!' The commander's face was red with fury. 'How *dare* you!' he repeated. 'You, a woman!'

Elen managed to collect herself. 'How dare you!' she echoed his words. 'You come into my house uninvited, and you question my actions? Yes, I am a woman.' She managed to keep her voice level. 'And I am a Christian woman. There is no place for Mithras in my world. Nor in any world. The worship of Mithras is forbidden. Christianity is the religion of the emperor; it is the religion of the empire. The temple was ruined. There has been

425

no worship there for years. The worship of Mithras is long for-gotten.'

He was too angry to speak for several seconds. 'You dare to call on the name of the emperor! You, whose husband was a traitor, whose lands and title and very existence have been annihilated by the senate.' His face twisted into a sneer. 'If you think the worship of Mithras is forgotten, you are much mistaken. You are alone here, you and your puny son.' To her horror she saw his hand go to his belt. He drew his sword, slowly and deliberately and held it out, waving it in her face.

'Put that away.' Somehow she kept her voice steady. 'You are dismissed.'

There was a moment of silence. She saw his knuckles tighten on the sword hilt and then as their eyes locked his face changed slowly into a rictus of agony. The sword fell from his hand and he pitched forward onto the flagstone floor. There was a dagger protruding from between his shoulder blades.

Fighting to draw breath, Elen turned. Rhys was standing behind them, his face a mask of anger. He had hurled the dag-ger from the doorway several feet away. 'Did he hurt you?' His voice was harsh.

'No,' Elen whispered. She was trembling with shock. 'You saved my life.'

'Your son sent me to tell you his favourite mare had foaled while you were both out at the Mithraeum. A son for Emrys.' Rhys gave a small moan which could have been amusement. 'He didn't want to leave her when he found her in the stable. He wanted you to go to him.'

Elen nodded. 'Of course. I will go at once. Will you send for someone to clear away this . . . mess.' She managed to stay upright as she walked towards the door, clutching her shawl around her shoulders. Behind her, Rhys bent over the dead man and withdrew his dagger. He wiped it on the man's tunic to remove the blood, and then again on his own sleeve. 'Thank you, Rhys,' she said as she left the chamber.

He nodded. 'The saints were with us, lady,' he murmured.

She crossed herself. 'They were indeed.'

The next morning the entire garrison was drawn up on the parade ground. Elen faced them, her shoulders squared. The second in command stood beside her, his face impassive. There was no point in pretending anyone was ignorant of what had happened. Elen stepped forward and took a deep breath. 'I have sent for King Cunedda to explain the behaviour of Marcus Quintus and, until he comes, Junius Secundus, beside me here' – she turned towards him, emphasising his position close to her and therefore supporting her – 'will take command of the garrison. It is to be understood that no one here, no one at all' – she surveyed the silent parade ground – 'is to continue in the worship of Mithras. Anyone who feels unable to obey my order should leave this place now.' She stared round, as though surveying every face drawn up in the ranks before her. No one moved. 'In future the men of this command will follow the orders of your emperor and worship as Christians wherever they are based. A church will be built on the site of the Mithraic temple to cleanse the site of the blood of its sacrifices and the water of the holy spring will be sanctified and dedicated to the care of Our Blessed Lady.'

The ensuing silence was broken only by the gentle moan of the wind outside the walls and the cry of gulls in the distance over the water of the strait.

The man standing next to her was the first to break the spell. He stepped forward and called the men to attention before dismissing them. As they marched away, Elen stood without moving, staring out towards the mountains. She was aware of Owain and Peblig slowly moving towards her to stand one on either side of her as the new commander saluted and marched away.

'Mama.' Peblig felt for her hand. 'That was well said. In any event, they will be gone in a matter of days. I suspect there are very few initiates amongst the senior officers, and none of them spoke out. Even if one or two disappear, most will stand firm with you. They are proud of you.'

'And loyal, as long as they are here.' Owain moved forward. 'You have nothing to fear here now.' He grinned. 'And my baby brother will have his church.'

'It's not my church!' Peblig contradicted him fondly, with a punch to his brother's shoulder.

'It will be. One day when you become a bishop.'

'I'm not going to be a bishop!' The affectionate scuffling between the brothers went unnoticed by their mother. Her eyes were fixed on the distant peaks.

Turning, Cadi followed Elen's gaze, towards the south. They were standing in the centre of the excavations of the Roman fort, surrounded by the carefully curated remains of centuries of Roman walls. She and Charles had found rooms at a small hotel only a short distance away from the site the night before, and met up with Meryn again over breakfast. She could feel Meryn's eyes on her as she dragged herself back into the present. She had been staring at the jagged outline of the mountain ranges of Eryri.

'Do you recognise it?' he asked softly.

She shook her head.

'But you sense her here now?'

She gave a wry smile. 'As always, you can read me like a book. The mountains are the same of course. And the blue of the sea. Even the cry of the gulls.'

'You're treading uncharted waters here,' he put in thoughtfully. Charles had wandered away from them and was staring round with interest. 'No one knows what happened to Elen after she left the presence of the emperor; you are perhaps the only person alive who has even the remotest clue to what happened later.'

Cadi shivered. 'She stood up to the commander of the garrison. He would have killed her.'

'An initiate of Mithras, I think you told me.'

She nodded.

'A bloodthirsty cult, if I remember rightly.'

'For the bulls, at least.' She shuddered. 'It seems she was still here at Segontium with her two youngest sons. Her two daughters had gone to their husbands and Anwn was off somewhere, presumably a cadet in the army. Owain wanted to train for the army as well and Peblig wanted to go into the church. I got the impression it was his idea to pull down the Mithraeum and put a church there instead.'

'And it appears he did. The church is close by.' Meryn nodded over his shoulder. 'I went there yesterday before you arrived. I looked it up online. It's reputed to be one of, if not the oldest in Wales. Its origins are supposed to be fifth century. Unfortunately it was locked, but we can try again this morning.'

Sadly the museum on the Segontium site was closed, as was the church when they walked down the road towards it. Frustrated, they stood in the churchyard looking round. Meryn had done his homework the night before. 'The Mithraeum was just over there somewhere. They discovered it when they were building those houses.' He waved towards an estate of houses built immediately below the ruins of the fort. 'They did an emergency excavation, though the site had already been badly damaged by then, and they found traces of the fire. They discovered a tremendous amount about it all, according to the article I read last night, and they found an altar from the Mithraeum somewhere over here, under the church.'

'So Peblig kept his word to build a Christian church over its ruins.'

'Or at least as near as makes no difference.' Meryn turned round slowly. 'It is after all, called St Peblig's.'

They walked slowly back up the road, which seemed to have cut the site of the fort in half. At the top of the hill they stopped. The view from there, down towards the brilliant blue of the Menai Strait was commanding. It was easy to see what a good position the fort must have had before the later town was built.

'I love the old pine trees round the ruins,' Charles commented at last, 'but I have to say, I could have done with some labelling of the various areas. It's all very well to put these places online, but it's hard to see one's phone when the sun's out. I was expecting it to be more like Caerleon.' He sighed.

Cadi hadn't forgotten her idea that they should try to find the Holy Grail. They pored over the Ordnance Survey map during lunch, sitting outside a pub beside the swing bridge over the River Seiont, tracing the lines of the Roman roads out of the fort. They were looking for narrow valleys and springs. Then

Meryn produced his pendulum. He glanced at Charles. 'Shall I go first?' Pushing aside their coffee cups, he put his finger over the spot where the fort was marked on the map.

Cadi sat back, staring into the distance across the water as the laughing cry of a gull rang out. They could hear the sound of rigging banging against the masts of the yachts moored against the quay. A couple of young women on a motorbike roared up the road near them and parked, removing their helmets and shaking out their hair as they squinted up at the high walls and towers of the castle.

Charles and Meryn were staring at the map. 'This way, I think,' Meryn murmured. 'Then they would have turned off the road here and ridden up the cwm, following the brook. My guess is there is some kind of a track.'

'You're right. It's a bridleway.' Charles stabbed at the map.

Cadi followed the line of his pointing finger. 'Ffynnon Fair,' she whispered. 'St Mary's well.'

It took twenty minutes to find the end of the bridleway. Charles parked his car in a gateway and they set off up the steep track.

'Do you recognise it?' Meryn stopped and waited for her. He was panting from the climb.

She stared round and shook her head. Charles took the folded map from his pocket. 'It's only about half a mile further. Worth a look?'

The waterfall still poured out of the cave mouth. Cadi stared up at it, speechless. 'This is it. I recognise it. This is where they picnicked. Where Emrys scared off the pirates. Where that poor boy was murdered.' She ran towards the rocks and began to scramble up towards the ledge where the spring bubbled out of the rock into a natural basin. People had obviously been there before them. They could see coins and pins, some new, some obviously old and corroded, scattered in the water; someone had hung a crystal rosary from a rocky projection near the cave.

Charles looked out across the woods back the way they had come. 'I can see my car down there, and way in the distance I can see the sea.' He sat down on the grass. 'I'll stay here. You

430

go in,' he said. She looked at Meryn and he nodded. 'Go on. We'll wait.'

The cave was damp and very dark. She stood still and listened. She could hear the two men talking quietly outside and the distant trickle of water. On tiptoe she walked deeper into the darkness towards the wall where Elen had tucked the little box on the far end of the rocky shelf with the little statue of the Virgin Mary.

There was nothing there.

As they began to make their way back down towards the car she paused and turned back. She habitually wore a plaited silver ring on her little finger. Pulling it off, she murmured a whispered prayer and dropped it in the water.

'I wonder where the grail went,' she said as Charles led the way back to the car. She sighed. 'I didn't really expect to find it, but still . . .'

'This is obviously recognised as a very special place,' Charles put in.

'Maybe it was its destiny to disappear,' Meryn added. 'People have been searching for it almost forever, perhaps it was never more than a memory?'

'Memory or legend?' Charles groped in his pocket for his car keys.

'Both presumably.' Cadi shook her head. 'I'm glad it wasn't there. Imagine if we had found it. They would have put it through all kinds of tests. Tried to find Christ's DNA. It doesn't bear thinking about. I'm glad it's still a mystery.'

'A mystery wrapped in the mists of time. Still, I can't help wondering who took it.' Charles clicked his key to unlock the car.

'A mystery that gave rise to a thousand folk tales.' Meryn smiled as he settled into the back seat. 'And a thousand and one legends. You know of course that the old name for this part of the world was Arfon, as in Caernarfon, as in, perhaps, Avalon.' He reached for his seat belt with a mischievous twinkle. 'And according to the legends, Arthur found the sword in a stone – perhaps an ancient altar stone that had once been in the temple of Mithras. And Sir Bedwyr was given Caledfwlch after the battle of Camlann, here in the mountains, and he took it up Yr Wyddfa to the ice-cold lake of Llyn Llydaw and there he threw it into the water, where it was taken into safekeeping by the lady of the lake. And even better, it was across those same ice-cold waters that the mortally wounded king was borne away to disappear into legend.' He fell silent for a while, mulling it over. 'Wonderful stuff. And in the meantime, if you could drop me off by my car, Charles, please. It's time for me to follow Sarn Elen south to my cottage in the hills.'

Charles and Cadi were nearly home when she felt the phone in her pocket vibrate and she pulled it out. 'It's Sally!' She listened for a moment. 'Oh my God! She came back to find Ifan outside her house shouting abuse.'

'Has she called the police?' Charles glanced across at her. She saw his knuckles whiten on the steering wheel.

'Yes. They're on their way.'

'Good. Tell her we're coming. Don't worry. By the time we get there they will have caught him. He's not going to get away this time.'

They saw a police car outside Sally's cottage as they turned into the village. There was no one in it.

Cadi leapt out of their car as Charles drew to a halt. 'Sally!' She ran up her neighbour's short path and banged on the door.

Sally opened it at once, a delighted Gemma jumping up and down at her heels. 'Come in! Come in.' She dragged Cadi in, then Charles, and slammed the door behind them. 'He's gone. I thought he was going to break my door down. I shouted that I'd called the cops and he turned and ran off down the road. I've no idea where he is. The policemen ran after him as soon as they arrived, but I've heard nothing since.'

Cadi sat down abruptly. 'What a welcome home! I'm so sorry.'

Charles turned back to the door. 'Perhaps we ought to check Cadi's house. Make sure he hasn't done any damage there.'

'From the noise he was making, he had something metallic in his hand.' Sally sat down beside Cadi. 'Thank God I had elbowed the door shut behind me when I brought my stuff in,

432

or he would have walked straight in. The police have told me to keep everything locked and not go out, even in the garden.' She looked near to tears. The bags and cases from her holiday were still standing near the front door with Gemma's dog bed beside them. 'Don't worry, they checked your house first. He doesn't seem to have managed to get in there.'

The police knocked on Sally's door half an hour later. They had found no sign of Ifan anywhere in the vicinity. 'We've searched the field and we've spoken to Mr Davies over the road there, who I understand is the man's father. He's seen nothing of his son since he came out of hospital. He's very concerned for your safety.'

Cadi raised an eyebrow. 'I doubt if we're in any more danger than he is. Ifan's never got on well with his father.'

The policeman nodded. 'So we understand. We've given him the same advice we're giving you; be very, very careful. Keep all your doors locked, and I think it would be best if you all stay together until we've located Mr Davies junior. He can't have gone far.'

'Isn't that the point?' Charles said drily as he closed the door behind the policemen. 'He can't have gone far, which means he's still close by. Why in God's name did they let him go in the first place?'

'It wasn't up to the local police,' Cadi said. 'When the DI spoke to me she said the decision had been made in London. She seemed very frustrated by it, and I'm not surprised. Think how much extra time and manpower this is going to take now he's disappeared. Do you think Branwen could be persuaded to come and watch over us as she seems to have done with Meryn? Come next door with us, Sally,' she added impulsively. 'He's right. You shouldn't be alone. Bring Gemma and we'll make a picnic supper.' She glanced uneasily at Charles. 'I'm sure the police will find him.'

'Who's Branwen?' Sally asked. 'I've got food.' She was unpacking a bag of French bread and cheeses and two bottles of wine. 'I brought you these from France.'

'This is lovely, Sal. Thank you so much.' Charles and Cadi exchanged glances. 'Branwen is a colleague of Meryn's,'

433

Cadi said after a slight hesitation. 'Part of his historical research project.'

'I almost feel inclined to climb in the car and drive straight back to France.' Sally scooped Gemma into her arms and kissed the top of the dog's head.

Clutching the bags of food they made their way next door. There was no sign that anyone had tried to break in. The house was quiet and safe and Charles brought in their bags before driving the car back to its hidden parking place with Annabel's friend. Coming in, he bolted the door behind him.

'We're OK here,' he said quietly. 'As long as we stay together.'

'But we're not together,' Cadi interrupted. 'Meryn is still out there. He will have gone straight home. He doesn't know about this. Supposing Ifan has gone back to his house to finish what he started?' She reached for her phone.

'He's not picking up,' she said at last. 'And no voicemail.'

'Ring the police.' Charles reached for one of Sally's bottles of wine. He rummaged in the drawer for a corkscrew.

Cadi watched. Part of her was wondering how she felt about him seeming to be so at home in her kitchen. Then she relaxed. She was actually quite pleased. 'He might not have got home yet.' She sat down next to Sally. 'It's a long drive and we don't know he left Caernarfon at the same time as us. He might have gone back to his B & B.' She took the glass Charles offered her. 'But you're right. I'll see if I can reach Gwen. She needs to know what's happening.'

As Sally took her glass from Charles her little dog struggled off her lap and ran to the doors that led into the garden. She whined softly and glanced back at Sally.

'Oh lord!' Sally put down her glass. 'She probably needs to go out for a pee.'

'Don't worry. We'll stand guard.' Charles stood up. 'At least its broad daylight. He can't creep up on us out there without us seeing him.'

'Keep her on the lead,' Cadi advised. 'We don't want her rushing off through the hedge.'

Charles and Cadi stood together on the terrace as Sally

wandered onto the lawn, the extending lead in her hand. They watched as the little dog sniffed her way round the flower beds, tail wagging. She looked better, Cadi noted. Happy. Perhaps Meryn's few minutes of super-Druid healing power had done her good before she left for her holiday. She hoped so. A few minutes later as Sally turned back towards the house, the dog raised her head, staring into the far corner behind the apple tree. At her sharp bark of warning, Sally hesitated and looked back over her shoulder.

'Gemma's seen something. Come back, Sally,' Cadi's whisper was frantic. 'There's someone there.'

As Sally reached the terrace and dived back through the doors, closely followed by Gemma and Cadi, Charles scanned the garden. He frowned. The branches of the apple tree were swaying in the breeze. The garden seemed empty but was that a patch of deeper shadow on the grass?

He followed the others inside and turned the key in the lock. 'I know this sounds a bit counter-intuitive but if there was someone out there, it was a woman,' he said.

48

Someone had swept most of the bracken and brush away from the doors, and Meryn's garden appeared untouched. The cottage felt relaxed and safe. The evening sun was moving slowly down into the bank of mist in the valley as he reached at last for his phone and picked up the message from Dai Vaughan. Then he answered the call from Cadi. She wasted no time on small talk. 'There's no sign of Ifan but he must be around here somewhere. Meryn, is it possible Charles saw Branwen in the garden? There was someone out there. Gemma barked at her.'

'I've no idea.' He sighed. He wanted nothing more than to relax into the gentle nurturing space that he had created up here on his mountainside, but he was going to have to climb back into the car yet again and head south through the mountains. That was where the danger lay.

He had not even got as far as unpacking the car. He grinned ruefully as he eased himself stiffly back into the driving seat. 'If Branwen is there, I would say it can only be helpful. I'm on my way.'

'Branwen again?' Sally took a gulp from her wine glass before bending to unclip Gemma's lead. 'You said she's a colleague of your uncle Meryn? I take it she's nothing to do with Ifan.'

'She's our ghost.' Cadi bent to rumple the little dog's ears. Had Gemma recognised her from her sojourn in the distant past? 'Long story. Nothing to worry about. The important thing is that it wasn't Ifan, and Meryn is on his way.'

By the time he arrived in time for their improvised supper a couple of hours later it had begun to rain.

They were all too stressed to enjoy their meal and it was only an hour later that Sally asked Charles to see her back home.

'Poor Sally,' he said as he reappeared five minutes later. 'She's still in quite a state. I've told her to ring us if she's the slightest bit worried. At least she has Gemma to warn her if there's anyone lurking around.' He walked over to the window and checked the blind before throwing himself down on the sofa. He was clearly exhausted.

Cadi was worn out too. They could hear the rain spattering on the terrace outside and she found herself shivering. Meryn had gone to sit down at her desk and she watched as he absent-mindedly pulled a file of papers towards him and glanced down at the contents.

'Those are Rachel's latest sketches,' she said slowly. 'For the poem.' After the shock of Ifan's reappearance in their lives it was a relief to go back to Elen's story.

Meryn shuffled through first one and then another. 'They're beautiful.' He looked up. 'I have two very talented nieces.'

'And Ifan has tried to ruin her life as well as mine,' Cadi said sadly. 'I can't believe the damage that man has done.'

'What's happened about her cottage?'

'Nothing. The owner's giving her three months to think of something and then he says he'll have to put it back on the market.'

Meryn nodded. 'Cadi, I've had an idea about that,' he said after a moment's hesitation. 'I've thought of a way of helping Rachel. I've been thinking about it for some time, and I wanted to discuss it with you first.' He chewed his lip. 'As you know, I have no children, so when I pop my clogs in this world and go on to better things, I would be leaving you and

Rachel to share my worldly goods. I've never had much need for stuff, but I have savings from my books and my teaching career. Quite a lot of savings. If I were to make a gift to you both, now, of your inheritance, that would enable her to buy her cottage and, if I live long enough, it would be a tax-efficient way of disposing of the bulk of my estate.' He paused, studying her face. 'It would give her the security she needs and take the worry off her shoulders. I know you have this house from your marriage to David, so you're set up, or you will be once Ifan's behind bars, so I'm assuming you don't need any cash now, but if I do it, I would want you to have your fair share.'

Charles climbed hastily to his feet. 'This is clearly personal family stuff. I think I should leave you two to discuss this on your own. I'll wander up to bed, if you don't mind. See you in the morning.'

Cadi gave him a grateful smile. She watched as he disappeared upstairs and then she turned back to Meryn. 'That is incredibly generous of you, Uncle Meryn. I think it's a wonderful idea for Rachel. But as you say, I don't need it. I think you should keep the rest of it. To do it for me as well isn't necessary. You might want it one day yourself and I would hate to think of you being left short.'

He gave her an impish grin. 'Don't worry. It won't leave me short and it would make me very happy. I've spoken to my accountant. It's all settled. All I need are Rachel's bank details.'

She stared at him, speechless. Meryn had an accountant. He was a rich man. It didn't seem possible.

He let out a yelp of laughter. 'I know exactly what you're thinking. That's my mystique gone for good. I only wish I could wave a wand to do more for you, but our problem here is altogether more complicated, I fear, than money.'

'Ifan?'

'Ifan.'

'But you're here in person, which makes me feel safe.'

'Oh, sweet Cadi, if only you knew how much it cheers me to hear you say that. Most people think that the trouble starts once I appear.' He sobered. 'But seriously, you know you have someone very special up there.' He nodded towards the stairs. 'He adores you, you do realise that.'

'But we hardly know each other.' Instinctively her voice had dropped to a whisper.

'That's not quite true, Cadi. Besides, it only takes a few minutes, so I'm told.'

'What, love at first sight?' She shook her head. 'I've cocked that up twice now after testing the water for much longer than a few minutes. David divorced me, and look at the mess my relationship with Ifan ended in.'

'Third time lucky?'

Cadi shook her head. 'No. If we're going for the clichés, it's twice bitten, thrice shy. I like Charles very much. I trust him. I hope we'll always be friends, but that's it.'

Meryn shook his head sadly. 'OK. We'll change the subject. Sorry.'

'Can I go back to being an eccentric lady author in your eyes, please?'

He laughed. 'Why eccentric?'

'I believe I'm taking dictation from a woman who's been dead for sixteen hundred or so years. Don't you think that's eccentric?'

'Ah.' He shook his head. 'You forget who you're talking to. To me such things are normal. All right, let's do a deal. You go back to being an eccentric lady author and I'll go back to being a penniless, mystical Druid.' He grinned. 'I'll ring Rachel in the morning and tell her what's happening.' He stood up wearily. 'It's been a long day. I suggest you go up to bed. I assume, from what you say, that you and Charles aren't sharing a bedroom, and I've seen the state of your boxroom so it will be easiest if I kip down here on the sofa. There's plenty of room and I'll be able to keep an ear open in case anyone's prowling around outside.'

Madelaine's house was in darkness. It was after midnight as Ifan crept up the drive. He groped in his pocket for the keys. Behind him the whole village seemed to be asleep; there were no signs of the police anywhere. There were no lights on in Cadi's house, nor his father's. He had held his breath as he tiptoed past Sally's in case the horrible little dog barked, but all had been silent there too. Quietly he inserted the key in the lock and let himself in, thanking his lucky stars he had not thought to set the alarms when he had left the house what seemed a lifetime ago. He pushed the door silently closed, listened for the reassuring click of the lock, and crept down the hall towards the kitchen. He was exhausted and his head was splitting. He needed painkillers and he needed sleep. Cautiously he turned on the lights and reached for the blinds. The house was isolated, but he couldn't afford to risk anyone glimpsing signs of life through the trees from the road. He found the tablets the hospital had given him when they discharged him still tucked in his inside pocket. Grabbing a glass of water he emptied several tablets out of the packet into his hand, swallowed them and headed for the door. Upstairs in the room he thought of as his own he was asleep almost before his head hit the pillow. He had not even had the strength to remove his shoes.

Gwen arrived next morning full of apologies. 'No sign of him. I've made it known how angry I am that it was decided to release him from the hospital. The CPS in their wisdom felt there wasn't enough evidence to charge him. So much of it was hearsay and without witnesses, without his wife's corroboration, we couldn't hold him. How is Mrs Davies, by the way? Has anyone heard?'

Charles nodded. 'I spoke to my sister this morning. No baby yet, but her midwife friend thinks it will appear fairly soon.'

There was a moment's silence. They had been sitting round the breakfast table, finishing off the last of the coffee. Cadi invited Gwen to sit down and she gratefully accepted a cup. 'Obviously Ifan came back here soon after that. Your neighbour Sally says he sounded very angry when he banged on her door. He hasn't been seen since. Which means,' Gwen sighed, 'that we'll have to circulate his details again and you'll all have to maintain the highest caution. I see no point in searching the countryside round here. I doubt he would have stayed anywhere close by. You don't think he could have got wind of where his wife is now?'

'Arwel knows, of course. But somehow I think he would have guarded that information with his life,' Cadi said at last. 'I don't think anyone else knows apart from us.'

'Well, if anyone is going to visit her, please make sure you're not followed. I suspect if he is still around here, he'll assume someone will go to see her sooner or later.' Gwen drained her mug and stood up. 'And if anyone hears that he's arrived on another planet, please be sure and let me know.' She glanced at Meryn.

'I'll check with my sources,' Meryn answered gravely.

'She probably thought you were joking,' Cadi said after she had gone.

'She probably thought she was, as well.' He sighed.

'I tell you what.' Charles was obviously restless. 'Why don't the three of us go out into the meadow and scout around. I don't know about you, but I'm feeling a bit claustrophobic. I think Gwen's right. I doubt Ifan's still anywhere round here and if he was, would he take on all three of us? He's probably miles away by now, and anyway, it's not us he wants at this point, it's Sue.'

It had rained itself out long since and the early morning mist had dispersed. The day had warmed up considerably. The air smelled rich and sultry and there was a haze over the top of the hill. The padlock on the gate was hanging open. Walking in, they stopped to look round.

'No sign of anyone,' Cadi whispered after a moment.

'You can almost hear the meadow holding its breath,' Meryn nodded. 'Too much has gone on here.'

They began to walk slowly towards the stream. The grass was crisscrossed with car tracks and trampled paths. The tent had gone, Cadi noticed, and it looked as though the grave had been filled in; there was a mound of soil where it had been. There had obviously been some activity there while they had been away in North Wales. She looked about her nervously.

Meryn stopped suddenly, holding out his arms to block their path. 'Look.'

The heat haze had deepened, it was getting harder to see the perimeters of the field.

Cadi caught her breath. The ground, some fifty metres ahead of them was beginning to shimmer. 'Oh God! It's happening,' she breathed.

'You two stay exactly where you are,' Meryn commanded. 'I'm going a bit closer.'

No! Cadi didn't actually cry out. It was too late, he was already walking determinedly towards the flickering light.

Charles reached out for her hand. 'He knows what he's doing,' he said.

'Does he?' She rounded on him. 'I don't think he does. I think he's like an excited schoolboy jumping off a cliff to see if he can fly.'

Meryn was very close to the strange phenomenon now and they saw him stretch out his hands towards it as though testing for heat. And then as suddenly as it had appeared it had gone. The mist around the field cleared and sunlight was pouring down on every corner of the grass. The silence was broken by a burst of song from the skylark high above them. Cadi stared up. 'I hadn't realised how quiet it was, but now listen.' The little bird soared higher until it was invisible against the glare of light.

Meryn turned and walked back towards them. 'Interesting.'

'Obviously,' Cadi said tartly. 'It could have sucked you in and we might never have seen you again.'

'I was careful,' he reprimanded her gently. 'Please give me credit for some common sense.'

'Did you see Ifan?' Charles asked. He realised he was still holding Cadi's hand and released it, embarrassed.

'No. I saw no one. It was opaque at the centre, a bit like steam, but it wasn't hot. I don't think it opened fully, maybe because I was there.' Meryn turned and walked back to where he had been standing, staring down at the ground. The other two followed him. He moved on a few paces. 'Look, here,' he said. 'This is where it was. Can you see anything?'

'Nothing.' Cadi stopped beside him. The grass was undisturbed.

'Fascinating.' Meryn beamed at them. 'Have either of you got a mobile phone on you. I'd like to have a picture of this exact place.'

Charles groped in his pocket. 'Here.'

Meryn held up his arms to demonstrate.

Charles clicked off several photos.

'Now. Show me.' Meryn went over to stand beside him.

'Nothing there,' Charles said after a moment. He scrolled down the pictures. Then he stopped. 'No. Look. That was the first. You can see something. A shadow.'

'The camera has caught the echo,' Meryn said, nodding. 'Excellent. The wonders of modern technology, eh?' He beamed at them both. 'I'll get you to email them over to me later.'

Charles was still gazing at his phone. 'Message from Steve. I had it on silent. It sounds as though the extra tests they ordered have produced quite a few new results. He wondered if I would like to go over to discuss them.' He glanced up at Cadi. 'He knows I love visiting the lab and how much this whole affair fascinates me.' There was a moment's silence. 'Would you mind if I went over there? I'd be back this afternoon.' They had turned towards the gate. 'I'll email those pics before I go,' Charles went on, glancing across at Meryn. 'Ah.' He grabbed his phone again. 'Another message. This one is from Margo.' He read it then beamed at them. 'Sue's had a little girl. Both doing well. Sue has asked us to tell Arwel. She doesn't dare phone him in case Ifan goes there.'

As they stopped outside Cadi's gate Sally's door opened. She looked pale and worn out. Gemma dived between her feet and rushed to the gate, her tail wagging. 'I was wondering if it was safe to go for a walk in the meadow,' Sally said. She stooped and picked up the dog.

'I wouldn't.' Cadi reached across to tickle Gemma under her chin. God forbid that the little dog race off down the tunnel again. 'We've just been up there and there isn't anyone around as far as we could see, but no one knows where he's gone.'

Sally nodded. 'I'll walk down to the village instead. Gemma loves meeting everyone so it won't be a hardship for her. She's her old self again, don't you think? She seems to have forgotten her ordeal.'

'Come over this evening and we can have some more of your lovely French wine,' Cadi called after her.

'I could feel the dog's aura,' Meryn said as they let themselves into the cottage. 'Sally's right. It is much stronger.'

'I'm so pleased.' Cadi threw herself down on the sofa. She in contrast felt completely drained.

'Shall I go and tell Arwel the good news before I leave?' Charles followed them in.

Cadi nodded. 'Please, Charles. I think it would come better from you as she's with your sister.'

'Say hello to the bones from us,' Meryn added drily as they watched him collecting some books from the table. 'You must know them quite well by now.'

Charles stopped in his tracks. He had picked up on the undertone. 'You're sure you don't mind me going? You'll be safe with the doors locked, and you've got Gwen's number.'

'Of course we don't mind.' Cadi put in sharply. 'In fact it will give me a chance to get on with my writing.' She leaned back against the cushions with a groan.

'Great.' He hesitated, in two minds about whether to drop a kiss on her head, reluctantly decided it would be a dreadful idea and headed for the door. 'I'll come straight back, I promise.'

And he was gone.

Meryn sat down opposite her. He refrained from commenting on Cadi's expression as she watched the door close behind him. She looked almost lost. 'Cadi, I haven't had the chance to speak to Rachel yet. Are you still OK with what we discussed yesterday?'

'You know I am.'

'Then I'll give her a ring now and tell her what I've decided. The sooner we get it sorted, the better as far as I'm concerned.' He walked over to the kitchen and retrieved his mobile from the charger.

Standing up she wandered across to her desk and looked down at the piles of notes and sketches, listening with half an ear to the conversation as she shuffled through Rachel's illustrations. It was clear they were trying to decide whether Meryn should drive over to the coast to see her or whether she should come here. She frowned, pausing at the picture of Macsen. How was it possible for Rachel to have drawn him so accurately, or was it, she looked up and stared at the ceiling, that Rachel had somehow picked up her own thoughts.

'Problem?'

She realised that Meryn had finished his call and was standing behind her. 'No. I just wondered how she had drawn him so true to real life. Or at least the real life as I saw it.'

'Did you describe him to her?'

'Yes, of course I did.'

'And did she read your manuscript?'

'Yes.'

'So, accept the fact that you're a good writer and she's an intuitive artist.' He sighed. 'You really must give yourself a bit of leeway, Cadi. You have tremendous talent. Acknowledge the fact.'

'I think Ifan had something to do with the fact that I don't have much confidence. He regarded my work as rubbish.'

Meryn let out a snort of derision. 'And you rate his opinion why?'

'I know. That was his way of destroying people.'

'Don't give him the satisfaction, Cadi. Seriously. Every time you doubt yourself, admit you're letting him win. Now,' he went on determinedly. 'Rachel and I have decided that I will drive over there this afternoon and I'll spend the night. We can then go to her bank and check with her solicitor about buying her cottage and set the whole thing in motion. Much easier to do it all in person. Charles will be back to keep an eye on you— No, sorry, I realise that is a sexist statement implying you're a weak and feeble woman.' He smiled. 'I only meant in the nicest possible way that, if you're fighting off any intruders, a bit of backup from someone who has a black belt would be helpful. I'll return tomorrow with more of Rachel's sketches, so you have no more than a few hours to produce more verses of your epic poem.'

It was Peblig who at last persuaded his mother that the time had come to move out of the fort altogether, leaving the commander's house to Cunedda, the king of the northern tribes. They collected the remaining members of their household and took up the offer of the king of the Ordovices to have their own round house within the great ramparts of Dinas Dinlle, their own home at last away from the malign atmosphere of the Roman legions. And they took Emrys and his mares with them. It was as though an overwhelming black cloud had been lifted. For the first time in her life Elen was living by the sea, able to stand on the high wall looking out over immeasurable distances, and feel the exhilaration of the wind in her hair and fizzing through her veins. The heaviness in her heart for little Victor was still there and always would be, but there was less of the sadness of loss now and more of the love and thankfulness for the time they had had together. She seldom thought about Macsen now but when she did she mourned the good times and the love they had experienced up here in this distant corner of the land.

Peblig had formed an intense and admiring friendship with the old king, listening to his stories of gods and heroes and days of long ago, so it was not all that much of a surprise when one day he called the young man outside to speak to him in private. 'My son, I want you to come with me.' The old man had been listening to Peblig's excited descriptions of the clearance of the Mithraic temple and the preparations under way for the foundations of his church and at last he had come to a decision.

Peblig found that rather than going to sit in their usual sheltered spot beneath the walls, they were heading down to the shore where a boat was waiting. He hadn't been at sea since he had been a little boy and crossed to Rutupiae with his family after the deaths of his father and his brother, and then he had been scared, lost and lonely, even surrounded as he was by his remaining family, but this was different. The fishing boat hugged the coastline of the peninsula as they sailed south-west, and the weather was fine, the tide and winds in their favour, waves of spray from time to time drenching the boat as it dipped and shuddered ever onward towards their destination. Eventually, after turning away from the coast across a stretch of rough water towards an island almost lost in the choppy seas, they headed in to an anchorage in a sheltered bay. 'Ynys Enlli,' the old man beamed. 'From here you and I will go on alone.'

The cave entrance was hidden in a heap of boulders near the

summit of a hill from which Peblig could see the entire island. He turned back to the old man who had seated himself on a rock to get his breath back. He grinned at Peblig. 'Not as young as I was, but I needed to do this one thing myself. My last duty as lord of these lands.'

'You still haven't told me why we are here.'

'We have come to collect something very special. Your mother has told you the story of Caledfwlch?'

Peblig caught his breath. 'Indeed she has.'

'Well, it has lain here, in this cave, these last centuries, except for the one time I brought it out to give to her. She took it in her hands, to acknowledge possession, and then she gave it back to me to keep safe until her children were grown.'

'Yet it is not for me.' Peblig shook his head anxiously, then he sat down next to the king. 'But you knew that.'

'I know. It will go to another, but you are called to be its guardian for your lifetime. You must hide it under a stone in your church at Segontium until one day, in the country's utmost hour of need, a future king will come to draw it forth. Come on.' The old man stood up, groaning. 'This is the hard bit. We have to crawl through the dark to the place I left it.'

Peblig followed him into the darkness, crawling close behind him down a narrow passage, aware of the oppressive silence all around them. When the king stopped at last he could only sense that the tight corridor had opened out into a much larger space. 'Wait.' The king's voice in the dark was strange, disembodied. He heard the strike of flint on metal, saw the spark, and saw with relief the light flare and the shadows draw back as the candle steadied in the old man's hand. 'See there. In the corner.' The king's voice echoed strangely. 'There is a pool of water.'

Peblig moved forward cautiously and looked down into the still depths of the blackest water he had ever seen. 'It is the purest water from the depths of Mother Earth.' The king was speaking in a whisper. 'No metal can rust in there. Reach down. Bring it out.'

Peblig fell on his knees and pulled back the sleeves of his tunic. The water was ice-cold. He groped around for a few moments, then he found it: the long narrow blade with its intricate hilt, just as Elen had described it to him, lying on a smooth shelf of rock. Carefully he pulled it out and held it up in the candlelight, seeing the glitter of gems, the reflection on the blade with its strange markings, hearing the slow drips of water falling from the blade back into the pool.

'We dried it and wrapped it up and I carried it back to the boat. Then we sailed home in the moonlight,' Peblig said as he presented it to his mother next morning. 'You and I will take it today to Segontium and we will set it under the stone which is now the foundation of my church, and we will dedicate sword, stone and church to Christ. And no one will know it is there until the rightful king comes to draw it out.'

49

'Of course, we still can't rule out contamination.' Steve was standing with Charles in the Cardiff laboratory. 'And when we submit our report that must be the way we describe the anomalies that have come up again and again in the tests. They have been repeated three times now – that's why it has all taken so long – and the same inconsistencies have appeared each time.' He moved a little further down the table with its neatly laid out skeletal remains and shook his head. 'Poor old Marius.' They had given him the name when Charles had finally explained the somewhat spurious evidence as to the man's identity. 'Some of the modern bones appear to have elements of the two age spans within the same sample.' He glanced up at Charles and raised an eyebrow. 'It must have happened when the body was buried in 1939. The young couple dug down into an ancient burial pit and without realising it, pushed the victim down amongst all the other stuff, and somehow the newer bones assimilated some of the ancient DNA.' He grinned. 'I would give my eye teeth to know what has really happened here. Someone has had a word with the local vicar, by the way, and she has agreed the bones should be reburied in the local churchyard. I expect you knew that. But we don't have to think about that yet. The law says we've got a couple of years before they need reburying. I expect you noticed we've been down to the meadow and filled in the grave for now. It was attracting too much attention. We're planning to lay on a full-scale excavation next year.'

'So, the development plans are on hold? For now.'

Steve nodded. 'Partly because of all this and the ongoing police interest in finding Ifan Davies, and partly because I gather there is some kind of confusion about the ownership of the property. I've had my suspicions that someone in the actual planning department has been deliberately trying to bypass the archaeology and wave this scheme through. It's not unknown, you know, for the odd hefty back-hander to speed things up a bit. It's not the sort of thing that happens round here, but we're dealing with a company we don't know. And didn't you tell me their manager let slip that arrangements had been made? Anyway, someone at the council has been doing some checking and they've discovered that the meadow is no longer an asset of the holding company that had originally applied for planning permission. It seems to have changed hands a couple of months ago and no one realised. My mate thinks it's probably some kind of tax fiddle. It's only a technicality, but when they consulted the Land Registry they found the land belongs to Mrs Susan Davies. That's John Davies' estranged wife. What?' He noticed Charles's expression. 'You knew?'

'No.' Charles shook his head. 'I didn't know. But I do know Sue Davies.'

'Very sweet.' Two hours later he was looking down at the tiny baby in the Moses basket in his sister's spare room.

'Oh, Charles!' Margo laughed. 'Can't you look a bit more enthusiastic? What is it with men and babies?'

Charles looked up helplessly. 'I can't help it. What else is there to say?' He turned as Sue made her way into the room. She looked pale and tired, but very happy. 'Congratulations! Have you got a name for her?' Surely that was the right thing to ask.

Sue nodded. 'I'm calling her Victoria Louise.'

'That's lovely.' He meant it. 'Solid nineteenth-century names.'

He didn't say anything else until they were all seated round the table having tea. Victoria Louise was sleeping peacefully and even Charles could see Sue was exhausted. It was time for him to leave. 'Can I ask you a couple of questions before I go?' He had thought very hard about what to say.

'I can tell it's not about baby care.' Margo was refilling his cup. She pushed it back towards him.

He grinned. 'No. The first is about a lady called Rachel Pritchard.'

'The painter?' Sue nodded. 'I remember Ifan talking about her. I think he wanted to arrange an exhibition of her work. He knew her back in the old days in Wales.'

'Oh, he knew her all right.' Charles grimaced. 'He didn't talk about buying her house, by any chance?'

She looked puzzled. 'I don't think so.'

'Never mind. I just needed to know he had her in his sights.'

Sue sighed. 'Oh dear, that sounds ominous.'

'Nothing to worry about.'

'And the other question?'

'It's about Camp Meadow.'

Both women looked puzzled. 'That's where that poor man's bones were dug up?' Margo said, realising where she had heard the name before.

Charles nodded. 'As you know, I'm a friend of Cadi Jones who lives next door to it. We've been closely involved in every-thing that's going on there. Too close sometimes.' He shook his head.

'These are the excavations you were telling us about and the skeleton you've just been to see.' Margo pushed the plate of biscuits towards him.

'I gather the council have recently discovered that you're actually the owner of the meadow, Sue.'

'Me?' Sue looked astonished.

'Ah. Didn't you know?'

She shook her head. 'Are you sure? How is that possible?' There was a moment's silence then her face cleared. 'I know what must have happened. A few months ago, before we separated, Ifan did tell me he was making me co-owner of some of his properties and he made me sign some papers. I didn't take much notice, to be honest. He said it was to give me security if anything ever happened to him, but I didn't believe him. I thought it was another of his nefarious plans, a way of putting them offshore or out of the taxman's reach. I wasn't as grateful as he thought I ought to be. We had a row about it. One of many. I wouldn't count on it being true. There's bound to be something fishy about it.'

Charles shook his head. 'It is true. Your name is on the deeds.'

'So, are you saying they should have asked my permission before digging up the field?'

'I'm saying Ifan had no right to apply for planning permission to build houses on the field in the first place. And I'm guessing you could forbid them to go ahead with the application. And yes, I expect you could stop them excavating in the field, although I'm hoping you won't do that.' He was tingling with excitement.

'And the council know about this.' Sue sat back in her chair with a heavy sigh.

'Charles, let's leave this till another time,' Margo said softly. 'You can see how tired Sue is.'

Charles stood up. 'I'm sorry. That was thoughtless of me. But yes, they do know. It was Steve, the head of the dig, who told me.'

'If it's true, I don't want it. I'll give it to the village. That nice man at the mill can arrange it all.' Sue stood up. She turned to the crib and scooped the baby into her arms. 'That should make up a little for all the anguish Ifan has caused.'

Meryn had gone to stand outside Rachel's cottage, staring out at the view. He was very tired. He had driven the length and breadth of Wales in the last couple of days, but seeing Rachel here in her clifftop retreat and knowing he had been able to make it secure for her had made it all worthwhile. The money was safely in her account and he was going with her tomorrow to meet up with her landlord to start the paperwork to transfer the property into her name. It was a lovely cottage with a beautiful little garden and best of all a wonderful studio overlooking the sea. He sat down on the bench, which was angled carefully to look out over the glorious green blue of Cardigan Bay.

It was almost no surprise to sense he was not alone. He glanced up. Branwen was there, standing where he had been standing, staring out towards the horizon just as he had, her silver hair streaming behind her in the wind off the sea.

'Greetings.' He whispered the word into the sound of the waves far below.

She gave no sign that she had heard him. He nodded comfortably. He was content just to be there watching the sun fall slowly into the ocean. He could see a distant wall of mist far out beyond the horizon. There was more rain on its way.

He heard Rachel behind him. She held out a glass. 'Welsh whisky. Local brew. Supper's ready when you are.'

He turned back towards the sea. Branwen had gone.

There were voices outside the window. Struggling out of the blackness of a drugged sleep, Ifan opened his eyes to daylight. For a moment he couldn't think where he was. Then he remembered. Madelaine's house. He sat up and swung his legs over the side of the bed. He was fully dressed. He must have lain down for a moment and dropped off. Putting his hand to his head, he groaned. Then he heard it again. Voices outside on the terrace. Men's voices. Shit! The police. He staggered to his feet and went over to the door, listening carefully. Silence. He crept over to the window and peered out. Two cops were heading across the lawn towards the summerhouse. The sound of their voices died away.

He stood on the landing for several seconds, peering down into the hall below. He could see the front door from there and it seemed to be closed. They weren't in the house. They must have rung the bell and decided there was no one inside. Perhaps that was what had awakened him. He ran down the stairs and into the kitchen. Grabbing a glass of water, he swallowed a couple of his painkillers and headed for the door. He paused.

Looking back over his shoulder he scanned the room. There on the wall was a rack of knives. He snatched one and tucked it into his belt, then he headed on into the living room where a pair of French doors led out onto a patio bordered with trellis hung with roses and honeysuckle. He groped for the hook behind the curtain where Madelaine hung the keys and cautiously he unlocked the doors and pushed them open. He listened. There was no sound from the garden save the rustle of leaves in the wind. It took only a few seconds to step outside, relock the doors, throw the key into the flower bed and then he was running between the hedges towards the road. There was no sign of the police; presumably they had assumed the house was locked and empty and they were busy searching the outbuildings.

He couldn't run far; his head was thudding and he felt sick. He ducked through a hedge and found himself in a copse. Collapsing on the ground, he lay back, gasping for breath, his arm across his eyes, aware at once that the ground was soaking wet and cold after last night's rain. He glanced at his wristwatch. It was just after five. Morning or evening? For a moment he couldn't remember. He screwed up his eyes and did a double take. Had he really slept through most of the day? He should probably still be in hospital. The NHS had been all too swift to discharge him once the police had lost interest. He gave a cynical groan. This was a ludicrous situation, when his own father lived just up the road in his warm safe house. He felt a wave of rage sweep through him. His father, who had driven up to London and collected Sue and his unborn baby from hospital. Except, it wasn't his baby, was it. It was some other man's. He sat up. He had a lot of scores to settle here. His attempt to burn down Meryn Jones's house had failed. His own stupid fault. He thought he saw someone there watching him and he had panicked. He had obviously been hallucinating. His head had been splitting. He groaned again. Then there was his father, Cadi and her interfering relations, that stupid cow who lived next to her. And Sue.

He climbed painfully to his feet. Well, he was here now and he was free. All he had to do was get to his father's house unseen.

As he pushed his way out of the copse he realised it had started to rain again. Even the weather was against him in this godforsaken place.

The story wouldn't come. Cadi sat staring down at the page. She had been writing all afternoon, about Peblig finding the sword hidden up there on Bardsey Island, and Elen's family and what had happened to her next and then between one word and the next the story had stopped. The pen was in her hand but it wasn't moving. Slowly she put it down and, pushing back her chair she stood up. Branwen. Why did her thoughts keep coming back to Branwen? It was Elen she was interested in. What had become of her now her children were gone and she was to all intents and purposes alone – except for Peblig, of course, but surely the time had come for him to leave home too and go off somewhere to study for the church.

Perhaps Branwen knew where the story led next, or perhaps she was just too exhausted to write anymore.

Sally arrived just after six with Gemma on the lead at her heels. Outside it had started to rain and the two women sat by the veranda doors staring out into the garden as the light faded. Cadi sighed. 'Charles promised he'd be back in time for supper,' she said at last. 'I have to say I'll feel safer with him back here.' There was a long pause. 'Stop it!' she had seen Sally's eyes twinkle.

'I never said a word,' Sally retorted. 'It will be interesting to hear what he has to say about your old bones. I don't know why they're so keen to date them. After all, there's no hurry now if they have postponed the dig.'

They didn't have long to wait. He pulled up in the car twenty minutes later, full of news.

Sally stayed on to have supper and it was some time after that and almost dark outside as they sat over a cup of tea when Gemma sat up and began to bark. They heard the gate crash open and there was a loud banging on the front door followed by a shout. 'Cadi, let me in! For God's sake. Quickly.'

'It's Arwel!' Cadi jumped to her feet.

'Don't open it!' Sally cried, but Cadi already had her hand on the latch. She pulled the door open. 'What is it? What's wrong?'

Arwel was standing on the doorstep, blood pouring from his nose. He threw himself into the room. 'Close the door, quickly! He's after me! And shut that bloody dog up!' Gemma was barking furiously from the far side of the room.

Cadi slammed the door and rammed the bolt across. 'Ring the police!' she shouted at Charles, but he was already on the phone. 'Where is he?'

'He broke in through my back door. I tried to stop him.' Arwel was groping frantically for a handkerchief. 'He thought Susie was still staying with me. When he ran upstairs to find her, I bolted. The boy's insane!'

'Did he see which way you went?' Cadi found a towel in the kitchen and handed it to him. 'Lean forward and pinch your nose. It looks worse than it is.' That wasn't true. The man's face was black and blue.

'They're on their way.' Charles was staring at him in horror. 'You haven't told him where Sue went, I hope.'

'Of course not!' Arwel snapped. 'He said he phoned the hospital in London and of course they told him that I'd come to collect her. They wouldn't have seen any reason not to. He came straight here. He guessed she's had the baby and I suppose I looked guilty or something and that confirmed it as far as he was concerned. I didn't tell him where she was, I swear it.' He was near to tears.

They all heard the gate clang back a second time against the garden wall. Then Ifan was banging on the door, shouting. There was total silence in the room. Cadi tiptoed towards the front window and stood there checking the blind was fully down. Sally had picked up Gemma, trying to quiet her as Cadi walked over to the back windows and then the garden door and checked the curtains. The banging on the door stopped.

They were all listening, holding their breath. Arwel moved quietly across the room and sat down at the table. He was visibly trembling. For a moment all was silent then there was a massive crash as the glass in the French doors shattered. The curtains billowed as Ifan stepped through the shards of glass and splintered wooden battens scattered all over the floor and stood staring from one to the other. He was drenched with rain. There was a large spanner in his hand. 'Where is she?' His voice was hoarse.

'She's not here, boy.' Arwel stood up shakily. His face was still smeared with blood. 'She's miles away. Go now. Quickly. The police are on their way and this time they won't let you go.'

'So I've nothing to lose.' Ifan's eyes were flicking round the room, his face was scratched and bruised, his clothes were torn and he was sweating profusely. 'I'm going to kill that dog if it doesn't shut up!' he added. He was shaking violently. He stepped towards Sally and raised the spanner.

'No!' she screamed.

It was Arwel who stepped in. 'Don't be stupid, Ifan. Don't you touch anyone here, d'you hear me? What's the matter with you? Don't you want to ever see your baby? Do you think they will let you near it if you hurt anyone else?'

'They won't anyway. That lying cow will tell them I hit her. Besides, it's not my baby.'

'If you're talking about your wife, Ifan, she has refused to testify against you,' Cadi put in. 'I think she still loves you, against all the odds.' She clenched her fists.

'Then why did she run away?'

'Because she's afraid of you.'

He was silent for a second or two, then he smiled. 'Are you afraid of me?' he said at last. His voice was low and somehow very menacing.

'No.' She could see his knuckles whitening as his fingers tightened on the spanner.

'Mistake,' he said. It was almost a whisper. 'Big mistake.'

'Cut it out, boy.' Arwel straightened his shoulders. 'Enough.'

'And what are you going to do, old man?' Ifan glared at his father with something approaching hatred in his eyes. Abruptly he shifted his glance towards Charles. He raised the spanner.

'I saw your baby today,' Charles put in calmly. The words stopped Ifan in his tracks. 'For what it's worth, she looks like you, poor little soul. And Sue promised me that you're the child's father. But that's of little consequence now. The police will be here any minute and they will remove you.' He glanced across at the kitchen window where a light had appeared behind the blind as a car drew up outside. 'In fact they're here now.'

Ifan followed his gaze and let out a vicious curse. He turned and ran back towards the broken glass doors. By the time the two policemen had entered the room he had disappeared into the dark.

50

The police guessed that Ifan must have a car and had left it hidden on the far side of the woods. It could be anywhere and in the dark there seemed no point in searching for him any longer. In the end they were called back to base, leaving Sarnelen Cottage to its own devices. The search would resume in the morning.

When they were alone at last, Cadi sat down with an exhausted sigh. 'He won't come back, will he.' They were all badly shaken. Arwel had returned to his house once the police had searched it and called someone to fix secure bolts on both back and front doors. Sally had gone too. 'I don't think he's interested in me, anyway,' she said as she left, Gemma in her arms. 'At least, I hope not. But I'll call if I get suspicious, I promise.' Once again Charles saw her next door and waited outside until he heard her turn the key and slot the bolt in place.

The broken French doors had been boarded up, thanks to a mate of Chris's who had arrived within what seemed like minutes of being alerted. He was a big man called Phil, with a bushy ginger beard and piercing blue eyes. He left them with a cheery grin. 'Call me if you feel the slightest bit worried,' he said, brandishing the hammer from his toolbox as he left. 'I'm only up the road and I can be here in three minutes. And I'll be back with new doors tomorrow.'

Charles reached out for Cadi's hand. 'I don't think Ifan'll be back this time. He won't dare.'

She gave a faint grin. 'I'm glad you're here.'

'So am I. And I'm going to sleep down here on the sofa to make sure you stay safe.'

Alone in her bedroom, Cadi picked up her notebook and her pen. She could hear the rain outside. Downstairs all was quiet. It felt inordinately comforting to know that Charles was there and briefly she wondered what it would be like if she had invited him to come upstairs with her. She smiled, glad that Sally wasn't there to guess at her thoughts. Sternly she turned her attention back to her story. And this time her pen was ready to move.

Elen had become a wanderer. No longer able to tolerate the memory of the legions at Segontium, she followed the road that came to bear her name south towards Y Gaer and then onwards to the place of her birth, where the echoes of invasion and fire hung over the ruins of the palace she had called home. The overgrown meadow that had once been a garden and a horse paddock was no place to dawdle; the atmosphere, strange and unsettled, drove her away. She moved on, always searching out the hidden places, staying a week, a month, perhaps the whole of a season here or there, to pray and meditate with the spirits of the earth and sky, of the waters and the winds, and dedicate these special places to the holy saints who now walked the mountains and moors of Britannia and to Our Lady, the special patron of the land, founding a hermitage here, a clas or a convent or a priory there, to continue her work.

Her children all kept in close touch with her, and somehow found her wherever she was, to sit and talk and tell her of their lives, all except Maxima, who lived in faraway Africa, but who still managed to write long vivid letters to her mother of her life in the sun. Sevira's husband Vortigern had become a powerful war leader and she wrote her mother letters from the Emperor Hadrian's wall, where he was fighting the incursions from the Picti and the Caledonii. Elen's little grandson Vortimer had been born amongst those northern hills. Peblig had indeed left home to study at colleges run by the greatest churches and would soon become a priest and the special sword had been hidden in the foundations of his church at Segontium until the time came for it to be wielded to save the land of Albion. Elen's stepson Victor had, to her great sorrow, died without leaving any children, but as if to make up for the loss his brother Constantine now had three sons. The eldest, Constans, had also dedicated his life to Christ and for a long time there had been no more children, but now there were two more little boys, Ambrosius and Uther.

It was near a fortress on a hill beside a lake in the foothills of Yr Wyddfa that her stepson Constantine found her one spring day. Her heart ached when she saw his smile; he was so like his father. He had left a troop of men to broach their rations on the roadside far below them, and, wandering up the long winding track, found her at last alone, sitting on a rocky outcrop, watching a black-and-white fish hawk hovering over the lake. He sat down beside her and they remained like that, in companionable silence, for a while.

She turned to him at last. 'You haven't come to find me to sit and watch the birds.'

He grinned. 'I was trying to think of words to break my news.'

She looked away. 'So, do I assume it's bad?'

He shook his head. 'Not for me. It's exciting. But for you, it may bring back unhappy memories.'

She looked back at him and he felt the full power of her intense scrutiny. His father had told him he always quailed when confronted with that look. He knew she could read his innermost secrets, however hard he had tried to hide them. He wondered if she was doing it now.

'So?' Just the one word.

He took a deep breath. 'The armies of Britannia, all that are left of the legions, all mercenaries and native troops, now, perhaps together some six thousand men, all that were left after my father led the rest overseas . . .' The words trailed off uncomfortably. That had not ended well for anyone. He straightened his back and announced, 'They have chosen me as their emperor.'

He waited for a response, glancing at her sideways, then looking away again, down towards the lake. The bird had caught a fish in its talons and was carrying it away towards the high peaks of the mountains. He could see it wriggling desperately as bird and prey disappeared and he thought with a bitter smile he knew how the fish must feel.

'Say something,' he said at last, under his breath.

'What is there to say?' she sighed. 'I assume you have agreed?'

'Of course.'

'And you are going to take that last remnant of the Britannic forces overseas, and leave this province defenceless, just as your father did?'

He shrugged his shoulders. 'Not quite defenceless. You have strong kings, natural-born kings of Britannia, to fill my place. Your father and Conan amongst them. And King Cunedda and Vortigern. All chosen and confirmed in their appointments by my father.'

'And you consider the numbers of the men you will take sufficient to defeat not only Honorius, who as I understand it, is currently recognised as emperor of the West, to say nothing of the vast barbarian hordes that, sensing its growing weakness, I hear, invade the empire from every side?'

'I know it is sufficient. They are well trained, they are keen, and they have not been paid, lately not at all, here, in this remote province. They are hungry. They will fight for me, Emperor Constantine III.' He paused, unable to hide his pride in the title.

'Then there is no more to be said. I wish you well, my son.' She gave him a look so full of sorrow that he shrank back.

'There is one other thing, Mama.' She always loved it when he called her that. 'I am taking Constans with me as my heir. We will form a new dynasty just as my father would have wished.'

She turned on him. 'Your son is a monk, Constantine! He serves God!' She was very proud of the young man she thought of as her grandson.

He nodded almost sadly. 'I have persuaded him. He understands that he will serve God better at his father's side. Ambrosius and Uther will go with their mother to Armorica. They are too young to go with me and they will be safe there.'

Under the full force of her disbelieving glance he looked away.

'And I don't suppose I can persuade you to change your mind?'

'No.'

'Go then.' She turned away. The great hawk had returned and was once more flying over the lake.

He stood up. 'Can I have your blessing?'

'Your father had my blessings, Constantine. That didn't save his life. Nor did it save your little brother.' Her eyes filled with tears. She brushed them away angrily. 'I will pray for you both,' she said eventually. 'God go with you, my son.'

She didn't watch him go, nor see the cohort of men march away along the road towards the south.

It was almost dark when Branwen came to find her. Elen was still sitting there, on the rocky outcrop watching the last crimson streaks of light in the sky.

'The colour of blood,' she said bitterly as Branwen sat down beside her.

'Such is the destiny of men,' Branwen replied softly. 'Nothing we say will ever change that.'

Cadi sighed. The sky in her story was almost dark and it was the same outside her bedroom window. The full moon was rising. Soon its light would flood the countryside. She stood looking longingly out of the window. She knew she wouldn't be able to pluck up the courage to go out alone. Not tonight. Perhaps not ever again. She wandered back to bed and climbed in. Pulling up her duvet and propped against the pillows she opened her notebook, illuminated in the pool of light from the bedside lamp. The rest of the room was in darkness.

Slowly and carefully she reread the last pages of her story, checking every word.

Constantine and his son Constans. And Ambrosius and Uther. Those names leapt out at her. Was this the Uther who would be the father of King Arthur? Arthur, for whom the sword, Caledfwlch – Excalibur – was waiting, hidden under the church of St Peblig. Arthur, whose knights spent so long searching for the Holy Grail. And Uther's brother Ambrosius – hadn't he had something to do with Merlin? She had thought it was Sevira who was the link to Arthur, but it was her husband Vortigern who was there at the start of the story of Merlin. Merlin who was so inextricably part of Arthur's story. Sevira was to be the mother of kings. It said so on the Stone of Eliseg, but not after all, of Arthur.

Was all this true? Was it real? But of course it was real. Everything in the dream world of her automatic writing was real, at least to her.

Outside clouds slowly drifted across the moon and once again the rain began to fall and once more her pen began to move.

It was the second time Elen had been back to her birthplace since her daughters had left Segontium. The villa was still in ruins, much of the building material gone, presumably quietly in the night to neighbouring farms and villages and some of it no doubt, to help build the clas, a tiny monastery she had founded in the cwm where an abbot and two monks prayed for the souls of those slaughtered by the invaders who had destroyed the area.

Her visit had taken her first up to the oppidum, the hill fort of Bryndinas, Branwen's home, then down to the meadow. On the way back along the track she stopped to say a prayer at the spring. The offerings were still to the local goddess and Elen knew it would be a long time before that would change, but in the meantime she could place a cross near the source and beg Our Lady or one of the holy saints to come and watch over it. It was nearly dark and she could hear the call of an owl from the trees. The bird of Minerva, and of Blodeuwedd. She smiled to herself, remembering the stories Branwen used to tell her all those years ago about the lady made of flowers who was punished for her crimes by being turned into an owl, and of the goddess Arianrhod who transformed herself into an owl in order to read the human soul. She found herself wondering if Jesus had a tutelary owl, but perhaps they didn't have owls in his part of the empire.

The hind tiptoed into the clearing, her head held high, her eyes enormous in the half-light. Elen smiled. She sat still, waiting until the animal drew close before quietly raising her hand to scratch the warm furry neck. 'So, my friend. You've come to greet me, you who walk between the worlds.' She reached out and felt the nibble of the soft lips on her hand. 'Do you want to drink at the spring? The water is blessed by God.'

'The water is blessed by older gods than yours.' She had not heard Branwen behind her. The deer raised her head, startled, but stayed for a moment longer to enjoy the touch of Elen's fingers before turning towards the bubbling spring and lowering her head to drink.

The shout from the field below brought Elen to her feet. She turned and peered down through the trees. A man was running for his life across the meadow, glancing over his shoulder behind him. He was being followed, she saw, by two pursuers, one of them somehow projecting a beam of light over the grass. She shivered. Crossing herself, she crept nearer to the edge of the wood. She could no longer see the ruins; the grass was flat and even; it was as if the palace had never been. As she watched, the man in the lead swerved aside as if dodging something she could not see, before he plunged into the darkness of the trees. The two men behind him skidded to a halt, staring round. Obviously they had lost him.

There was a quiet chuckle behind her and Elen turned swiftly to see Branwen leaning against the bole of a nearby tree, her arms folded, wrapped as always in a cloak of dark-dyed wool, the colour of which melded seamlessly into the shadows of the woods. 'What is happening? Who is he?' Elen asked. She turned back to peer through the trees. The man and his pursuers had gone. Below them the meadow was empty and peaceful once more, the misty ruins wet with rain and wrapped now in darkness.

'That is the man who tried to burn down the house of the seer Meryn,' Branwen replied, thoughtful now. 'He came very close to the time gate in the meadow and he dodged round it as if he saw it. Very few manage to do that.'

'The time gate?' Elen turned to face her.

'That is where your little dog Gemma came from and where she went back to her own people.' Branwen smiled. 'It is closed again now. The meadow is quiet.'

Elen glanced back. The rain had cleared and she could see the ruins of the palace clearly visible in the moonlight as black clouds raced across the sky.

'That man was in another time, wasn't he?' Elen asked quietly, her eyes on the animal drinking near her.

Branwen nodded. 'He's hiding in our woods, but he is in his own world. It would have been better if he had come to us so that he could disappear into the mountains. I doubt if he would be missed by those he has left behind. He has evil intentions.'

'You too could feel his heart is black.' Elen smiled at the hind as she turned away from the water, her mouth dripping diamond droplets in the moonlight, and melted back into the woods.

She glanced up at the sky. The cloud had cleared and she could see the glittering zigzag of stars in the sky which was the court of the goddess Dôn. Which had been, she corrected herself sharply. She wondered what names Christ had for the great constellations of the stars which, Branwen had taught her, were the dwelling places of the old gods.

Branwen was watching her with a quizzical smile.

Elen felt a twinge of guilt, just as she had when she was a child, sure that Branwen could read her every thought. 'So, what is the answer?' she asked sharply. 'Where has he gone? What will happen to him?'

Branwen shook her head. 'I can't answer that question. Perhaps it is one for your god. Does he not answer your prayers?'

Elen was silent. She had prayed for God to keep Macsen safe. She had prayed for God to keep Victor safe. But then he had answered her prayers to keep the other children safe.

He had brought her back to Britannia and he had helped her and Peblig hide the sword for a future king, and he had watched her stow the little dish in the cave in the mountains, blessed by the ghost of the old hermit, who by now must surely be numbered amongst the saints.

'He answers everyone's prayers,' she said at last, almost to herself. 'But he judges what the answer should be for the best.'

'And it was best that little Victor die?' Branwen homed in on the one question that could never be answered.

'Just because I cannot see his reasoning it doesn't mean there isn't any,' Elen snapped back.

Branwen inclined her head. 'So he will judge that man and decide his future.' She looked back towards the woods on the lower slopes of the hill. 'Tell me, does your Christ love the animals as our gods do?' she asked at last.

Both women glanced back at the trees where the hind had disappeared, leaving not even the tremble of a leaf to show where she had gone.

'I am sure he does.' Elen didn't remember Bishop Martin ever mentioning animals, but how could a merciful god not love animals?

As though to emphasise her words the silence of the woods was broken by the lonely howl of a wolf far away to the north.

Below them, hiding on the wooded slopes of Bryndinas, in another place and another time, Ifan Davies heard the sound and shivered. He hid for a long time in the woods, heart thudding uncomfortably as he hunkered down and waited. The police were still out there looking for him. They had powerful torches. As they appeared in the meadow behind him he had watched the beams flashing across the grass as he splashed across the brook and crouched amongst the bushes. He saw the lights stop near the centre of the field, scanning the meadow, forward, back, round. They hadn't seen which way he went. Slowly his breath steadied as he listened for any sound of his pursuers but there was nothing to hear but the pattering of rain on the leaves all round him. He glanced nervously over his shoulder. He had a feeling he was being watched, but the police were far away down in the field. Surely there was no one up here in this godawful place. From the depths of the alder brake a blackbird shrieked its indignation. Nearby an owl hooted. It was watching him as it sat above him in a tree, hiding from the rain. Its mate replied from far away, the call echoing through the night. He huddled deeper into the undergrowth and only then did he realise his teeth were chattering.

Above him on the hillside, near the source of the spring, Branwen was watching. Wrapped in her dark cloak, her arms folded into its deep folds, her hair hidden beneath her hood, she was no more than a silent shadow.

So, Elen and Branwen had seen Ifan out there on the hill-side. Cadi read over the passage again. Two women from another age had watched him run across the field, followed by the police. They were close by, interacting with the world of another time. They had recognised the blackness of his heart and argued about the powers of God to interfere in the affairs of men. And Elen? Had she glimpsed, just for a moment, a possible reason why in some versions of Elen's legend she was remembered as the personification of the antlered goddess. Was she, this passionate Christian, who was credited with bringing the idea of isolated monasteries and lonely hermits to the sacred isles of Britain, in reality a Saint Francis type figure who talked to the animals?

51

Only when the lights of the police car had at last disappeared round the bend in the lane and the sound of its engine had faded away did Ifan stand up and make his way stiffly back the way he had come and haul himself over the gate. He was soaked to the skin, bleeding from the clinging brambles, and shivering. He stood for a while, listening. There was silence now. The rain had stopped and the moon had appeared between the streaming black clouds. There was no sign of any traffic. As he moved away from the gate and began to limp back towards the village he groped in his pockets to check Madelaine's keys were still there. They had gone. He swore under his breath. He had thrown away the keys to her garden doors but he had been so sure his own set was tucked safely in his pocket. He must have lost them while he was crouching in the woods. Where was he going to go now?

He paused outside Cadi's cottage. He had so many scores to settle with that woman, but they could keep. The windows were dark, as were his father's; pathetic little man. A car's headlights appeared in the distance, coming from the direction of the mill. He was almost opposite the shadowy turning into Church Lane and, keeping close to the hedge, he crept into it, huddling there as the car drove past the end of the road.

It was then he spotted a faint light in the distance. As he staggered up the lane he realised it came from the church, not a place he had ever chosen to frequent. Limping up the path towards it, he stood outside the great oak door, listening. The porch light wasn't on. All was dark in the churchyard and there were no cars parked nearby that he could see. There was no sound from inside the church. Cautiously he turned the heavy iron handle and pushed the door open. The light he had seen through the high window came from a single lamp near the altar, and a stand of votive candles nearby, of which three were lit. He could smell the melting beeswax and a slight hint of smoke. Closing the heavy door behind him, he stood and listened, shivering. The church was silent. There was no one there. Slowly his eyes grew used to the candlelight; he could make out the altar at the far end of the nave, the pulpit, the rows of shadowy pews, and nearby, along the back wall, a table. It was being used as some sort of second-hand book stall, presumably to raise cash for the church, and there at the far end he spotted a kettle and some mugs. A closer examination disclosed a bowl containing teabags, little plastic tubs of milk, sachets of sugar and an unopened packet of biscuits. A notice bade him welcome, invited him to make himself a hot drink and after that to sit quietly and perhaps say a prayer. He gave a snort as he switched on the kettle. 'Thank you, God!' he said out loud. His voice was heavy with sarcasm. He scrabbled in his pockets for his pills, terrified they too might have fallen out somewhere on the hillside. They were still there. With a sigh of relief he pulled them out. Perhaps they would help the pain in his head to go away.

The candles were burning down when he discovered the side room up near the altar. It led to a loo, and seemed to contain a lot of junk, beside a small safe, which was locked. There were some choir robes and various dusty old cloaks hanging on a line of ornate hooks. He grabbed them thankfully. They might at least serve to keep him warm and, shivering fitfully, he had already decided to spend the night in here out of the rain. Here he was near his father's house, and Cadi's. Tomorrow at dawn he was going to pay them both a visit they would never forget.

It took him a long time to fall asleep on his improvised bed on the floor, but when he was awakened by the sound of the main door opening at the far end of the church, the early sunlight was pouring in through the windows. He heard the door close and footsteps headed towards his hiding place in the vestry. Flinging his make-do coverings aside he staggered to his feet and tiptoed towards the vestry door just as it opened. A woman was standing there. She let out an exclamation of surprise at the sight of him.

'Oh my goodness, you gave me a fright.' She was middle-aged, pretty in a faded understated way, and wearing a raincoat. It was a moment before he spotted the dog collar.

'Sorry. I came in out of the rain.' He was flooded with resentment at the sight of this complete stranger invading the space he had thought of as safe.

'No problem.' He saw her glance at him more closely and wondered if she'd guessed who he was. After all, the police in about four counties were probably after him, so why not the clergy as well. He felt his chest tightening and he clenched his fists.

'Why don't we have a hot drink?' she said quietly. 'We have a kettle on the table at the back of the church there, and tea bags and coffee. And biscuits, unless the local children have scoffed them.' She had obviously not noticed his depredations of the night before.

'You know who I am, don't you,' he murmured.

'I don't care who you are,' she replied. 'I know it's a bit of a cliché, but this is the house of God. All are welcome here. And safe.'

He stared at her incredulously. He felt himself sneer. 'That's a cliché. And no doubt you have your phone on speed-dial to the police as we speak.'

She had put her hands in her pockets. She shook her head and pulled them out to show him they were empty. 'My phone is in my car.' She nodded behind her. 'I came in to pray and see to the candles.' She hesitated. 'One of my prayers was for you and your family, Ifan. It is Ifan, isn't it. I'm Kate. I know your father. He's desperately worried about you.'

He laughed derisively. 'I doubt it! Not after I thumped him yesterday. Besides, he's never cared about anyone apart from himself in his whole life.'

She gave a sigh. 'So, what are you planning to do next?'

'Get away from here.' He was hardly likely to tell her. 'Car keys.' He held out his hand. 'Give me your car keys.'

She shook her head. 'I left my car the other end of the village. I'm going to visit some of my parishioners later, so I parked outside the almshouses. There's a huge amount of unrest and distress around here at the moment.'

'My fault, no doubt.'

She nodded slowly. 'You haven't helped, with your plans for our lovely meadow, but mainly it's not you, it's to do with the man they found in the field. He was killed before the war but this is a village. Local families were involved. People are still upset.'

'But they all hate me as well, because of the housing development.' Ifan could feel himself beginning to shiver again. His clothes were clammy with damp.

'Some of them do, of course. It's probably fifty-fifty.' She smiled. She had a gentle voice. He could imagine her coaxing people into confession.

He scowled. 'Well, Cadi has always hated me. Do you know her? Probably not, she was never a God-botherer. I used to love her, you know. But oh, no, she was so wrapped up in her own world. So snug in her little cottage. So smug. She was scared of me though. That always gave me a buzz. I suppose that's what originally gave me the idea for my plan. I needed a new place to invest and out of the blue it occurred to me to buy Cadi's field. That would really upset her.' He gave a malicious grin. 'I wanted to give her a reason to remember me!' He paused for a fraction of a second, aware that he was ranting. 'She was like my wife. Bitches, both of them. Why was I attracted to bitches? You should know, you're probably one yourself.' His smile was very cold. 'Though I can't say I'm attracted to you.'

'I do know Cadi, and she doesn't hate you, Ifan.' Kate refused to rise to his taunts. 'I can't think why not, though, after all you've done. You terrified her yesterday.'

'Good! And it's going to upset her a whole lot more when my builders arrive.' He sighed. 'I've had enough of all this. I didn't mean to hit my father, you know. But no one's going to believe me, are they.'

He felt her eyes on his face, her gaze very steady. 'Funnily enough, I do believe you,' she said at last. 'Why don't we go up to see him now, together, see if he'll talk to you. See if we can't sort all this out.'

Cadi and Charles had both awakened early. She had tiptoed downstairs, hoping not to wake him, but he had already made himself a cup of tea and was folding up his blankets when she appeared.

'Why don't I nip up to the mill and collect some breakfast,' he said. 'I need to put Chris in the picture about the meadow. I still can't get my head round the fact that Ifan put it in her name.' He grinned. 'I bet he's regretting that now.'

Unlocking the front door, he stepped outside. It promised to be a lovely day. He turned back to her. 'I won't be long. Be careful, and for God's sake don't open the door to anyone else.'

Cadi stood on the doorstep watching as he set off up the road before she retreated inside and closed the door. The living room was dark. It felt depressingly gloomy and claustrophobic with boards nailed across the broken French windows and, picking up the mug of tea Charles had made her, she made her way through into the pantry to unlock the side door. Surely there was no danger in broad daylight. Opening the door a crack and looking carefully left and right up and down the side passage to make sure all was quiet, she stepped outside.

The rain had cleared away in the night but the garden was still dripping wet, the raindrops sparkling in the sunlight. The mist had dispersed. She stood for a while on the terrace, sipping her tea, slowly feeling herself relax. She could see her robin hopping round the rose bush near the boarded-up windows. If there was anyone out there he would have let her know. She took a deep breath, smelling grass and roses and the lavender bush in the corner near the fence. In a moment she would go back inside. Charles would be home soon with some warm croissants and the builder would be arriving to mend the doors.

Behind her the robin let out a cry of alarm.

'It's cold out here, isn't it.' The voice almost gave her a heart attack. She dropped her mug of tea. Broken china scattered across the flagstones. Ifan was standing in the passage between her and the side door watching her. He must have vaulted over the gate. 'There's no need to call the police.' He saw her groping in her pocket for her phone. 'Let me say my piece and I'll get out of your hair.'

Cadi was speechless with terror. 'What do you want?' she managed at last. 'Where did you come from? Where have you been hiding?'

He grinned. 'You won't believe it, but I spent the night in the church.' He threw himself down on one of the garden chairs and she saw him flinch as the ice-cold rain soaked into his jeans. 'So where are your minders this morning?'

'Back any minute.'

He gave a grim smile. 'I need to be quick then. The vicar found me and the nosy cow insisted on going with me to see my father. I don't think she trusted me not to kill him this time.' He gave an exaggerated sigh. 'He gave me this hideous shirt as my other one was bloody.' He was wearing a black-and-grey striped T-shirt. 'My blood, I may say, not anyone else's. From brambles up there on that sodding hill. And for the record, I apologised for hitting him and he and the vicar have promised they won't call the police until I've had the chance to speak to you. I suppose I believe the vicar when she says that with her big sincere eyes, though I wouldn't believe him further than I could throw him. I didn't let them out of my sight even to find the horrible shirt. But the old so-and-so's coughed up all the cash he had hidden in that desk of his to get rid of me and he's given me his car keys. So, I'm off. I don't want to go to prison; you won't see me again. I've stashed enough money abroad and I've even bought a house in the sun. I hoped Sue would like it, but that didn't work out.' He paused and she saw a wave of anger cross his face. 'I won't pester Sue. They'll be better off without me. I've already made most of my property in this country over to her.' He gritted his teeth. 'That was a bloody mistake, but too late to change it all now.' He stood up. 'But there are still things I need to tell you. The vicar is right behind me. She thinks I've come to apologise for having frightened you so much.' He gave a cold smile. 'As if!'

Cadi stared at him. 'I didn't think this sounded like you!' She clenched her fists.

'No.' He gave a bitter laugh. 'The God lady from the church thinks she can reform me with a little lecture, the naïve do-gooding bitch, just like every woman in my life, even my goddam mother, who died rather than stay to look after me when I was a child!' He took a step towards her. 'I told the vicar what I thought of all the women I know and she still thought she could sweet-talk me round. She thought it would be nice for me to say goodbye to you politely and apologise for being nasty. She thought my soul would feel better.'

Cadi could hear the anger in his voice mounting. She took a step back. Her pulse rate had rocketed.

'You took everything from me,' he went on. 'My home, my father, my self-esteem, my happiness. And all for this poxy little house and that stupid bloody field!' He was shouting now. 'I'm going to say goodbye, Cadi, oh yes, I'm going to say goodbye, but in a way you'll remember for the rest of your life!' He was feeling under his T-shirt and as he raised his hand she realised to her horror that he had had a knife tucked into the belt of his jeans.

'Stop it, Ifan!' The voice that rang out was sharp. Kate was standing in the passageway behind them. 'I'm not that stupid, my friend. I didn't believe a word you said. You may not have given me the chance to ring them in his house but your father managed to slip me his phone and I've just called them.' She held it up. 'Pretending it was to let you speak to Cadi gave me the chance I needed. Leave her alone. You've said your good-byes.'

He let out a shout of laughter. 'Stupid bitch, I haven't nearly said my goodbyes. Not yet!' He raised the knife and lunged at Cadi. She jumped back with a scream, but he managed to land a blow to her shoulder that sent her reeling to the ground. 'Good-bye, sweetheart,' he shouted, then he turned and ran across the lawn. In seconds he had forced his way through the hedge and was running across the meadow.

'Oh God! Cadi, Cadi, are you OK?' Kate threw herself towards her.

'I'm all right.' Cadi managed to stagger to her feet, clutching her shoulder. There was blood welling between her fingers. She bit her lip against the pain, her eyes filling with tears.

'The police are on their way.' Kate put her arm round her and already they could hear the distant siren. 'Come inside. It's OK. You're safe now. He's gone.' As she helped Cadi inside, leaving the bloodstained knife lying on the terrace amid the broken china, they heard the police banging on the front door. Gently pushing Cadi down on the sofa Kate ran to open it and Cadi saw the strobing light of the police car parked outside. 'He ran across the field. That way.' Kate gestured wildly and Cadi saw the blurred shapes of two officers turn away and vanish back towards the gate. Kate was about to close the door when Charles appeared. At the sight of the police car outside the house he had broken into a run.

'My God, what's happened?' He threw the bag he was carry-ing onto the table and hurried over, falling on his knees beside Cadi as she lay back against the cushions.

'I'm OK. I don't think it's serious.' She gave a watery smile. 'We had a visitor.'

Kate brought the phone out of her pocket. 'I'll call an ambulance. Then I'm calling Gwen.'

'No, don't, please.' Cadi managed a faint smile. 'No ambulance. I'll be fine. Don't fuss!' She pushed Charles away. 'I'm OK. I was stupid. It never occurred to me he might come back. I was standing there in the garden. Happy. Drinking my tea. He just appeared round the back of the house.' The tears began to flow again. 'Sorry. I'm being an idiot! It's the shock.'

'Here, let me see. After her brief call to Gwen, Kate repocketed the phone. She sat down beside Cadi. 'Let me help you take off your blouse.'

'It's OK. It's not deep. I dodged in time.'

Kate shook her head. 'I'm so sorry. I was just determined to keep things calm. I needed him out of sight for just a couple of minutes so I could call the police. Have you got a first aid box?' She glanced across at Charles. He scrambled to his feet.

Cadi gave him a weak grin. 'It's under the sink. Stop fussing. Please. I just need a plaster.'

Kate helped her peel off the blood-stained blouse to reveal a long shallow cut across the top of her arm. 'Thank God, I don't think it's too bad.' She glanced up at Charles. 'There's a lot of blood, but I don't think it's deep. Are there any bandages in there?'

Between them they mopped up the blood and managed to staunch the bleeding before tying a dressing across the wound.

'We went to see Arwel,' Kate talked quietly as she tidied up after disappearing upstairs on Cadi's instructions to find her a fresh shirt. She helped her put it on. 'We talked for quite a long time. Ifan was like unstable dynamite, terrified we'd try and call the police, but slowly things were calming down. He said he'd go quietly and Arwel seemed to believe him; he found an envelope full of cash in his desk and gave it to Ifan with his car keys. Anything to get him out of the house. Then Ifan said there was one more thing he wanted to do and that was apologise to you. I could see it might be the only chance we had to get help, and after we'd talked for such a long time—'

'In the church, I gather.' Cadi was sitting back in the sofa, her face very pale. Charles sat down opposite her. He seemed as shaken as she was.

Kate nodded with a smile. 'I didn't think I'd converted him. I'm not that naïve. But he was at his wits' end. Exhausted. Miserable. I thought genuinely scared.'

'And you believed that?' Cadi was incredulous. 'Far more likely, if he felt anything at all, it would be sorry for himself.'

'Well, he'd said he was sorry for Sue and for you, Cadi. He admitted it gave him a sense of power to know how frightened you both were of him, to say nothing of his poor father. Arwel burst into tears as we left. Imagine.' Kate gave a grim smile. 'I told Ifan I was coming over here with him but I hung back. The moment he was out of sight round the corner I dialled 999. It was the first chance I'd had. He'd said all he wanted was to apologise. I'm not stupid; I knew I couldn't trust him. He knew I was right behind him. But I wasn't quick enough. I'm so sorry.'

'Even if you had been there I doubt if you could have stopped him,' Cadi said. 'Don't beat yourself up. He would have done it anyway. And at least you managed to call the police.'

Kate gave Cadi a gentle smile. 'Is there anyone else I can call to be with you?'

Cadi shook her head. 'Charles will look after me.' He had gone over to make her more tea.

Kate nodded uncomfortably. 'OK. I'll nip back to check on Arwel. He was in an awful state. You've got his number, haven't you. Call me if you need me. I'll only be across the road. Gwen is on her way.'

Charles followed her to the door and locked it behind her then he came back to Cadi and sat down, next to her this time. He could see her hands shaking as she reached for the tea.

'I could see the police lights flashing in the lane. There are two cars. They're parked up by the meadow. You're safe now, Cadi. Hopefully they've caught him.'

She nodded. 'I'm fine,' she whispered. 'Just a bit shocked. I was stupid to go outside.' She gave a shaky laugh. 'I know you told me not to. Bossy old Charles!' Her eyes filled with tears again.

'It's OK.' Tentatively he reached out to put his arm round her. She didn't resist.

Gwen appeared fifteen minutes later. 'Are you all right, Cadi? Are you sure you don't want an ambulance? It's lucky the man's father had already rung the police the moment he and Kate left the house and they were already on their way. There's a land line there which apparently Ifan didn't know about.' There was a long pause. 'There is absolutely no excuse. They should have caught him.' She looked furiously angry.

'What do you mean?' Cadi stared at her. She had gone cold all over. 'Please tell me he hasn't escaped.'

'They saw him on the far side of the field. He had made a run for it along the hedgerow and at the last minute he swerved into the open, sprinting towards the hill. Apparently they were that close to him!' Gwen held up her hand, her finger and thumb two inches apart. 'And yet' – she looked from Cadi to Charles and back – 'they maintain that he vanished in front of their eyes. I have four experienced police officers out there, about to have a nervous breakdown,' she went on. 'So, what happened?'

Cadi and Charles looked at each other. Cadi took a deep breath. 'He vanished?' she echoed.

'That can happen out there.' The awkward silence was broken by Charles. 'There's something about the lie of the land that makes it easy to misjudge distances.'

'Really? Four experienced officers are searching that field for a man who disappeared in front of their eyes.' Gwen was incredulous. 'That field is flat and open. They were fifty yards away from the woodland perimeter. And you say they misjudged the distance?'

'We don't know. We weren't there.' Charles looked at her uncomfortably.

'So, you're not claiming he went down your wormhole?'

'How do you know about the wormhole?' Cadi stared at her.

'Word gets round.'

'Kate?'

Gwen shook her head in despair. She gave a tight smile. 'I'm protecting my sources.' She folded her arms 'So. Tell me. What do you think happened? Where could he have gone?'

'The trouble is,' Charles went on without missing a beat, 'we know no more than you do. Surely the chances are he ducked into the woods? They weren't really that far away. If one knows the area, which Ifan must have once as he was brought up here, there are thousands of acres of mountains and forest over there in the national park.' He waved towards the wall.

Gwen nodded. She sat down abruptly on one of the kitchen chairs. 'Well, assuming we have discounted a wormhole, I've told them to bring in dogs. I've had enough of chasing Mr Davies round in circles. Now, Cadi, are you sure you don't want someone to look at that shoulder?'

Cadi had been cradling her elbow and Gwen caught sight of her wincing with pain. Cadi shook her head. 'I'm OK. Is Arwel all right?'

'I have no doubt he's still in a state of shock. I'll go over there now. I gather Kate's with him. We owe him a lot. It was courageous of him to ring the police to come and arrest his own son.'

She was walking across the road when a van pulled up outside. Phil the handyman climbed out. 'What's happened? There are police everywhere.'

'What's happened is that you're not a moment too soon. We're extremely glad to see you.' Charles met him at the gate.

Phil nodded. 'Well, I got to the suppliers first thing and found some new doors for you. They're in the van. Luckily they're a standard size. Proper toughened glass this time.'

Charles and Cadi watched as he carried them in, both wordlessly reassured by his quiet presence. 'Those old things you had, nice though they looked, would be illegal nowadays,' he muttered as he opened his toolbox. 'And, can I make a suggestion?'

Cadi nodded. 'Anything.'

'Shutters. I think they would look rather nice on your downstairs windows here at the back. And although I know I said these new doors are toughened glass, it would add a layer of safety.'

It was Phil who swept up the broken china. He used a plastic bag to pick up the bloodstained knife and handed it to Charles. 'Sabatier,' he commented. 'Nice. Better keep it for fingerprints.'

By lunchtime there was still no sign of Ifan having been caught. Charles had strolled up the lane to the meadow and reported that a police dog unit was there, together with reinforcements who were heading towards the hillside, each man with a long pole to help them probe the undergrowth. A little later Kate phoned to tell them Arwel's cousin had arrived to take him to stay with him in Swansea and that she would call in again that evening.

The doors were installed by mid-afternoon. Unable to concentrate while Phil was at work, Cadi went upstairs to her bedroom, leaving Charles sitting downstairs, his ears firmly clamped into an audiobook to block the sound of hammering. Her shoulder was aching unbearably, and she longed for sleep.

She took a couple of paracetamol, lay back on her bed and closed her eyes, but sleep wouldn't come. The pain was too intense and she couldn't stop herself shivering, imagining Ifan creeping back towards the house intent on finishing off whatever fate it was he had planned for her. After a while, she gave up trying and sat up propped against her pillows. It had become almost second nature to pick up her notebook and painfully she reached for her pen.

52

Branwen crept closer to the edge of the meadow, watching as the man stood staring round. Slowly he began to scramble up the hill, clearly trying to get his bearings. Once or twice he glanced over his shoulder to make sure he wasn't followed. She smiled. He was this side of the time gate. In her world.

Ifan stopped, leaning against the trunk of a tree to try to regain his breath. He was somewhere on the hill with the Iron Age fort on top, near Camp Meadow, but in a landscape he didn't recognise. He dabbed crossly at the deep scratch on his arm, smudging blood onto his fresh T-shirt. He was completely exhausted, disorientated and desperately thirsty. He glanced back the way he had come. Somehow he seemed to have lost most of the day. The sun was nearly gone. Soon the light would have disappeared completely. The forest, lapping against the slopes of the hill, was dark and somehow very sinister. He shuddered. He needed to get out of these woods. There had been no sight or sound of the police following him for some time. Pushing himself away from the tree trunk he headed downhill, trying to pick his way through the brambles, feeling them catching at his jeans. As he pulled himself free of yet another clinging tendril he felt the cloth rip and he realised he was near to collapse.

He paused, trying to calm himself, and it was then he heard the trickle of running water. He must be near the stream that ran along the foot of the hill on the edge of the meadow. He turned slowly, cupping his hand round his ear, trying to make out where the sound was coming from and carefully he began to make his way towards it. It was much darker down here and he held out his hands, warding off the tangled undergrowth. If he could find the stream he could follow it until he came to the edge of the meadow and what is more he could have a drink. Even the thought of water made his thirst rage more desperately. The police seemed to have given up and gone.

On the hillside where Ifan had hidden, the stag stepped forward, his nostrils flaring. Intent on her prayers Elen hadn't noticed the creature standing on the edge of the clearing. She watched him with a smile. He was obviously looking for his hind. He was aware of her there, on her knees by the spring, and was keeping half an eye on her but he didn't seem alarmed as he took another step forward. She didn't move. This was his territory, his world.

She became aware of the man standing in the shadows at the same moment the stag saw him. The creature froze, his eyes huge, his head with its great span of antlers raised. Was it possible the man hadn't noticed the animal? He was watching her and she saw him take a step forward towards her, then another. She hastily rose to her feet, brushing the moss from her skirt as she faced him. At first she thought it was one of the robbers who had attacked them so long ago, but then she realised it was the man she had seen earlier being pursued across the meadow and up through the woods. He was wearing oddly-styled trousers and a striped shirt covered in the marks of fresh blood. Seeing she had noticed him, he took another step forward.

'Help me. I'm lost.'

* * *

483

So, Ifan was there in Elen's world. Cadi lay back against the pillows and, looking down at her page, read those two last words again.

'I'm lost.'

For a moment she felt quite sorry for him. What would he do if he really was lost there in that ancient world of hidden forests where wolves still roamed?

At the sound of his voice the stag let out a great bellow of rage. It thumped the ground with a forefoot and took several steps into the clearing.

'Hush. He's no danger. You are safe here,' Elen said, but whether to the stag or the man she wasn't certain. With a cry of terror the man turned and fled back into the woods. She could hear the sounds of his racing footsteps, the crashing of branches and the alarm calls of the birds receding into the distance. When she glanced back towards the stag it had vanished as silently as it had come. She smiled. 'Thank you,' she whispered.

Meryn returned that evening. Stepping inside and setting his case down on the floor, he glanced round anxiously. 'What's happened?' The atmosphere in the room was jagged. He could feel the circling remnants of torn emotions: fear, anger, exhaustion.

Cadi bit her lip. 'Long story. I had a visitor. Ifan was here. We talked. And he left.'

Meryn frowned. 'And?' He glanced from Cadi to Charles and back.

'He disappeared.'

'Did he hurt you, Cadi?' He didn't need to be psychic to see that she was nursing her arm as she sat hunched over the table, and she was very pale.

'A bit.' She nodded. 'It's OK. He had a knife but he didn't do too much damage. I managed to dodge the worst. And I'm a bit bruised where I fell. Nothing serious, I promise. Kate was here. She and Arwel called the police. The sirens frightened him off.'

'But they haven't found him?' One look at their faces told him the answer to that one.

Cadi grimaced. 'They brought in tracker dogs. They followed his trail around the village to the church and here, and across the garden into the meadow, but . . .' She looked across at Charles, her eyebrow raised. 'There was no sign of him after that. Of course he might have got into a car somewhere – Arwel had given him his car keys – but the car is still there, and they seemed to think – that is, one of the dogs seemed to think – the trail petered out in the middle of the meadow. The dog handler said it was strange. It sniffed around that area, and its hackles went up. It didn't like it. It was scared.'

'They're not going to find him, are they,' Charles put in softly.

'I wonder.' Meryn shook his head. He sat down abruptly and reached a comforting hand across the table to Cadi.

There were a few long moments of silence, then, 'Meryn, can I ask you something,' said Charles. 'In all seriousness, if he has somehow slipped through our hidden door into another world, is there any way we can close it off? For good. It's not a nice thing to have on one's doorstep.'

'And trap him in the past, you mean?' Cadi snorted. 'I wish.'

'It's an interesting thought,' Meryn said. 'I believe it's generally assumed these portals aren't consistent. I don't even know how common they are, but I believe people think they come and go. This one certainly seems to. There is a suspicion they could be seasonal, or respond to geological stress of some kind. Nobody knows. And as to shutting them for good, I've no idea.'

'You could ask Branwen,' Cadi said quietly. 'Surely the ancient Druids would have known all about this sort of thing.'

'Or,' Meryn said thoughtfully, 'it's a scenario you could write into your novel and then we can see what happens next. Imagine, you're one of the three Fates. You're spinning the story, deciding what will happen to us mortal men.' He was still holding her hand. His grasp was gentle and soothing. Cadi relaxed and found herself wondering if he was a hypnotist as well as all his other talents. She had already seen he was a healer when he had soothed little Gemma. Her improvement had started with that moment.

485

'When I came in,' he went on quietly, 'you were both bent over your notebooks, Cadi. Did you manage to write some more while I was away, before all these cataclysmic interruptions?'

She nodded. 'I wrote a bit this afternoon. Post cataclysm.' She managed a smile. 'I couldn't sleep so I asked Branwen what had happened to him.'

'Excellent. You're fulfilling your destiny as a spinner of tales. So, may I see how far we've got?' Gently he withdrew his hand from hers and he groped for his glasses.

As Cadi pushed the notebook towards him and sat back in her chair she remembered something. 'With all this excitement I haven't had a chance to ask how your trip to see Rachel went. Is she happy now?'

Meryn smiled. 'I think you could say so. As I hope you will be when you check your bank balance.' He picked up her notebook. 'My solicitor has set everything in motion and as far as Rachel is concerned it's all arranged. It's amazing how quickly one can buy a house when everyone's working from the same page.' He put his glasses on. 'So, let's see what's been happening.'

It seemed an age before Ifan fought his way through the last tangle of undergrowth and found himself on the shallow pebbly beach on the bend of the brook. With a groan he dropped to his knees and began to scoop water into his mouth. When at last he sat back on his heels he realised he could see the edge of the wood. Beyond, there was an area of grass, bounded by a broken fence. In the twilight he could just see some ruined buildings on the far side of the paddock. Damn. He must be in the wrong place. There were no ruins in his meadow, and as far as he was concerned there never would be. New houses, yes. He grinned to himself. Cadi might think his disappearance would save the field. She was wrong. He would make sure somehow that Sue pushed the plans through. Climbing stiffly to his feet, he looked for a place to ford the stream and it was only then that he realised he was not alone at the water's edge. A pair of yellow eyes were watching him from the shelter of the trees. Dear God! It was the wolf.

With a yelp of fear he flung himself forward across the brook, splashing carelessly through the deeper pools, scrambled up the bank on the far side and ran towards the fence. As he climbed over it, aware that the rotten wood was splintering under his weight, he glanced back. The animal had followed him, soundlessly leaping in one bound across the water. It was gaining on him. He began to run across the field towards the ruined walls, imagining he could feel its breath on the back of his neck. The twilight thickened as the sun dropped out of sight behind the hills in a blaze of crimson cloud and he became aware of a column of mist rising from the grass. Desperately he made for it.

Behind him the wolf watched, puzzled. Its hackles began to stand up on its neck and it backed away. It turned and, running back the way it had come, jumped the brook and padded lightly into the trees. In seconds it had melted silently back into the woods.

Branwen saw the man look round, confused. The mist had vanished. Almost, the gateway had reopened, but then, as always unpredictable, it had closed again. The field was clear now in the moonlight.

There was nowhere to hide. The ruins near him smelt sour and lifeless. Slowly he turned back towards the steam. The wolf had gone, if it ever existed. That was one of the madder schemes of the dotty rewilding people, which could never happen. He followed the track back in the moonlight towards the stream, then up over the rocks until he found the spring. He stopped near the spot where the woman had been standing and, gazing round, he saw the gentle gleam of silver in the moonlight. It was a little Celtic cross. He stooped and picked it up. There was no sign of the woman now. Holding it in his hand he looked around again. 'Hello?' His voice was hesitant, flat. It held no resonance.

He stared up towards the top of the hill where the glow from the oppidum's cooking fires showed through the trees, half hidden by the surrounding walls, and Branwen saw him head purposefully up the path towards it.

Quietly, almost soundlessly, she pursed her lips and gave a low whistle. The wolf wasn't far away. She heard the pad of its paws on the forest path and she smiled. As it approached the man he let out a scream of fear, plunging off the path and away down the hillside over the heather and rocks, not caring where he went as long as he could escape.

He ran until, exhausted, he collapsed at last, lying motionless in the undergrowth as the rain began to fall. The wolf had followed effortlessly. It approached him and cautiously sniffed at his hair, then it turned and trotted away into the darkness.

The holy men from the clas found him eventually and managed to carry him to the shelter of their little house. They would care for him.

Branwen smiled.

If he ever returned, looking for his way back to that other world where he had made so many people unhappy, he wasn't going to find it. At least for now the pathway had closed.

Taking off his glasses, Meryn sat back on the sofa. 'So. He's gone.'

'That's what it says.' Cadi laughed uncomfortably.

'Perhaps we should tell Gwen.'

Charles shook his head. 'I suggest we give it a day or two. Let's see what happens. I know she asked to be informed if he ever turned up on another planet, but I'm not sure where he's gone counts as another planet.'

'I think it's near enough,' Meryn said with a chuckle. 'And in the meantime, perhaps you might take a look at these.' He reached for the folder that he had brought in with him when he had come in from the car. He had dropped it on the table when, with a bolt of real terror, he had caught sight of Cadi lying injured on the sofa and he'd forgotten about it until this moment. It contained a selection of new watercolour sketches. Cadi reached across and picked one up. She stared at it for a few seconds then put it down and picked up another. She looked up at the two men. 'She's painted Ifan!'

Meryn was still smiling. 'In a monk's habit.'

'Did she ever actually meet Ifan?' Charles frowned. 'I know he had her in his sights.'

Cadi nodded. 'Oh yes. She met him.'

'But, certainly not as he is now.' Charles was trying to keep a straight face. 'It looks to me as if he's met his match. You, Cadi, or Rachel, or both of you between you, have written that man's fate into history, just like Meryn said. I think he's found God. Or God has found him.' He stood up. 'D'you know what I'm going to do? I'm going to nip up to the pub to buy a bottle of bubbly and we're going to drink to Ifan's conversion. If your story is to be believed, and I do so hope it is, he's warm, he has shelter. He'll be fed, and who knows, before long he may well meet Elen again and perhaps it's her destiny to talk some sense into him, and his destiny to listen.'

Meryn and Cadi looked at each other after he had gone. 'The more I see of your Dr Ford, the more I like him,' Meryn said with a quiet laugh. 'He's confronted by evil beyond reckoning, attempted murder and something that, to the average layman, cannot be anything other than genuine out-and-out witchcraft, and the man goes out to buy champagne. As I may have said before, he's a keeper, Cadi. You hang on to him.'

That night Cadi heard the marching feet again. She sat up in bed with a shock of recognition; the sound still had the ability to scare her. Her gaze went automatically to the window. Outside, the moonlight was very bright. Silently she slid out of bed and tiptoed to look out. There was something different about the sound tonight and it was a moment before she realised what it was. It was coming from the other direction, from the meadow, heading back towards the village from where it would continue on down Sarn Elen towards the distant coast. The cohort was on its way to join the ragged remnants of the armies of the Roman province of Britannia to follow the standard of the Emperor Constantine III over the sea and into oblivion.

And Elen? Would she write any more of her story? Cadi had a feeling that, as far as she was concerned, her role in Elen's life was finished. She, together with the magic isle of Albion, were to be left to their legends.

Known Dates

Roman Emperors

Gratian	375–383
Valentinian II	375–392
Magnus Maximus	383–388
Flavius Victor	384–388
Theodosius I, The Great	379–395
Honorius	395–423
Constantine III	407–411

Christianity

313 Constantine I makes Christianity legal through the Edict of Milan

325 Council of Nicaea confirms Christianity legal

380 Edict of Thessalonica. Theodosius makes Christianity the official religion of the Roman Empire

St Martin of Tours 316–397 is recorded by his biographer, Sulpicious Severus, his contemporary, as meeting Magnus Maximus and his wife in 384. It is stated in the writings of St Ambrose – bishop of Milan from 374–397 and therefore a contemporary of the family – that after the defeat and execution of Magnus Maximus, the lives of his mother, his wife and his two daughters were spared. They are not named.

Author's Note

As Cadi discovers in her research, the history of Britain during the late Roman period is frustratingly complicated. We know much from the records of the four hundred years of Roman rule, but as the organisation which prevailed when it was part of the empire began to disintegrate, so did the written accounts of what was going on. The names and genealogies of the native rulers are inconsistent and muddled and muddied by the enthusiastic contributions of later historians and bards; tradition and wishful thinking. This story is my version of what might have happened.

Just as complicated is the confusion between the churches, chapels and Holy Wells, roads, and footpaths (even a mountain) dedicated to Elen (presumed to be our Elen), 'St Elen of Caernarfon,' and St Helen, the mother of the Emperor Constantine I. It is 'our Elen' who is remembered as the patron saint of British roadbuilders (and some would say of potholes) and a patroness of travellers.

The idea of the meadow and its voyage into planning law came to me from my own experience of applying some thirty years ago to plant a wood in a meadow and receiving in the reply to my request, secure in the knowledge that no one could possibly object to such a wonderful and worthy cause, those magic words 'you've got archaeology'. In our case I walked the land with the county archaeologist who came to do the survey, and he told us that sadly many years of deep ploughing while the site was in the care of a neighbouring farmer, had rendered any remains unsalvageable. Picking over the ploughland with him revealed shredded evidence of history dating to pretty much every era, as far back as the Bronze Age. I was thrilled with the evidence, sad that so little had survived, and pleased that the results were not sufficiently preserved to doom my plan, so I was able to plant my beautiful wood.

I want to thank my present day neighbour, and real-life archaeologist Adrian Hadley, for his advice on modern approaches, techniques and problems with archaeology and planning. He brought expertise, logic and a gently lifted eyebrow to my questions on reconciling the realities of serious archaeology with wormhole theories. He also pointed out that in real life all the archaeological, scientific and planning aspects of the story would have taken far longer than depicted here. In the interests of telling a fast-paced story I have taken liberties with both the facts and the time scale – an aspect of my story telling which is, let's face it, always fairly elastic.

Many thanks also go to my lovely agent Isobel Dixon for her steadfast advice and support, and to her assistant, Sian Ellis-Martin, and to my patient editors, Susan Opie, Belinda Toor and Anne O'Brien and a special mention and thank you must go to Kim Young who has seen me through many years of writing, helped to keep me sane and taken overall care of at least five of my books. She is moving on to other things and I wish her every success in the future. And thanks of course as always to my son Jon who is there on the end of the phone, or linked in on the mysterious ether, to help with every succeeding glitch in the computer system and who enters with so much enthusiasm and down to earth restraint into our research trips to all the places (at least on this plane) mentioned in the story. Our trips to Roman Wales and to the wild beauties of Eryri were especially memorable – and so much fun.

This has been the most complex of any of my books to research. As Cadi frequently bewails, history is confused and sparse when discussing Elen both as a real person and as a legend and assumptions are profuse and multifaceted when addressing her many alternative personas. I have taken huge liberties with both history and legend but to be fair so have story tellers and historians throughout the ages, as Cadi found out. Please don't go basing any theses on my story.

I first studied the Mabinogion some twenty-five years ago as part of a course I was on and it never ceased to intrigue and beguile me, especially as the stand-out story of Macsen appeared to cover such an unlikely slab of real events within the frame of folk memory. I hope my telling of the story has, if nothing else, succeeded in capturing your imagination.

As to wormholes: we had one once, in a previous house. They are interesting to say the least. Unsettling. And real. We considered underlying geology, which was very special, the crystalline content of bricks which was very high, the presence of malign or mischievous spirits, which was possible and the theories of quantum physics which were beyond our under-standing. We consulted experts and on one occasion declined a TV documentary. Overall we reached no conclusions apart from being very careful where we put things down. I shall say no more in the interests of others who live there now.

And finally, a heartfelt thank you again to everyone who has shared with me their love of Wales and its wonderful landscape, history and stories. *Diolch yn fawr*.